TRUE EVIL

Look for more
heart-stopping stories from

FEAR STREET.....

The Perfect Date

Secret Admirer

Runaway

The Confession

Night Games

The Wrong Number

Who Killed the Homecoming Queen?

FEAR STREET

TRUE EVIL

THE FIRST EVIL · THE SECOND EVIL
THE THIRD EVIL

R.L. STINE

SIMON PULSE
NEW YORK   LONDON   TORONTO   SYDNEY   NEW DELHI

SIMON PULSE

An imprint of Simon & Schuster Children's Publishing Division

1230 Avenue of the Americas, New York, New York 10020

This Simon Pulse paperback edition April 2023

The First Evil, *The Second Evil*, and *The Third Evil* copyright © 1992 by Parachute Press, Inc.

Cover illustration copyright © 2023 by Marie Bergeron

FEAR STREET is a registered trademark of Parachute Press, Inc.

All rights reserved, including the right of reproduction in whole or in part in any form.

Simon Pulse and colophon are registered trademarks of Simon & Schuster, Inc.

For information about special discounts for bulk purchases, please contact Simon & Schuster Special Sales at 1-866-506-1949 or business@simonandschuster.com.

The Simon & Schuster Speakers Bureau can bring authors to your live event.

For more information or to book an event contact the Simon & Schuster Speakers Bureau at 1-866-248-3049 or visit our website at www.simonspeakers.com.

Series designed by Sarah Creech

Cover designed by Heather Palisi

Interior designed by Mike Rosamilia

The text of this book was set in Excelsior LT Std.

Manufactured in the United States of America

10 9 8 7 6 5 4 3

Library of Congress Control Number 2022946101

ISBN 9781665932639 (pbk)

ISBN 9781442407459 (*The First Evil* ebook)

ISBN 9781439120965 (*The Second Evil* ebook)

ISBN 9781439120811 (*The Third Evil* ebook)

These titles were previously published individually.

CONTENTS

THE FIRST EVIL

PART ONE
THE CHEERS

1

THE EVIL SISTER

*Y*ou are evil," Corky said in a hushed whisper. "You are truly evil."

The words made Bobbi grin, her green eyes lighting up with pleasure. She gripped the rat tighter around its rib cage.

"Where are you going to put it?" Corky asked, still rubbing the sleep from her eyes. The floorboards felt cold beneath her bare feet. "Right in front of Sean's door?"

Bobbi nodded and tiptoed down the narrow hall toward their brother's room. Her blond hair was still tangled from sleep. Both girls were in long cotton nightshirts.

"Sean is terrified of rats," Corky whispered, her eyes on her little brother's door, expecting him to burst out and ruin Bobbi's little surprise.

"I know," Bobbi said with an evil snicker. She carefully set the rat down in the center of the doorway. When Sean came out for breakfast, he'd have to walk right into it.

"It looks so real," Corky whispered. "It doesn't look like rubber." The floor creaked noisily, and Corky stopped. She set one hand against the peeling wallpaper and leaned on it.

"It's the hair that makes it," Bobbi replied. Having set down the realistic-looking creature, she and her sister started to back away, their eyes on Sean's closed door. "It's very good rat hair. Very authentic."

"Girls? What are you doing?" Their mother's voice interrupted them from downstairs, startling them both. "Are you dressed yet? You're going to be late. Come down for breakfast. And make sure Sean is up."

"Don't worry," Bobbi whispered, grinning at her sister. "Sean will be wide-awake real soon!"

Chuckling about Bobbi's little joke, both girls descended the creaking staircase and joined their parents in the kitchen. Mr. Corcoran—their handsome, young-looking father—was already at the table, wiping egg off his chin with a paper napkin.

"Yuck. Not poached eggs again," Bobbi groaned.

Mrs. Corcoran turned around, a pale reflection

of her vibrant blond daughters. She stared at their nightshirts, frowning. "That's how you're going to school?"

"Yeah," Bobbi answered quickly. "All the girls are wearing nightshirts. It's sort of a trend."

"Why do we have to have poached eggs?" Corky asked, pouring herself a half glass of orange juice.

"You need a lot of energy," their mother replied, dumping two runny eggs onto two pieces of toast with a plastic spatula.

Mr. Corcoran yawned loudly. "I don't sleep well in this house."

"No one does," Corky muttered, taking her place at the breakfast table. The two eggs on her plate stared up at her like giant runny eyes. "It's the ghosts."

"Yeah. This place is definitely haunted," Bobbi quickly agreed.

"Haunted? That's ridiculous." Mrs. Corcoran set down a plate in front of Bobbi, who made a disgusted face.

"This girl I met at school—Lisa Blume— she told me that *all* the houses on Fear Street are haunted," Corky said, poking her eggs with her fork, watching the yellow run over the toast.

"Just because a house is old and creaky, it doesn't mean it's haunted," Mr. Corcoran replied.

"I think someone was murdered in my room,"

Bobbi said, glancing across the table at her sister. Bobbi was the one with the wild imagination. "Someone keeps whispering to me late at night, whispering and crying."

"Probably the wind," their father said, straightening his tie with one hand and taking a sip from his coffee cup with the other.

"Yeah, sure. The wind," Bobbi said sarcastically.

Sitting across from each other, Corky and Bobbi looked like twins, even though Bobbi was a year older. Both had blond hair, very light, very fine, which they wore brushed straight to their shoulders or sometimes in ponytails or single braids. Both had lively green eyes; creamy, pale skin; and high cheekbones like models.

Bobbi was seventeen but nearly two inches shorter than her younger sister, which annoyed her no end. Corky, on the other hand, was envious of her sister's figure. Corky was tall but boyish. Sometimes she felt gawky and wished she'd hurry up and fill out.

"Well, your brother is certainly not having any trouble sleeping in this house," Mrs. Corcoran said, heading toward the front stairs. "Didn't you wake him up?"

They heard a deafening shriek, a hideous scream of terror from upstairs. Sean had obviously discovered the rat.

"I think he's up," Bobbi said dryly.

Both girls collapsed in laughter, lowering their heads to the table.

"What did you two do?" Mrs. Corcoran demanded. She hurried to the rescue.

"We didn't do it! The ghost did it!" Bobbi called after her.

Mr. Corcoran simply shook his head. He was used to having his daughters play tricks on Sean. They loved to take advantage of their brother's trusting personality.

Taking another sip of coffee, Mr. Corcoran sighed, wondering what hideous thing they had just done to make poor Sean scream like that.

The girls were still snickering when Sean entered the kitchen, fully dressed in faded jeans and a red Gap T-shirt, swinging the rat by the tail. "It didn't fool me at all," he told his sisters.

"You always scream like that when you get up, right?" Bobbi teased.

"I just did that so you wouldn't be disappointed," Sean said, avoiding their eyes.

Mrs. Corcoran followed him into the kitchen and rested her hands on his slender shoulders. "This house is creepy enough," she scolded the girls. "Do we really need *rats*?"

Sean set the rat down on the breakfast table.

Mrs. Corcoran quickly grabbed it away. "Not on the table. Please!"

"It's not as disgusting as these eggs," Bobbi griped.

Sean glanced from one plate to another. "Looks like rat puke."

"Sean—*please*!" his mother exclaimed.

"Another delightful Corcoran family breakfast," their father said, pulling himself up and scraping his chair noisily back along the faded old linoleum.

"Have your breakfast," Mrs. Corcoran told the girls, glancing at the clock. "Don't you have cheerleader tryouts this afternoon?"

"*If* they'll let us try out," Corky said glumly. The light in her emerald eyes faded. "The squad is already full. They say they picked everyone last spring. Before we moved here."

"But you girls are the best!" their mother declared, plopping two eggs onto a plate for Sean. "You were both all-state back home in Missouri. You practically took your squad to the national championships."

"You both stink," Sean said flatly.

"No one asked your opinion," Mr. Corcoran told Sean. "Hey—I'm outta here." He gave his wife a quick kiss on the cheek and disappeared out the kitchen door. "Good luck this afternoon, girls!" they heard him call from outside.

"We'll need it," Corky muttered.

"When you jump up, everyone can see your underpants," Sean said nastily.

"Sean—eat your eggs," Mrs. Corcoran replied sharply. She pushed the plate closer to him, then glanced down at the girls, concern wrinkling her pale face. "They *should* let you try out at least. When they see how good you are—"

"Miss Green said it was up to the girls on the squad," Corky said.

"Who's Miss Green? The advisor?" their mother asked, pouring herself a cup of coffee.

"Yeah. We met her and we met the squad captain—Jennifer something-or-other," Bobbi said. "She seemed really nice."

"So they'll let you try out?" Mrs. Corcoran asked, motioning for Sean to eat faster.

"Maybe," Corky said doubtfully.

"We'll see after school," Bobbi said. She took a final bite of toast, pushed her chair back, and hurried upstairs to get dressed.

"You two could put Shadyside High on the map," Mrs. Corcoran yelled after her.

Corky laughed. "Mom, if it were up to you, we'd have it made."

"But you stink," Sean said quietly. Then he opened his mouth wide so Corky could see the yellow egg inside.

"You're gross," Corky said, frowning.

"You stink," he replied. It seemed to be the refrain of the morning.

"Knock it off," their mother scolded, rolling her eyes. "Hurry. Get dressed. You're all going to be late."

Corky took a last sip of orange juice, then headed upstairs, trying to decide what to wear. The kids at Shadyside were a lot more into clothes than her friends back in Missouri. She had the feeling that she'd need some new things, some short skirts, some tights, some leggings.

"Oh!"

She stopped on the landing and stared up at the hall railing. It took her a while to realize that she was staring at her sister.

"Bobbi!" she called.

Bobbi was dangling over the wooden railing, motionless, her arms hanging down. Her eyes were open in an unseeing stare, her mouth twisted in a wide O of horror.

"Bobbi!" Corky repeated, calling in a shrill voice she didn't recognize. "Bobbi!"

But her sister didn't move. Didn't blink.

Didn't breathe.

2

NERVOUS TIME

"Bobbi!"

Her heart in her throat, Corky lurched up the final stairs to her sister.

Bobbi raised her head and blinked, and an amused smile formed on her face. "Gotcha," she said softly. Pushing with both hands against the railing, she raised herself to a standing position.

"Bobbi—you rat!" Corky screeched, her heart still thudding.

"*You* weren't supposed to find me," Bobbi said, still grinning delightedly that her little joke had worked so well. "Sean was supposed to come upstairs first."

"Don't ever do that again!" Corky cried, giving her sister a playful but hard punch on the shoulder.

"You *know* I'm nervous about this house and trying out for cheerleading and everything."

"Nervous?" said Bobbi, following her sister into the room they shared. "Come on, Cork—lighten up. I mean, what's there to be nervous about?"

Her friends at Shadyside High were always telling Jennifer Daly that she looked like a movie star. In fact, Jennifer did have the easy grace of an actress, as well as large, dark eyes and sensual full lips.

A friendly girl with a soft voice and a high, tinkling laugh, Jennifer had been the popular choice for captain of the Shadyside High Tigers cheerleading squad. She and Kimmy Bass, the squad's energetic assistant captain, had been good friends since elementary school. But Jennifer also got along well with the other cheerleaders. She was so easy to know and to like, and as Kimmy put it, "She isn't stuck-up about anything."

Kimmy buzzed around Jennifer like a frenetic bumblebee. With her round face topped by a mop of crimped black hair, her full cheeks that always seemed to be pink, and her slightly chunky shape, she proved a striking contrast to her friend.

Their personalities were quite different too. While Jennifer was soft-spoken, serene, and graceful, Kimmy was loud, enthusiastic, and so full of energy that she seemed unable to stand still.

Standing under the basketball backboard, Jennifer straightened her T-shirt over her gray sweatpants and waited for the other members of the squad to enter the gym. She glanced up at the big clock next to the scoreboard. 3:20. School had just let out. Time for cheerleading practice to begin.

Kimmy was the next to arrive, the swinging double doors banging behind her as she hurried across the gym floor, waving to Jennifer. The bright overhead lights gave Kimmy's face a greenish tinge, Jennifer noticed. And as Kimmy drew closer, Jennifer saw that she had tiny beads of perspiration above her upper lip, a sure sign that Kimmy was worked up about something.

Jennifer didn't have to guess what Kimmy was upset about. It had to be the two Corcoran sisters, who, Jennifer noticed, had slipped into the gym and were huddled together on the far side of the floor near a section of wooden bleachers that had been lowered during the last gym class.

"I just don't think it's right!" Kimmy exclaimed, tossing her backpack to the floor, her round cheeks pink with excitement. "We already have our squad, Jennifer. We've practiced all summer. They can't just barge in. I don't care who they are!"

Jennifer closed her eyes briefly. Evidently Kimmy didn't realize how far her voice could travel in the big, empty gym. Or perhaps she didn't care. But she was talking loudly enough for the Corcoran sisters to overhear every word.

"Shh," Jennifer whispered, gesturing with her eyes to the bleachers.

Kimmy turned quickly, following Jennifer's gaze. "I don't care," she repeated just as loudly as before. She shook her mop of hair, as if shaking away Jennifer's warning. "We can't let them try out, Jen. We can't. It just isn't fair."

The other cheerleaders were filing into the gym now, dropping their books and backpacks beside the wall, greeting one another in low tones, leaning against the tile wall to stretch out. Kimmy's friend Debra Kern entered and gave Kimmy a wave. She was followed by Heather Diehl and Megan Carman, who were best friends and always together. Entering last was Veronica (Ronnie) Mitchell, the only freshman to have made the squad.

"Kimmy—they can *hear* you!" Jennifer repeated, embarrassed. She turned to the bleachers, where the Corcorans were now sitting side by side on the bottom bench, their hands clasped tensely in their laps. "You know, they're supposed to be terrific cheerleaders."

"Says who?" Kimmy snapped, crossing her arms in front of her chest.

"They were all-state back in their old hometown," Jennifer told her. "And you know that cheerleading competition that's on ESPN every year?"

"Yeah. We watched it together, remember?" Kimmy said almost grudgingly.

"Well, their cheerleading team won it last year. That's how good the Corcorans are."

"But who cares, Jen?" Kimmy cried emotionally, uncrossing her arms and gesturing with her hands. "We have a *great* team, don't we? We work together so well. We've practiced together for so long and—"

"But maybe they can make our team even better," Jennifer said, refusing to raise her voice. "After all, we want the very best girls we can get, don't we? I mean, maybe we could be all-state this year. Or be on ESPN or something."

"I agree with Kimmy," Debra broke in, stepping up beside her friend. She was beautiful but cold-looking, with straight blond hair cut very short and icy blue eyes. Debra was an unlikely cheerleader. Short and thin, almost too thin, she seldom smiled. The only time she ever really seemed to come alive was when she was performing a cheer or a routine.

"Look at them," Jennifer said softly, turning

her eyes to Corky and Bobbi. "They're here. We can at least let them do their stuff, don't you think? It won't hurt to watch them."

"But we had tryouts last spring," Kimmy insisted.

"Yeah," Debra chimed in. "We can't hold tryouts every week, you know." She fixed Jennifer with an icy stare.

"Is this a cheerleading squad or a debate team?" a harsh voice rang out loudly.

All of the cheerleaders turned to see Miss Green, their advisor, step quickly from her small office in the corner and move toward them with long, quick strides. Dressed in tight white tennis shorts, a gray short-sleeved T-shirt, and black high-tops, Miss Green was a compact woman with frizzy brown hair, a plain face that naturally seemed to fall into an angry expression, and a husky voice that always sounded as if she had a bad case of laryngitis.

She taught health and phys ed, and had a reputation for being tough—a well-deserved reputation.

"We have three new routines to learn by Friday night," she called out loudly, her voice echoing off the tile walls of the vast gym. "So what's holding things up? Or have you learned the new routines already?"

"We're trying to decide about *them*," Kimmy said, glancing first at Jennifer, then pointing to the Corcoran sisters, who had climbed to their feet.

"It's up to Jennifer," Miss Green said, staring at Jennifer. "The captain decides."

Kimmy, obviously miffed, made a face.

"I'd like to see what they can do," Jennifer said, staring defiantly at Kimmy. "I really think we should give them a chance."

"Okay. End of debate," Miss Green said brusquely. She waved to Corky and Bobbi. "You two!" she shouted. "You're on!"

"I don't believe this," Kimmy muttered darkly to Debra as they went to join the other girls against the wall. They stood beside Ronnie, and the three girls whispered among themselves, their expressions unhappy, as Corky and Bobbi made their way across the gym.

"Are you nervous?" Corky whispered to Bobbi, her eyes on the cheerleaders huddled against the wall.

"Who? *Me?*" Bobbi replied with a peal of nervous laughter. "Hey, come on. Why should *we* be nervous, Cork? We know we're good!"

"Tell that to my shaking knees!" Corky exclaimed.

Their sneakers squeaked as they hurried across

the gleaming wood floor. The gym suddenly grew silent. The air felt heavy and hot.

"Show us whatever you like," Jennifer told them, flashing them an encouraging smile.

Corky and Bobbi each took a deep breath, glanced at the other for luck, stepped to the center of the floor, and huddled together.

"What should we do first?" Corky asked her older sister.

"Let's start with some synchronized walk-overs," Bobbi suggested. "Then let's show them our double cartwheel."

"Why are they staring at us like that?" Corky asked, glancing over Bobbi's shoulder at the silent cheerleaders. "Like they hate us or something."

"Let's give them something to stare at," Bobbi replied, grinning.

"Break a leg," Corky said.

3

FIRST SCREAM

"Ohh!"

The cry from one of the cheerleaders told Bobbi that her spread eagle was as spectacular as she had planned.

Up, up she leaped until she felt as if she could take off and fly. And then she shot out both legs, raising them up until they were perfectly straight. And then, in her most startling move, Bobbi kept her legs outstretched as she gracefully floated down, hands high above her head like a diving bird, into a perfect split.

Then, before her stunned audience had recovered, she and Corky were into a powerhouse chant:

"First and ten,
Do it again!

First and ten,
Do it again!
Go, Tigers!"

It's going okay, Bobbi thought. *At least they're not glaring at us anymore.*

She glanced at her sister, gave her a quick nod—their signal for their big finish—and jumped.

Onto Corky's back. A perfect pony mount.

Then one swift move. Up. Arms up. And up again. Into the shoulder stand they had practiced day after day until their shoulders and backs were red and sore.

Good, Bobbi thought, standing straight and tall on Corky's shoulders, feeling Corky's hot hands lock on to the backs of her legs. She smiled confidently, hands on hips. Then, without losing her smile, she suddenly dove off Corky's shoulders.

The cheerleaders gasped as she plummeted straight out. She completed a perfect flip and landed, standing on both feet. And then the sisters moved into a repeat of their double cartwheel. Corky grasped Bobbi's ankles as Bobbi grasped Corky's ankles, and the two girls cartwheeled across the floor. They stood up with a final shout: "Go, Tigers!"

The two sisters ran off clapping. Bobbi smiled

at Corky as they leaned against the wall, catching their breath.

"Wow! They're incredible!" she heard one of the cheerleaders exclaim.

"How'd they do that?" she heard another ask in a loud whisper.

"You're putting on weight," Corky grumbled, rubbing her shoulders.

"Wow, that was great!" Jennifer said, smiling warmly, her dark eyes lighting up with genuine excitement.

"Thanks," Corky and Bobbi said in unison, smiling back at her.

They were standing awkwardly in Miss Green's office, a small glassed-in enclosure in the corner of the gym. Seated at the wooden desk, Miss Green was searching the top drawer for some forms.

The routine had been one of their best ever, Bobbi thought. Sometimes she and Corky just clicked, and that day had been one of those days.

All of the cheerleaders had been really impressed. Except for the one named Kimmy and her short, blond friend. They had remained stone-faced, even when all the other girls had burst into appreciative applause.

"That was fabulous!" Miss Green had called

out in her husky voice. "Of course your shoulder dive is impressive, but I also liked the height you got on those spread eagles." She'd turned to the squad members along the wall. "I'd like to see everyone work on the new routines now. I hope Bobbi and Corky have inspired you to keep your energy up. Up!"

"Let's go!" Kimmy had yelled, clapping and running past Corky and Bobbi, avoiding their eyes as she'd led the squad to the center of the floor.

As the girls had started to chant one of their new cheers, the two sisters had followed Jennifer and Miss Green into the corner office.

Jennifer motioned for the sisters to sit down on the folding chairs against the wall. Corky glanced quickly at Bobbi as they sat, a questioning glance.

"Do you mean we made the squad?" Bobbi asked Jennifer.

"Ah, here they are," Miss Green interrupted before Jennifer could reply. "You'll need to fill out these forms. This one's a health form," she said, pulling out a green sheet of paper. "And this one is the release form. Your parents have to sign that one."

"We made the squad?" Bobbi repeated, to Jennifer.

"Yeah. You were amazing!" Jennifer gushed. Then she added: "I used to be the star here. But no one's going to notice me with you two around."

Bobbi couldn't decide if she was kidding or not. The girls reacted with embarrassed laughter. "We'll show you how to do the shoulder dismount," Bobbi offered.

"I think we can all learn something from you two," Miss Green added, shuffling through the sheaf of forms.

Jennifer's eyes flared just then, and Bobbi suddenly felt uncomfortable. Jennifer was making it clear that she was jealous of the Corcorans.

"Where did you get that double cartwheel thing after the dive?" Jennifer asked, leaning back against the yellow-tiled wall.

"We sort of made it up," Corky told her.

"Some other girls were doing something like it at the state finals back in Missouri last year," Bobbi added, "and we kind of adapted it."

"I hope *we* can get to the state finals," Jennifer said wistfully.

"With these two on the squad, it's a lock," Miss Green said, smiling one of her rare smiles as she handed the forms to Corky and Bobbi. As she stared at the girls, her expression changed to one of concern. "Uniforms. Uniforms," she muttered. "This might be a problem. Quick." She pulled a pad of paper from her top drawer. "Write down your sizes. This will have to be a rush order."

A short while later Bobbi and Corky were thanking Jennifer and Miss Green; with the chants of their fellow cheerleaders ringing through the gym, they hurried out of the building, eager to congratulate each other.

Jennifer and Miss Green continued to confer over the low wooden desk, their expressions serious, concerned. Miss Green spoke heatedly, her eyes turning occasionally to watch the practice on the other side of the glass partition.

"The squad is supposed to be six," she told Jennifer. "I guess we can squeeze one more girl on. But not two. We don't have the funds for eight cheerleaders."

Lowering their voices, Jennifer and Miss Green continued to discuss the problem.

"Hey—what's going on?"

Startled by the intrusion, both the captain and the advisor whirled around to see Kimmy standing in the doorway, hands on hips, her cheeks pink, breathing heavily.

"Can you ask Ronnie to come in?" Jennifer asked Kimmy. "We can only make room for one more girl, so Ronnie will have to—"

"Huh? You're putting those sisters on the squad?" Kimmy demanded, her voice rising several octaves.

"Of course," Jennifer replied. "You saw how good they were. They're awesome!"

"But I thought—" Kimmy stopped, letting the news sink in.

"We're very lucky they moved to Shadyside," Miss Green added with unusual enthusiasm.

"And that means—Ronnie's out?" Kimmy asked, her voice revealing her outrage. "She's off the squad? Just like that?"

"Kimmy—" Jennifer started.

But Miss Green took over, climbing to her feet as if prepared to fight. "Ronnie is only a freshman," she said firmly. "She'll be an alternate. She'll practice with the squad. And she'll go on if one of you gets sick or something."

"Oh, she'll *love* that," Kimmy said bitterly. "I really don't think it's fair. I mean—"

"Kimmy—you *saw* how good Bobbi and Corky are!" Jennifer cried. "We *need* them. We really do."

Kimmy started to reply, thought better of it, and uttered a sigh of exasperation. Glaring at Jennifer, she turned away from the office and called to Ronnie.

"You wanted to see me?" Ronnie hesitated in the doorway, nervously pushing back her curly red hair with both hands. She had small brown eyes, a tiny round stub of a nose, and a face full of freckles.

She almost collapsed when Miss Green told her of her demotion. Angry tears formed in the corners of her eyes, which she quickly wiped away with the backs of her hands.

"We really don't have a choice," Jennifer said softly.

"Yes, you do," Ronnie snapped back, her dark eyes flashing.

"We have to think of what's best for the squad," Miss Green said, twirling a pen nervously between her fingers. "You'll have plenty of opportunity—"

"Yeah. Sure," Ronnie interrupted, and fled toward the locker room.

"She feels bad," Jennifer said, staring through the glass as the other girls stopped their practice to watch Ronnie run off.

"She'll get over it," Miss Green said flatly.

"I'll never forgive them!" Ronnie cried. "Never!"

Kimmy and Debra huddled around the freshman, trying to ignore the steamy, junglelike air of the locker room. The other girls had showered and left. These three remained, talking, commiserating with one another, trying to decide what, if anything, they could do.

"Those sisters had no right to try out," Kimmy

agreed heatedly, putting a comforting hand on Ronnie's shoulder.

"Not them," Ronnie insisted angrily. "Jennifer and Miss Green. It was *their* idea to kick me off."

"We should all get together," Debra said heatedly. "You know. Sign a petition or something. I'm sure Megan and Heather would sign it too." She sat down on the bench and began to pull off her sneakers.

Kimmy removed a white towel from her locker and mopped her forehead with it. "Wow, do I need a shower! Yeah, maybe you're right, Deb. If the whole squad protests, if we all stand together, I'll bet we could get them to change their minds."

Ronnie groaned and rolled her eyes. "What dream world do you live in?" she muttered. "The Corcoran sisters were all-state, remember? Did you see the look on Miss Green's face when they did that shoulder stand and all those double cartwheels?"

"She was practically drooling," Debra said, shaking her head. "She could probably see the championship trophy on her shelf."

"But what's Jennifer's problem?" Kimmy demanded, pulling her heavy sweater off over her head.

"She's *your* friend," Ronnie said bitterly.

"I can't *believe* her," Debra added. "Maybe

being captain has gone to her head or something. She thinks she's such a big deal."

"My parents are going to be very upset," Ronnie said with renewed sadness. "They were more excited about my making the squad than I was. And now—"

Kimmy and Debra continued trying to comfort Ronnie as they undressed, tossing their clothes onto the benches. They carried their towels over the concrete floor to the shower room.

"I don't *want* to be an alternate," Ronnie complained, her voice breaking with emotion. "That's just stupid. I'd rather—"

"If only the Corcorans would just go back where they came from," Debra said. "With their long blond hair and their big eyes and phony smiles." She put a finger down her throat and pretended to puke. "Yuck."

"They're not that bad," Ronnie muttered. "It's Jennifer. She had no right—"

Kimmy stepped under the chrome showerhead. She turned the knobs on the wall with both hands.

The water burst out in a loud rush.

Kimmy froze, open-mouthed, for a brief second.

Then she started to scream.

4

A TRAGIC ACCIDENT

Kimmy staggered back until she hit the tile wall.

Panting loudly, she pointed to the water rushing in a broad stream from the showerhead.

"Kimmy—are you okay?" Debra cried in alarm. "What *is* it?"

"The water—it's scalding hot!" Kimmy told her.

The three girls turned off the taps and hurried out, clutching their towels.

"Ow, that *burned*!" Kimmy declared, starting to breathe normally.

"Should we get the nurse? Are you all right?" Debra asked, staring at Kimmy's chest and neck, which were scarlet.

"I think I'll be okay," Kimmy said, relieved,

covering herself with the towel. "It was just such a shock."

"We'll have to remember to tell Simmons," Debra said. And then she added sarcastically, "Maybe he'll get around to fixing it in a year or two."

Simmons was one of the Shadyside High custodians. He also drove a school bus. A laid-back young man with a blond ponytail and headphones that seemed to be permanently glued to his ears, he wasn't terribly reliable in either job.

"Hey—did you drop this?" Ronnie asked. She bent down and picked something shiny off the floor.

"Oh. Thanks." Kimmy reached out for it. It was her silver megaphone pendant. Her parents had given it to her for her sixteenth birthday. She struggled to put it back around her neck, which was still red from the scalding shower. "The clasp is loose," she said, frowning. "I really have to get it fixed. Don't want to lose it."

The three friends hurriedly got dressed in silence.

Hoisting her backpack onto her shoulder, Ronnie sighed and headed for the door, her sneakers thudding heavily on the concrete.

"You feeling any better?" Kimmy called after her.

"No" was the sullen reply.

"This is so exciting!" Bobbi declared.

It was a Friday evening, two weeks later, and the cheerleaders were boarding the small yellow-and-black school bus that would take them to the Tigers' first away game.

Corky followed her sister onto the bus. She said hi to Simmons, who was slouched in the driver's seat, fiddling with his ponytail. He grunted in reply.

Raindrops dotted the windshield. A light rain had started to fall. The sky was a gloomy charcoal color, but not gloomy enough to darken the sisters' moods.

They had been working hard for that night, practicing the new routines after school and at home, learning the cheers, working up a few new wrinkles of their own.

"Go, Tigers!" Bobbi yelled, tumbling into a seat near the back.

"Go, *who*?" Megan yelled back.

The bus quickly filled with loud voices, happy laughter. Simmons leaned forward and pulled the handle to close the door.

"Hey—where's Miss Green?" Debra called.

Jennifer turned around in the front seat. "She's driving in her own car tonight. She had to take some friends."

Kimmy sat in the window seat next to Debra. She rubbed her hand over the glass, trying to clear the thin film of steam away so she could see out.

"Hey, Simmons—how about some air-conditioning?" one of the girls yelled. "We're melting back here!"

Simmons, obviously lost in his own thoughts, ignored the request, as usual. He started the bus up and clicked on the headlights.

Corky, seated in the aisle beside her sister, turned to stare out their window as the bus backed out of its parking space and headed out of the student parking lot. Rivulets of rainwater ran down the glass, distorting her view.

The rain picked up, drumming noisily on the roof of the bus. A gust of wind blew water through the window, which was open an inch or two at the top. Bobbi raised herself up and, with great effort, pushed the window shut.

"Now we'll suffocate," Corky complained.

"Take your pick—suffocate or drown," Bobbi told her.

"Tough choice," Corky replied.

"Go, Tigers!" someone yelled.

Someone started a cheer, and everyone joined in.

>"*Tigers are yellow,*
>*Tigers are black.*
>*Push 'em back, push 'em back,*
>*Push 'em waaaaay back!*"

Bobbi smiled at her sister. She settled back in her seat, happy and excited.

The past two weeks had been difficult. The other girls were aloof at first, even resentful. But Bobbi was confident that she and Corky had won most of them over. Kimmy and Debra were still cold to them, still acted as if they were unwanted intruders. But she felt sure that she and Corky would eventually win those two over too.

As the bus rattled down Park Drive away from the school, the rain pounded harder. The trees and shrubs exploded in a white flash of lightning. The thunder seemed to crack right above them.

Heather and Megan began chanting, "Rain, rain, go away."

Jennifer turned in her seat to face the rest of the cheerleaders. "It's not going to last," she announced. "It's just a flash storm. They said on the radio it's going to pass quickly."

Another loud thunderclap made two girls scream.

Everyone else laughed.

The big wipers scraped noisily, rhythmically, across the windshield, which was covered with a curtain of white steam. Simmons didn't seem to mind—or notice—the poor visibility.

Holding on to the seat back, Jennifer stood up. "I have a few announcements to make," she called out, shouting to be heard over the driving rain.

Kimmy and Debra were giggling loudly about something. Jennifer waited for them to get quiet.

"First of all, unless it's still drizzling, we'll do the fire baton routine at halftime as planned," Jennifer said, cupping her hands like a megaphone.

Simmons made a sharp turn onto Canyon Road, causing Jennifer to topple back into her seat. She pushed herself back up, flashing the driver an annoyed look, which, of course, he didn't see.

"If the storm doesn't blow over—" Jennifer continued.

"Oh no!" Corky cried. "The fire batons!"

All eyes turned to the back of the bus.

A flash of lightning seemed to outline Corky and her sister.

"We have to turn around!" Corky declared, shouting over the clap of thunder.

"What?" Jennifer called, her face filled with confusion.

"We have to stop at my house," Corky explained. "The fire batons. Bobbi and I brought them home to practice. We forgot them. Can we turn around?"

Several girls groaned, Kimmy the loudest of all.

"It's only a small detour," Bobbi said, coming to her sister's defense.

"No problem," Jennifer said, her expression troubled. Standing in the aisle beside Simmons, she tapped him hard on the shoulder.

No reaction.

So she tugged his ponytail. "We have to make a stop on Fear Street," Jennifer told him.

"Huh?"

"Fear Street," Jennifer repeated impatiently. "Just turn here."

Simmons turned the wheel, and the bus skidded into a turn over the wet pavement. Holding on to the seat back, Jennifer turned back to Corky and Bobbi. "Direct us when we get to Fear Street, okay?"

The two sisters agreed, apologizing again for the detour.

"Oooh, Fear Street," someone said, uttering a spooky howl. Some other girls laughed.

Kimmy made some kind of wisecrack to Debra, and the two girls giggled together.

The rain fell in heavy sheets, driven by unpredictable, powerful wind gusts. For some reason Simmons sped up. In front of him the big wipers swam mechanically across the steamy windshield.

Jennifer resumed her position in the aisle beside him. "I have just a few more announcements to make," she shouted.

Staring out the window at the storm, Bobbi saw the passing houses and trees grow darker, as if a heavy shadow had lowered itself over them, over the whole world. Trees bent in the strong wind. The rain suddenly shifted and blew against the window, startling Bobbi and blocking her view.

Up at the front, Jennifer continued with her announcements. Bobbi couldn't hear her over the pounding rain, the thunder, the angry rush of wind.

Simmons reached out and pulled the lever to open the door. The sound of the rain grew louder. Cold, wet air cut through the bus.

"Why did he open the door?" Corky asked her sister.

"I guess to see better," Bobbi replied thoughtfully. "The windshield is totally steamed."

"Are we near home?"

The bus sped up. Simmons had his head turned to the open door, his eyes on the cross street, which passed by in a gray blur.

Bobbi stared hard out the rain-blotted window, trying to read a street sign.

Suddenly she realized that something was wrong.

The bus—it began to skid.

There was no time to scream or cry out a warning.

One second they were moving along through the rain. The next second they were sliding, sliding out of control toward the curb.

"Whoa!" Simmons shrieked over the squeal of tires. "The brakes—!"

The tire squeals grew to a roar in Bobbi's ears. She covered them with both hands. She tried to scream, but the sound caught in her throat.

The impact was fast and hard.

What had they hit? A tree? A rock? The curb?

The bus seemed to bounce, to fly up off the road, to bounce again.

Staring in horror and surprise at the front, Bobbi saw Jennifer's eyes open wide. And then as the bus jolted and spun, she watched as Jennifer flew out the open door.

Jennifer's startled scream was drowned out by the squeal of the skidding tires.

By the crunch of metal.

By the shatter of glass.

5

DEATH OF A CHEERLEADER

It all took a second. Maybe less.

Bobbi blinked—and it was over.

The screams swirled around her, surrounding her.

She wasn't sure whether she was hearing the squeal of the tires or the cries of the cheerleaders.

And then the world tilted onto its side.

With a silent, choked gasp, Bobbi toppled onto Corky. And the two of them, arms flailing helplessly, fell sideways toward the far window.

Which was now the floor.

No time to scream.

It took only a microsecond. Or so it seemed.

The window glass beneath them cracked all the way down the pane like a jagged bolt of lightning.

And still the bus bumped and slid, metal grating against pavement, invading their ears.

Bobbi felt another hard bump. A stab of pain jolted her entire body, made her shake and bounce.

And then all movement stopped. Such an abrupt stop. Such a shattering stop.

I'm okay, Bobbi realized. Her first clear thought.

She was on top of her sister, their arms and legs tangled.

Corky is okay too.

Corky stared up at her, open-mouthed, her green eyes wide with fear.

All sideways.

She heard muffled cries. Whimpers, like from frightened puppies.

"Oh man." A loud groan from the front of the bus. From Simmons.

Bobbi pulled herself up. Simmons was trying to stand. But everything was tilted. Everything was wrong.

"Are you okay?" Corky asked in a tiny voice.

"Yeah. I think so," Bobbi replied uncertainly.

"Then get *off* me!" Corky cried.

She sounded so angry, it made Bobbi laugh.

Hysterical laughter, she realized, and forced herself to stop.

Got to keep control. Control. Control.

Bobbi looked up to find a row of windows above her head.

"Oh," she said out loud. She finally realized what had happened. The bus was on its side.

It had rammed into a tree or something, bounced off, and toppled onto its side, then skidded to a stop.

"How do we get out?" Bobbi heard Kimmy call even though she couldn't see her.

In the darkness she saw a tangle of arms and legs.

She heard a girl crying. She heard groans and whispers.

"The emergency door. In back!" someone shouted.

Bobbi reached for the emergency door, and tried pushing it open. It was stuck.

"The windows are faster!" someone else cried.

Kimmy stood up, raised both arms high, struggled to slide one of the windows open. Bobbi, balancing uneasily, tried to do the same.

"Can't you get *off* me?" Corky asked impatiently.

"I'm *trying*, okay?" Bobbi replied, not recognizing her own tight, shrill voice.

The window slid open.

Raindrops hit Bobbi's upturned face. Cold. Fresh.

So clean.

"Is anyone hurt?" Simmons was calling, a tall shadow in the front. "Is anyone hurt? Who's crying?"

Bobbi raised herself up, grabbed hold of the window frame.

"Is anyone hurt?"

The rain was just a drizzle now. The rumble of thunder was low and far in the distance.

Bobbi pulled herself halfway out of the bus.

The whole world was shimmering, glistening, wet. Fresh and clean.

The bus tires were still spinning.

Where are we? Bobbi wondered. It all looked so familiar and unfamiliar at the same time.

Another face appeared. Debra was emerging from a window closer to the front. "Are you okay?" she called, squinting at Bobbi as if she were far away.

"I think so," Bobbi replied. "You?"

"Yeah. My wrist—I think it's sprained. That's all."

They pulled themselves out, smiled at each other, buoyed by the fresh air, the cool wetness, being alive. Then, standing on the overturned side that was now the roof, they leaned down into the windows to help other girls escape.

Time seemed to stand still.

Corky joined her sister, slid to the ground, stretched and yawned as if emerging from a long sleep.

The bus headlights, one on top of the other, cut through the air, casting twin spotlights on the jagged tombstones poking up through tall weeds.

Tombstones? Weeds?

Bobbi lowered herself to the ground, her sneakers sinking into the wet grass. Gripping Corky's ice-cold hand, she turned back toward the street.

Behind them, a tilted street sign read: FEAR ST.

"Oh." She let go of Corky's hand. "Look."

The bus had careened off the road and slid over the grass of the Fear Street cemetery. A thick yellow mist, catching the light from the headlights, lingered between the old gravestones, which rose up like arms and legs from the twisting, bending weeds.

"We're . . . in the cemetery," Corky said, her voice a whisper, her expression stunned. "How?"

"We're only a block from home," Bobbi said.

"Is everybody out?" Simmons called. He came toward them, taking long strides, his jeans stained at the knees, a bandanna wrapped tightly around a bleeding cut on his arm. "You okay?" he asked the two sisters.

"Yeah," Bobbi told him.

"Everyone got out," Simmons said. "No one's hurt too bad."

Then Bobbi and Corky cried out at the same time: "Jennifer!"

Where was Jennifer?

In the horror of the crash, in the noise and tilting darkness of it, they had forgotten about her.

Jennifer. Bobbi saw her again. Saw her arms jerk up as she flew out the open bus door—almost as if being pulled out.

"Jennifer?" Corky began calling, cupping her hands around her mouth. "Has anyone seen Jennifer?"

"Jennifer. Jennifer."

The word buzzed through the group of dazed, frightened girls as they huddled together, squinting against the bright headlights, trying to turn things right side up in their minds.

Trying to make sense of everything.

Trying to convince themselves that they were okay. That everything was going to be fine.

"Jennifer. Jennifer."

And then Corky saw her.

From behind.

Saw her body sprawled facedown, her head resting on the earth in front of an old tombstone, her arms stretched above her head as if she were hugging the stone.

"Jennifer!" Bobbi shouted.

A sudden gust of wind made Jennifer's skirt ruffle. But Jennifer didn't look up, didn't raise her head.

Corky and Bobbi reached her before the others. Bobbi grabbed Jennifer's shoulders to roll her onto her back.

"Don't move her!" someone yelled.

"Don't touch her! It isn't safe!"

Bobbi looked up to see Simmons standing beside her, staring down at Jennifer sprawled so awkwardly across the old grave site.

"Let's carefully roll her over and get her face out of the mud," he said quietly.

They tugged her gently by the shoulders.

As they turned Jennifer over, the words etched on the old grave marker came into Bobbi's view: SARAH FEAR. The dates beneath the name had been worn away nearly beyond legibility: 1875–1899.

They laid Jennifer gingerly onto her back.

"Call an ambulance!" Heather was screaming. "Somebody—call for help!"

Bobbi leaned over Jennifer's unmoving form. "It's too late," she said, choking out the words. "She's dead."

6

"IT'S YOUR FAULT!"

No!"

Corky's anguished cry cut through the air. She dropped to the wet ground beside Jennifer and grabbed her pale, limp hand.

"No!"

At first Bobbi thought the low wail she was hearing came from her sister. But as the sound grew louder, cutting through the crackle and whisper of the wind bending the ancient trees of the cemetery, Bobbi realized it was the siren of an ambulance.

Someone in one of the houses across the street must have seen the accident and called for help.

A few seconds later three ambulances and a police cruiser pulled onto the wet grass, their flashing red lights washing over everyone, making everything seem too bright, the colors all wrong, too frightening, too vivid to be real.

The white coats of the paramedics, scrambling through the wet weeds, flashed red and gray, red and gray. The light caught their hard expressions like those in artificial-light snapshots, freezing them in Bobbi's mind. She knew she'd always remember every somber face, every flash of light, every second of this dark, wet nightmare.

Behind the tilted tombstone, Ronnie stood crying, sobbing loudly, her mouth open wide, her eyes round. Kimmy and Debra huddled around her, trying to comfort her, their faces distorted by the flickers of red light too.

The rain had stopped now, leaving the air heavy and cold.

On the ground in front of the tombstone, several paramedics worked over Jennifer, speaking softly among themselves, softly but urgently.

Gentle hands pulled Bobbi and her sister back. Two young police officers were questioning Simmons, who was shrugging and gesturing to the overturned bus. He appeared very frightened and upset.

Radios crackled from the ambulances and the police car. A paramedic leaning over Jennifer spoke rapidly into a cell phone. The wind blew a shower of ice-cold rainwater down from the trees. Bobbi took a reluctant step closer.

Was Jennifer alive? Were they bringing her around? She had to see.

The white coats had formed a protective circle around Jennifer. Bobbi tried to make sense out of the buzz of low voices. She made her way to just outside the circle, her sneakers sinking into soft earth.

One of the paramedics stood up. In the blink of red light, Bobbi saw his eyes close, his teeth clench. "She's gone," he said.

Another white-coated young man climbed to his feet, shaking his head.

"Gone."

Radios crackled. Ronnie's sobs cut through the air.

"No!" Bobbi screamed.

Without realizing it, without even realizing she was moving, Bobbi pushed past the grim-faced paramedics. She knelt at Jennifer's side, stared down at her pretty, expressionless face.

And Jennifer opened her eyes.

"Hey!" Bobbi cried. "Whoa!"

Jennifer blinked. And stared up at Bobbi.

"Hey—" Bobbi called. "Hey—"

Jennifer blinked again. Her lips trembled. Her dark eyes moved from side to side.

"Hey—she's alive!" Bobbi called. "Hey—"

Corky was holding on to Bobbi's shoulders, leaning over her, staring down at Jennifer.

Jennifer smiled up at them both.

"Hey—"

Cheers and cries. Urgent voices. The crackling of the radios. A low voice speaking rapidly into a cell phone.

The sounds were drowned out by a rush of wind. It started to rain again.

Bobbi stared at the flashing colors, the darting yellow cones of light from the flashlights, the pale white beams of headlights. The lights all melted into one and grew brighter and brighter until she had to close her eyes.

Jennifer was alive. Okay. She was going to be okay.

Her eyes still shut tightly, Bobbi said a silent prayer.

When she opened her eyes, Jennifer's gurney was being slid into an ambulance. Two more squad cars had pulled up. Several officers stood outlined in headlights, inspecting the overturned bus, shaking their heads.

"Lucky no one was killed."

The words floated through the air and repeated in Bobbi's mind.

The rain came down harder, swirled by the wind. The ambulance siren started with a cough. Then the shrill wail corkscrewed through the rustling trees. The ambulance roared away.

"How will we get home?" Ronnie was asking, still flanked by Kimmy and Debra.

"What about the game?" Heather asked.

"We have to get *home!*" Ronnie insisted.

"Will Jennifer be okay?"

"Has anyone called our parents?"

"Someone should call Miss Green."

"She's probably at the game."

"They won't play in this rain."

Let it rain, Bobbi thought, raising her face to it. *Let the rain wash everything away. Everything.*

She turned, and was startled to see Kimmy standing beside her, a cold, grim expression on her face, her eyes locked on Bobbi's.

"Kimmy—?" Bobbi started.

"This is all your fault," Kimmy said, speaking through clenched teeth. Her hands were balled into tight fists at her sides. The rain had matted her black hair against her forehead.

"Huh?"

"All your fault," Kimmy repeated, continuing to glare at Bobbi. "If you hadn't made us turn onto Fear Street—"

"Now, *wait* a minute!" Bobbi cried. "That isn't fair!"

She realized the other cheerleaders were all staring at her, their faces grim and unhappy, lit by the flashes of red light.

"Kimmy, that's not fair," Corky cried, rushing forward to join her sister.

Kimmy walked quickly back to Ronnie and Debra.

"That's not fair!" Corky repeated.

The rain fell harder, making it difficult to see. The ambulance carrying Jennifer was far in the distance now, its siren a lingering cry that refused to fade away.

PART TWO
THE FALL

7

THE NEW CAPTAIN

The cheers thundered down from the bleachers as the cheerleaders ran out onto the floor. As the seven girls bounded across the gym, the noise rose and echoed until it felt as if the roof might be blown off.

Kimmy led the girls onto the floor, and they immediately went into what they called their clap-clap routine. The girls clapped out a rhythm—and everyone in the bleachers repeated it as loudly as possible.

As she clapped, Kimmy stared up at the colorful blur of kids filling the bleachers, spilling out onto the gym floor, standing along the walls. The entire school was at the pep rally.

The hand clapping gave way to foot stomping.

The bleachers quaked and trembled. The rhythm picked up. Faster. Louder.

What a thrill! Kimmy thought, an excited grin spread across her face. What a thrill to perform for the entire school! What a *sound!* Like an earthquake or the stampede of a thousand elephants!

She knew she looked great in her new uniform. They all did. The maroon-and-gray was so sharp, the skirt so crisp, and the sweater so bright. Their old uniforms had been ruined that night in the rain.

But here it was, two weeks later, and everything was fresh and new again. And everyone was cheering. Cheering their lungs out.

Well . . . almost everyone.

"Give me a T!"

"T!"

"Give me an I!"

"I!"

"Give me a G!"

"G!"

What a sound! Kimmy thought, her grin growing even wider as her shiny black hair bounced around her face every time she jumped.

They finished the cheer in a wavelike ripple, the girls going down in splits one after the other. Kimmy glanced down the row of cheerleaders, all

so happy, so fresh and enthusiastic, as if that terrible night had never happened.

There was Ronnie down at the end, radiant,
shouting her heart out. Her curly red hair, caught
in the bright lights, seemed to glow on its own. How
happy she'd been to be back on the squad.

And Debra, normally so cool, so withdrawn,
was cheering at the top of her lungs.

Only cheerleaders, Kimmy thought, *know
what this is like. A lot of people put us down. They
think we're wasting our time. Or we're out-of-date
or something. But that's because they don't know
this special excitement, the special thrill of getting a huge crowd to forget itself and go wild.*

The cheer ended to raucous shouts and applause.

Kimmy peered down the line of girls to see
Corky and Bobbi do their special double cartwheel.

Ugh, she thought bitterly. *What show-offs.
They really make me sick. With their blond hair
and sweet, innocent faces. Always prancing around
together, trying to make the rest of us look second-
rate. I could throw up. I really could.*

The echoing drums of the marching band
brought Kimmy out of her dark thoughts.

No, she decided. *I'm not going to allow those
two to ruin this day. I'm not going to give them
another thought.*

Everyone stood and clapped along as the band played the Shadyside High marching song.

I want only good memories of this pep rally, Kimmy thought, clapping as hard as she could. *After all, the rally is in honor of us, in honor of how brave we were, in honor of how we survived that terrible night.*

The band ended its number to wild applause. Corky and Bobbi did their cartwheel again, and Kimmy forced herself not to react.

The girls all turned to her to begin the next cheer routine.

"Let's go, let's go, let's go, let's go. . . ."

Kimmy's eye caught Miss Green leaning against the wall of her office and clapping along with them, a big smile on her usually dour face.

In a few minutes Miss Green will name me as the new captain, Kimmy thought. The thought sent a shiver of anticipation down her back.

It's something I've wanted for so long. I've worked so hard for it, so hard.

I'm not knockout beautiful like the other girls. I'm not tall and well built. I don't have straight blond hair like the Corcorans or look like a movie star like . . . Jennifer.

But I'm going to be captain. I'm finally going to be captain.

She wished her parents could have been there to see it, to see the pep rally, to see their daughter, to see how thrilling it all was. She had begged them to come. But, as usual, they'd claimed they couldn't get away from their jobs.

Just an excuse, Kimmy thought bitterly.

Then she forced those thoughts out of her mind. Nothing was going to spoil her day. Nothing.

The routine ended. The band started up immediately. Kimmy turned toward the far side of the gym, and the other girls followed her lead.

As the band finished its number, a deafening cheer went up as Jennifer wheeled herself out onto the floor. She was wearing a new uniform too, Kimmy saw. In her hand was a maroon-and-gray pennant with her name embroidered on it, the pennant the cheer team had given her in the hospital.

She waved it from her seat as she wheeled herself across the gym. The applause grew and grew until Kimmy felt like covering her ears.

Jennifer has been so brave during all this, Kimmy thought, staring at her in her wheelchair now lined up with the other cheerleaders.

Kimmy wondered if *she* would have been so brave, so smiling, so . . . accepting.

Kimmy realized that the gym had grown silent.

Jennifer had wheeled herself to a microphone and begun a short speech.

"I'm not good at making speeches," she was saying, her voice a bit unsteady. "I'd much rather be cheering than talking!"

Nervous laughter rolled down from the bleachers. One of the drummers in the band hit a rim shot.

"I just want to say thank you to everyone at Shadyside High," Jennifer continued, her voice breaking with sudden emotion. "You've all been so good to me . . . all my friends . . . everyone . . . with all the cards and presents and stuff. . . ." She waved the pennant. "And I just want to tell you all that . . . I feel *great! Go, Tigers!*"

She pushed back from the microphone, waving her pennant, as the entire school erupted in applause. The band played the marching song again. Maroon-and-gray streamers came flying down from the bleachers.

Kimmy wiped away the tears that were rolling down her cheeks. She could feel herself begin to lose control, feel the loud, choking sobs try to force their way up.

But she cut them off.

This wasn't a sad day. It was a happy day.

Everyone was smiling and cheering.

This was a celebration. A celebration that they were all alive.

So why did Jennifer's smile make Kimmy feel like bawling?

She turned away from Jennifer. It was the only way to keep the sobs down, to keep herself in control.

I'm just excited, she thought. *Overexcited, I guess.*

She took a deep breath and held it.

Miss Green was approaching them, taking long strides across the gleaming wood gym floor, an intent expression on her face. She wore a maroon-and-gray Shadyside sweatshirt over gray sweatpants. As she neared the microphone, her face flushed, she clasped her hands together behind her back.

Miss Green hated public speaking. She seldom spoke at assemblies or pep rallies, and when she did, she always rocked back and forth on her feet and her voice quavered, and everyone could tell she was really nervous.

She smiled at Jennifer, stopped, and made a short bow to her. Then, her face nearly scarlet, she stepped close to the microphone.

"I have an announcement to make!" she shouted, her voice echoing off the four walls. It

took a while for the crowd to quiet down. She
stood silently, waiting until they did. Kimmy
could see a muscle twitch in her jaw from nervousness.

Poor woman, she thought sympathetically.

Kimmy felt the emotion begin to tighten her
own muscles. She realized she was smiling with
trembling lips. She hoped no one could see them
shaking.

"This is a day of celebration," Miss Green
began. "We are celebrating the great spirit of these
Shadyside cheerleaders. And we are celebrating the
spirit shown in particular by Jennifer Daly."

The gym grew absolutely silent. So silent,
Kimmy could hear a car horn honking outside in
the parking lot.

"We are all celebrating today because Jennifer
is back with us," Miss Green continued, rocking on
the heels of her white high-tops. "Her indomitable
spirit is an example for us all."

Applause.

"Now it's time for me to announce a new captain to lead the team while Jennifer continues to
heal," Miss Green said, glancing at Jennifer, who
flashed her an encouraging smile.

Kimmy took a deep breath. Her heart was
thudding so hard, she thought she might pass out.

She gave Jennifer a big smile, but Jennifer had turned to stare up into the bleachers.

"I have spent many hours thinking about this selection," Miss Green continued. "And I know that the young lady I have chosen will lead the Tiger cheerleaders with the same courage and spirit that Jennifer Daly has shown."

Yes! Yes! Thank you! Kimmy thought, about to burst.

She took another deep breath and let it out slowly.

Miss Green cleared her throat and then, speaking loudly and enthusiastically, announced the name of the new cheerleader captain.

"No!" Kimmy shrieked out loud. "Please—no!"

8

KIMMY QUITS

Kimmy's cries of protest were drowned out by the applause that rang down from the bleachers. Several of the other cheerleaders, including Ronnie and Debra, had turned to Kimmy to watch her mouth drop open and her expression turn to shock and dismay.

Bobbi Corcoran?

How could Bobbi Corcoran be named cheerleader captain?

Unfair, Kimmy thought, feeling her surprise turn to rage. *Impossible!*

After all, Kimmy had been named assistant captain last spring. She had been on the squad for two years. She had worked so hard. So hard.

So how could she be passed over for a flashy newcomer?

Bobbi had been on the squad for only a few weeks. She didn't know the school. She didn't know any of the routines.

So how could Miss Green and Jennifer have chosen her?

Kimmy stood with her shoulders slumped forward, allowing her unhappiness, her anger, to show on her face. She was miserable and upset, and she didn't care who knew it.

As the applause died down and Miss Green continued talking, Kimmy glanced down the line of cheerleaders. There was Corky hugging her sister joyfully. Heather and Megan had rushed over to congratulate Bobbi. And Bobbi had the widest smile on her face, her eyes brimming with happy tears.

Yuck, Kimmy thought bitterly.

I know why she was named captain. Because she's so pretty, and I'm not. She's so blond and skinny and disgustingly all-American.

Okay. So I'm not skinny, and I don't have long blond hair and look like a Seventeen *model. But how could Jennifer and Miss Green do this to me? I'm a better cheerleader than Bobbi Corcoran will ever be!*

I deserve to be captain. Everyone knows I deserve to be captain.

Kimmy realized then that her entire body was

trembling. Gazing up into the bleachers, she felt her anger turn to embarrassment.

Everyone is staring at me, she decided. *Everyone in the entire school. They're all staring at me. They know I deserve to be captain. They know I've been cheated.*

She turned and saw Debra and Ronnie studying her, their faces locked in sympathy, their eyes on Kimmy's face, trying to determine how Kimmy was taking the awful news.

Everyone is watching me, Kimmy thought, forcing back the loud sobs that pushed at her throat. *Everyone is feeling sorry for me.*

I've never been so embarrassed.

This is the worst day of my life.

I'll never forgive Bobbi. Never.

And I'll never forgive Miss Green, either.

I just want to disappear. I just want to die.

And as bitter thoughts continued to spin through Kimmy's mind, Miss Green finished her remarks and stepped back from the microphone with a relieved sigh. There was a scattering of applause.

Kimmy saw Jennifer smiling, always smiling that brave smile of hers, wheeling herself to the side of the gym.

And then Bobbi—*Bobbi!*—led the girls into

a circle to begin their final routine.

No! Kimmy decided.

No way.

I can't do this. I'm too embarrassed. Too humil-iated. I won't do it. I won't!

I quit, she decided.

I quit the cheerleaders.

She had joined the circle, followed the others automatically like some kind of sheep. But now, as they raised their arms high in the air to begin their routine, Kimmy uttered a cry of disgust—and took off, running across the polished wood floor. Running, running as fast as she could, her eyes narrowed, nearly shut, her heart pounding in rhythm with each thud of her sneakers.

Were those gasps of surprise from the bleach-ers? Were those startled questions? A worried buzz of voices?

Kimmy didn't care. She was escaping. Escap-ing and never coming back.

As she reached the double doors to the cor-ridor, running so hard that she nearly collided with them, she turned and glanced back. The cheer had begun without her; Corky Corcoran had moved around to close up the circle.

I'll pay her back too, Kimmy decided.

Jennifer. Bobbi. Corky. All of them.

She was through the doors and running down the empty corridor when the first anguished sob finally burst from her throat.

9

BOBBI AND CHIP

*C*ongratulations!"

Bobbi pulled open her locker door and turned to greet a girl she didn't know. "Thanks," she said, smiling.

"I'm Cari Taylor," the girl said, shifting the books she was carrying. She was a pretty, fragile-looking girl with blond hair, even lighter and finer than Bobbi's, and a warm, friendly smile. "I have science lab sixth period too. I've seen you there."

"Yeah. Right," Bobbi replied. "I've seen you too."

"I just wanted to say hi and congratulations," Cari said with a shrug. Then she added, "That accident must have been scary."

"Yeah," Bobbi said. "It was."

"Well, see you tomorrow."

"Right. See you."

The long corridor was emptying out as kids headed for home or after-school jobs. Bobbi could still hear the ringing applause in her ears, the cheers, the shouts, the pounding of the drums echoing off the walls.

Wow! I just feel so great! Bobbi thought, pulling some books and a binder from the top shelf of her locker. *I feel as if I could* fly *home!*

A few other kids, kids she'd seen around school but didn't really know, called out congratulations as they passed by. *Maybe Shadyside High is an okay place,* Bobbi thought happily.

During her first weeks in school, she had wondered if she'd ever get to like it. The kids all seemed so snobby. They all seemed to have known each other their whole lives. Bobbi had wondered if she'd ever fit in or find friends of her own.

But that day had erased all of her worries. It was going to be a great school year, Bobbi decided. Great. Great. Great. Everything was great.

Still in her cheerleader uniform, she looked up and down the hall. Seeing that it was empty, she performed a high leap, landed, and did a cartwheel that nearly carried her into the wall.

Having gotten that out of her system, she collected her books, stuffed them into her backpack, and, humming to herself, headed out the back door to the student parking lot.

Even the weather is great today, she thought, stopping to take a deep breath. The afternoon sky was still high and cloudless. The air felt warm and dry, more like summer than a day in autumn.

Near the fence, two girls sat on the hood of a car, talking to a boy in a maroon-and-gray letter jacket. Beside them, another car revved up noisily. Two boys were puzzling over a bike with a flat rear tire, scratching their heads and scowling.

Beyond the student parking lot, Shadyside Park stretched out, still green and vibrant. A broad, grassy field with an empty baseball diamond set in one corner led to thick woods.

I wish Mom and Dad were home, Bobbi thought. *I can't wait to tell them the news.*

I'm still in a state of shock, she told herself. *It was such a surprise. I never* dreamed *that Miss Green would name me captain!*

The other girls must have been shocked too, Bobbi realized. *Especially Kimmy.*

Kimmy.

She hadn't stopped to think about Kimmy. But now the thought descended on her like a heavy cloud, bringing her back to earth.

Had Kimmy come over to congratulate her?

Bobbi struggled to remember. Bobbi had been surrounded by everyone all at once. But no. She didn't
remember Kimmy being one of them.

I'd better call her or something, she thought.

Just then a hand touched her shoulder, startling
her out of her thoughts.

"Hi."

She stared into a boy's face. He was handsome,
with friendly dark brown eyes that crinkled at the
corners, a shy smile, and lots of unbrushed brown
hair that seemed to be tossed around on his head.

"Hi." She returned the greeting.

It was Chip Chasner, quarterback of the Tigers.
She had seen him a lot during outdoor practices.
He was friendly with the other cheerleaders, but he
had never said a word to Bobbi.

He fell into step with her as she crossed the
parking lot. He was broad-shouldered and tall,
especially in his shoulder pads and cleats.

"I just wanted to say, way to go," he said shyly,
his dark eyes smiling at her.

"Thanks," she said, suddenly shy too. "I was
really surprised. I mean, I didn't think they'd pick
me. Since I'm new and all."

"We haven't really met. I'm Charles Chasner,"
he said. "But everyone calls me Chip."

"I know," Bobbi replied, feeling her face grow

hot. "I think you're a really good player."

"Thanks." He beamed at her. Her compliment seemed to make him forget his shyness. "I've watched you too."

"Tough game Friday night," Bobbi said, watching the two boys dispiritedly walk the disabled bike away.

"Yeah. Winstead is always tough," Chip said, waving to a couple of girls who had just emerged from the building. "They'll probably cream us."

Bobbi laughed. "Wow, you've sure got confidence," she said sarcastically.

"No. Come on," he replied. "I'm pumped for the game. But you've got to be realistic. They went to the state finals last year."

"How'd you learn to throw the ball so far?" Bobbi asked, stopping at the edge of the parking lot, shifting her backpack on her shoulders. "Just practice a lot?"

"Yeah." He nodded. "My dad and I used to practice throwing in the backyard. We still do, when he has the time. He's working two jobs these days, so it's kind of tough."

"My parents both work all the time," Bobbi told him. "But I'm usually at cheerleading practice or studying, so I wouldn't see them much even if they were home."

"I guess my dad got me my first football when I was five," Chip said, leaning against the parking lot fence. The wind ruffled his thick, brown hair, his dark eyes studying Bobbi as he talked. "He loves football, but he never had a chance to play. Always had to work. So I guess he wanted to do his playing through me."

"That can be a lot of pressure," Bobbi said thoughtfully.

Chip's expression hardened. "I can handle it," he said softly.

"I just meant—" Bobbi started, surprised by his abrupt answer.

"Are you going out with anybody or anything?" Chip interrupted.

Caught off guard by the change of subject, Bobbi hesitated. "No," she finally managed to reply. "Are you?"

He shook his head. "No. Not anymore. Want to meet me after the Winstead game?" He stared at her intently. "We could go get a pizza. You know. Hang out with some other guys?"

"Great," Bobbi replied. "Sounds good."

"Well, okay. Excellent." He glanced up at the clock over the back door of the school. "I've got to practice," he said, pushing away from the fence. "After the game, wait for me outside the stadium locker room, okay?"

He didn't wait for her to reply. Instead he slipped his helmet on and began jogging toward the practice field across from the baseball diamond, taking long, easy strides.

What an amazing day! Bobbi thought, watching him as he ran. So many good things happening at once!

She shook her head, somewhat dazed by it all. Her next thought was: *I'll probably be hit by a truck on the way home.*

The next evening, a warm, almost balmy Thursday night, Bobbi finished her dinner, then hurried to Jennifer's house to study. Since the accident, she and Jennifer had become close.

Unlike some of the other girls, who wanted to shut the accident out of their minds and forget it had ever happened, Bobbi had visited Jennifer in the hospital every day. Bobbi had been touched by her new friend's bravery and serenity. Soon she and Jennifer were talking easily, sharing their thoughts and feelings as if they had been longtime friends.

Bobbi parked her car on the street and made her way up the drive. Jennifer lived in a sprawling modern ranch house in North Hills, the wealthiest section of Shadyside.

What a contrast to Fear Street, Bobbi thought

wistfully, her eyes taking in the manicured lawns, raked clean, and the well-cared-for houses.

The streetlights flickered on as Mrs. Daly opened the door to her. "Oh, hi, Bobbi," she said, looking tired and drawn in the pale porch light. "Jennifer's waiting for you in the den."

Bobbi eagerly made her way across the carpeted living room with its low, sleek furniture of chrome and white leather and into the small den, and closed the door behind her. "Did you talk to Kimmy?" she asked Jennifer, skipping any greeting.

Jennifer was seated in her wheelchair, between two red leather couches that faced each other. She was wearing navy-blue sweats, the sweatshirt sleeves rolled up above her elbows. Her reddish brown hair was tied behind her head in a single braid. She had a textbook in her lap.

"I talked to her," she replied, her face expressionless. Slowly a smile spread across her full lips. "She's coming back."

"Oh good," Bobbi said, breathing a long sigh. She dropped her backpack onto the checkered tile floor and plopped down on the red couch on Jennifer's right. "I can't believe I didn't even notice that she had run out."

"You were a little excited," Jennifer said dryly.

"But I should have known Kimmy would be

upset," Bobbi insisted, rubbing her hand against the smooth leather of the couch arm. "But I didn't see her. I didn't see anything. It was all so . . ." She didn't finish her thought.

"Anyway, I talked to her," Jennifer said, wheeling herself closer until she was right in front of Bobbi. "She's not a happy camper, but I got her to come around." Her mouth fell into an unhappy pout. She avoided Bobbi's eyes. "Kimmy and I used to be so close. But not anymore."

"I'm really sorry," Bobbi said quickly. "If it's my fault, I—"

"No, it isn't," Jennifer interrupted. "You didn't do anything. Really."

"How did you get her to come back on the squad?" Bobbi asked.

"I told her we needed her. I said, 'What would happen if Bobbi fell and broke her leg?'"

"And what did *she* say?" Bobbi wondered.

"She asked if I would put that in writing!" Jennifer said.

Both girls burst out laughing.

"Kimmy isn't your biggest fan," Jennifer said.

"*Duh*," Bobbi replied, rolling her eyes, imitating her little brother, Sean. "Well, I'm glad she's not quitting," Bobbi said.

"Really? Why?" Jennifer demanded, closing the

textbook on her lap and tossing it onto the couch opposite Bobbi.

"Because . . . because it would make me feel really bad," Bobbi said with emotion.

Jennifer snickered. "Having her around might make you feel a lot worse, Bobbi. She won't talk to you. You know that. And she'll probably try to turn the other girls against you. I'm sure she's been on the phone night and day with those two pals of hers, Debra and Ronnie."

Bobbi sighed and pulled both hands back through her hair. "You know, it's only a cheerleading squad. It's supposed to be fun."

"Tell that to Kimmy," Jennifer said softly. She shifted her weight in the wheelchair. "Ow."

"Are you okay?" Bobbi asked, leaning forward, preparing to jump up if her friend needed help of some kind.

"Yeah. Fine." Jennifer forced a smile. "Let's change the subject, okay?"

"Yeah. Okay." Bobbi settled back on the couch. "Do you know Charles Chasner?"

"Chip? Sure." Jennifer's smile broadened. "Chip is a real babe. I've had a crush on him since third grade. He's cuter now, though."

"He asked me out for tomorrow after the game," Bobbi confided.

Jennifer's eyes widened in surprise. "Huh? Chip?"

Bobbi nodded. "Yeah. He asked me out. Yesterday. After the pep rally."

"Really?" Bobbi was startled to see Jennifer's eyes narrow and her features tighten. Jennifer glared at Bobbi. "You didn't say yes—*did* you?"

HORROR IN THE HALL

"Jen—what's wrong?" Bobbi asked.

Jennifer shook her head, then locked her eyes on Bobbi's. "Don't you know that Chip is Kimmy's boyfriend?"

"Huh?" Bobbi's mouth dropped open in shock. She suddenly could feel the blood pulsing at her temples.

"I mean, he *was* Kimmy's boyfriend," Jennifer said, gripping the sides of the wheelchair, "until a couple of weeks ago."

"A couple of weeks?"

"Yeah." Jennifer frowned. "Then he dumped her. Just like that. After more than two years."

"Oh my gosh." Bobbi slumped down on the soft leather couch. She seemed to deflate. The shock of this news made her feel weak. "She'll think—"

"She'll think Chip dumped her for you," Jennifer finished the thought for her.

Bobbi moaned. "One more reason for Kimmy to hate my guts."

They stared at each other in silence for a while. Jennifer squeaked her wheelchair back and forth on the floor.

Finally Bobbi asked, "What should I do?"

Jennifer shrugged. "I don't know. He's *really* cute!"

"Girls, how about getting up a little energy?" Miss Green said. It was more of a complaint than a question, and she said the words with disgust.

Having blown her whistle and stepped onto the floor to interrupt the practice, she did an imitation of the way they looked to her, moving her arms and legs in weary slow motion, her eyes half-closed, her mouth drooping open.

The cheerleaders watched in sullen silence. Bobbi felt embarrassed. She was leading the practice, after all. It was *her* job, not Miss Green's, to get the girls to show some spirit.

But Bobbi was finding it difficult to get some of the girls to listen to her, even though it was the last practice before the game that night.

Kimmy had done a good job of turning the girls against Bobbi. It hadn't been hard, Bobbi realized unhappily. The girls had all known Kimmy for years. Bobbi was a newcomer, an intruder.

Most of the cheerleaders hadn't wanted to allow the Corcorans on the squad in the first place. And now here was Bobbi, giving them instructions, leading them, or *trying* to lead them, *trying* to get them to cooperate.

"When you do 'Ssssssssteam Heat' like that," Miss Green was scolding them, "it makes me think your boiler's broken."

It was supposed to be a joke, but it fell flat on the dispirited squad. No one even cracked a smile.

Standing beside Miss Green, Bobbi let her eyes wander down the row of girls. She stopped at Kimmy, who was glaring at her, her eyes narrowed. Kimmy's stare was so hard, so cold, it forced Bobbi to look away.

The gym doors opened, and Jennifer wheeled herself in. Smiling at Bobbi, she made her way silently along the far wall, her maroon-and-gray pennant on her lap, her backpack attached to her wheelchair.

Bobbi wished Jennifer hadn't come. She felt embarrassed to have Jennifer show up while the girls were being lectured by Miss Green. Jennifer would see that Bobbi didn't have control, that the girls weren't with her.

She knew Jennifer would be sympathetic. She was Bobbi's best friend, after all. But it was still embarrassing.

Bobbi felt a hand on her shoulder. It was Corky, who gave her an encouraging smile and then quickly resumed her place.

Bobbi took a deep breath. "Okay, guys," she shouted, clapping her hands enthusiastically and moving in front of Miss Green, "let's try it again! Let's really get sssssteamed up!"

She saw Kimmy roll her eyes and sarcastically mutter something to Debra. Then the girls lined up and began the Steam Heat routine, this time with a little more enthusiasm than before.

The routine wasn't great. Ronnie was out of step for the entire last part, but Bobbi didn't think it was worth making them do the dance again.

As the routine ended with a cheer and a spread eagle, Bobbi turned to see Jennifer and Miss Green talking heatedly near the wall. Miss Green was leaning over the wheelchair, close to Jennifer's ear. Both of them were shaking their heads as they spoke.

Are they talking about me? Bobbi wondered, dread building in the pit of her stomach. *Is Miss*

Green complaining about me, about how I haven't been able to win over the girls?

"Are we finished?"

Kimmy's shrill question made Bobbi turn back to the line of girls.

"Yeah. I guess," Bobbi said distractedly.

"Well, can we *go*?" Kimmy asked impatiently. "I mean, the game's in a few hours. We have to go home and have dinner and everything, *don't* we?"

Kimmy was making no attempt to hide her dislike of Bobbi. To Bobbi's dismay, she saw that some of the other girls seemed to adopt Kimmy's attitude.

They all agree with her, Bobbi thought, her head suddenly pounding, her temples throbbing. *They probably* all *think that Kimmy should be captain, not me.*

And now even Jennifer and Miss Green are talking about me.

"We'll meet here in the gym at seven," Bobbi announced dispiritedly, avoiding their eyes by glancing up at the scoreboard clock. "Ronnie will be in charge of equipment."

Ronnie rolled her eyes and cast a glance at Kimmy.

"No fire batons tonight," Bobbi announced. "That routine needs a lot more work. We'll try it for homecoming next week."

The girls picked up their belongings and

quickly made their way out of the gym. Bobbi stood in the middle of the floor, her shoulders slumped, feeling discouraged, watching the girls exit.

"I thought it went a lot better, that last time," Corky said, offering an encouraging smile.

"Liar," Bobbi muttered.

Corky shrugged. "No. Really."

"Thanks," Bobbi said dryly, watching Jennifer and Miss Green still talking animatedly.

"You coming straight home?" Corky bent to scratch one knee. Her hair was damp from perspiration.

At least one cheerleader is really trying, Bobbi thought miserably. "Go on without me," she told her sister. "I've got to get all my stuff."

After giving her a quick, playful salute, Corky obediently headed to the door. With a sigh, Bobbi turned and saw that Jennifer and Miss Green had disappeared into the advisor's office in the corner.

She pulled the whistle from around her neck and, swinging it by its cord, began walking slowly toward the door. *Being cheerleader captain is supposed to be fun,* she thought regretfully.

Well, she told herself, *I'll find a way to win them over. Maybe even Kimmy.* Once again she remembered Kimmy's cold stare, and shuddered.

She stepped into the hallway, which was empty

and silent. Her sneakers squeaked along the hard floor. She turned a corner, climbed the stairs to the first floor, and headed to her locker to collect her books and jacket.

The long corridor stretched before her like a tunnel. The lights had been dimmed to save energy. Gray lockers lined both walls. The classrooms were dark and empty.

Bobbi coughed, and the sound echoed through the long tunnel.

The loud crash behind her made her jump and cry out.

She spun around in time to see a locker door swing open, then slam shut.

"Oh!"

Another crash. In front of her.

She turned to see two lockers against the right wall swing open.

As she stared in disbelief, two more lockers pulled open. The doors seemed to hesitate, then slammed shut with deafening force.

Her mouth open in a silent cry, Bobbi gaped in astonishment.

Doors slammed, then swung open again.

Bang. Bang.

The sound echoed until it became a terrifying roar.

Bang. Bang. Both rows of locker doors swung open at once, as if pulled by invisible hands.

"No!" Bobbi cried.

This isn't happening. I'm imagining *this!*

Her heart pounding, she dropped the whistle and began to run. Past swinging, slamming locker doors. Through the echoing sounds, a barrage like gunfire.

"No! Stop!"

The wall of lockers on her left swung open in unison, then slammed shut with a deafening *crash.*

"No! Please!"

She held her hands over her ears and ran.

And then she heard the screams.

A girl, screaming in horror.

High-pitched, shrill screams of anguish, of pain.

Who's there? Bobbi wondered, running between the slamming lockers. *Who* is *it?*

The girl screamed again, the sound rising above the thunder of the lockers.

And again.

Bobbi's sneakers pounded against the floor. She ran blindly through the dark hallway, locker doors swinging open, then slamming shut on both sides of her.

Another scream of agony.

Bobbi reached the end of the corridor, turned the corner, and stared in surprise.

11

WHO WAS SCREAMING?

No one there.

The front hall was deserted.

Silence.

"Hello?" Bobbi called.

No reply. No screams. The only sound now was that of her loud, gasping breaths.

"Hello? Anyone there?" she called out in a hoarse, choked voice.

Silence.

No one.

Confused and frightened, her hands pressed tightly to her burning cheeks, Bobbi turned back. And peered cautiously down the long, dim corridor.

The dark lockers along the walls were all shut tight.

Her ears rang from the crashing, banging sounds they had made. But now they stood still and silent. She took a reluctant step, then another, expecting them to fly open again, to begin their frightening symphony.

Silence.

No lockers banging. No girl screaming in terror.

Her legs trembling, Bobbi made her way to her locker. She opened the combination lock with a shaking hand and pulled the door open.

She glanced down the hall. Still silent and empty.

The silence seemed to echo in her mind.

Am I cracking up?

Am I totally losing it?

She pulled out the things she needed, stuffed them into her backpack, locked the door, and ran.

At home, in the upstairs room they shared, Corky didn't believe her. "You're very tired," she said sympathetically from her desk, where she was trying to cram in a little homework before she had to leave for the game. "You've been under a lot of pressure."

"You don't believe me?" Bobbi shrieked, immediately angry at herself for not keeping her cool.

Corky stared at her sister thoughtfully. "Locker doors flying open?"

"I know it sounds crazy—" Bobbi started.

"The hall was dark, right?" Corky interrupted, tapping her pencil against her open textbook. "It was late. You were tired. Practice was rough. You're nervous about the game tonight."

Bobbi started to protest, then changed her mind. With a loud sigh, she tossed herself onto her bed. "I wouldn't believe me either," she muttered softly. "I wouldn't—"

She stopped and gasped in horror, staring across the room.

Corky followed her sister's frightened gaze.

Both girls watched in silent terror as the closet door swung open.

12

CHIP IS BURIED

"It's—it's happening again," Bobbi uttered, her voice a choked whisper.

Corky raised her hands to her face, her eyes wide with fear, and stared, open-mouthed, as the closet door continued to move.

And Sean stepped out, a triumphant grin spread across his face, his eyes sparkling with evil glee. "Hi," he said, giving them a nonchalant wave.

"Oh!" Bobbi jumped up, her hands balling into fists at her sides.

"You little creep!" Corky screamed. She grabbed Sean by the neck and pretended to choke him.

He collapsed to his knees in a fit of giggles.

"How long have you been in the closet?" Bobbi

demanded, joining Corky in holding him down on the floor.

"It wasn't me. It was a ghost," he said.

Both girls began tickling him furiously.

"Ow! Ow! Ow!" he cried, squirming and laughing.

All three of them were laughing hysterically now, wrestling on the floor.

Digging her fingers into Sean's bony ribs, Bobbi glanced up at the clock. "Oh." She rolled away and stood up. "Come on, Corky. We've got to eat dinner and change. We'll be late for the game."

Corky gave Sean one last hard tickle, then climbed to her feet.

"Shadyside's going to lose," Sean called after them, following them downstairs. "Shadyside stinks."

The excitement of the game, the cheers of the Shadyside fans who filled the stadium, the white lights cutting through the chill of the night, making the field brighter than daylight under the starless black sky, forced all thoughts of that afternoon from Bobbi's mind.

>"Tigers growl! Tigers roar!
>Do it again—more, more, MORE!"

Across the field the Winstead High cheerleaders, in their blue-and-gold uniforms, were
clapping and cheering, rousing the few hundred
Winstead fans in the away-team bleachers. Their
cries barely carried over the cheers and shouts
that roared down from the Shadyside support-
ers, and the loud blasts and drumrolls from the
Shadyside marching band in their own bleachers
near the end zone.

"Tigers roar! Tigers growl!
We want a touchdown—now, now,
* NOW!"*

Her eyes darting back and forth from the game
on the field to the crowd in the stadium, Bobbi led
the girls through their cheers. They were onstage
now, in full view of everyone. The bitterness and
rivalries that had created so much ill feeling in
practice were all forgotten.

Bobbi was in charge, and no one questioned
her commands. She called out the cheers and routines they were to perform as she carefully watched
the action on the field.

"Go team, go team, go-go-go-go-go-
* GO!"*

The cheers thundered down from the stadium, punctuated by applause and excited shouts. Bobbi glanced quickly down the line of cheerleaders, catching a smile of encouragement from Corky at the far end.

Before the game, Ronnie had complained that she wasn't feeling well, that she thought she was coming down with the flu. But Bobbi saw that she was giving 100 percent, cheering with her usual enthusiasm.

At the far end of the players' bench, Bobbi spotted Jennifer. She was in her wheelchair, a maroon blanket over her lap, waving her Shadyside pennant. Their eyes met. Jennifer, smiling happily, waved. Bobbi waved back.

Whistles blew on the field. Bobbi heard laughter spread across the stadium bleachers. She turned to see the cause of the interruption. A white wire-haired terrier had run onto the field.

Two Shadyside players were trying to chase it to the sidelines. But the dog, enjoying the attention, ran in wide circles, its stub of a tail wagging furiously.

Finally one of the referees managed to pick the dog up. He jogged to the sideline with it, to a loud chorus of good-natured boos. Then whistles rang out for the game to resume.

Bobbi stared over the heads of the players on the bench, watching Chip lead the offense out of the huddle. The first quarter had been pretty even. Both teams had been able to move the ball, although neither team had scored.

Now, as the second quarter began, the Tigers were starting on the Winstead thirty-five-yard line. Good field position. The cheers grew louder. The noise level in the stadium rose as if someone had turned up the volume control.

Watching Chip step behind the center, Bobbi wondered what he was thinking. Was he thinking about the Winstead linemen staring at him from under their helmets, about to come charging toward him? Was he thinking only about the play he had called? Was he nervous? Was he scared to death?

She decided she'd have to ask him these questions when she met him after the game.

After the game. She forced that thought out of her mind. She couldn't think about that now. She had to concentrate, stay alert, stay on the ball.

She heard Chip call out the signals in his loud, high-pitched voice. Then she saw him take the snap from center. He took a few steps back. He raised his arm to throwing position.

Another step back, his arm ready to throw.

The crowd roared. Bobbi held her breath.

Chip seemed to freeze, his arm cocked, his feet planted firmly on the grass.

He stood there until two Winstead tacklers swarmed over him and pushed him to the ground.

Bobbi realized she had been holding her breath the whole time. She exhaled, turned to the cheerleaders, and called out a clapping cheer.

What had happened to Chip? she wondered, moving in line and clapping. The crowd responded half-heartedly. The cheer was drowned out by muttering and heated voices. *People in the stands must be asking the same question,* she realized.

Chip had had plenty of time to throw, but he hadn't even pumped his arm. He hadn't seemed to be looking for a receiver. And he hadn't tried to scramble away when the line had come crashing in on him.

Oh well, thought Bobbi, *it's just one play.*

She and the cheerleaders finished the cheer and turned back to the game. Some of the players on the bench had climbed to their feet, so Bobbi had to move closer to see the playing field.

The stadium grew quiet as Chip stepped up to the center, quiet enough for Bobbi to hear the Winstead cheerleaders on the far side of the field.

Again Bobbi held her breath as Chip took the ball and stepped back. It appeared to be a running play. Dave Johnson, the Tigers' big running back, came crunching forward, his arms outstretched.

But again Chip froze in place. He didn't hand off the ball. Johnson ran past him into the line. Chip stood with the ball in his hands. He didn't run or step back to pass.

"Oh!" Bobbi exclaimed as Chip was tackled hard around the knees and dropped for a loss.

Voices in the stadium bleachers cried out in surprise. The entire stadium seemed to buzz. Bobbi heard a scattering of boos.

She shook her head hard as if trying to force the play from her mind. "Let's do Go, Tigers," she called out.

The girls lined up quickly. Except for Kimmy, who remained just behind the players' bench, staring on to the field.

"Kimmy!" Bobbi called.

But Kimmy didn't seem to hear her. She was staring straight ahead with the strangest expression on her face.

"Kimmy!" Bobbi repeated. But it was too late to do the cheer anyway. Chip was leading the team out of the huddle for the third-down play.

Again the stadium grew quiet.

The wind suddenly picked up, blowing the flag and the big Shadyside pennant beneath it on the

pole, making them flap noisily, the rope clips clang-
ing against the metal flagpole.

Come on, Chip! Bobbi thought, crossing her
fingers.

Across the field the cheerleaders in blue and
gold were standing in a tight line, staring in rapt
silence at the field.

Chip took the ball from the center. Johnson
came rolling toward him. But Chip kept the ball. It
was a fake run.

Chip backpedaled quickly and started to roll out.

"Throw it!" Bobbi screamed, cupping her
hands to form a megaphone. "Throw it!"

Chip stopped.

He froze.

"Throw it! *Throw it!*"

Chip didn't move. He was holding the ball at
his waist.

"Throw it!"

Shadyside players were shouting to him.

"I'm open! I'm open!" Johnson was yelling
downfield.

Chip was frozen like a statue.

Bobbi's mouth dropped open in a silent cry as
she saw the Winstead players close in on him.

Several tacklers got to him at the same time.

The ball dribbled out of Chip's hand as they

covered him, pulled him down, and piled on top of him.

Players scrambled for the ball.

Whistles blew.

The stadium remained eerily silent.

"They *buried* him!" Bobbi heard Kimmy say.

Buried him.

Bobbi moved closer to the sidelines, stepping in front of the players' bench. The Winstead players were slowly climbing off Chip, making their way triumphantly to their bench across the field.

Buried him. Buried him.

Bobbi suddenly felt cold all over.

The tacklers were all gone now.

But Chip, sprawled flat on his back, wasn't getting up.

13

"I WAS DEAD"

Bobbi showered and changed quickly into a green turtleneck sweater and a short, straight black skirt, which she pulled over green tights. She brushed her hair, frowning at herself in the water-spotted locker room mirror.

Feeling excited, she made her way out of the room, calling out good night to the few girls who were still there. As she half walked, half jogged back outside to the football team's locker room, she relived that second-quarter nightmare, seeing the scene repeat in her mind.

There was Chip frozen in place. And there were the Winstead tacklers swarming over him. And there was Chip out cold on the ground, sprawled so flat, so still.

And then there came the stretcher. The worried coach and players forming a tight circle around their fallen quarterback. And then Chip being carried away. Under the bright—too bright—stadium lights, Bobbi had seen his hands dangling limply, lifelessly, over the sides of the stretcher, had seen that his eyes were closed, his head tilted at such a strange angle.

He's dead, she'd thought.

It had been so silent in the stadium. So unearthly silent.

We're all dead. All.

But then whistles had blown. The game had resumed.

"Chasner injured on the play," the stadium announcer had informed everyone. Old news already.

The voices came back. The cheers and shouts. The band revived, blared out the Tigers' fight song, the tubas punctuating each beat with a raucous *blat.*

Bobbi, feeling shaken and stunned, called out the cheers. Somehow, she knew, she had to keep going.

But is he okay? she wondered.

Is he okay?

Winstead scored quickly. The Tigers came back with Overman, Chip's backup. They tried some running plays that didn't work. After three plays, they had to punt.

Again Bobbi heard scattered boos. The cheer-leaders across the field were leaping high, shouting with renewed enthusiasm.

Is he okay? Is Chip okay?

The game lost all interest for her. She called out cheers, kept the routines going, all on auto-matic pilot.

Word on the bench was that Chip had proba-bly suffered a mild concussion and was feeling fine now. Everyone was very relieved.

She saw that he didn't come out for the sec-ond half.

Did they take him to a hospital? Bobbi won-dered. *Is he still in the locker room? Does he still expect me to meet him?*

The Tigers lost, twenty-one to six.

And now here she was, nervously waiting in the student parking lot, in front of the door to the team locker room. The stadium lights dimmed, then went out, casting the stadium, the parking lot, the entire back of the school, into sudden night.

As if someone had turned off the sun, Bobbi thought.

As her eyes adjusted to the new darkness, she saw Debra and Ronnie heading across the parking lot. Involved in conversation, they didn't notice her. Bobbi watched them disappear around the corner, both of them talking animatedly, gesturing with their hands.

Strange that Kimmy isn't with them, she thought. Maybe Kimmy had a date.

The locker room door swung open. Bobbi recognized Dave Johnson, the running back. He came bouncing out, carrying a small knapsack, his hair still wet from the shower.

"Is Chip—is he in there?" Bobbi stammered.

"Yeah. He's coming out," Johnson told her.

"Is he okay?" Bobbi asked.

But Johnson was already halfway across the rapidly emptying parking lot.

Bobbi started to shout after him, but the door opened again and Chip appeared. He moved forward unsteadily, smiling at her, his face pale, almost bloodless under the parking lot lights. He was wearing faded jeans and a Shadyside letter jacket that he had snapped up to the collar.

"Hi," he called. "How's it going?" His smile was forced, she saw. His eyes weren't quite focusing on her.

"Are you okay?" she blurted out.

The question seemed to catch him off guard. "I'm not sure," he replied, wrinkling his forehead.

He stepped closer to her.

"What happened?" Bobbi asked. "I was . . . well . . . worried."

"Me too."

She waited for him to say more, but his face fell into a thoughtful, faraway stare.

"So what happened? I mean—you're okay?"

"I guess," he said. "Maybe a slight concussion. That's what they said. I'm supposed to go right home. I feel kind of funny."

"Oh." She couldn't hide the disappointment from her voice. "I have a car," she said. "Can I give you a lift?"

"Yeah. That would be great. My parents are out of town. Actually, I'm glad my mom wasn't at the game. She worries."

"Do you feel kind of weird?"

"Yeah." He nodded. "Kind of. You know, spacey."

"It looked so scary when you didn't get up," Bobbi said, leading the way to her parents' Accord, which was parked around the front on the street. "Were you knocked out?"

"I guess." He put a hand on her shoulder as if he needed to steady himself as he walked.

She slowed down. He waved to a couple of players from the team.

"Did it hurt?" she asked.

"No. Not really."

"Am I asking too many questions?" she asked. He didn't reply.

Wow, this is sure going great, Bobbi thought unhappily. *I'm asking question after question, and he's staring off into space. He can barely walk or even answer me.*

They made their way in silence to the car. She unlocked the passenger door and held the door open as he slid into the front seat.

A few seconds later she started up the car and turned on the headlights. "I don't know where you live," she said, turning to him, adjusting her shoulder seat belt.

"It was like I was dead," he replied.

She stared into his eyes. "Huh?"

"It was like I was paralyzed or something. I couldn't get my body to move, to do *anything*." He turned his eyes to the windshield. A group of kids crossed in front of the car. One of them tapped on the hood as he passed.

"Chip—are you feeling okay? Should I call your parents or something?" she asked, feeling a stab of worry in the pit of her stomach.

"Well, aren't you wondering why I didn't pass the ball? Or hand it off?" he asked heatedly. "Isn't that what everyone wants to know?"

"The doctor said you had a concussion, right?" Bobbi said, a little frightened. She started to pull away from the curb, but he stopped her, placing his hand over hers. His hand was ice-cold.

"Before I got the concussion," he said, more quietly. "Before. When I was playing. I wanted to throw the ball, but it was like I had no control. Like I was paralyzed or something. Just for that moment."

"I don't understand," Bobbi said, shaking her head.

Oncoming headlights filled the car with light. Bobbi and Chip both shielded their eyes. A car roared by filled with Shadyside kids, all the windows down, everyone singing along to a blaring radio.

"I couldn't hand it off either," Chip said. She realized he was explaining it to himself. She wondered if he even cared whether she was in the car. "I didn't freeze. I just wasn't there. I mean, I was and I wasn't. I knew where I was, but I couldn't move."

"Uh, Chip . . . ," Bobbi started, reaching again for the gearshift. They still hadn't moved from the curb. "Maybe we'd better—"

He startled her by turning in the seat, leaning toward her, and grabbing her shoulders with both of his hands.

"Chip—" she began.

"I'm kind of scared," he said, his eyes wild and unfocused, his face moving closer and closer to hers. "You know? I'm really kind of scared."

And then he pulled her down to him and

started to kiss her. His lips felt hard and dry against hers. His hands held on to her shoulders, pulled her to him.

Bobbi started to pull away. But he seemed so needy, so frightened. Returning his kiss, she raised her hands to his wrists and removed them from her shoulders. Then she slid her hands around the back of his neck.

To her surprise, he was trembling all over.

The kiss ended as suddenly as it had begun. Chip, his expression a little embarrassed, leaned back against his seat. "Sorry. I—"

"That's okay," Bobbi replied, realizing her heart was pounding.

"Maybe we'd better get me home," Chip said, avoiding her eyes, staring out the passenger window, which was beginning to steam up. "I just feel so weird."

"Okay." Bobbi put the gearshift into drive and pulled away from the curb. As he directed her to his house on Canyon Road, she repeatedly glanced over at him. He seemed to flicker on and off in the light of the passing streetlights, so pale, so ghostly pale and worried-looking.

"Bobbi, what *happened* to me tonight?" he whispered, staring out the passenger window.

Bobbi had no reply.

14

KIMMY HAS A PROBLEM

"Bobbi—can I talk to you?"

Kimmy came bounding across the gym before practice on Monday afternoon, her cheeks flushed, her eyes angry.

"I just got here," Bobbi said distractedly, searching the gym. Everyone seemed to be ready. Megan and Heather were already working on one of the new routines. Miss Green was standing behind her desk in her office, talking on the phone.

"Sorry I'm late," Bobbi called to the others.

"I really need to talk to you," Kimmy insisted, hands on her waist. Her black crimped hair was more disheveled than usual. The sleeves of her sweater were rolled up, one above the elbow, the other below.

Bobbi waved to Corky. She tossed her backpack against the wall. "What about, Kimmy?" she asked impatiently. "I've had the *worst* day. First I forgot about a chemistry quiz. Then—"

"About Chip," Kimmy said through clenched teeth.

Bobbi's eyes widened in surprise. She could feel her face growing hot. "Chip? What about him?"

Kimmy glared at her.

"Well—what about him?"

"You made a little mistake, Bobbi," Kimmy said, tapping her sneaker nervously on the gym floor, like a thumping rabbit foot. One hand played with the silver megaphone pendant she always wore around her neck.

"Huh?"

"Chip is *my* boyfriend," Kimmy said heatedly.

Bobbi glanced past Kimmy and saw that the other girls had stopped their practicing and were standing around staring with unconcealed interest at this unpleasant confrontation.

"Could we talk about this *after* practice?" Bobbi asked, gesturing to the audience they had attracted.

"No way," Kimmy insisted, fingering the silver pendant. "Chip is my boyfriend. We've been going together for a long time. Ask anyone." She gestured back to the other girls, who shifted uncomfortably and avoided Bobbi's eyes.

"Kimmy, listen—" Bobbi said quietly, backing away.

"You made a little mistake, Bobbi. A little mistake," Kimmy repeated, raising her voice, following Bobbi, moving very close to her.

Bobbi felt herself losing her temper. What right did Kimmy have to do this to her? She was only trying to embarrass Bobbi in front of the other cheerleaders. She was only trying to turn the girls against Bobbi even more.

"*You're* the one who made the mistake," Bobbi blurted out. "You're forgetting one little detail, Kimmy—I didn't ask Chip out. He asked *me*!"

Kimmy's eyes grew wide. Then, uttering a cry of anger, she lunged at Bobbi, grabbed the sides of her hair with both hands, and pulled hard.

Startled, Bobbi gasped. She tried to duck out of Kimmy's hold. But Kimmy had a firm grasp on her hair. Bobbi yelped in pain and struggled to pull Kimmy's hands off.

Suddenly a voice was calling, "Stop! Girls—stop! *Please!*"

And Jennifer wheeled her chair right between the two combatants. "Stop it—please! Kimmy! Bobbi!"

Both girls stumbled backward. Surprised to see Jennifer appear out of nowhere, they hesitated, panting noisily.

Bobbi's head throbbed. She raised a hand and tried to smooth her hair.

"Girls—what is going on?" Miss Green came trotting out of her office, a look of alarm on her face. "I was on the phone, and when I looked up—"

"It's okay," Jennifer told her, backing her wheelchair up, her eyes on Bobbi. "A slight disagreement."

"Good Lord!" Miss Green cried, staring first at Bobbi, then at Kimmy, who had bent down to pick the silver megaphone pendant up off the floor.

Embarrassed and upset, Bobbi stared at the bleachers at the other end of the gym. Taking in big gulps of air, she struggled to catch her breath. Her throat felt as dry as cotton.

Kimmy fiddled with the clasp of the pendant chain, her hands shaking visibly. Her face was crimson, and a damp clump of her hair had fallen over one eye.

"I think you two had better apologize to each other right now," Miss Green said sternly, talking to them as if they were four-year-olds.

Neither girl replied.

Jennifer backed her wheelchair out of the way.

Kimmy fastened the megaphone pendant around her neck, glaring at Bobbi as she did it.

"This is very bad timing," Miss Green said, crossing her arms in front of her chest. "Especially since you two have to work together so closely on the new routine."

The new routine.

Bobbi had forgotten they were going to work on the new routine. She sighed. The new routine was long and difficult. And it ended with Kimmy doing a pike, diving off Corky's shoulders—and being caught by Bobbi!

"Maybe we should practice something easier today," Bobbi muttered glumly.

"We're not practicing anything until you and Kimmy apologize to each other for acting like spoiled babies," Miss Green said, frowning.

Bobbi glanced past Miss Green at the other girls. Corky was making funny faces at her. Helpful. Very helpful.

The other girls all looked terribly uncomfortable. Debra and Ronnie had gone back to practicing their splits. They were pretending that the little drama wasn't taking place.

"There's nothing to apologize about," Kimmy said defiantly.

Nothing to apologize about? Bobbi thought, rolling her eyes. *She* attacked *me!*

"Well, if you really feel that way," Miss Green

said angrily, her arms still crossed, "I'll have no choice but to suspend both of you from the squad."

A few of the girls gasped. Ronnie and Debra stopped their exercises.

"Well . . . ," Kimmy said slowly, avoiding Bobbi's eyes.

"I'm willing to apologize," Bobbi said. *Even though this is entirely Kimmy's fault,* she added to herself.

"I guess I am too," Kimmy said grudgingly, her blue eyes flashing.

"I should hope so," the advisor said, lowering her arms. "After all, this is a cheerleading squad— not the wrestling team."

Bobbi glanced at Jennifer, who had backed up nearly to the wall. Jennifer flashed Bobbi an encouraging smile.

"I'm sorry," Kimmy said sullenly, and extended her hand.

Bobbi took her hand. It felt hot and wet. "I'm sorry too," she said softly.

"That's better," Miss Green said, more than a little relieved. "I'm sure you girls can find a more civilized way to work out your differences."

Bobbi and Kimmy both nodded.

Bobbi let go of Kimmy's hand. The two eyed each other warily.

Kimmy will never *be my friend,* Bobbi realized. Her next thought: *Will she always be my enemy?*

"This new routine is so tricky," Miss Green was saying, "so complicated. The timing is split-second. You two girls have to be able to rely on each other. You have to have confidence in each other." She called the other cheerleaders over to begin the practice.

Bobbi wasn't in the mood to work on anything new. She still felt strange, out of sorts. How could Kimmy have attacked her like that? Didn't she have any pride?

"Let's try the last part of the routine first," Miss Green suggested. "Why don't you explain it again, Bobbi."

"Actually, Corky should explain it," Bobbi replied, turning to her sister. "Corky invented it. We used it at the state finals last year, and it really got a big reaction."

Bobbi saw Kimmy mutter something to Debra. Both girls snickered quietly to themselves.

"It's easier to demonstrate it," Corky said. "Bobbi—do a shoulder stand. We'll do this now without the rest of the pyramid. But in the real routine, she'd be up much higher. We'll show you how the pike works. Miss Green, will you catch Bobbi when she dives?"

Bobbi and Miss Green obediently moved into

place as the other girls watched intently. "You'll be doing this pike, Kimmy," Miss Green said, "so watch carefully. If you have any questions—"

"I'm watching," Kimmy said sharply.

Bobbi stepped behind Corky and grabbed Corky's hands. Then she placed one sneaker on Corky's bent knee and, with a boost from Heather, who was standing behind her, raised her other sneaker to Corky's shoulder, and pulled herself up until she was standing on Corky's shoulders. Corky brought her hands up to Bobbi's ankles and gripped them tightly, locking Bobbi in place.

Miss Green moved in front of Corky and readied herself to catch Bobbi as she dove. "Ready, Bobbi?" Corky asked, keeping her shoulders steady, bracing herself.

"Here goes," Bobbi said. She leaped up off Corky's shoulders, bringing her feet up, folding her body into a perfect *V*, and dropped in a sitting position right into Miss Green's waiting arms.

Some of the girls burst into enthusiastic applause. "Excellent!" Miss Green cried as Bobbi lowered her feet to the floor. "You really made it look easy."

"We've practiced it a lot," Bobbi said modestly.

"Kimmy—are you ready to try it?" Miss Green asked.

"I guess so," Kimmy said reluctantly, eyeing Bobbi.

"Bobbi will catch you. Run through it slowly," Miss Green instructed as Kimmy stepped behind Corky. "Take as long as it takes. Don't worry about the number of beats. We'll practice the timing later."

The girls who were not involved in this part of the routine stepped back to make room. Ronnie was talking excitedly to two of them, shaking her head, glancing at Bobbi.

"I really don't believe this. My life is in your hands," Kimmy told Bobbi dryly.

"No problem," Bobbi replied. "I haven't dropped anyone in weeks."

Kimmy didn't smile at Bobbi's joke. Corky braced herself. Kimmy pulled herself up quickly into a standing position on Corky's shoulders. Corky grabbed her calves to brace her.

Bobbi moved into position to catch Kimmy. "I'm ready whenever you are," she called up to her.

"Shouldn't she go on a diet first?" Debra cracked.

Kimmy glared down at her. "Since when do *you* make jokes?"

Debra shrugged. "Ronnie made me say it."

"Let's get serious, girls," Miss Green scolded. "This stunt could really be dangerous."

"Corky and I have done it a million times," Bobbi reassured her, looking up at Kimmy. "Ready?"

"I guess," Kimmy replied with a shrug. "Wish I had a safety net."

"You can do it!" Jennifer yelled encouragement from against the wall.

"Okay. On three," Corky said. "One, two—"

Bobbi braced herself, spreading her feet far apart in preparation for the catch. She arched her back. And started to raise both arms above her head.

"Three!"

Bobbi sucked in a mouthful of air. *My arms,* she thought. *What's wrong? What's happening to me?*

I can't raise my arms, Bobbi thought, frozen in horror.

I can't move. I can't move anything.

She could feel beads of cold sweat run down her forehead.

Stop! Bobbi thought. *You've got to stop this! Hold everything! Please! Just stop!*

But to her horror, she couldn't speak. She couldn't make a sound.

I can't move. I can't speak.

She strained to raise her arms, to get into position.

No! Please—no! Bobbi cried, only no sound came out.

What is happening to me?

She could see herself standing there, as if she had floated out of her own body.

She could see herself looking up as Kimmy prepared to dive, looking up with her arms still at her sides.

Unable to move them, to raise them.

Unable to catch Kimmy.

Unable to warn her.

No! Please—Kimmy, don't dive! Don't dive!

Can't you see I'm paralyzed here?

Can't you see something is holding me here? Holding me in its grip? Holding me so I can't move a single muscle, cannot even blink?

Can't you see?

Corky's shoulders bobbed under Kimmy's weight as Kimmy bent her knees and began her jump.

No! No! Kimmy—don't!

Kimmy's eyes narrowed, her features tight in intent concentration. Her knees bent, and the muscles tightened.

No! Stop!

Kimmy—stop!

I can't catch you!

I can't even move to break your fall.

Kimmy—please!

Kimmy took a deep breath. Held it.

And then she leaped off Corky's shoulders.

15

THE ACCUSATIONS FLY

Kimmy hit the floor hard.

She landed first on her knees and elbows.

Everyone heard a sickening crack. And then a heavy thud as her forehead smashed against the floor.

Her head snapped back and her mouth let out a *whoosh*, like air escaping a blown-out tire.

And then her eyes closed, and she didn't move.

At first no one reacted. Everyone seemed as paralyzed as Bobbi.

But then Heather's shrill scream pierced the air, echoing off the high gym ceiling.

Several other girls cried out.

Corky dropped to her knees beside Kimmy's unmoving body and stared up at Bobbi.

Her eyes locked on Kimmy, Bobbi stumbled back. One step. Two.

She raised her hands to her cheeks.

I can move, she realized.

I can move again.

I'm me again.

Jennifer was wheeling her chair frantically toward Kimmy.

Miss Green leaned over Kimmy, took her hand, slapped at it.

Kimmy groaned.

"She had the wind knocked out," Miss Green announced. She raised her eyes to the girls huddling around the fallen cheerleader. "Quick—call for an ambulance. Call nine-one-one."

Megan and Heather, pale and shaken, went racing from the gym.

I can move now, Bobbi thought. *But what happened to me?*

"You didn't *try* to catch her!" Debra's words stung Bobbi. Stepping close, Debra pointed an accusing finger. "You didn't even *try!*"

"No—" Bobbi didn't know what to say. She took a step back, away from Debra's accusing finger.

"You just let her fall!" Ronnie cried shrilly. She had tears running down her cheeks.

"No!" Bobbi cried. "I tried, but—"

"You didn't try!" Ronnie screamed. "We saw you. We all saw you!"

"You just *stood* there!" Debra cried angrily.

"It was deliberate," Ronnie said. "She did it deliberately."

Corky, still on her knees beside Kimmy, stared up at her sister. *What happened?* She mouthed the words silently.

"I couldn't catch her," Bobbi explained, knowing how lame her words sounded. "My arms—"

Bobbi stopped. It didn't make any sense to *her*. How could she make it make sense to *them*?

"You were mad at her. So you let her fall," Ronnie accused.

"How *could* you?" Debra cried.

Kimmy stirred and opened her eyes.

"You had the wind knocked out of you," Miss Green said softly, still holding her hand.

Kimmy groaned. Her eyes darted from face to face. "My arm," she groaned.

"Your arm?" Miss Green lowered Kimmy's hand to the floor.

"The other one," Kimmy groaned. "I can't move it. I think it's—"

"We heard a crack," Miss Green said. "Maybe you broke it."

Kimmy tried to raise herself.

"No." Miss Green pushed her gently back down. "Don't try to get up. There's an ambulance on the way."

"Ohhh, it hurts." Kimmy stared up at Bobbi. "You—you did this to me. On purpose," she said, her voice a pained whisper.

"No!" Bobbi protested.

"You just let me fall," Kimmy accused, wincing from the pain in her arm.

"Lie back," Miss Green instructed her. "You're going to be okay, dear. You're going to be just fine. Don't worry about Bobbi now, okay?" She glanced up at Bobbi, and her expression became hard and cold. "Bobbi and I will be having a good, long talk. Bobbi has a lot of explaining to do."

"I'm sure it was an accident," Corky said, suddenly bursting into the conversation. "We've done this dive a million times. Really."

"She tried to hurt her," Debra insisted. "I watched her the whole time."

"It's attempted murder!" Ronnie said, deliberately loud enough for Bobbi to hear.

"Ronnie—you're going too far!" Miss Green scolded.

"We *saw* her!" Ronnie shot back angrily.

"No!" Bobbi screamed, tugging at the sides of her hair. "No! No! NO!"

She couldn't take any more of this.

She couldn't take the eyes, so many eyes, staring at her with so much hatred.

She couldn't take the accusing frowns, the pointing fingers.

She couldn't take the sting of their words.

"No! No!"

And without realizing it, she had turned away from them, away from their eyes, away from their hatred. And now she was running—her sneakers loud against the hard floor—running blindly, her eyes blurred by hot tears, running with her arms outstretched, running to the double doors.

And pushing through them. Into the coolness of the hallway. Out of the heat, away from their eyes, their unforgiving eyes.

She turned and ran toward the stairs. Past the white-coated paramedics hurrying toward the gym, carrying a stretcher and black bags of equipment. Past a surprised group of students gathered in the middle of the hall.

Up the stairs and out of the building, without stopping for her jacket, without stopping for her books.

Out into the cold, gray afternoon. Her sneakers crunching over dead leaves, hot tears stinging her eyes.

She ran as fast as her heart was pounding.

She just wanted to run forever.

But then two hands grabbed her roughly from behind.

Bobbi gasped and flailed out with both hands.

"No—don't!" she cried.

16

STRANGE SHADOWS

Bobbi—what's wrong?"

Chip let go of her shoulders and backed away, startled by her wild reaction.

"Oh. Chip. I—"The words caught in her throat.

"I'm sorry. I didn't mean to scare you," he said, his eyes studying her, his expression alarmed. "I saw you running and—"

"Chip—it happened to me, too!"Bobbi blurted out, half talking, half crying. She grabbed the sleeve of his letter jacket, pressed her face against it.

"Huh? Where's your coat? Aren't you cold?"

"It happened to me, too,"she repeated, not recognizing her shrill, frightened voice. She straightened up, saw that her tears had run onto his jacket sleeve. "I—I couldn't move."

"You? Really?" Chip stared at her, as if he didn't quite know what to make of her words, as if he didn't understand. Or didn't believe her. "I'm going to the doctor's. For tests. Right now," he said awkwardly. "I was just telling Coach I had to miss practice. He said—"

"I couldn't move," Bobbi repeated, as if repeating it would make him believe her. "I couldn't raise my arms. Just like you, Chip."

She stared into his eyes imploringly.

"You should get to a doctor too," he said softly. "Mine thinks it's some kind of muscle thing. These tests—"

A horn honked loudly, insistently, behind them.

"Hey—that's my brother. He's taking me to the doctor," Chip said, turning to wave to the driver. "I've got to go."

"Can I call you later?" Bobbi asked. "I mean, I've really got to talk to you. About . . . what happened."

"Yeah. Sure," he said, jogging to the car. "I'll be home later." He stopped suddenly and turned back to her. "You need a lift?"

"No." She shook her head. "I want to walk. Thanks!"

He climbed into the passenger seat. The car sped off.

He's the only one who will believe me, Bobbi thought, watching the car until it disappeared around the next corner.

He's the only one.

It happened to him, too. I'm not cracking up. I'm not.

"I'm not cracking up," she told Jennifer. "It happened to Chip, too."

Jennifer's eyes flared for a brief second when Bobbi mentioned Chip's name. She wheeled herself back against the wall, giving Bobbi room to pass her and enter the den.

"Thanks for letting me come over," Bobbi said gratefully. She tossed her backpack onto the floor beside a couch and started to pull off her coat. "My parents took my little brother to a Cub Scouts dinner, and Corky is babysitting tonight. I just didn't want to be alone."

"That was so awful this afternoon," Jennifer said, speaking slowly, cautiously. "You must have felt terrible." She wheeled herself back into the den, banged into the frame of the narrow doorway, backed up, and succeeded on the second try.

Bobbi dropped her coat on top of her backpack and rubbed the sleeves of her blue, long-sleeved pullover to warm herself. "Yeah. I—I was— " She stopped, unable to describe how she had felt.

"So did you talk to Chip about it?" Jennifer asked.

"I—I tried to call him. There was no answer. No one at his house."

"Would you like some tea?" Jennifer asked softly. "You look chilled."

"No. No, thanks. Maybe later," Bobbi said. "Do *you* believe me, Jen? Do *you* believe that I didn't deliberately let Kimmy fall?"

"I talked to her mother," Jennifer said, avoiding the question. "She has a broken wrist. It's in a cast. But it's her left hand, so it isn't so bad."

"Do you believe me?" Bobbi demanded, sitting on the edge of the couch, leaning forward expectantly, her hands clasped nervously in front of her.

"I really don't know what to believe," Jennifer replied reluctantly.

"It was like someone was holding me down, holding me in place, smothering me. My arms were useless," Bobbi said, explaining for the hundredth time. "Useless. My whole body was useless."

"I know what *that's* like," Jennifer said with sudden bitterness. She stared down at her legs.

"Oh, Jen—I'm *sorry!*" Bobbi cried, jumping to her feet, feeling her face grow hot. "That was so *thoughtless* of me. I—"

Jennifer gestured for her to sit back down. "You've had a hard day, Bobbi. A horrible day."

"Do you think Miss Green will let me stay on the squad?" Bobbi asked, dropping back onto the couch.

Jennifer shrugged. "Do you want to try to study or something? Take your mind off what happened?"

Bobbi sighed. "I don't know if I *can* take my mind off it."

"Let's try," Jennifer said, tossing her beautiful wavy hair behind her shoulders. "I'll make us some tea, and we'll try."

Jennifer tried valiantly, but she couldn't rouse Bobbi from her frightened, unhappy thoughts. No matter what they talked about, Bobbi's mind trailed back to the gym, back to her mysterious, terrifying paralysis, back to Kimmy's plunge to the floor.

Again and again Bobbi heard the *crack* of Kimmy's wrist breaking. She heard the *thud* of Kimmy's forehead hitting the floorboards, saw Kimmy's head snap back and her eyes close.

Again and again she saw the accusing eyes of the other cheerleaders and heard their outraged cries.

A little after eleven o'clock, Bobbi glumly pulled on her jacket, hoisted her backpack to a shoulder, and headed for the front door. "Thanks for keeping me company," she told Jennifer, and leaned down to give her friend a hug.

"Anytime," Jennifer replied with a yawn.

"Where are *your* parents?" Bobbi asked.

"Visiting some friends," Jennifer said sleepily. "They'll probably be home soon."

"Well, thanks again," Bobbi said, pulling open the front door, feeling the chill of the night air against her hot face. "See you tomorrow, Jen."

"Get some sleep" were Jennifer's parting words. She wheeled herself to the door.

Bobbi closed the door behind her. She looked out into a dark, starless night. The air was cold and wet. From the driveway she could see a white covering of frost on her car windshield, reflecting the streetlight.

Shivering, she made her way down the drive, her high-tops crunching over the gravel.

Crunch, crunch, she thought. *Like the crunch of bones.*

When she got down to the car, she rubbed a finger over the frost on the windshield. It wasn't very frozen. She didn't need to scrape it off. The windshield wipers would take care of it.

She pulled open the car door. Then, before climbing behind the wheel, she glanced back at the house.

And gasped.

"Whoa!" she exclaimed out loud, her breath steamy white in front of her as she squinted at the large living room picture window.

It was the only lighted window in the front of the house. A window shade had been pulled down, covering the entire window. The bright living room lights made the shade bright orange and cast shadows onto it.

Moving shadows.

Squinting hard, Bobbi realized that she was seeing Jennifer's shadow against the shade.

And Jennifer was walking.

Pacing back and forth in front of the window.

"Whoa," Bobbi repeated.

She blinked several times.

But when she reopened her eyes and directed them back to the window, the shadow didn't change or fade away.

Jennifer, Bobbi knew, was the only one home. And Jennifer was out of her wheelchair. Jennifer was walking!

"What's going on?" Bobbi asked out loud.

I'm definitely cracking up, she decided. *I've got to get help. I'm seeing things.*

She took a step up the driveway. Then another. Her sneakers slid over the wet gravel.

I'm crazy. Crazy. Crazy.

But, no. As she drew closer to the house, the gray shadow against the orange shade continued to move steadily back and forth. The image grew clearer. Sharper.

It was Jennifer. She was *walking*, her hands knotted in front of her.

What's going on? Bobbi wondered, her mind whirring with wild ideas.

Did Jennifer just this second discover she can walk?

No. That wasn't likely. Then . . .

Has Jennifer been faking all along?

Why? Why would she fake paralysis?

Why?

Bobbi stepped back onto the stoop. She rang the doorbell.

She had to know. She had to ask Jennifer what was going on.

She leaned toward the door and listened for Jennifer's footsteps.

Silence.

She rang the bell again.

Finally the front door was pulled open, revealing a widening rectangle of light.

"Jennifer!" Bobbi cried.

17

CRACKING UP

Standing on the front stoop, Bobbi stared into the yellow light of the front hallway. Jennifer held the door open, her face filled with surprise.

"Bobbi—what's the matter?"

"Oh . . . uh . . . ," Bobbi stammered. "Nothing. I . . . thought I forgot my gloves."

Jennifer's face relaxed. She wheeled herself back a few inches, still gripping the doorknob. "Do you want to come in and look for them?"

"No," Bobbi replied quickly. "I just remembered I didn't bring any gloves. Sorry."

Jennifer laughed. "You're really in a state, aren't you?"

"Yeah. I guess." Bobbi felt totally embarrassed. And confused.

And worried.

Jennifer was in her wheelchair, a small blanket over her lap. Why had Bobbi imagined that she'd seen her pacing back and forth near the window?

Had Bobbi imagined it all, imagined the moving shadow, imagined the dark figure walking across the living room?

What's wrong *with me?* Bobbi asked herself, saying good night to Jennifer again and trudging back down the gravel driveway.

Her breaths rose in puffs of white steam in the cold night air.

But Bobbi didn't feel the cold.

In fact, she felt hot. Feverish. Her forehead throbbed, a sharp pain just behind her eyes.

Why am I seeing things?

Am *I seeing things?*

Am *I cracking up? Really cracking up?*

The headlights seemed to skip and dance as she drove through the silent darkness back to her house on Fear Street. The house was dark except for the porch light. She realized everyone must have gone to bed.

After tossing her jacket onto the banister, she hurried up to her bedroom and, without turning on the light, shook Corky awake.

"Huh?" Corky cried out, frightened, and sat up stiffly.

"It's me," Bobbi whispered. "Wake up."

"You scared me to death!" Corky cried angrily. She never liked to be awakened.

Bobbi clicked on the bedside lamp. "I saw Jennifer walk!" she blurted out.

Corky yawned. "Huh?"

"I think I saw Jennifer walk. I'm not sure, but—"

"What time is it?" Corky asked crankily. "You must have been dreaming."

"No. I wasn't asleep," Bobbi insisted. "I was standing outside her house. I saw shadows."

Corky stretched, turned, and lowered her feet to the floor. She brushed a strand of blond hair from over her eyes. "You saw shadows?" Her face filled with concern. "Bobbi, I'm really worried about you."

"No! Really! I saw her," Bobbi said, not realizing that she was almost shouting. She stood over her sister, her hands knotted tensely in front of her, feeling hot and trembly, the pain still pulsing behind her eyes.

"Maybe we should tell Mom and Dad," Corky said, glancing at the bedside clock. "I mean, just stop and think for a minute, Bobbi. First you told me you saw all the lockers at school open and close when you walked down the hall. Then you told me you were paralyzed at practice this afternoon. You couldn't move. You couldn't even speak. And that's why you let Kimmy fall."

"But, Corky—"

"Let me finish," Corky said sharply, holding up a hand as if to fend Bobbi off. "Then there was that weird story about Chip, about how he froze too and couldn't move. And now you come home from Jennifer's and—"

"But it's *true!*" Bobbi cried. "It's all true. I mean, I *think* it's true. I think—I— Don't you *believe* me, Corky?"

Corky was holding her hands over her ears. "Stop shouting. You're screaming right in my face."

"Sorry. I—"

"Let's go tell everything to Mom and Dad," Corky urged. "I really think you have to go talk to a doctor or something. I think you need help, Bobbi. I really do."

"You don't believe me," Bobbi accused heatedly, bitterly, her head throbbing. "You don't believe me."

Without thinking about it, she picked up Corky's pillow and heaved it at her angrily.

"Hey—" Corky cried, grabbing the pillow and tossing it back into its place.

"Just don't talk to me!" Bobbi snapped. "Traitor!"

"Oh, fine!" Corky screamed. "That's just fine with me! You're crazy, Bobbi! Crazy!"

Bobbi stormed over to the closet. "Shut up! Just shut up! Don't talk to me! Ever again!" She began to tear off her clothes, tossing them onto the closet floor, muttering to herself.

Corky punched her pillow, fluffed it, and slid back under the covers, turning her back on her sister.

She's gone totally crazy, she told herself. *She's just so weird!*

Imagine—calling me a traitor because I think she should talk to someone and get help.

Me, a traitor.

And now she's gotten me so upset, I'll probably be up all night.

I hate her. I really hate her, Corky thought darkly, struggling to get comfortable. *She just makes me so mad.*

Corky might have been more sympathetic. She might have been more understanding. More caring. More believing.

But Corky had no way of knowing that this was the last night she would ever spend with her sister.

PART THREE
THE EVIL

18

IN HOT WATER

"Okay, everyone—some aerobics to warm up!"

Bobbi trotted enthusiastically onto the gym floor, clapping her hands, trying to get the girls up for their after-school practice.

But they lingered against the wall, clustered in pairs, talking quietly.

"Come on, everyone—line up! Let's warm up!"

Bobbi's eyes wandered from girl to girl. *Where's Corky?* she wondered, and then she remembered that Corky had to stay late in Mr. Adams's science lab. Bobbi saw Jennifer wheel herself in, concentrating as she maneuvered her wheelchair through the double doors. Jennifer saw Bobbi and smiled, giving her a little wave.

"Line up!" Bobbi insisted.

"Where's Miss Green?" Kimmy asked, stepping forward slowly, awkwardly holding her wrist with the white cast on it.

"I don't know," Bobbi told her. "Are you going to warm up with us? Or does your wrist—"

"My wrist is no concern of yours," Kimmy snapped. "I'm not quitting the squad because of it, if that's what you mean." Her eyes burned angrily into Bobbi's.

"Let's warm up! Come on, everyone!" Bobbi called out, ignoring Kimmy's anger.

Slowly the girls moved away from the wall and formed a line in front of Bobbi. Bobbi started up the music. They began their exercises, the same routine they had followed since school had begun.

But they performed half-heartedly, grudgingly, without enthusiasm.

"Come on—let's work up a sweat!" Bobbi cried, working doubly hard, as if to make up for their feeble effort. But the girls ignored her. Debra and Ronnie, she saw, were carrying on a conversation while going through the motions.

Bobbi glanced toward the wall. Jennifer gave her a thumbs-up, but it didn't cheer her. The girls, she knew, were deliberately not cooperating.

She stopped the music. "Let's work on Steam

Heat," she suggested. "Ronnie, do you want to take the end this time?"

"Huh?"

"Do you want to take the end? You can lead it."

"I don't know." Ronnie shrugged. "Whatever." She turned back to her conversation with Debra.

Without Corky, I don't have anyone on my side, Bobbi realized, suddenly overcome by a powerful wave of depression. *Only Jennifer, I guess. But even she doesn't want to speak up for me in front of the girls—not after what happened to Kimmy.*

"Okay, line up for Steam Heat," Bobbi called out, struggling to keep up a show of enthusiasm.

"I think we should wait for Miss Green," Kimmy said defiantly.

"Yeah. Let's wait," Debra added quickly.

"No reason to wait," Bobbi said unsteadily. She glanced up at the scoreboard clock. Three forty-five. "We know what we have to work on, don't we?"

"I still think we should wait," Kimmy said, a definite challenge to Bobbi's authority.

"Yeah. Wait," Debra muttered nastily. Heather and Megan nodded in sullen agreement.

It's a mutiny, Bobbi realized, suddenly dizzy.

"Line up!" she insisted, glancing at Jennifer, whose smile had faded. She was watching the proceedings with a look of concern. "Kimmy, if you have something to say to me—"Bobbi started.

"I think Miss Green has something to say to you," Kimmy replied smugly. Beside her, Ronnie snickered out loud.

The double doors swung open, and Miss Green entered, taking long, rapid strides, carrying a bulging briefcase. "Sorry I'm late," she called out, heading to her office in the corner.

Seeing them on the floor, Bobbi by herself in front of the sullen-looking group, Miss Green stopped. "You've started?"

"Not exactly," Kimmy told her, shooting Bobbi a meaningful glance.

"No one seems to be in the mood to work today," Bobbi reported reluctantly.

Miss Green shifted the heavy briefcase to her other hand. "Bobbi—could I see you in my office for a minute?"

"Yeah, sure," Bobbi replied, dread building in the pit of her stomach, her throat tightening.

"Everyone—let's cancel practice for today, okay?" Miss Green said, her eyes on Kimmy.

Uh-oh, Bobbi thought. She could feel the blood pulsing at her temples.

"We'll regroup tomorrow afternoon," Miss Green said.

Talking quietly among themselves, the cheerleaders obediently moved off the floor and began to collect their belongings. Bobbi realized that all of them were avoiding looking at her. She caught a smug grin on Kimmy's face, but Kimmy quickly turned her head and walked away with Debra and Ronnie.

They all know what Miss Green is going to say to me, Bobbi realized.

And I know too.

As the gym quickly emptied out, Bobbi followed Miss Green to her office, her heart pounding, her legs suddenly feeling as if they weighed a thousand pounds.

Miss Green dropped the briefcase onto her desk. She sifted through a few pink phone-message sheets, then looked up at Bobbi. "Health forms," she said, patting the briefcase. "They weigh a ton. You've got to be strong to be in the phys ed department."

Bobbi stood awkwardly in front of the desk, nervously toying with a strand of her hair. When Miss Green motioned her toward a seat, Bobbi obediently lowered herself into it, folding her hands in her lap.

She realized she was perspiring. It was so hot in the gym, and she had been the only one to really work during the aerobics warm-ups.

"Bobbi, I'm really sorry," Miss Green said abruptly, setting down the pink message sheets and leaning with both hands on the desktop. "I have to ask you to step down from the squad."

"Oh!" Bobbi uttered a short cry.

She had anticipated those very words. But somehow they had come as a surprise anyway.

"I really don't—" Bobbi started.

Miss Green held up a hand to silence her. "I don't want to discuss what happened yesterday. I know you wouldn't deliberately try to injure one of the girls. But what happened, happened. Whether it was a loss of concentration or whatever. It happened."

She sat down, leaning forward over the desk, playing with an opal ring on her right hand. "You're a very talented cheerleader, Bobbi," she continued. "You and your sister. I like you both. But after yesterday, I'm afraid—well, I'm afraid you've lost the confidence of the squad."

"Confidence?" Bobbi managed to utter in a tight, choked voice. She suddenly realized she was breathing hard. Drops of perspiration were sliding down her forehead, but she made no attempt to wipe them away.

"A squad is built on trust. And the girls just don't feel they can trust you," Miss Green said, lowering her voice, her face expressionless. "They've made it very clear to me. Whether it's true or not, *they* believe that you deliberately didn't catch Kimmy yesterday." She cleared her throat noisily, covering her mouth with one hand. "I'm really sorry, Bobbi. I have no choice. I have to ask you to quit."

Bobbi lowered her head, struggling to stop her body from shaking, struggling to hold back her tears. "I understand," she managed to whisper.

"If you'd like to talk to someone," Miss Green offered, her eyes sympathetic, "a doctor, I mean. If you'd like me to recommend someone you could . . . confide in—"

Bobbi rose to her feet. She had to get out of there, she realized. She felt hot and cold and shaky and sick. "No, thanks. I'll just leave now," she said, turning to the door, avoiding Miss Green's stare.

"I know how you must feel," Miss Green said, standing too. "If there's anything I can do . . ."

A few seconds later Bobbi found herself in the locker room. Alone. Her footsteps echoing on the damp concrete floor. She choked back a sob.

I'm wringing wet. Wringing wet.

I'll take a shower, she decided. *Change into street clothes.*

That'll make me feel better.

She thought she heard a scraping sound from

another row of lockers. "Anybody here?" she called
in a quivery voice.

No reply.

"Now I'm *hearing* things too," she said out loud.

Oh well, she thought, pulling her sweatshirt
over her head, *at least now I'll have more time to
study.*

With that thought, the sob she'd been holding
back burst out.

*How could this happen to me? How could this
happen?*

Am I really going crazy?

Leaving her clothes on the bench, she pulled
a towel from her locker and padded over the damp
floor toward the shower room. A warm shower
would be soothing, she decided. She'd make it nice
and hot. It would stop the trembling, stop the chills
down her back.

She turned at the entrance to the showers,
thinking she heard someone again. She listened.
Again, silence.

She stepped into the large shower room with
its stained tile walls, its row of chrome showerheads. The floor was puddled with cold water, left
over from last-period gym class.

Bobbi shivered.

I'm so cold. So cold.

As she reached up to turn on the water, metal doors nearby slammed shut with a *clang*.

"Huh?"

At first Bobbi wasn't sure what had happened. She jumped, startled by the loud, unexpected noise. Maybe someone had entered the dressing area outside, she decided.

But then she saw that the shower room doors had been closed.

That's weird, she thought. She turned on the water.

And screamed as scalding water burst out of the showerhead with a roar, striking her chest, her shoulders.

"Ow!"

She dodged away. But the next showerhead was spraying down hot water too, scalding hot, burning hot.

"Help!"

All the showers were turned on now. Scalding hot water shooting out of all of them.

Something's wrong, Bobbi realized, stumbling back in a panic, her chest burning, her legs burning. *Something's terribly wrong.*

"Ow!"

She slipped, toppled backward, and landed with a splash in a steaming puddle.

"Help!"

Scrambling to her feet, she saw that the hot water was rising rapidly. The drain appeared to be clogged.

"Ow!"

The water was nearly an inch deep already, and so hot that it burned her feet.

The steam rose like a thick, choking curtain.

Gasping in the hot, wet air, Bobbi lunged for the doors. She tugged on the handles. "Hey—" They wouldn't move.

"Hey—"

She struggled to push open the doors. But they were stuck. Or blocked. Or locked.

"Hey—!"

The steam was thick. She felt as if her lungs were burning, filling up. It was so hard to breathe.

Crying out from the pain of the scalding water, she hopped back to the wall of showerheads, reached for the first control knob, turned it, turned, turned. . . .

To her horror, the water didn't slow. Didn't grow colder.

Frantically she turned another knob. Another. Another.

"Ow!"

She couldn't shut them off.

"I can't *breathe*!" The steam was so thick, so hot. "I can't *see*!"

She slipped, stumbling back to the double doors.

"Help me!" She choked out a desperate cry. "Somebody—help!"

The water was up over her ankles. Why wouldn't it drain? She danced wildly, a dance of unbearable pain.

"Help me! I can't—breathe!"

The rush of water became a roar.

She closed her eyes and covered her ears.

The roar didn't go away.

The pain didn't go away.

The roar grew louder.

Then all was silence.

19

WHAT CORKY FOUND

Where'd everyone go? Corky wondered.

She stepped into the gym, shifting her backpack to her other shoulder. "Anyone here?" she called, her voice echoing against the high ceiling.

Her sneakers squeaked on the shiny polished floor. She glanced up at the scoreboard clock. Not even four thirty.

Practice usually lasted until five, she knew.

So where *was* everyone?

Had they moved the practice outdoors? Sometimes they did that on nice days. It was good to practice in the stadium, get some fresh air, get out of the gym, which was usually stifling hot.

But it was gray and blustery outside today, not a day for an outdoor practice.

Her footsteps echoed as she made her way to Miss Green's office and peered in through the big glass window.

Empty. The papers all neatly stacked on one corner of the desk. The chair pushed in.

I guess practice ended early for some reason, Corky thought, shaking her head.

Well, Bobbi must be glad. She wasn't in any mood to face the girls anyway.

Bobbi. I want to talk to her, to make up, Corky thought.

She pushed open the door to the locker room and stuck her head inside. "Bobbi? Anyone?"

The locker room seemed empty too.

Corky was about to close the door when she heard the sound of rushing water.

Someone's taking a shower, she decided.

She made her way into the locker room, warmer and steamier than usual. Past a row of lockers.

Corky spotted someone's clothes tossed onto one of the long benches that stretched in front of the lockers. On the other side of the lockers, she could hear the rush of shower water going full force. She picked up the sweatshirt, recognized it as Bobbi's.

So Bobbi was taking a shower.

By herself?

Where were the other girls?

This didn't make any sense.

Corky took a step toward the shower room, then stopped. She had spotted something on the floor under Bobbi's things. Something shiny.

She bent down and picked it up, bringing it up close to her face to examine it. It was Kimmy's silver pendant, the shiny little megaphone.

It must have fallen off again, Corky decided. She rolled it into a tissue and stuffed it into the pocket of her jeans.

I'll have to remember to return it to her.

She walked past the lockers, turned toward the shower room, and then stopped in surprise. The shower doors were closed.

Weird, she thought.

The shower doors were *never* closed. She hadn't even known they *could* close.

As Corky drew nearer, the rush of water on the other side of the door grew louder. Could one shower make all that noise? she wondered.

She knocked on the metal door. "Hey—Bobbi!"

No reply.

"Bobbi?" She pounded harder.

She can't hear me over the water, Corky decided.

She put a hand on each of the two door handles and pulled.

The doors swung open easily.

"Hey—!" Corky shrieked as a tidal wave of hot water came spewing out at her. "Whoa!"

Startled, she staggered back until she bumped into the side of a locker. The hot water rolled over her sneakers, washed up onto the legs of her jeans.

"Ow! Hey—" It was boiling hot.

She looked up to see thick white steam floating into the locker room, like a fog rolling over a beach.

What's going on? she wondered, more angry than frightened. *Who closed the doors?*

Where is Bobbi?

The steaming hot water flooded through the locker room, but it sounded as if the water had been shut off. Walking on tiptoe, Corky made her way back to the shower room.

Holding on to the tile wall, she peered inside, squinting against the swirling steam.

And saw Bobbi.

Lying facedown against the wall under the showerheads.

"Bobbi—?"

Through gaps in the parting fog, her body slowly became visible.

Her arms were crumpled beneath her. Her legs were folded. Her hair was soaked and matted over her head and onto the floor.

Her back, her legs, her skin—her entire body was as red as a lobster.

"Bobbi—?"

Gripped with fear, Corky plunged into the room, and dropped to her knees in the scalding water.

"Bobbi—?"

With a loud gasp, she reached down and gently pulled her sister's head up.

"Bobbi—? Bobbi—? Please?"

Bobbi stared back at her with vacant, wide-eyed terror, her flesh swollen and red, her mouth locked open in a silent scream.

"Bobbi—?"

No. No answer.

The heavy steam settled over Corky, making her shiver.

Holding her sister tightly in her arms, Corky knew that Bobbi would never answer her again.

20

CORKY FIGURES IT OUT

A pearly full moon seemed to hover over the Fear Street cemetery, casting pale, ghostly light over the jagged tombstones. Trees whispered and shook their nearly leafless branches in the cold, gusting wind.

Corky slipped on wet leaves, and she almost lost her balance. A light rain had just ended, leaving the weed-choked ground between the graves soft and muddy.

Like quicksand, she thought. She had a sudden picture of sinking into the ground, of being pulled down, down, until only her head poked out. And then it, too, would be sucked into the mud to join the corpses.

Something slithered through the clump of dead leaves near her feet. A squirrel? A mouse?

Even in a graveyard, there are living things, she thought. She shivered and dug her bare hands deeper into her coat pockets.

The wind died down as she made her way along the path through the old section of graves. Bobbi was buried in a new section up a little hill, away from the street. Corky knew the way well.

The old tombstones, poking up from the ground like rotting teeth, cast long shadows on the ground at Corky's feet. At the end of the first row, she stopped. Why did the stone on the end look familiar?

Creeping closer, her boots sinking into the mud, Corky read the inscription: SARAH FEAR. 1875–1899.

"Sarah Fear," Corky said aloud, staring at the carved name. She suddenly remembered. This was the grave that Jennifer had been found sprawled on, on that horrible night when she had been thrown from the bus.

"Sarah Fear."

And what were these four stones behind Sarah Fear's grave?

Corky leaned down to read the low stones. The names had been worn off over the years. But the dates were clearly readable. They had all died in the same year: 1899.

Four grave markers with the same year that Sarah Fear had died.

What had happened? Corky wondered. Had Sarah Fear's entire family been wiped out at once?

People died so young back then, Corky thought, climbing back to her feet. *Sarah Fear would have been only twenty-four.*

Without realizing it, she uttered a loud sob.

Bobbi was only seventeen.

Hands shoved into her jacket pockets, Corky turned away from the old graves and made her way along the familiar path up to the new section.

The wind picked up again, cold and wet. She could hear a dog howling mournfully somewhere down the block. The trees shivered their wintry limbs. Dead leaves scattered as if trying to flee.

"Here I am again," Corky said, placing a hand on top of her sister's temporary marker. "You're probably getting tired of seeing me."

How many times had Corky visited her sister's grave since the funeral two weeks before? Nearly every day?

"I just miss you so much," Corky whispered, holding on to the cold marker, feeling the tears well up in her eyes.

She thought about the funeral, saw it all again. The flowers, so bright and colorful and out of

place on that gray, mournful day. Her parents, holding hands, leaning against each other, hiding their
faces so outsiders couldn't see their pain.

Again Corky saw the cheerleaders, huddled
together, silent and pale. Jennifer had stayed by
herself in the wheelchair, a wool blanket over her
legs, tears trickling down her cheeks.

Chip had been there too, looking awkward
and uncomfortable. He had been nice to Corky, had
tried to say something comforting but had ended
up stammering about how sorry he was and hurrying off.

And Kimmy. Kimmy had been there too. Standing a little way off from the other cheerleaders, her
arms crossed tightly in front of her, her expression
grim, unchanging, her eyes on Chip.

A cold drizzle had begun to fall when they lowered Bobbi's coffin into the ground. Corky had felt
her mother's arms go around her and Sean. They
were all weeping, she realized, their tears dropping
into the open grave.

Corky had looked up through tear-clouded
eyes to see Kimmy again, still staring at Chip. And
then, as the drizzle had turned to a hard, steady
rain, people had started to leave, pushing up their
coat collars, ducking under black umbrellas.

Jennifer's father had appeared and wheeled

her away. Chip had hurried off, taking long, awkward strides over the mud. Kimmy had left with the other cheerleaders, their heads lowered, bent against the wind and rain.

Corky and her family had been left alone.

Without Bobbi.

Without Bobbi forever.

And now it was two weeks later, and Corky still couldn't get used to the idea that she no longer had her sister to talk to.

"I'm back again," Corky said, turning her eyes up to the full moon. "I know you can hear me, Bobbi. I—I just wish you could answer."

Her next words caught in her throat. She stopped, took a deep breath, taking in the sweet, cold air.

"I just wanted to tell you the news," she continued after a long pause. "They made Kimmy captain of the cheerleaders. You probably guessed that would happen, right? Well, everyone seems real happy about it. Especially Kimmy. The news sure made her wrist get better in a hurry."

Corky sighed. She rubbed her palm against the cold marker.

"Everyone turned to look at me when Miss Green made the announcement," Corky continued. "As if I would throw a fit or storm out or something."

And then she added bitterly, "As if I would care."

She kicked away a leaf that had blown onto a leg of her jeans. "I don't care anymore, Bobbi. I really don't," she said with growing emotion. "I don't know what I care about now. I just wish you were here. So that I could apologize for being mean to you the night before . . . the night before you died. I just wish you were here so you could tell me what happened."

Corky sobbed. "What happened in that shower room? Why didn't you open the door and come out? The police say you had some kind of seizure and died instantly. I was glad you didn't suffer, but I just can't understand it. Why? How did it happen? You weren't sick. You were in great shape. What happened, Bobbi? What happened?"

Then she was crying, big tears rolling down her cheeks, her nose running, the sound of her own cries pushed back at her by a rush of cold wind.

"I'm sorry. I'm sorry," she apologized to the silent, unanswering gravestone. "I keep coming here day after day, saying the same things. It's just—just—"

Corky shoved her hand into her jeans pocket, searching for a tissue. Digging deep, she found one, balled up. She pulled it out.

And saw something shiny fall out.

TRUE EVIL 163

She bent down and searched the wet ground at her feet until she found it. Then she stood to examine it.

Kimmy's megaphone pendant.

She had found it that day. On the locker room floor. Near Bobbi's clothes.

On that horrible day.

She had tucked it into her jeans pocket, forgotten all about it.

As she stared at it, watching it gleam in the cold, white moonlight, Corky realized that here was a clue.

Here in her trembling hand.

Kimmy had been there. Kimmy had been in the locker room. Had been near Bobbi's things.

"Oh no," Corky said aloud, squeezing the pendant tight in her fist. "Oh no. Oh no."

Had Kimmy had something to do with Bobbi's death? No one had had more motive, Corky realized.

No one had resented Bobbi more than Kimmy.

In fact, it wasn't just resentment. It was hatred.

Open hatred.

Kimmy had hated Bobbi because she was cheerleader captain. Because Chip had dropped Kimmy and asked Bobbi out. Because Bobbi had been pretty and blond and talented, and Kimmy wasn't.

Because of *everything*.

"Yes, Kimmy was there," Corky said aloud. "Kimmy was there when Bobbi died, and I have the proof in my hand."

And then, without realizing it, she was running, running between the rows of graves, her boots sliding and slipping in the mud. With the pendant wrapped tightly in her fist, she was running down to the street.

Soon she was home and in the car, starting it up, the engine roaring to life, the headlights cutting through the dark night air.

I have the proof. I have the proof.

And she squealed away from her house, following the curve of Fear Street, past the dark, old houses, past the trembling, nearly bare trees, and turned toward Kimmy's house.

A few minutes later, her heart pounding, the pendant still clutched tightly in her fist, she was staring up at the large white-shingled house, the windows all lit up, a silver Volvo parked in the drive.

Kimmy's mother opened the door, surprised to see Corky there so late, unannounced. Corky rushed past her without any explanation, tore through the front hallway, swallowing hard, gasping for air, and burst into the den.

Kimmy was there with Debra and Ronnie.

"Hey—" Kimmy called out as Corky entered.

"Here," Corky screamed accusingly. Then she unwrapped her fist and thrust the silver megaphone pendant into Kimmy's face.

Kimmy started, and her eyes grew wide with surprise.

21

KIMMY'S SURPRISE

It's my proof!" Corky cried.

Ronnie jumped to her feet. Debra stared up at Corky from the floor, a notebook in her lap.

"My proof!" Corky repeated, holding the pendant in front of Kimmy's startled face.

"Where'd you get it?" Kimmy asked, locking her eyes on to Corky's.

"You left it somewhere," Corky said, shaking all over from her anger.

"Huh?"

"You left it somewhere, and now it's my proof!" Corky exclaimed.

"Corky—are you okay?" Ronnie asked, moving over to her and putting a hand gently on her trembling shoulder.

"You'd better sit down," Debra said, closing her notebook. "You don't look very well."

Corky pulled away from Ronnie's hand. "You were there. You were there when Bobbi died," she snarled, staring accusingly at Kimmy.

Kimmy's mouth dropped open, but she didn't reply.

"Here's my proof," Corky said, waving the pendant in Kimmy's face.

"Listen to Debra," Kimmy said finally. "Sit down." She pointed to the couch. "You're not making any sense, Corky."

"I found this in the locker room," Corky said, ignoring Kimmy's words. "On the day Bobbi died. I found it on the floor. I found it."

"Corky—please!" Kimmy insisted. "Sit down. Let me get you something hot to drink. You're shaking like a leaf!"

"Don't change the subject!" Corky screamed, realizing she was out of control, not caring, not caring at all. "I have the proof, Kimmy. I have the proof! I found your pendant under Bobbi's things."

Kimmy's expression changed from surprise to concern. "Corky," she said softly, "that pendant isn't mine."

22

JENNIFER'S SURPRISE

H uh?" Corky took a step back, her expression
one of suspicion and disbelief.

"It isn't mine anymore," Kimmy said, her
eyes on the pendant.

"But—but—"

"I gave it to Jennifer," Kimmy said.

"She's telling the truth," Debra said quickly.
Holding her notebook, she climbed to her feet and
stepped up beside Kimmy, as if taking sides. Ronnie
had moved back to the window and was leaning
against the sill, a troubled look on her face.

"Jennifer?" Corky asked weakly, suddenly feeling as if she were falling, falling down a dark, endless hole.

"I gave it to Jennifer. A couple of weeks ago,"

Kimmy said, resting her hands on her hips. "She was always telling me how much she liked it. So one day I saw her in the hall before school, and I just gave it to her."

"No," Corky insisted. "You always wore it—"

"She's telling the truth," Debra insisted. "I was there when Kimmy gave it to Jennifer. Jennifer was really happy."

"I was tired of it anyway," Kimmy said with a shrug. "The clasp was loose. It was always falling off."

Corky stared hard into Kimmy's eyes. She was telling the truth, Corky realized.

But that meant . . .

"You *hated* my sister!" Corky declared, unwilling to let Kimmy off the hook.

Kimmy shook her head. She turned her eyes to the window. "I didn't like her very much, Corky. But I didn't hate her. I guess I resented her a lot. I guess I was a little jealous of her."

"A *little*?" Corky cried.

"Okay, okay. A lot," Kimmy admitted. "But I'm not a murderer! I wouldn't kill someone because of cheerleading!"

"J-Jennifer—" Corky stammered.

"Jennifer isn't a killer either," Kimmy said softly. She shook her head. "You know that, Corky. Poor Jennifer—"

"But the pendant—" Corky said, staring down at it in her hand.

"Jennifer must have dropped it," Kimmy replied. "Just like I always did. I told you, the clasp was loose."

Corky's mind whirred crazily from thought to thought. She stared at the pendant as if hypnotized by it. The room started to tilt, then spin. Once again she felt as if she were falling, falling down into a bottomless, dark pit.

"Corky—!" Kimmy grabbed her arm.

"Jennifer couldn't change her clothes in the locker room," Corky said, closing her eyes, trying to make the room stop spinning, trying to make the falling sensation stop. "Jennifer always changed at home. She wouldn't go into the locker room."

"Yeah. Maybe," Kimmy agreed. "But, Corky—"

"Why would Jennifer go into the locker room? Why? What was she doing there?" Corky screamed.

"Corky—stop! You're not thinking clearly!" Kimmy cried.

"Sit down," Ronnie said from across the room. "Somebody make her sit down."

"Maybe we should call her parents," Debra said at the same time.

"No!" Corky screamed, pulling out of Kimmy's

grasp. "No! I have to talk to Jennifer! I *have* to! I have to know the truth!"

"Corky—please—let us call your parents," Kimmy pleaded.

But Corky had already run out of the den and was making her way down the front hallway. The three girls called to her, begging her to come back.

"What on earth is going on?" Kimmy's mom cried, poking her head out of the living room.

Corky flew past her—and out into the dark, cool night.

"Corky—come back! Come back!"

"Come back and talk!"

She ignored their pleas, their frantic, high-pitched shouts.

The car started quickly. The lights shot on. And she headed the car toward Jennifer's house in North Hills.

Past houses darkened for the night. Past empty yards and woods filled with silent, bending trees. Past Shadyside High, dark except for the spotlight out front, throwing a shimmering cone of light onto the front doors.

Jennifer's house was on a side street just north of the school. As Corky turned the corner, her headlights swept over the low ranch-style house. She braked hard, stopping the car down the street from the house, and stared across the smooth lawn.

Dark.

All the windows were dark, the shades drawn, curtains pulled.

Corky glanced at the dashboard clock. Eleven o'clock.

"Guess they all go to bed early," she said out loud.

And then she saw the headlights of a car parked at the curb in front of Jennifer's house flash on.

It was a red Volkswagen, Corky saw.

The car pulled slowly away from the curb and edged into the driveway to turn around. The interior lights came on for a second, and the girl in the car was illuminated.

It's Jennifer! Corky's mouth dropped open.

I didn't know she could drive.

I didn't think she could move her legs enough to push the pedals.

Corky watched Jennifer pull the car halfway up the drive, then back into the street, and then pull off in the other direction.

Jennifer's headlights filled Corky's car with blinding white light. *She's coming right at me,* Corky thought. *She'll see me.*

Corky ducked her head, covered her face with the sleeve of her coat.

Jennifer didn't seem to notice her. The

Volkswagen rolled slowly past, then turned right, heading toward the school.

Where could Jennifer be going by herself at eleven o'clock at night? Corky wondered.

Deciding to follow her, she eased the car into Jennifer's driveway and turned around just as Jennifer had done. Then she floored the gas pedal and shot around the corner, eager to catch up.

Racing down Park Drive, Corky quickly saw that their cars were the only two on the road. She slowed down, deciding to keep at least a block between her car and Jennifer's.

Where is she going? Where?

The question repeated and repeated in her mind.

The full moon floated at the top of the windshield, as if leading the way. A raccoon scooted into the road, hesitated in Corky's headlights, and then just made it safely to the other side as Corky rolled by.

As she followed a block behind the red Volkswagen, Corky's thoughts went back to her emotional encounter with Kimmy. Kimmy had appeared to be telling the truth about the silver pendant. And she truly seemed to be concerned about Corky.

What did that mean?

Had Jennifer been in the locker room the afternoon Bobbi was killed?

Bobbi and Jennifer had become best friends. There was no reason to suspect that Jennifer might have killed Bobbi. No reason at all.

So what had Jennifer been doing there that afternoon?

And what was she doing *now*?

Corky followed the Volkswagen as it turned onto Old Mill Road. As an oncoming car's headlights shone forward, Corky could see Jennifer's shadow reflected on the back window of the little car.

She's heading for Fear Street! Corky realized.

But why?

Is she going to my house? An unexpected visit?

No. Jennifer isn't my friend. She was Bobbi's friend.

Bobbi's friend. Bobbi's friend. Bobbi's friend.

The words repeated until they didn't make any sense.

Nothing made any sense.

Corky followed Jennifer's car as it turned onto Fear Street. Past the sprawling, ramshackle old houses. Past the burned-out ruins of the old Simon Fear mansion high on its sloping weed-covered lawn.

And then suddenly, after Fear Street curved

into the thick woods, Corky saw Jennifer pull her car to the side of the road. Her headlights dimmed, then went out.

Corky hit the brakes, and her car slid to a stop less than a block behind. Quickly she cut her lights.

Corky wondered, *Why is she stopping here?*

Leaning forward to get a better view through the windshield, she saw where Jennifer had stopped.

The cemetery. The Fear Street cemetery.

Squinting through the darkness, she saw Jennifer's car door swing open. Saw Jennifer's hand on the door handle, pushing the door open, holding it open.

Then she saw Jennifer turn and put her feet down on the pavement.

"Oh, I don't *believe* it!" Corky muttered to herself as Jennifer pulled herself to her feet.

Stood up.

Stepped away from the car. Slammed the door. Walked onto the grass of the cemetery.

Walked.

"I don't believe it," Corky repeated, gaping at the slender, dark figure disappearing behind the gravestones.

"She walks. She can walk. Bobbi was right. That night in front of Jennifer's house. Bobbi was right. And I thought she was crazy."

Corky leaped out of the car and closed the door silently behind her. Then she began jogging along the curb, running as quietly as she could, staying in the shadows thrown by the tall trees.

She stopped and knelt behind a gnarled old oak, and peered toward where Jennifer had gone.

Wisps of fog floated over the graveyard. The moonlight filtering through the fog tinged everything with a pale, sickly green. Shadows shifted and shimmered in the eerie green light. The jagged tombstones glowed.

As Corky leaned against the cold, damp tree trunk, peering intently into the dimly lit scene, Jennifer reemerged. Dancing.

Dancing a strange silent dance.

Her arms over her head, her legs—those legs everyone believed to be paralyzed—twirled and kicked. A silent, cheerless tango.

She was wearing her cheerleader costume. The short skirt flew up as she spun. Her dark hair flew behind her as if alive.

And what was that she was waving in her hand?

Corky squinted into the misty green light.

It was the pennant. The Shadyside pennant they had made for her after the accident. The crippling accident.

And now here was Jennifer, twirling wildly in the green moonlight. Kicking and twirling. Waving the pennant high.

Dancing in a narrow circle. Bending her back, raising her face to the moon, her long hair flowing down nearly to the ground.

Round and round.

Around a tombstone, Corky realized.

Jennifer was circling a tall tombstone surrounded by four other stones.

Sarah Fear's tombstone.

Waving the pennant, she kicked her legs high as if leading a silent parade. Then, once again, she arched her back, raising her face to the moon.

Her eyes closed, the pale green light played off her face. She bowed deeply, crossing her legs as she dipped, a strange curtsy to the moon. And then she rose up and began moving slowly to an unheard rhythm, twirling around the gravestone, her eyes closed, a strange tranquil smile on her face.

Corky couldn't stand it any longer.

Pushing herself away from the tree, she lurched forward into the graveyard, her boots sinking into the wet mud.

"Jennifer—" she called, her voice sounding tiny and hollow on the wind. "Jennifer—what's going on?"

23

"I'M NOT JENNIFER"

Jennifer halted her strange dance and opened her eyes. Her smile faded. She lowered the pennant to her side.

Corky ran, then stopped before the first row of gravestones. "Jennifer—what are you doing?"

Jennifer's eyes reflected the green moonlight as she turned to face Corky. "I'm not Jennifer," she said, her voice husky, almost breathless.

"Huh? Jennifer—I saw you dancing," Corky cried.

"I'm not Jennifer," she repeated darkly, standing directly in front of Sarah Fear's tombstone. And then she screamed: *"I'm not Jennifer!"*

"Jennifer—I *saw* you!" Corky insisted.

As if in reply, Jennifer lifted one hand high

above her head and waved it as if summoning someone.

"Oh!" Corky cried out, raising her hands to her face as the grass flew off Sarah Fear's grave and the dirt began to rise.

Jennifer waved her hand high above her head, and the dirt rose up like a dark curtain, flying off the grave, flying high into the black sky.

And then the dirt was swirling around them both, thicker and thicker, until Corky couldn't see beyond it, until Corky was forced to move closer to Jennifer.

Faster and faster the curtain of dirt swirled, until it became a raging dark whirlwind, like a tornado funnel.

Covering her eyes with her arm, Corky staggered forward, forward—until she was standing face-to-face with Jennifer. Jennifer held her hand high as if directing the swirling dirt, her eyes aglow with excitement, the excitement of her power.

"Jennifer—what are you doing? Stop it! Stop it—*please!*"

Corky's frightened plea was drowned out by the roar of the spinning dirt. The roar drowned out all sound, all thoughts. She could no longer see the moon or the sky, the graves, the trees.

Inside the dark funnel of dirt, she could see

only Jennifer. Jennifer, her eyes glowing with an eerie green light, glaring at Corky, her expression hard, angry, her hand still raised high over her head.

They were alone, the two of them, trapped inside this frightening storm of graveyard dirt.

And then the roar faded and died as the dirt continued to whirl around them. And Jennifer's throaty voice, a voice Corky had never heard before, rose in the fresh silence. "I am not Jennifer," she repeated, glaring coldly at Corky. "Jennifer is dead. Jennifer died weeks ago."

"What are you saying?" Corky cried, wrapping her arms around herself as if for protection. "What is *happening*?"

"Jennifer died in the bus accident," the husky voice revealed, her eyes lighting up, as if the words were giving her pleasure. "She was dead that night in the rain. She died on top of Sarah Fear's grave."

"Jennifer—what are you *saying*?" Corky cried. Her eyes darted around, searching for an escape route. But the swirling black column of dirt offered no hope of escape.

"I waited so long, so long," the husky voice said, deepening with sudden sadness. "I waited so long—and then Jennifer came along. . . ."

"I don't understand," Corky started. "I don't—"

"Buried for so long," the voice continued.

"Buried down there for more than a hundred years with Sarah Fear. Waiting. Waiting."

"You're—you're *Sarah Fear?*" Corky stammered, staring into the angry glowing eyes.

"Not anymore," came the reply.

Corky shuddered and hugged herself tightly.

This isn't happening.

The heavy funnel of dirt from the grave continued to swirl silently around the two girls, blocking out all sound, all light, all evidence that the rest of the world existed.

"I—I don't get it," Corky stammered. "Are you some kind of ghost? An evil spirit?"

Again Jennifer threw back her head in laughter. "That is a quaint way of putting it," she replied, sneering. She pointed down to the grave. "For more than a hundred years I waited down there for a new body. And then Jennifer came along."

"Please—" Corky cried, lowering her hands to her sides. "Stop. Let me go now, okay?"

Jennifer shook her head, her eyes lighting up with pleasure.

"No—please," Corky begged. "Let me go. What do you want with me?"

A thin smile played over Jennifer's lips. "It's *your* turn to go down there," she said, pointing into the grave.

24

INTO THE COFFIN

"No!" Corky tried to back away. But she was trapped, trapped inside the spinning dirt as thick as a garden wall.

Jennifer leaned forward until her eyes burned so close to Corky that she could feel their heat. "For more than a hundred years I waited. But now I'm alive inside Jennifer, and Jennifer's enemies will pay." Again she pointed down into the grave. "Now it's your turn, Corky."

"But why?" Corky cried. "I haven't done anything to you."

"Haven't *done* anything? You and your sister—with your perfect faces? Your perfect bodies? Your perfect lives?"

"But—" Corky turned her head, tried to get

away from the searing heat of the evil burning eyes.

A bitter smile formed on Jennifer's eerily glowing face. "But I showed Bobbi. I showed Bobbi and that boy, Chip."

"You frightened them," Corky said, realizing what had happened, realizing that her sister's wild stories were all true. "You paralyzed them. And then—you killed Bobbi," Corky said, choking out the words.

Jennifer nodded once and locked her eyes on Corky. "Now it's your turn."

"No! Jennifer—*wait*!" Corky screamed.

The evil spirit inside Jennifer's body laughed scornfully. She pointed at her feet. "Look down there, Corky dear. Look down at your new home."

Corky, too frightened to disobey, turned her eyes down.

With another wave of Jennifer's hand, more dirt flew up into the swirling dirt funnel. As the dirt rose up in eerie silence, Corky stared down into a deep hole. To her horror, the hole revealed the top of a coffin, the dark wood swollen and warped.

"See your new home—and your new friend!" the evil spirit cried in its hoarse dead voice.

"Oh!" Corky moaned weakly as the coffin lid creaked open.

Still compelled to peer down into the darkness,

Corky watched the lid lift all the way up.

Inside the coffin, she saw a rotting skeleton, its eyeless skull staring up at her with a toothy grin.

The skeleton was moving. Quivering all over.

No.

Staring hard, unable to remove her eyes from the ghastly sight, Corky saw why the skeleton appeared to quiver.

Those were worms moving on the bones, thousands of white worms slithering over the skeleton, crawling over the rotting remains of Sarah Fear.

"Oh!" Corky felt her stomach heave, felt her throat tighten in disgust.

She shut her eyes and turned away, but the sight of the thousands of slithering white worms stayed with her.

Swallowing hard, trying to shake away the horrifying picture, she suddenly heard voices. Far away yet familiar.

For a brief terrifying moment, she thought it was the voice of Sarah Fear, calling to her from down in the open grave.

But then she recognized Kimmy's voice. And heard Debra's reply. And Ronnie's frightened shout.

The voices sounded far away because they came from outside the wall of dirt.

They must have followed me, Corky realized.

"Your friends are too late to save you," Jennifer said calmly, without urgency. She raised both hands.

"No—please!" Corky screamed. "Please—don't!"

Ignoring her cries, Jennifer shoved Corky with startling strength, inhuman strength.

Still screaming, Corky toppled into the hole, down to join Sarah Fear in the open worm-ridden coffin.

25

CORKY LOSES

own into the hole. Into the warped, swollen coffin.

Down to the white worms.

But even in her screaming terror, Corky's body responded, remembering the cheerleading skills, the moves her body had practiced over the years until they had become reflexive, a part of her.

She landed hard on her feet. Absorbed the pressure of the landing by bending her knees. Then pushed up, up—into a high standing jump. Raised her hands. Caught the top of the open grave as the wall of dirt began to swirl back down onto her. Pulled herself up and out as the dirt began to lower itself back into the hole.

Panting loudly, she crawled away from the hole, away from the horror.

Jennifer had already turned away, turned around to face the three cheerleaders.

Still acting by reflex, her mind still paralyzed by the horrors of the open grave, her body forced to act on its own, Corky flung herself onto Jennifer. Caught her from behind. Wrapped her arms around Jennifer's waist. Swung her back toward the open grave.

She struggled to wrestle Jennifer into the hole. Into the coffin. To wrestle the evil spirit back to where it belonged, as the dirt continued to rain down, down, down.

Jennifer cried out in her husky, deep voice, trying to pull out of Corky's desperate hug.

The pennant, which she had clutched all the while, fell from her hand. Corky watched it drop into the hole. It landed silently among the bones and worms.

They wrestled nearer to the edge of the hole. Corky pulled, pulled with all her strength, tightening her arms around Jennifer's waist, trying to throw her down.

Jennifer pulled back, crying out in protest.

Closer to the hole. Closer to the edge.

I can do it! Corky thought. *I can do it!*

But then Jennifer turned to face her, her eyes wild with fury. She opened her mouth wide, wider—and a wind blew out, a stench, a vapor, a wind that howled over Corky, covered her face, filled her nostrils.

Jennifer tilted her head, closed her eyes, and the vapor roared out of her, reeking of death, of decay, of all that is foul.

It blew into Corky's face, hot and wet and sour. Corky gagged and turned her face.

But the wind still howled out of Jennifer's mouth, encircled Corky and choked her in its thick, hot stench.

I'm going to suffocate, Corky thought.

I can't breathe. I'm going to suffocate. The smell. The smell is too sickening!

Corky realized she was weakening, about to lose the fight.

One last tug. She held her breath and braced herself, summoned all her remaining strength for one last tug.

Now! she told herself.

And heaved with all her might, her arms wrapped tightly around Jennifer's waist.

Into the grave! Corky thought. *Jennifer—go down into the grave!*

But Jennifer was too strong.

The foul wind raged and howled from her open mouth.

Jennifer didn't budge.

I'm lost, Corky thought.

26

BURIED

*C*orky felt her arms slip off Jennifer's waist. *I'm lost. I'm lost.*

As the dirt rained down, she could suddenly hear the terrified cries of the three other girls.

Jennifer's eyes were open wide as the sour wind howled from her mouth. She knew she had won. She knew her evil had triumphed.

First Bobbi. Now me, Corky thought.

Bobbi. Bobbi.

The thought of her sister filled her with renewed anger. With an anguished cry, Corky threw herself onto Jennifer's back and wrapped her hands around Jennifer's throat from behind.

Jennifer struggled as Corky tightened her grip, tightened her hands, began to choke Jennifer, choke the evil spirit inside Jennifer's body, pushing her head down.

The raging stream of foul vapor from Jennifer's mouth blew into the hole now, into the open grave. Corky could see it, blowing the worms around in the coffin.

"Yes!" she cried aloud, hearing the wind lose its howl, feeling it weaken as it poured into the coffin.

All the evil pouring down into the coffin.

And as Corky continued to choke her, Jennifer felt lighter, lighter. As light as air.

And the wind stopped. Jennifer uttered a feeble groan, and the wind stopped.

"Yes!" Corky cried, not loosening her grip on Jennifer's throat.

The evil spirit is abandoning her, Corky thought.

She could feel it leaving, could feel Jennifer's body growing light.

Corky let go.

Jennifer lay facedown in the dirt.

Corky watched as the coffin lid slammed shut, trapping the evil vapor, trapping the evil spirit inside.

The dirt rained down in a dark, thunderous avalanche, filling the hole, re-covering the grave.

Buried. The evil spirit is buried again, Corky

thought, gasping in the cool, sweet air, the clean air, letting the fresh night air fill her lungs.

She realized she was still on her knees in the soft dirt.

"Corky—!" Kimmy was screaming.

The three girls were standing right in front of her, peering at the grave in horror. They had seen it all, seen every moment of Corky's desperate battle. Now they huddled around her.

"Corky—are you *okay*?" Ronnie cried.

All four of them turned their eyes to Jennifer's body. Slowly Corky rolled her over so she was faceup.

"Ohh," Kimmy groaned.

Ronnie gagged and held on to Debra to keep from sinking to her knees.

As the girls gaped in silent horror, Jennifer's skin dried and crumpled, flaked off in chunks. Her long hair fell off, strands blowing away in the breeze. Her eyes sank back into her skull, then rotted into dark pits. Her cheerleader costume appeared to grow larger as her flesh decayed underneath it, and her bones appeared.

Before Corky realized what was happening, she felt Kimmy's arm slide around her shoulders. "It's okay, Corky," Kimmy whispered. "You're okay now. It's all going to be okay."

And then they heard a man's voice calling from the street. "What's going on here?"

Darting beams from flashlights danced over the ground. The girls looked up into the suspicious faces of two uniformed Shadyside officers.

"What's going on here? One of the neighbors reported a—"

Both of the young officers gasped in surprise as they saw the body sprawled on the ground beside the four girls, the body draped in a cheerleader's costume.

"What on earth—?"

"It's Jennifer," Corky managed to say from the midst of her confusion. "It's Jennifer Daly. I followed her here. She—"

"Huh?" Both police directed their lights from the body to Corky's face. "You followed her here? Are you sure, miss?"

"Yes. I followed her here. She was dancing—"

"You didn't follow this girl, miss," one of the police officers said, eyeing Corky intently. "This girl hasn't been dancing tonight. Take a good look at the corpse. This girl has been dead for weeks!"

Jennifer's anguished parents, awakened and summoned to the police station, demanded answers.

But there were no reasonable answers, no logical answers.

Corky's parents also arrived, as upset and confused as everyone else. They waited patiently with
their daughter during the hours of questioning, the
police asking the same questions again and again,
dissatisfied with the answers they received from
Corky and the other three girls.

"Fear Street," one of the police officers said
grimly, shaking his head. "Fear Street . . ."

A few minutes later he allowed them all to go
home.

As Corky climbed the stairs to her room, the
room she had shared with her sister, she thought of
Bobbi.

Bobbi had died because of the evil spirit's
jealousy.

And now Corky was alone. Left alone to
remember forever the horrors of this night.

She turned on the light and glanced at the
bedside clock. Three o'clock in the morning. Wearily, feeling numb, she tugged off her clothes and
let them fall to the floor, and pulled a nightgown
over her head.

"Bobbi—I miss you so much!" she cried out
loud.

Trying to force back the sobs that threatened
to burst out of her throat, she turned off the light
and lowered herself into bed.

Bobbi is gone forever, she told herself miserably.

But so is the evil spirit.

The evil spirit is buried once again, buried in the old grave, locked in the coffin under six feet of dirt, where it can't harm anyone ever again.

She sighed, pulling the covers up to her chin.

"Hey—"

There was something in her bed.

With a startled cry, she reached down, grabbed it, held it tightly.

She clicked on the lamp and stared at it, blinking as her eyes adjusted to the light.

It was the maroon-and-gray pennant with Jennifer's name stitched across the front.

She stared at the pennant, reading the name again and again.

Then it fell from her hand and she started to scream.

THE SECOND EVIL

PART ONE
WHERE IS THE EVIL?

1

BURIED HOPES

Kimmy Bass slowed her car to a stop at Division Street and tapped her fingers impatiently on the wheel. "I never make this light," she complained.

Her friend Debra Kern stared out the passenger window at a boy in a blue windbreaker, walking a large Doberman across the street. "What's your hurry?" she asked, wiping steam off the window with her wool-gloved hand.

"You're always in such a hurry," Veronica (Ronnie) Mitchell chimed in from the back seat.

The light changed. Kimmy pushed hard on the gas pedal, and the pale blue Camry lurched across the intersection. "I'm not in a hurry. I just don't like to stop," Kimmy said.

Debra shivered even though the heater was on high. She was very thin, and no matter how many T-shirts and sweaters she wore, she was always cold.

Ronnie looked completely lost inside the fake raccoon coat that had once belonged to her mother, but it kept her really warm. With her curly red hair, tiny snub of a nose, and freckles, she appeared to be about twelve.

Outside, the wind picked up, blowing dead brown leaves across the road. It was cold for late November. Heavy clouds hovered low in the evening sky, threatening snow.

"Want to do something Saturday night?" Kimmy asked, making a sharp turn onto Old Mill Road. "Hang out or something?"

Debra smoothed her straight blond hair with a quick toss of her head. Her blue eyes, normally pale and icy, lit up. "No. I actually have a date Saturday night."

"Hey, with who?" Ronnie asked, leaning over the front seat, catching the coy look on Debra's face.

"Eric Bishop," Debra said after a suspenseful pause.

Kimmy reacted with surprise. "Eric? Isn't he going out with Cari Taylor?"

Debra's face assumed a smug grin. "Not anymore." She trailed her gloved finger along the steamed-up window, drawing a star across the glass.

Ronnie settled back in her seat. "Eric Bishop!" she exclaimed. "He's definitely okay." She snuggled inside the big furry coat. "Could you turn the heat down a bit?"

Kimmy ignored her.

"Who are you interested in these days?" Debra asked Kimmy, adjusting her seat belt.

"I don't know," Kimmy replied wistfully. "Nobody, really."

"You're not still hung up on Chip, are you?" Debra asked, turning to study Kimmy's round face. In the light of the passing streetlights, she could see Kimmy's cheeks redden.

"No way!" Kimmy protested loudly. "Corky is welcome to him. Really."

Debra stared hard at her. Ronnie hummed to herself.

"Really!" Kimmy repeated. "I mean it. I'm over Chip. I'm glad he dumped me."

"Chip seems to like Corcorans," Debra said dryly, turning back to the houses passing outside the window. "First Bobbi, now her sister, Corky."

The mention of Bobbi's name brought a chill to the car. Debra reached out to turn up the heat, but saw it was up all the way.

"Bobbi was so great-looking," Ronnie said thoughtfully.

"She was the best cheerleader I ever saw," Debra added.

"I was so jealous of her," Kimmy admitted. "I still can't believe she's dead."

"Poor Corky," Debra said, lowering her voice nearly to a whisper. "She really looked up to her sister. I can't imagine what it would be like. I mean, if *my* sister died, I'd . . ." Her voice trailed off.

"Corky's been kind of weird lately," Kimmy said, keeping her eyes on the twin beams of white light ahead of her. "She barely talks to anyone."

"I was jealous of her and her sister, too," Ronnie confessed. "I mean, they were so perfect with their perfect blond hair, and their perfect white teeth, and their perfect figures."

"I've tried being friendly with Corky," Kimmy said. "But she just keeps that sad expression on her face and isn't friendly at all. That's why I thought maybe the three of us could—"

"We've got to get Corky back on the cheerleading squad," Debra said, interrupting. "It was so strange when she quit last month. If she'd quit right when her sister died, I'd understand. But she waited a while to drop out."

"We'll get her back to normal," Ronnie said. "At least I hope she'll listen to us."

Kimmy made a right turn onto Fear Street, and the sky immediately appeared to darken. Gusting winds swept around the small car.

"Too bad you're not in sixth-period study hall. In the library," Debra said. "You should have seen Suki Thomas with Gary Brandt. Well, Suki was giving Gary a sex ed class. They didn't even bother to go back to the stacks."

"She was kissing him?" Ronnie asked, leaning forward to hear Debra's soft, whispery voice.

"I guess you could call it that. I thought Mrs. Bartlett was going to have a cow."

All three girls laughed.

Their laughter was cut short as the car approached the Fear Street cemetery. Behind a weather-beaten rail fence, the weed-choked graveyard sloped up from the street. Eerie wisps of gray mist rose up between the crooked tombstones.

"Corky's family should move," Debra said, shuddering. "I mean, living so close to where Bobbi is buried. It's like a constant reminder."

"Corky visits Bobbi's grave all the time," Kimmy said, shaking her head.

"We've *got* to talk to her," Ronnie said heatedly.

"We've got to make her forget about Bobbi and the evil spirit—"

"The evil spirit isn't dead," Debra said suddenly. "I can still feel it."

"Debra, stop," Kimmy said sharply.

"I know the evil spirit that killed Bobbi is still alive," Debra insisted quietly.

"Don't say that!" Ronnie cried.

"You've got to stop reading those stupid books," Kimmy said. "I can't believe you spend so much time with that stuff."

"I want to learn all I can about the occult," Debra replied. "Both of you should too. You were there that night. You were there in the cemetery and saw the evil spirit."

"I saw Corky fight it. And I saw it go back down into its grave," Kimmy replied impatiently, almost angrily. "Oh, I don't know *what* I saw. It was all a bad dream. I just want to forget about it. I don't want to read any of that occult mumbo jumbo, and I don't want to hear about it."

Debra fingered the crystal she had begun wearing around her neck soon after Bobbi's funeral. "But I can feel—" she started.

"*I want to get on with my life!*" Kimmy declared loudly. "I want—" She stopped midsentence, her mouth open.

Ronnie and Debra followed Kimmy's gaze through the still-cloudy windshield. In the darkness of the cemetery they could see a solitary figure near the top of a small hill where the ground leveled out and some new graves stood.

Wisps of gray mist snaked along her feet. She had one hand on the top of a gravestone, her head lowered as if talking to someone in the grave.

"It's Corky," Debra whispered. "What's she doing there?"

"I *told* you," Kimmy said, slowing the car to a near-stop. "She visits Bobbi's grave all the time."

"But she'll *freeze!*" Debra declared with a shiver. "Honk the horn." She reached out to pound on the horn, but Kimmy pushed her hand away.

"No. Don't."

"Why?" Debra insisted.

"I think it's bad luck to honk at a cemetery."

"*Now* who's the superstitious one?" Debra scoffed. She peered out into the darkness.

"Does she see us?" Ronnie asked.

"No. She's still staring at the grave," Kimmy said. She rolled down her window. "I'll call to her."

She stuck her head out the window and called Corky's name. The gusting wind blew the name back into her face.

"She didn't hear you," Debra said, staring out

at Corky's unmoving figure, frail and small, surrounded by the rows of crooked gravestones.

Kimmy rolled up the window, her cheeks red,
her expression troubled. She tossed back her black
crimped hair and continued to watch Corky's dark
figure among the gravestones.

"What do we do now?" Ronnie asked in a tiny
voice.

Debra fingered her crystal as she stared out
at Corky.

"I don't know," Kimmy replied. "I don't know."

Unaware that she was being watched, Corky
Corcoran leaned against the cold granite of
Bobbi's tombstone. Her face was wet with tears,
silent tears that came without warning, without
crying. Tears that spilled out like the words she
spoke to her dead sister.

"I shouldn't come here all the time," Corky
said, bending low, one arm resting on top of the
stone. "I know I shouldn't. Sometimes I feel as if
I'm pulled here. Almost against my will."

The wind howled through the bent trees that
clung to the sloping hill. Corky didn't feel the cold.

"If only I could sleep," she said. "If only I could
fall asleep and not dream. I have such frightening dreams, Bobbi. Such vivid, frightening dreams.

Nightmares. Of that awful night here in the cemetery. The night I fought the evil spirit."

She sighed and wiped away the tears with her open hands. "I feel as if I'm still fighting the evil, Bobbi. I'm still fighting it even though I sent it down to its grave."

Corky pressed her hot face against the cool granite. "Bobbi, can you hear me?" she asked suddenly.

As if in reply, the ground began to shake.

"Bobbi?" Corky cried, pulling herself upright in surprise.

The entire hill trembled, the white gravestones quaking and tilting.

"Bobbi?"

A crack formed in the dirt. Another crack zigzagged across the ground like a dark streak of lightning.

As Corky gaped in disbelief, the ground over Bobbi's grave split open. The crack grew wider.

Wider.

A bony hand reached up to the surface.

Bits of flesh clung to the arm that followed the hand. Another hand clawed through to the surface. A heavy stench filled the air, invading Corky's nostrils.

The bony hands grappled at the edge of the

crack, pulling, straining, until a head appeared, then two shoulders.

"It's *you*!" Corky cried in horror as her dead sister pulled herself up from the grave.

2

SOMEONE IS WATCHING

Bobbi?"

Corky uttered the name in a choked whisper. Her breath caught in her throat.

As her dead sister rose up in front of her, Corky staggered back, bumping against Bobbi's gravestone, almost toppling backward over it.

"Bobbi, it's you!" she cried again, dropping to her knees on the hard, frozen ground.

Her sister rose up, up, until she hovered over Corky. Then she glared down with sunken eyes. The skin on her face, green and peeling, sagged, ready to fall off. Her straight blond hair was caked with wet dirt and twigs.

"Ohh!" Corky uttered a low, horrified moan. Her entire body convulsed in a tremor of terror.

Her dead sister stared down at her as the winds swirled and the ground shook.

"What is it, Bobbi?" Corky managed to cry out. She stared up at the hideous rotting figure of her sister, not wanting to see what had happened to her but unable to turn away.

"What is it, Bobbi? Why did you leave your grave? Do you want to tell me something?"

Corky was so horrified, so overcome by Bobbi's decaying form, she didn't know whether she had spoken the questions out loud or only thought them.

As she stared up at the sunken-eyed green face, Bobbi's mouth slowly began to open. The flaking, blackened lips parted as if about to speak. No sound emerged.

"Bobbi, what *is* it?" Corky demanded. "What do you want to tell me?"

The black lips opened wider.

The sunken eyes rolled back.

The winds swirled loudly.

Corky stared up expectantly, unable to get off her knees, gripped by horror.

The lips parted even wider, and a fat brown worm curled out from Bobbi's mouth.

"Nooooooo!"

Corky's shrill scream rose and swirled with the raging wind.

She covered her eyes and lowered her head, fighting the waves of nausea that rolled through her body.

When she looked back up a few seconds later, blinking hard, struggling to breathe, Bobbi was gone.

The ink-black sky was clear. Pale moonlight filtered down.

The winds had stopped.

The cemetery was deserted. Silent.

The ground over her sister's grave wasn't split or cracked open.

It didn't happen, Corky realized.

It was another dream. Another nightmare about Bobbi.

I was asleep, Corky thought.

I was leaning against Bobbi's gravestone, and I fell asleep.

I'm always so tired these days. I never can fall asleep at night. I never sleep the night through because of the nightmares.

Yes. I was asleep.

She stared at the dark ground, solid, silent. *I must have dreamed it,* she thought. The ground trembling, the gravestones shaking and tilting. The bony hand reaching up through the crack in the earth. The grotesque figure of her sister, green and rotting, covered with dirt and insects.

All a hideous dream.

"What am I going to do?" she asked aloud. "What *can* I do to make these nightmares end?"

She turned back to the gravestone, lowering her head to talk once again to Bobbi. "I'm not going to visit for a while," she said softly, her voice muted by the heavy chill in the air. "At least I'm going to try to stay away."

The wind picked up and gently stirred the trees. There seemed to be whispering all around.

"It's not that I want to forget you, Bobbi," Corky continued with a loud sob. "It's just that—It's just that I'm still alive, and I have to—"

She stopped abruptly. "I'm sorry. I'm not making any sense. I have to go. It's late, and I'm cold."

Bobbi is even colder, she thought. The grim thought made her shudder.

"Bobbi, I really—"

She stopped short and uttered a brief cry.

Something moved behind a tall marble monument. A squirrel?

No. It was too big to be a squirrel.

Staring into the darkness, surrounded by the ceaseless whispers, Corky saw a dark form hunkered down behind the monument. A hand moved, then was quickly pulled back. A head, the face hidden in shadow, poked out, then disappeared just as quickly.

Someone is here, Corky realized.

Someone is watching me.

The whispers grew louder as once again the wind swirled around her.

Before she realized it, she had pushed herself away from Bobbi's gravestone and was running down the sloping hill. Panting loudly, she made her way through the crooked rows of tombstones, her sneakers slipping on the wet grass, on the flat, dead brown leaves. Tall wet weeds swished against the legs of her jeans.

Without slowing, she glanced back.

And saw that he was following her.

It was a man, or maybe a boy. He had the dark hood of his sweatshirt pulled up over his head.

He was running fast, breathing hard, his breath steaming up over the dark hood.

She could see only a triangle of his face. Saw part of his nose and eyes. Hard, determined eyes. Angry eyes. Gray eyes, so pale that they were almost colorless.

Pale gray ghostlike eyes.

Somebody—help me! Corky wanted to cry out, but she could only pant in terror as she fled.

His shoes pounded the ground. So close behind her.

Or was that the pounding of her heart?

Who was he? Why was he spying on her? Why was he chasing her?

The questions made her dizzy as she ran, gasping in mouthfuls of the heavy, cold air. Ran through the darkness. Ran toward the street. Fear Street.

Her house was only a block away.

Would she make it?

She was nearly to the street.

Running hard. Her right side aching.

The footsteps pounding behind her.

"Ow!"

She cried out as her leg hit a low tombstone.

As the pain shot up her leg, she fell and toppled forward, her arms and legs sprawling out as she dropped facedown into a pile of wet leaves.

3

"PLEASE COME BACK"

*C*orky!"

At first she didn't recognize the voice.

"Corky!"

She raised her head, scrambled to her feet, frantically brushing at the wet leaves clinging to the front of her coat.

"Hey, Corky!"

The voice came from the street. From the little blue car just beyond the curb.

"Kimmy!" she cried. "Oh, Kimmy!"

Kimmy was running toward her, her eyes wide with concern. Behind Kimmy, Corky could see Debra and Ronnie climbing out of the car.

"He—he's chasing me!" Corky cried breathlessly. She skidded to a stop.

Kimmy protectively threw her arms around Corky's shoulders. "What's wrong, Corky?"

"What *is* it?" Ronnie called, hurrying up to them.

"He's chasing me!" Corky turned and pointed behind her.

No one.

No hooded man. No pale, pale eyes.

Vanished.

Or was he another nightmare?

Corky shuddered. Her side ached. Her ankle throbbed from its collision with the granite tombstone.

Another nightmare? Just a hallucination?

"We've got to get you home," Kimmy said, her arm still around Corky's shoulders. "Come on, Corky. Come with us," she urged softly.

"It's freezing out here!" Ronnie exclaimed, wrapping her big coat tightly around herself.

Debra remained silent, staring up at the crooked gravestones in an old section of the cemetery. Intense concentration froze her face. She reached for the crystal she wore around her neck and, still gazing up at the old stones, moved her lips in some sort of silent chant.

"Debra, come *on*!" Kimmy's voice from near the car interrupted Debra's concentration. She turned, still distracted, and followed her friends to the car.

A short while later Kimmy pulled the Camry up the gravel drive beside the Corcorans' rambling old house and cut the engine.

The four girls jogged to the front porch. Corky fumbled with her keys before finally managing to push open the front door. They all stepped inside.

"Brrrrrr!" Debra shivered and stamped her feet.

"Debra, it isn't *that* cold," Kimmy scolded.

"Yaaaaii!"

A screaming figure leaped out at them from the living room.

"Sean, give us a break," Corky told her little brother, rolling her eyes.

"I scared you." Sean grinned, his blue eyes lighting up. With his straight blond hair and high cheekbones, he looked like a smaller, more angelic version of Corky.

"We don't really feel like being scared right now," Kimmy told him, tossing her coat onto the banister.

"Wanna play hide-and-seek?" Sean asked, tugging her arm.

"Hide-and-seek?"

"Yeah! I've got *great* hiding places."

"Not right now," Kimmy told him.

"Just a short game," Sean insisted, pulling Kimmy toward the stairs.

Kimmy turned helplessly to Corky.

"Sean, take a hike," Corky said sharply. "We can't play with you now." She poked her head into the living room. "Where are Mom and Dad?"

Sean reluctantly let go of Kimmy's sleeve. "Next door."

"Come on in," Corky told the three girls, motioning to the living room. "I'm going to run into the kitchen and put on the kettle. I'll make hot chocolate."

"That sounds great!" Debra exclaimed, rubbing her shoulders, still shivering.

"I *hate* hot chocolate," Sean offered loudly.

"Sean, please!" Corky cried. She pointed. "Upstairs. Now."

"You're a jerk" was his reply, one he used about a hundred times a day. He stuck his tongue out at her, then loped up the stairs to his room.

Corky clicked on the floor lamp beside the leather couch against the wall. Pale light washed over the living room, which was decorated mainly in greens and browns.

"I'll be right back," she told the others. She hesitated at the doorway. "What were you doing there? I mean, at the cemetery?"

Debra flashed Kimmy a hesitant look. "Well . . ."

"We were looking for you," Kimmy explained. "We were headed to your house. But we stopped when we saw you . . . uh . . ." She hesitated to finish her sentence.

Corky's pale cheeks reddened. "I was at Bobbi's grave. I go there sometimes."

No one could think of a reply. A heavy silence hung over the room.

"I'll go put on the kettle," Corky said, and hurried out of the room.

As she held the kettle under the tap, her mind whirred from thought to thought. She tried to figure out why the three cheerleaders had come to find her.

Corky hadn't spent time with any of them since dropping off the cheerleading squad. They always acted very friendly when she passed them in the halls at school. But Corky really hadn't talked with them in weeks.

Hearing an odd noise, Corky glanced out the kitchen window into the darkness. Two cats were chasing each other over the deep carpet of brown leaves that covered the backyard. Their chase reminded her of being pursued by the strange hooded man with the cold gray eyes. With a shudder she hurried back to her visitors.

She found Kimmy and Debra seated on opposite

ends of the couch. Kimmy was tapping her fingers nervously on the arm. Debra had her hands clasped tightly in her lap.

Ronnie was standing by the window, hands on her slender hips, staring out at the driveway. She turned when Corky reentered the room. "I think we're warming up," she said.

Corky moved quickly to the armchair that faced the couch. She sat down, and a rude noise erupted from under the chair cushion.

"Sean!" she screamed angrily, jumping to her feet. She reached under the cushion and pulled out her brother's pink whoopee cushion.

Her three visitors laughed.

"My family *loves* practical jokes," Corky explained, rolling her eyes. She tossed the flattened whoopee cushion across the room.

"Your brother's funny," Debra said, tucking her legs under her.

"You want him?" Corky offered. She resumed her place on the chair. Ronnie moved in front of the couch and flopped down on the carpet, crossing her legs in front of her.

"Corky, how *are* you?" Kimmy asked finally in a concerned tone.

"Okay, I guess," Corky replied quickly, avoiding Kimmy's eyes.

"Were you at the game last night?" Ronnie asked.

"No. Uh-uh." Corky shook her head.

An uncomfortable silence.

Corky cleared her throat. The repetitive electronic music of Sean's Nintendo game drifted down from upstairs.

"So why'd you want to see me?" Corky asked.

"We want you to come back on the squad," Ronnie blurted out.

"Yeah. That's why we came," Kimmy said, locking her blue eyes on Corky's.

"I don't know," Corky replied, shaking her head. She brushed away a strand of blond hair that had fallen over an eye.

"The squad really needs you," Kimmy said. "It isn't the same without you."

"Really," Ronnie added earnestly.

"That's nice of you," Corky said, avoiding their eyes. "But . . ."

Her mind suddenly returned to the days when Bobbi was on the squad. She remembered how angry Kimmy had been when Bobbi was named cheerleader captain. She remembered how Kimmy had tried to turn the other girls against Bobbi.

Now Kimmy was the captain. Bobbi was dead, and Kimmy had gotten what she always wanted. So why was she here begging Corky to rejoin the squad?

"Why not give it a chance?" Kimmy urged her.

"Yeah. Just come to practice a few times," Ronnie suggested, twirling a ring on her index finger.

"Let's be honest," Corky blurted out. "You girls all resented Bobbi and me."

Her blunt words seemed to freeze in the air. Kimmy and Ronnie looked stunned for a brief moment. Debra swallowed hard.

"Things have changed, Corky," Kimmy said finally. Then she added, "Since that night."

Debra dropped her hands to her lap. She stared out the window with her icy blue eyes, her face pale in the harsh light of the floor lamp.

"We've all changed, I think," Kimmy continued, lowering her voice. "I know I have."

Corky sighed but didn't say anything.

"I was there with you that night," Kimmy said heatedly. "I saw the evil spirit too. I saw the dirt flying up from that old grave. I—I can't get it out of my mind."

"I can't either," Ronnie added. "I still have nightmares about it."

"Me too," Debra whispered.

"It's changed me," Kimmy said, continuing to stare at Corky. "I didn't lose a sister like you did, but it's changed me. I used to be angry a lot of the time. You're right when you say I resented you and Bobbi. I'm not as thin or as pretty or as talented as you. But after that horrible night in the cemetery, I don't care so much about that stuff. I saw how fragile life is. I saw—"

"It made us all stop and think about what's important," Ronnie interrupted. "I've changed too."

"And you've changed too," Kimmy told Corky. "We've all seen it. We understand."

Debra nodded but remained silent.

"That's why we think it would be good for you to come back to the squad," Ronnie said. "We really want to help."

"We should be friends," Kimmy said, round spots of pink growing darker on her cheeks. "We went through something really frightening together. Now we should be friends."

Corky stared at them one after another.

They're sincere, she decided. *They really mean it. They came here out of friendship, out of concern for me.*

They really have changed.

Corky had a sudden urge to leap across the coffee table and hug all three of them. Instead she stammered, "It—it's really nice of you. To come, I mean. I mean, to ask me back. I'll think about it. I really will."

"Come to practice after school," Kimmy urged. "You can just watch, if you want."

"Well . . ." Corky climbed to her feet and, wrapping her arms over the front of her sweater, crossed over to the window.

"The spark is just missing without you," Ronnie said, her eyes following Corky across the room.

"We haven't replaced you," Kimmy added. "Your place on the squad is waiting for you. Really."

"Thanks," Corky said, sincerely moved.

She gazed out the window—and gasped. "Ohh! It's *him*!"

The hooded man with the strange ghostly eyes—he must have followed her home.

As Corky gaped in fright, he strode over the shadowy front lawn, moving quickly toward the house.

4

THE EVIL IS ALIVE

*C*orky, what *is* it?"

Seeing the horrified expression on Corky's face as she stood frozen at the window, Kimmy and Debra leaped off the couch and darted across the room. Ronnie, who had scrambled to her feet, was right behind them.

"He—he's there!" Corky managed to cry. She pointed toward the middle of the yard.

Kimmy put a protective arm around Corky's shoulders and drew her aside.

The other two girls pressed their faces close to the glass and peered out.

"Huh?"

"Where?"

"He's there!" Corky insisted, her voice trembling.

"He stared at me with those empty eyes. Like ghost eyes."

"I don't see him," Debra said, cupping her hands around her eyes to shut out the glare from the living room.

"I don't see *anything*," Ronnie agreed. "The wind is blowing the leaves around. That's all."

"Hey, there are two cats down at the end of the drive," Debra reported. She turned away from the window to face Corky. "Is *that* what you saw?"

"No!" Corky insisted, shaking her head. "I saw him. I *did*! He was there, walking on the grass toward the house."

"Well, he's gone now," Ronnie said, flashing Kimmy a puzzled look.

Corky breathed a loud sigh of relief. "He must have seen us all staring at him and run away," she said.

"Yeah. I guess," Debra said doubtfully.

"I guess," Ronnie repeated.

They don't believe me, Corky thought miserably. *They don't believe I saw him.*

They think I'm seeing things.

And then she added, *I'm not so sure I believe me.*

She shuddered and started back to the couch.

"Guess we'd better get going," Kimmy said,

starting toward the front hallway. "I promised my parents I'd be back half an hour ago."

"Me too," Ronnie said, forcing a smile for Corky.

"It was really nice of you to come," Corky said, a little embarrassed at how stiff the words sounded. "I mean, I'm so glad you came by. With that guy and everything—"

Again Ronnie met Kimmy's eyes.

None of them believe me, Corky thought again, catching Ronnie's expression. *They think I'm cracking up.*

She glanced at the front window, half expecting to see the hooded guy peering in at her.

The window was dark and empty.

Kimmy and Ronnie had pulled on their coats.

"Is that fake fur? It's really neat!" Corky ran her hand up and down the sleeve of Ronnie's coat.

"You like it? There's room for you in here too," Ronnie joked.

"Hey, aren't you coming?" Kimmy called to Debra, who had hung back at the living room doorway.

"I thought I'd stay a few minutes and talk with Corky," Debra told Kimmy. She turned to Corky. "If that's okay?"

"Yeah. Sure," Corky replied quickly, smiling at Debra.

"I'll walk home," Debra told Kimmy.

"I can drive you," Corky said.

"Well, think about what we said," Kimmy told Corky, pulling open the front door. "Come to practice, okay?"

"I'll think about it. I really will," Corky said.

More good-nights. Then Kimmy and Ronnie disappeared out the door.

Corky followed Debra back into the living room. They both headed for the couch. The beams of Kimmy's headlights rolled up the wall, then disappeared.

Debra tucked her legs under her slight frame and settled onto the cushion. "How *are* you, Corky? I've been meaning to come over for a long time."

"I'm okay, I guess," Corky said, sitting on the arm of the couch at the far end from Debra.

"No. I mean *really*," Debra said, her blue eyes suddenly glowing with intensity, burning into Corky's. "I mean, how are you *really*?"

"Not great," Corky admitted. "I mean, it's been hard. Real hard. You were there that night, Debra. It must be hard for you, too."

Debra nodded solemnly. "Kimmy and Ronnie think I've gone weird." Her hand went up to the crystal at her neck. "They think I'm weird because

I've become so interested in the occult. But I can't get over what happened."

Corky uttered a dry laugh. "We've all gone a bit weird, I think."

Debra didn't smile. "They told me not to tell you this, but I have to. They made me swear I wouldn't say it, but I don't care. I have to let you know, Corky."

Corky walked to the window, turned, and rested her back against the sill. "Let me know what? Why are you being so mysterious, Debra?"

"The evil is still here," Debra said flatly, her eyes suddenly dull as if someone had turned off a light inside her.

Corky's mouth dropped open, but no words came out.

Debra shifted uncomfortably on the couch.

The awful jangling music from the Nintendo game upstairs seemed to grow louder.

"You were there, Debra," Corky said, her voice nearly a whisper. "You saw me fight poor Jennifer. You saw the evil spirit pour out of her mouth. You saw the evil go down into Sarah Fear's coffin, where it was buried again. You saw it all, Debra."

Debra nodded, keeping her lifeless eyes locked on Corky's. "I saw. But I know the evil didn't die, Corky. You didn't kill it. Believe me. It's still around."

"But, Debra, maybe . . ."

Corky wasn't sure *what* to say. Kimmy and Ronnie were right—Debra had gotten strange. She had always been a little quiet, a little cold even. But sitting there so straight on the couch, her legs tucked under her, dressed all in black, her pale face frozen in that stare, Debra looked positively frightening.

"Kimmy and Ronnie don't believe me," Debra said, clasping her hands in front of her almost as if preparing to pray. "But I'm right, Corky. The evil spirit is still around. I can feel the evil. I can feel it so strongly—right now—right in this house!"

"Please stop!" Corky cried. She pushed herself away from the window and walked back to the couch, but stopped a few inches in front of Debra. "These books you've been reading. About voodoo and the occult—"

"I've been studying," Debra replied, sounding defensive. "I know what I'm talking about, Corky." She suddenly reached up and grabbed Corky's hand. "We were never friends. I know I was never nice to you, or to your sister. But we have to be friends now. We *have* to trust each other."

Debra's hand was burning hot.

Corky pulled away.

Debra let her hand fall back into her lap.

Corky sat down beside her on the couch. "We have to forget what happened," Corky heard herself say.

Debra shook her head, frowning. "We can't. Not while the evil is still here."

"Maybe you should stop reading all that stuff," Corky said softly. "We've all been through a terrible experience. But we have to get on with our lives now. We have to force ourselves. I know that's why Kimmy and Ronnie asked me back on the squad."

"You're not *listening* to me," Debra insisted. "The evil spirit is alive. You didn't kill it, Corky. There's no way we can get on with our lives—not while it's still here. You've got to believe me!"

"Debra, your hand is so hot. Do you have a temperature?" Corky asked.

A shrill whistle interrupted their conversation.

"Oh no! I forgot all about the hot chocolate!" Corky hurried toward the kitchen.

"Let it whistle. I've been reading about ancient spirits," Debra said. "I—"

"Sit still. We need something hot to drink," Corky interrupted. "I'll be right back."

She hurried out of the room, her mind spinning, Debra's words echoing in her ears.

Poor Debra, Corky thought. *She seems as*

troubled as I am. She looks so pale, so tense, so . . . frail.

What can I say to her? Corky asked herself after turning off the teakettle. *What does she expect me to say?*

I don't believe the evil spirit is still alive. I saw it buried.

I saw it. We all saw it.

But what if it's true? What if it isn't buried? What then?

Is Debra trying to scare me? Corky suddenly wondered. *Is she saying all this just to keep me from going back on the squad?*

No. Debra believed what she was saying. It was obvious from the expression on her face, from the dull horror in her eyes.

Corky pulled two mugs down from the cabinet and glanced out the kitchen window.

Was that a figure she saw in the backyard? Was someone out there?

She looked again and saw nothing. *It must be my imagination,* Corky reasoned. She poured the chocolate powder into each mug, all the while peering nervously out the window into the dark yard.

"Hey, Corky?" Debra called from the living room.

"Be right there!" Corky shouted back to her.

"I'm just going to pour the hot water."

She lifted the kettle off the stove and carried it to the mugs on the counter.

As she reached the counter, her arm suddenly flew straight up.

Without wanting to, she raised the steaming kettle over her left hand.

"Hey!" she cried out.

She tried to lower her right arm, struggling to push the kettle back down.

To lower it.

To move it away from her left hand.

But her arm wouldn't obey her.

She had no control over it.

And her left hand wouldn't move away from the countertop.

"What's happening? What's *happening* to me?"

Holding the kettle high, her right hand tilted the kettle down.

Down.

Down.

Steam rose from the spout. Then the scalding water began to shower down onto her left hand.

"Help! Ow!"

She couldn't lower her arm, couldn't move her hand out from under the boiling waterfall.

"Help me—please!" she cried.

The scalding water gushed over the back of her hand and splashed up her arm.

"I can't stop! Can't stop!"

The scalding water splashed onto her skin.

Burning.

Burning.

Burning beyond pain.

Beyond all sensation.

5

OUT OF THE GRAVE

She's up in her room," Sean told Chip.

Chip tossed his Shadyside High letter jacket onto the banister and pulled down the sleeves of his bulky sweater. "Is it okay to go up?" he asked.

Sean blew a large pink bubble before replying. "Yeah. Kimmy's up there too."

Chip frowned. He glanced up to the top of the stairs. He didn't really want to see Kimmy. It had been two months since he'd broken up with her and gone out with Bobbi Corcoran. But Kimmy still treated him coldly and made him feel uncomfortable every time they bumped into each other. When they passed in the halls at school, she always turned away, cutting him dead.

"Is Corky feeling okay?" Chip asked Sean, delaying the confrontation.

Sean nodded, unsticking bubble gum from his cheeks. "Yeah, she's okay. Only, she can't wrestle."

"That's too bad," Chip replied, chuckling. He was trying to decide whether to go upstairs or not. "Maybe I'll come back later," he told Sean.

"Chip, is that you?" Corky's voice called from upstairs.

Trapped, he thought.

"Hi!" he shouted, and stepped past Sean to climb the stairs.

He stopped in the doorway to Corky's bedroom. She was sitting on the edge of the bed, her bandaged hand resting in her lap. Kimmy was standing by the dresser, zipping up her down coat.

"How you doing?" Chip asked Corky, flashing her a broad smile.

"A lot better," Corky said, smiling back.

Chip crossed the room and bent down to give her a quick kiss on the cheek. After Bobbi's death, he and Corky had become friends. Corky had found that he was someone she could talk to, about her sister, about her feelings of grief, about her fears. After a while they had become more than friends.

A tall, athletic-looking boy with an open, friendly face, Chip was wearing a heavy wool plaid sweater, all greens and blues, which made him look big and broad-shouldered. His thick brown hair was unbrushed as usual.

"So the hand is better?" he asked Corky.

"Don't mind me. I'm just leaving," Kimmy interrupted, her voice dripping with bitterness.

"Oh, hi, Kimmy," Chip said, trying to sound casual. He didn't turn to her. He didn't want to see the disapproval on her face.

"Thanks for coming," Corky told Kimmy, standing up. "And thanks for bringing my homework."

"See you Monday," Kimmy said. With a toss of her black crimped hair, she strode quickly from the room.

As soon as she was gone, Chip stepped forward and wrapped his arms around Corky's shoulders, drawing her into a hug.

"Ow. Be careful. My hand!" she exclaimed.

"Hey, what are you two doing?" a voice shouted from the bedroom doorway.

They both looked around to see Sean, hands on hips, staring suspiciously at them.

"We're not *doing* anything," Corky said defensively.

Sean glared at her. "I thought you said you couldn't wrestle. You were wrestling with *him*." He pointed accusingly at Chip.

"We weren't wrestling," Corky said, laughing. "Now get lost."

"Make me." Sean's standard reply.

"Go on. Beat it," Corky insisted.

Sean put his tongue between his lips and made a rude sound. Another of his standard replies.

Chip laughed.

Corky elbowed Chip in the ribs. "Don't encourage him," she chided. She glared at her brother. "Go on. Get lost."

"Okay," he said, pouting. "I'm going." Sean started out of the room, but turned at the doorway. "But no wrestling, you hear?"

He disappeared, and Corky heard him clomping back down the stairs.

"He's funny," Chip said, still chuckling.

"Who needs funny?" Corky asked dryly. She dropped back onto the edge of the bed.

Chip sat down beside her. "So the hand—it's really better?"

"Yeah. It's still pretty tender. You have no idea how hard it is to dress yourself with one hand!" She laughed, a forced laugh. "I'm going back to school on Monday," she told him. "It's been a long week. A long week."

He started to say something, but the phone on the night table rang. Corky sprang up to answer it.

"Oh. Hi. Yeah. Can I call you back later?" she said, holding the receiver in her right hand. "Chip just arrived. . . . Okay. Bye."

She hung up the phone and, catching a glimpse of herself in the dresser mirror, ran her uninjured hand through her blond hair, smoothing it back.

"Who was that?" Chip asked, lying back on the quilted bedspread, resting his head on his hands.

"Debra," she replied. "She calls me every afternoon now. Ever since I burned my hand and she ran next door to get my parents, I think she feels responsible for me or something."

"Is she still insisting that the evil spirit made you burn yourself?" Chip asked, frowning.

Corky crossed to the window and looked down on the backyard. The late-afternoon sun had lowered itself behind the trees, making shadows stretch all across the leaf-covered lawn.

"Don't make fun of Debra," she said in a quiet voice.

"Hey, I'm sorry," Chip replied quickly. "It's just that she's gone weird or something. People accidentally burn themselves all the time, Corky. Your right hand slipped. The water poured onto your left hand. And—"

"My hand didn't slip," Corky said shrilly. "It

wasn't an accident, Chip." She decided she had to tell him what had really happened.

Chip pulled himself up to a sitting position. His face revealed his surprise. "You mean you *believe* her?" he asked, his voice rising several octaves.

"I don't have to believe her," Corky said sharply, staring at him now. "I was there. I *know* what happened. I could feel the evil, Chip, I could feel it paralyze me. The evil spirit was there. It forced me to scald myself. It held my hand there and *forced* me!"

"Okay. Okay. Sorry," Chip muttered. He didn't like to fight with her. He almost always backed down or changed the subject. "That scary guy hasn't shown up again?" he asked. "The one with the gray eyes?"

"No sign of him," Corky replied. She shook her head bitterly. "Kimmy and Ronnie are sure that I made him up. Every time I started to point him out, he'd vanish. Poof." She snapped her fingers.

"Weird," Chip said. He couldn't think of anything else to say. "So do you—"

"I never told you, I talked to a psychiatrist," Corky interrupted, walking back to the bed and sitting down next to him.

"Huh?"

"At the hospital," she told him, "when I told the

emergency room doctors how I burned my hand, they called for a psychiatrist to see me. I guess they thought I did it deliberately or something." She rolled her eyes.

Then Corky's expression grew thoughtful. As she talked, she smoothed the bedspread with her unbandaged hand.

"He was a young guy. Really nice. His name was Dr. Sterne. He was the psychiatrist Mayra Barnes saw for a while."

Chip reacted with surprise. "Mayra? What did *she* need him for? She's got to be the most normal person in Shadyside!"

"She told me she started sleepwalking suddenly a couple of summers ago," Corky told him. "This Dr. Sterne helped her a lot."

"So what did he say to you?" Chip asked. "Did you tell *him* about the evil spirit?"

Corky turned her eyes to the window, avoiding Chip's stare. "Well, actually . . . no."

"Huh?"

"I just didn't want to get into it with him," she confessed. "I mean, I wasn't ready. I didn't want him to think I was totally crazy. I told him about Bobbi dying and everything—"

"And what did he say?" Chip demanded.

"He said I should try to return to a normal

routine. He said I've been through a lot. But I have to stop dwelling on the past. I have to try to get my life back on track." She grabbed Chip's hand and squeezed it. "He was very understanding."

"What's a normal routine?" Chip asked. "You mean like early to bed, early to rise, or something?"

"Don't be dumb. He means I should try to do things the way I did before—before Bobbi died and that evil spirit . . ." Her voice trailed off. "I mean, I'm thinking of going back on the cheerleading squad."

"Outstanding!" Chip exclaimed with genuine enthusiasm.

"Well, I thought I'd give it a try," Corky said, still resting her hand on his. "Kimmy and Ronnie have been insisting, so . . ."

"Excellent," Chip said, squeezing her hand. "Excellent."

"I'm going to rejoin for two reasons," Corky said, her voice a whisper, her expression thoughtful. "I know I have to adjust to not having Bobbi around anymore. Getting back on the squad will keep me busy. You know, give me something to think about."

"And what's the second reason?" Chip asked.

"I have to find the evil spirit," she said, locking her eyes on his. "The evil is back. It must be inhabiting someone else. Maybe someone I know."

"Huh? What makes you so sure?" Chip demanded.

"Because it was right in my house the other night," Corky said in a whisper, staring down at the floor. "I'm going to find it before it kills again."

Chip stared at her thoughtfully but didn't reply.

She raised her eyes to his. "I have one favor to ask. Sort of a big one," she said reluctantly.

"Yeah?" Chip eyed her warily. "What is it?"

"Come with me to the cemetery tonight after dinner?" she asked in a tiny, pleading voice.

"Huh?" He swept his hand back through his thick disheveled hair.

"Come with me. I want to go to Bobbi's grave. Just one more time. I promised myself I'd stop going there so often. But I just want to tell Bobbi my decision. About going back on the cheerleading squad."

Chip sighed. "Bad idea," he said softly.

Corky squeezed his hand. "Come on, Chip."

"It's a bad idea, Corky," he repeated heatedly. "You said that shrink wants you to get back to a normal routine. Well, going to the cemetery all the time isn't normal. I don't think you should go."

She leaned over and pressed her cheek against his. "Come on," she pleaded. "One last time. I promise."

She kept her face pressed against his. He turned toward her. She kissed him tenderly. A long kiss. A pleading kiss.

When she finally pulled her face away from his, she could see his features soften.

"Okay, okay. I'll go with you after dinner." And then he added, "I guess there's no harm. What could happen?"

It was a warm night for early December. Thousands of tiny white stars dotted the charcoal sky. A huge full moon cast bright light over the Fear Street cemetery.

Since the cemetery was little more than a block from Corky's house, she and Chip walked. He carried a flashlight, in case the moonlight wasn't enough, swinging it as they walked.

She asked him about last Saturday's basketball game, the first preseason one. He told her about the center on the opposing team who repeatedly slam-dunked even though he was the smallest guy on the floor! She told Chip how Sean had slipped green food coloring into the mashed potatoes just before dinner.

Neither of them talked about what they were doing, where they were headed. It was as if they were pretending they were out for a pleasant walk, and not going to the Fear Street cemetery so Corky could talk to the dead sister she couldn't get out of her thoughts.

After leaving the sidewalk, they made their way through an old section of the cemetery, past rows of low, crumbling gravestones, jagged shadowy forms in the gray moonlight. Chip's flashlight sent a cone of bright light over the tall grass ahead of them.

Corky stopped and grabbed Chip's arm as two eyes appeared in that light. A scrawny white cat stepped timidly out from behind a granite gravestone. It mewed a warning, then scampered away and disappeared into the darkness.

Corky held on to Chip's arm and led him up a hill toward a section of newer graves on a flat grassy area bounded by low trees. "This way. We're almost there," she whispered.

Chip suddenly held back.

She stopped and followed the direction of his gaze. He was shining the light on a grave marker, its smooth whiteness revealing that it was new.

Jennifer Daly's grave.

Corky sighed and tugged the sleeve of Chip's sweater. Every time she passed that grave, terrifying memories flooded her mind. She didn't want that to happen now. She didn't want to think of poor Jennifer or the evil spirit that had inhabited her body.

She wanted to tell Bobbi her decision and then leave the cemetery. Leave the horror behind. Leave the memories behind.

Or at least try to.

Hearing a sound on the street, she turned around. Just a passing station wagon.

When she looked back down toward the old section, her eye caught a tilted old tombstone lit up by the bright moon. Corky knew it well. Surrounded by four other graves, Sarah Fear's stone, worn by time and the weather, stood silent.

It was over Sarah Fear's grave that Corky had battled the evil spirit on that dreadful, terrifying night. Over Sarah Fear's open grave, she had fought and won—and sent the evil pouring out of Jennifer Daly's body, back into the grave forever.

Or so she had thought.

But the evil hadn't remained in the grave.

The evil was back.

Somewhere.

Corky shuddered.

I don't want to think about this now.

I don't. I don't. I don't.

"This way," Corky said, turning away and striding with renewed purpose up to her sister's

rectangular grave marker. Remnants of the flowers
Corky had brought there a week ago lay shriveled
at the foot of the stone.

Suddenly chilled, Corky shoved her hands
deep into the pockets of her windbreaker and
turned back to Chip. He was leaning against a tree
several yards away, his arms crossed over his chest,
his eyes on the sky.

I guess he's giving me a little space, Corky
thought.

She turned to face her sister's gravestone. "It's
me, Bobbi," she said in a low voice. "I'm really not
going to be coming here for a while. At least I'm
going to try not to come. I need to get my life back
to normal. I know you'd want me to."

Corky paused; glanced at Chip, who was still
staring at the heavens; took a deep breath; and continued. "I just wanted to tell you about the decision
I've made. I hope it's the right one. I've decided to go
back on the cheerleading squad. You see, Bobbi — "

Corky stopped. She heard a sound. She turned
and peered down the hill.

Her breath caught in her throat.

She froze.

And stared in horror as a woman floated out of
Sarah Fear's grave.

6

FIVE MYSTERIOUS DEATHS

As the woman materialized in the shadows, Corky struggled to find her voice. Finally she managed to call out Chip's name.

Uncrossing his arms, he turned to her, startled. Corky pointed.

Would Chip see the woman too? Or was she seeing things again?

Corky was suddenly filled with dread. Was she losing her mind completely? Had she really seen this woman float up from Sarah Fear's grave?

"Hey!" Chip shouted. He saw the woman too.

Corky realized she'd been holding her breath. She let it out with a loud *whoosh*.

"Oh. Hi!" the woman called up to them.

The beam from Chip's flashlight played across

her face as he made his way down toward her. She was young and kind of plain, Corky saw. She had straight black hair that hung down over the turned-up collar of her trench coat.

She raised her hands to shield her eyes from the light. "You scared me," she called out. "I didn't know anyone else was here."

Chip lowered the light to the ground and stood waiting for Corky to catch up. Reluctantly she followed.

"You scared us too," Chip said as he and Corky joined the young woman.

"I thought you were a ghost or something," Corky said, trying to make it sound light.

The young woman didn't smile. "I'm just doing a gravestone rubbing," she said. She had a scratchy voice, a voice that sounded older than she looked. "Did you two come here to be alone?"

Without waiting for an answer, she knelt in front of Sarah Fear's gravestone, then lay down on her stomach to work.

"Oh!" Corky couldn't help but utter a cry. The young woman was lying in the exact same place over the grave where Jennifer Daly had died.

Stop! Stop! Stop! Corky cried silently to herself. *Stop thinking about it!*

But how could she not be reminded when

this woman was lying in the exact place?

"What are you doing?" Corky asked, speaking loudly to try to force away the horrible memories.

"I just told you—I'm doing some gravestone rubbings," the woman answered, rapidly moving a piece of black chalk over a thin sheet of paper she had taped over the tombstone. "There are some wonderful stones in this graveyard. Some of them are truly unique. Many are very revealing of their time, I think."

She finished quickly, then climbed to her feet, examining her work. Seemingly pleased, she rolled up the paper and smiled at Corky. "I'm kind of glad not to be alone," she said pleasantly. "This cemetery has an *amazing* reputation."

"I know," Corky said dryly.

"How can you work in the dark?" Chip asked, pointing to the rolled-up paper in her hand.

"I do most of it by feel, and I have a flashlight and, of course, the moon."

Chip wanted to ask more but didn't.

"I'm a graduate student doing research on Shadyside history." She stuck out her hand to Chip. "I'm Sarah Beth Plummer."

Chip and Corky shook hands with her and introduced themselves.

She seems quite pleasant, Corky thought, *once*

you get used to the old-lady voice with her young face. Corky guessed that Sarah Beth was in her early twenties.

"Do you know anything about Sarah Fear?" Corky asked, staring at the gravestone in front of them.

The question seemed to surprise Sarah Beth; she narrowed her dark eyes and shook her head. "Not very much. I've read a little about her. In old newspapers, mostly. I know she came to a strange and mysterious end."

"Huh? Really?" Corky asked with genuine interest, her voice rising several octaves. "What happened to her?"

Sarah Beth pulled the collar of her trench coat tight. She shivered. "It's getting chilly, don't you think?" she asked, glancing toward the street. Then she added, "Are you really interested in Sarah Fear?"

"Yeah," Corky replied quickly. "It's . . . it's a long story, but I'm very interested." She cast Chip a look, urging him to respond.

"Uh . . . me too," Chip said obediently, placing a hand protectively on Corky's shoulder.

"Well, there's a small coffee shop on Hawthorne," Sarah Beth said, buttoning the top button on the coat. "It's within walking distance. It's called Alma's. It's sort of a college hangout."

"I know where it is," Chip said. "It's just a couple of blocks from here."

"If you want," Sarah Beth continued, "we could go there and get something hot to drink. I'll tell you all I know about Sarah Fear."

"Excellent," Chip said, glancing at Corky.

"Okay," Corky agreed.

The image of Sarah Beth floating up from Sarah Fear's grave flashed into Corky's mind again. She hesitated.

I imagined it, she told herself. *Just as I imagined Bobbi rising up from the ground.*

Sarah Beth seems friendly and interesting.

Taking one last glance up toward Bobbi's headstone, she turned and followed Chip and Sarah Beth to the street.

It took only a few minutes to walk to the restaurant at the corner of Hawthorne and Old Mill Road. "See that place over there?" Sarah Beth asked, pointing to a small redbrick house across the street. "That's where I'm living. It's not a mansion, but it's cozy."

Alma's coffee shop was small but cozy too. A long counter ran along the right wall. Narrow red vinyl booths lined the other wall. The restaurant smelled of strong coffee and grilled onions.

Four teenagers at a booth near the front were

laughing loudly, drumming on the tabletop and clattering their silverware. Two white-haired men nursing mugs of coffee at the counter were the only other customers.

Sarah Beth squeezed into the last booth at the back. Corky and Chip slid in across from her. Sarah Beth ordered tea, while Corky asked for hot chocolate. Chip ordered a Coke float with chocolate ice cream. "I have a craving," he said, shrugging his broad shoulders in reply to the stares of the other two.

The conversation was awkward at first. Corky began to wonder why she had agreed to come with this complete stranger. Sarah Beth seemed friendly enough. But Corky had an uneasy feeling about her, a suspicion she couldn't put into words.

"Why do you have to do your gravestone rubbing at night?" she asked Sarah Beth.

Again Sarah Beth's eyes narrowed, as if the question displeased her. "Oh, I'm just running late, as usual," she said, stirring her tea. "The assignment is due tomorrow morning, so of course I waited till the last possible minute."

It seemed like a perfectly reasonable explanation. But to Corky's mind, it just didn't ring true.

"Oops! Sorry." Chip dropped his ice cream spoon onto the seat. Moving to retrieve it, he accidentally bumped Corky's hand.

She cried out in pain, startling Sarah Beth.

"It's my hand. I . . . uh . . . burned it," Corky explained, holding up her bandaged hand.

Sarah Beth continued to stare at her. For a frightening moment Corky had the feeling that Sarah Beth knew *how* Corky had burned it.

But of course that was impossible.

Stop being so suspicious, Corky scolded herself. "Please tell us about Sarah Fear," she urged Sarah Beth. "I'm really interested."

Sarah Beth took a long sip of tea, then set the mug down. She reached for the aluminum sugar dispenser. "Okay, here's the little information I've been able to find," she said, pouring a stream of sugar into the tea.

"There isn't much information available about her. Strangely enough, I've been able to find out a lot more about her *death* than about her life.

"She married a grandson of Simon Fear, a mysterious man who moved to Shadyside and built an enormous mansion back in the woods, away from everyone else in—"

"That's the burned-out old shell across from the cemetery," Chip interrupted, busily scooping ice cream out of the tall soda glass.

"There wasn't much of a cemetery when Simon built his house," Sarah Beth replied. "He was all

alone out here for a while. Then they built the mill
in this area. Soon after that, the city built a road
through the woods, right past the Fear mansion.
And it came to be named Fear Street."

"Wow, I never knew any of this," Corky said,
intrigued. "Of course, my family is new in town. We
just moved here this fall from Missouri. Have you
lived in Shadyside a long time? Is that why you're
so interested in the town?"

Sarah Beth took a sip of her tea, staring over
the booths to the front window of the restaurant.
"I've lived here on and off," she said curtly.

Am I being too nosy? Corky wondered. *Is that
why she got so cold?*

"As I said, Sarah Fear married Simon's grandson. She and her husband lived in a house near
Simon's mansion, a large house on Fear Lake."

"That's the small lake with the island in the
middle of it," Chip explained to Corky. "It's back in
the woods, two or three blocks from your house."

"As I mentioned earlier, little is known of
Sarah Fear's life," Sarah Beth continued, rolling the
sugar dispenser between her long, slender hands.
"Her husband died suddenly of pneumonia just
two years after they were married, leaving her quite
wealthy, according to the newspaper reports from
the time. She had servants. Her house was always

filled with people. After her husband died, her two brothers moved in with her, as did several cousins.

"Despite her wealth, she was never mentioned on the social pages of the newspaper. Nor was she ever mentioned as being involved with charitable functions, the way wealthy people often are.

"I haven't found much personal information about her," Sarah Beth continued. "I don't know if she ever remarried. There isn't any mention of it in the Fear family records I've seen. Of course, she didn't live long enough to have much of a life."

"She died young too?" Corky asked in surprise.

"Very," Sarah Beth replied somberly. "In her twenties. Sarah died in 1899. The whole thing was very mysterious. The Fear family pleasure boat capsized on Fear Lake—for no apparent reason. It was a calm, sunny summer day. The lake was as flat as glass. There were no other boats in the water.

"Yet the boat turned over. All on board were drowned. Sarah Fear, her brother, her niece and nephew, and a servant."

"Whew!" Chip let out his breath, shaking his head.

Corky stared at Sarah Beth, listening to her story in rapt silence. *So that explains the four graves around Sarah Fear's grave*, she thought. *A brother, a niece, a nephew, and a servant.*

"They all drowned," Sarah Beth said again, speaking softly, leaning over the table. "All within view of the shore. Maybe a five- or ten-minute swim at most."

Sarah Beth sipped her tea, then licked her pale lips. "No one knows why the boat turned over; no one knows why everyone drowned. It's all a mystery."

Corky stared down at her mug of hot chocolate, thinking hard, Sarah Beth's scratchy voice still echoing in her ears.

It was the evil spirit, Corky thought. *It had to be the evil spirit that was responsible for that accident.*

She was tempted to tell Sarah Beth about the evil force, but it was late. Her hand ached, and she suddenly felt tired. Besides, she realized she didn't really trust the young woman. She didn't know enough about her to confide in her.

"There's more," Sarah Beth said suddenly. Corky saw Sarah Beth staring at her as if trying to read her thoughts. "After Sarah Fear's death, there were all kinds of stories—stories about how she and the servant who'd drowned had been lovers. Stories about how Sarah and the servant were seen walking in Shadyside, walking in the woods behind her house, even walking in town—long after their deaths.

"You know," Sarah Beth scoffed, "the usual ghost story mumbo jumbo that the Fear family is known for."

Her attitude surprised Corky. "You don't believe it?" Corky demanded.

Sarah Beth chuckled. A smile formed slowly on her lips. "I think it's all kind of funny," she replied, locking her dark eyes on Corky's, as if trying to gauge her reaction.

Funny? Corky thought. *Five people drown? Their boat capsizes on a calm lake for no reason? Such a horrible, tragic story. And Sarah Beth thinks it's kind of funny?*

Corky took a final sip of her hot chocolate. "It's pretty late. My mom is probably worried. I didn't tell her I'd be gone this long." She gave Chip a push to get him moving.

"Nice meeting you," Chip said to Sarah Beth. He slid out of the booth and reached for Corky's windbreaker, hanging on a hook on the back wall.

"I enjoyed talking with you," Sarah Beth said, her eyes on Corky. "I usually don't meet such nice people in a cemetery."

"Are you leaving too?" Corky asked, standing up and allowing Chip to help her put her coat on.

"I think I'll stay and have another cup of tea," she replied. "I live so close. I haven't far to walk."

They all said good night again, and Chip and Corky made their way down the narrow aisle, past the counter where the two white-haired men still sat hunched over their coffee mugs, and out the front door.

"She's nice," Chip said, glancing up at the moon, which was now pale white and high in the black sky.

"I guess," Corky said without enthusiasm. "But there's something odd about her, don't you think?"

"Odd?" Chip shook his head. "Just her voice."

Corky stared through the restaurant window and focused on the back booth. She could see Sarah Beth Plummer sitting alone against the back wall, her slender hands wrapped around a white mug of tea.

To Corky's surprise, she had the strangest smile on her face.

Not a pleasant smile.

A cruel smile.

Even from that distance, even through the hazy glass, Corky could see the gleam in Sarah Beth's dark eyes, the unmistakable gleam of . . . evil.

7

CHEERS AND SCREAMS

After school on Monday, Corky hesitated at the double doors to the gym. On the other side she could hear shouts and the thunder of sneakers pounding over the wooden floorboards. *The basketball team must also be practicing in the gym,* she realized.

Taking a deep breath, she closed her eyes, said a silent prayer, and pushed open the swinging doors. As if on cue, the voices of the cheerleaders rang out:

> *"Hey, you!*
> *Yeah, you!*
> *Are you ready?*
> *Our team is tough and our team is*
> *steady!*

We're on the way to the top
And we'll never stop!
The tigers are on the hunt.
Hear them growl, hear them roar!
You'd better hold your ears,
'Cause the Tigers will roar
All over,
All over you!"

The cheer ended with an enthusiastic shout, and each of the five girls performed a flying split, their legs shooting out as they leaped into the air one at a time.

"Pretty good. Pretty good," Miss Green, the advisor, called out with her usual restraint, hands on the hips of her gray sweats, her expression thoughtful A compact woman with frizzy brown hair and a somewhat plain face, Miss Green had a husky voice that always sounded as if she had laryngitis.

"Try it again," she told them, "and this time get more height on those jumps. And *enunciate*. I want to hear consonants, guys! We're not entering the Mumbling Olympics."

On the other side of the gym, Coach Swenson was blowing his whistle. The shrill sound echoed off the tile walls. Corky watched the basketball players form a line to practice running layups.

She turned her attention back to the cheer-leaders, who were in position to do the cheer again. As Corky's eyes moved from girl to girl, a flood of memories washed over her, holding her in place, frozen against the doors.

There was Kimmy, the captain, her round face pink as usual, her black crimped hair bobbing on her head as she enthusiastically jumped into place and checked to make sure the other girls were lining up correctly.

Beside her stood freckle-faced, redheaded Ronnie, looking like a kid, in gray sweat shorts and a white sleeveless T-shirt, whispering something to Debra.

Debra smiled slowly, her cold blue eyes lighting up. Beside her, Megan Carman and Heather Diehl, best friends who always seemed to be together, were chatting animatedly.

Kimmy blew a whistle, and the cheer began.

Corky watched them run through it again. It was crisper this time, and the flying splits were higher. Ronnie started hers too soon and landed awkwardly, but everyone else was right on the money.

As the cheer ended, Kimmy noticed Corky. She jogged over. "Hi! You came!"

"Yeah. I'm here," Corky said, smiling. "The routine looks excellent!" She took a few steps away from the door.

A basketball bounced toward them. Kimmy caught it on the bounce and tossed it back to Gary Brandt, who was waving for it across the floor.

"Good to see you, Corky. We've missed you," Miss Green said, joining Kimmy. She turned back to the others. "Hey, look who's here!"

"Are you coming back?" Heather asked as the girls surrounded Corky. They all began asking her questions at once.

"Give her a break!" Kimmy cried, laughing. She whispered to Corky, "Hey, it's like you're a superstar or something."

"With Corky back, we can do the diamond-head pyramid," Megan said excitedly. "You know, the way you and Bobbi showed us." She blushed, instantly regretting mentioning Bobbi's name.

"We can try," Corky said quickly, seeing how uncomfortable Megan was. She smiled at her. "But it's going to take me a while to get in shape." She patted her stomach. "Pure flab. I feel as heavy as a bag of potatoes."

"You look *great*!" Kimmy gushed. The others quickly agreed.

Did Miss Green coach them to encourage me? Corky suddenly wondered. *Or are they really happy to have me back?*

Only Debra seemed unenthusiastic. As Corky

went over to the wall to toss down her backpack, she saw that Debra was following her.

"I can feel it," Debra said quietly.

"Huh?" Corky propped the backpack against the wall near the other ones lined up there and turned to face Debra.

"I can feel it right now," Debra whispered, her intense blue eyes staring into Corky's. She nervously fingered the crystal she wore around her neck.

"Feel what?" Corky asked edgily. She felt nervous enough coming back to the squad. She didn't really need Debra acting so mysterious, did she?

"The evil spirit," Debra whispered, glancing at the other cheerleaders, who had begun practicing roundoffs.

"Debra—" Corky started.

"I'm not trying to scare you," she said sharply. "But I'm into these things, Corky. I know the evil is here. In this gym. I can feel it." She clasped the crystal so tightly, her hand turned white.

Corky turned her eyes to the other girls. "Let's discuss this later," she said. "I really need to talk to you about it. But not now."

"Okay." Debra looked hurt. "I just thought you'd want to know."

Kimmy blew her whistle. Corky saw Miss Green standing in front of her glassed-in office in the corner of the gym. She was watching them, a curious expression on her face.

"Corky, come on!" Kimmy called enthusiastically. She turned to the others, pushing her hair away from her eyes. "We'll work on roundoffs in a little bit. Let's run through that same cheer so Corky can try it. You know it, don't you, Corky?"

Corky shook her head. "Not really. I just saw you do it twice. I could try to pick it up as we do it."

"Good," Kimmy said, flashing her a warm smile. "It's pretty simple, actually. Try it." She motioned for Corky to get in line.

Corky could feel her heart flutter as she took her place at the end of the line, next to Heather. "Here goes nothing," she said aloud to herself.

Heather gave her an encouraging pat on the shoulder. "Just watch me," she said, smiling. "Then you'll be *sure* to mess up!"

She and Corky burst out laughing.

Everyone's being so nice to me, Corky thought happily. But then her smile quickly faded.

Everyone's being so nice. It's hard to believe that the evil spirit may be hiding inside one of these girls.

"Okay. Ready?" Kimmy stepped forward to inspect the line, then moved back into place. "On three. One. Two. *Three.*"

"*Hey, you!*" the cheer began, followed by two loud, sharp claps.

"*Yeah, you!*" Stomp, stomp.

Corky shouted out the words, watching Heather to get the rhythm.

I think I can get into this, she thought.

And then the screaming began.

A girl shrieking in horror, so loud, so frightening. So *close*, as if she were right inside Corky's head.

The cheerleaders' voices faded as the hideous noise drowned out everything.

Corky covered her ears with her hands, but the shrieking continued.

"Help her! Somebody help that girl!" Corky cried, closing her eyes tight, trying to shut out the terrifying screams.

Opening her eyes, she saw that the girls had stopped cheering and were all staring at her in open-mouthed confusion.

8

CORKY IS CAPTURED

Corky, what's *wrong*?" Kimmy rushed over to her.
As soon as the cheering stopped, the screaming stopped too. Corky blinked hard, her heart pounding. She felt dizzy. Even though the shrieks had quieted, the sound echoed in her mind, refusing to fade.

Kimmy gently gripped Corky's shoulders. "What happened? Are you okay?"

Corky's eyes moved from one startled face to another. "Didn't you hear the screaming?" Corky asked.

Heather and Megan shook their heads and glanced at each other. Debra stared hard at Corky. Ronnie lowered her eyes. Miss Green had disappeared into her office before the cheer had begun.

"We didn't hear anything," Kimmy said softly. "Do you want to go sit down?"

"No." Corky shook her head and forced a smile. "Guess I'm hearing things."

"Really. Sit down. Get yourself together," Kimmy urged, gesturing toward the sideline.

"No. Let's start again," Corky insisted.

Debra was fingering her crystal, squeezing it in her fist. When she saw Corky looking at her, she tucked it back under her T-shirt.

"Really," Corky insisted, stepping back into the line. "I want to try it again."

Reluctantly Kimmy moved back to the other end of the line. Ronnie asked her a question. Kimmy shrugged. The other girls moved into place.

I'm going *to do this*, Corky told herself. *I'm* going *to succeed.*

She arched her back, straightened her legs, and waited for Kimmy's count.

I'm going *to do it this time.*

But as soon as the girls started cheering, the frightening screams returned.

Again. Again. A terrified girl in some kind of terrible trouble. High-pitched, shrill—screaming for her life. Inside Corky's head.

"No! Please, please!" Corky cried, covering her ears, dropping to her knees.

The cheer stopped. So did the screams.

Kimmy reached down, took Corky's hand, and helped her to her feet. "Corky, what *is* it?"

"The screams. I—I heard them again," Corky managed to stammer, her voice breaking.

The gym spun in front of her. At the other end of the gym, some of the basketball players had stopped practicing and were asking what the problem was.

It was all a blur to Corky now. A blur of colors and hushed voices.

Kimmy led her gently to the wall. "Do you have a headache?" she asked.

"No," Corky said uncertainly. "I don't think so. I mean—I just heard someone screaming." She stared at Kimmy. "You really didn't hear it?"

Kimmy shook her head. "I'll go get Miss Green. Maybe we should call a doctor or something."

"No!" Corky said sharply. "I mean—no doctor. I'll be okay. I'll just sit down and watch for a bit. Then maybe I'll do some roundoffs with everyone. You know—limber up."

What am I saying? she asked herself, the brightly lit gym still spinning in front of her. *I'm babbling like an idiot.*

What is happening *to me?*

Her face taut with worry, Kimmy spread out

her coat for Corky to sit on. "You want some water or something?" Kimmy asked.

Corky could see the other girls huddled together, talking excitedly. They'd steal quick glances at Corky, then look away, shaking their heads.

They all think I'm crazy, she thought glumly.

"Corky, can you hear me?" Kimmy asked, standing over her.

"Oh. Uh . . . sorry. No, thanks. I don't need water." She stared up at Kimmy, forcing a smile. "I'll be okay. Go ahead—do the cheer. I'll watch."

Kimmy turned and started to jog back to the others.

What is that strange smile on Debra's face? Corky wondered. Debra was once again fingering the crystal on her neck. Her smile was smug.

Why does she look so pleased? Corky asked herself.

Debra caught Corky staring at her, and whirled away.

Kimmy shouted for the girls to line up. "Everyone ready?"

Seated on Kimmy's coat, Corky pressed her back against the tiles of the gym wall. She shut her eyes and took a deep breath.

"Hey, you!" The girls began the cheer.

The hideous screams returned.

So loud. So close.

Corky leaped to her feet, trying to locate the screaming girl.

No one there.

The cheerleaders continued their cheer. But the terrified shrieks drowned out their voices.

"No!" Corky shrieked. "No!" Covering her ears, she ran to the door.

The screams followed her as she pushed open both doors and burst out of the gym—into the arms of the young man with the strange gray eyes who had chased her in the Fear Street cemetery.

9

"DON'T YOU KNOW WHO I AM?"

With a loud gasp, Corky stared up into his startled face.

His eyes really were gray. Like those of a ghost. Like monster eyes.

He gripped her arms tightly above the elbow.

He was wearing a brown leather bomber jacket. The leather felt cool against her arms. His breath smelled of peppermint.

"Let go!" Corky cried, regaining her voice.

His strange eyes narrowed. His expression changed from surprise to menace.

"Let go!" She pulled back out of his grasp.

"Hey!" he cried angrily.

She spun around and started to run, her sneakers thudding hard on the concrete floor.

"Stop!" he shouted, his voice reedy, high-pitched.

Who is *he?* Corky wondered. *Why is he following me? How did he* find *me?*

She glanced back and saw that he was chasing her, his expression angry, his arms out as if preparing to grab her.

She ran wildly past a blur of lockers and up the stairs at the end of the corridor.

"Stop!" he called, close behind her. His boots pounded thunderously over the floor.

At the top of the stairs Corky gasped in a mouthful of air, turned to the right, then changed her mind and took the corridor to her left, running as fast as she could.

"Help me! Somebody!" she called breathlessly.

But the hall was deserted. The wall clock read 4:25.

"Somebody—*please!*"

She glanced back to see the young man emerge at the top of the stairs. He looked to the right, then spotted her in the hallway to the left.

"Wait!" he called, and began running toward her, his expression hard, angry.

She uttered a low cry and turned the corner, searching frantically for a hiding place.

An idea flashed into her mind—she could duck

into an open locker and pull the door shut. But the lockers on both sides of the hall were all locked.

"Hey!"

She could hear him calling to her. He was about to turn the corner.

A sharp pain stabbed her side. She sucked in a mouthful of air, her mouth dry, her forehead throbbing.

I can't keep running, she thought, hearing his footsteps near the corner. She hurled herself through an open classroom door to her right and pressed her back against the wall.

Had he seen her? Would he burst in after her?

Seeing the long tables, the tall stools, the Bunsen burners and other equipment, Corky realized she had ducked into the science lab. She wanted to call to Mr. Adams—sometimes he stayed late, grading papers in the small office at the back.

But she could hear the footsteps of the young man right outside the lab door. She couldn't call out. She could only hold her breath and pray, her back pressed against the wall, her side still aching with pain, her forehead still throbbing.

Would he run past the door—and keep on running?

Would he give up and leave?

She listened hard.

His footsteps stopped. "Hey!" he called.

He was just outside the lab door.

Corky shut her eyes and silently repeated, *Don't come in, don't come in, don't come in. . . .*

She heard him hesitate.

She heard him kick a locker door.

Would he notice the open lab door? Would he look inside? Would he see her standing there, hiding from him?

If he came in, she'd have no way out, Corky realized.

She'd be trapped. Trapped like one of the mice Mr. Adams kept in the cages on the windowsill.

Don't come in, don't come in, don't come in. . . .

And then she heard him begin to run again. She heard his heavy boots heading on down the hall.

Corky moved away from the wall, allowing the breath she had held so long to escape her body in a loud sigh.

He's leaving.

He's heading down the hall.

I fooled him.

Leaning against a lab table, lowering her head, she took a slow, deep breath. Then another.

She raised her head and listened.

Silence.

She waited.

Silence.

She waited to hear him return. But the hall remained silent. "I'm okay," she said aloud. "I'm okay." Except that her knees trembled and her head still throbbed.

She took a reluctant step toward the door—and a bell went off in the hallway right outside the door. Like a metallic siren, it clanged out four thirty.

Corky jumped, startled. She backed into a lab table with a hard jolt. "Ow!"

When the bell finally stopped, the silence seemed deep and heavy.

"I needed that," she said sarcastically. "Stupid bell."

Her heart still pounding, she made her way to the lab door, then stepped cautiously out into the silent hallway.

A hand grabbed her shoulder roughly from behind.

The young man spun her around. His almost blank eyes burned into hers.

"Let *go* of me!" Corky cried in a tight, high voice she didn't recognize.

"We have to talk," he said. "Don't you know who I am?"

Corky shook her head. "No. Who are you?"

His eyes narrowed. He tightened his grip on her shoulder.

"I'm the evil spirit," he told her.

10

"I'M THE EVIL SPIRIT"

uh?" Corky's mouth dropped open. She could feel her knees start to buckle.

He was gripping her with both hands now, staring into her eyes, studying her face—studying her *fear*.

"I'm the evil spirit," he repeated, smiling for the first time.

"No," Corky whispered. "Let me go. Please."

To her surprise, he let her go. She toppled backward into the wall. She rubbed her arms, uttering a soft cry.

"You really looked scared," he said, the lower half of his face covered in shadow. His eyes continued to stare at her like two car headlights coming out of the darkness. "I think you really believed me for a moment."

"Why—" Corky waited for her heart to stop thudding. "Why did you say that? Who are you, really?" She pressed her back against the wall, her eyes darting down the hall as she thought about an escape route.

"You ran away from me as if I *were* the evil spirit," he said. "You were scared of me. You were terrified, weren't you? And you had good reason to be!"

"Who are you?" Corky repeated impatiently.

"I'm Jon Daly," he told her. "Jennifer's brother."

Corky uttered a cry of surprise. "Her brother? I didn't know she had a brother."

"Now you do, and now you know why I followed you," Jon said, enjoying her shock.

"No," Corky told him, her voice trembling. "No, I don't. Why did you follow me? Why did you chase me?"

"Because I don't believe all the garbage I heard," Jon said bitterly.

"Garbage? What garbage?" Corky cried, genuinely confused.

"All the garbage about how my sister was invaded by an evil spirit. I don't believe in evil spirits."

"I do," Corky said softly. "I was there that night in the cemetery. I had to fight with Jennifer, with the evil that was inside her."

"Sure, *you* want to believe it," Jon said angrily.

He balled his fists at his sides as if preparing to attack her. "You want to believe you killed an evil spirit *because you don't want to admit that you killed Jennifer*!"

"Now, wait—" Corky started. She could feel the fear returning, feel her knees go weak, her temples start to pound. "Wait a minute, Jon. I'm not a murderer. Your sister—"

"You killed her," Jon said, inches from her, leaning into her. "You killed my sister. Then you made up that ridiculous story. My sister wasn't evil, and she didn't deserve to die. *You* are evil—and I'm going to prove it."

"No. Your s-sister—" Corky stammered in protest. "The spirit—"

He gripped both of her shoulders. "I told you," he said angrily, "I don't believe in spirits. But you know what, Corky? I'm going to be *your* evil spirit."

"Huh? What do you mean?"

"I'm going to watch you. I'm going to follow you—you and your friends—until I find out the *truth*. Until I can *prove* that you killed my sister!"

"What's going on?" a voice called urgently from down the hall. Corky turned to see a large figure jogging toward them.

Jon released her shoulders and spun around to face the intruder.

"Corky, are you okay?" It was Chip.

"Chip!" Corky called gratefully.

As Chip approached, Jon turned away from Corky and started off in the other direction. As Chip caught up to her, Jon disappeared around a corner.

Corky sank back against a locker, trying to catch her breath.

"Who *was* that? Are you okay?" Chip asked, his eyes focusing down the hall, watching to see if Jon returned.

Corky nodded. "Yeah. I'm okay, I guess."

"But who *was* that?" Chip demanded. "What did he want?"

Corky took a deep breath. She held on to Chip's broad shoulder. He felt so solid, so safe. "He's Jennifer's brother," she told him. "Jon Daly. He's the one who's been following me."

Chip slapped his forehead with an open palm. "Jon Daly. Of course. How could I forget him?"

Corky leaned against Chip as she asked him to walk her to her locker. She'd forgotten to take her jacket to the gym earlier. "What do you mean?" Corky asked. "You know him?"

Chip shook his head. "No. But I remember him. He's the guy who went ballistic at Jennifer's funeral. Remember—they practically had to hold him down?"

"It's all a blur," Corky admitted. She tugged at her locker door.

"He's a strange guy," Chip said, shaking his head, glancing back down the hall. "He's messed up, I think. He was always in trouble. He even got kicked out of school."

"Huh? He did?" Corky asked, holding Chip's hand tightly.

"Yeah. Four or five years ago when he was a senior. I don't remember the whole story. He got into some kind of trouble—beat up a teacher, I think. Got suspended from Shadyside. Then his parents sent him away, to a military school."

"Wow." Corky let out a long breath. Her hand trembled as she worked the combination to open her locker. "He thinks I killed Jennifer."

"Did he threaten you?" Chip asked, hovering over her as she picked up her jacket, which had fallen to the locker floor.

"Kind of. He said he's going to watch me," she answered. "He said he's going to watch all of us—until he finds out the truth."

"Lots of luck," Chip said dryly.

"He's really messed up about his sister. He doesn't believe what happened. But—but—I lost a sister too," Corky said bitterly, slamming her locker door shut. "That's what I *should* have said to him."

Chip put a comforting hand on her shoulder. "We'll have to watch out for him," he said quietly. "He seems like a bad dude."

They made their way back downstairs, where Chip picked up Corky's backpack. Then they went out of the building, into a blustery gray afternoon. "He's a bad dude," Chip repeated.

How bad? Corky wondered. *Bad enough to do her harm?*

11

TWO ON A GRAVE

After dinner that night, Corky went upstairs to Sean's room, to play a Nintendo basketball game with him. The phone rang and interrupted them. "Don't answer it," Sean ordered, his eyes on the screen, his fingers furiously pressing the controller.

"I have to answer it," Corky said, setting her controller down and hurrying across the room. "We're the only ones home, remember?"

"Well, I'm not going to pause it. I'm going to keep playing," Sean threatened. "You're going to lose."

Corky hurried across the hall to her room and picked up the phone on her night table. It was Kimmy.

"Oh, hi," Corky said unenthusiastically. The Nintendo game had managed to push the frightening events of the afternoon from her mind. Hearing Kimmy's voice brought them all flooding back to her.

"I just wondered how you're feeling," Kimmy said.

"Okay. I guess," Corky answered. "I mean, I can't really explain—"

"No need," Kimmy said quickly.

"I really wanted to come back on the squad," Corky said, nervously twisting the phone cord around her wrist. "But the screams—"

"Don't give up," Kimmy told her.

"I don't know. I—"

"Don't give up," Kimmy repeated. "You can do it, Corky—I know you can. Come to practice tomorrow."

Corky unwound the cord from her wrist, then twisted it around again. "I don't know. I don't think so."

"Give it another try," Kimmy urged. "Come after school tomorrow."

"I—I can't," Corky said, letting go of the phone cord and pressing her hand flat against the green-and-yellow-patterned wallpaper. "I just remembered. I have to take a makeup exam tomorrow. In the science lab."

"Then come on Friday. That's our next practice," Kimmy insisted. "Don't give up, Corky. Try
one more time. We really want you back."

Corky felt her throat tighten with emotion.
Kimmy was going out of her way to be nice to her.
"Thanks, Kimmy," she managed to utter. "Maybe I'll
come. I really don't know what to do. I just want
things to be normal again. But every time I try,
something happens and—" She just had to blurt it
out. "It's the evil, Kimmy. The evil spirit. It's back. It
didn't disappear that night."

"What? Corky, listen—" Kimmy sounded very
concerned.

"No. Listen to me," Corky insisted, more shrilly
than she had intended. "What do you think caused
those awful, frightening screams in my head? The
evil spirit did. It was *there*, Kimmy. It was right
there in the gym with us!"

"Corky, what are you doing now?" Kimmy
asked softly, calmly.

"Nothing. Just playing with Sean . . . putting
off doing my homework. Trying not to think about
anything," Corky told her.

"Want to come over here? We could talk. You
could tell me what you've found out about the evil.
We could try to make a plan," Kimmy suggested.

"Well . . ." Corky couldn't decide.

"You don't want to be alone in this," Kimmy said. "If the evil is back, all of us are in danger, Corky. We're *all* in this. We're all involved. We have to work together to find it before anyone else gets hurt."

"Well, I have to stay with Sean till my parents get back," Corky replied. "But, yeah, sure. I'll be over in half an hour or so."

"Okay," Kimmy said. "We can talk then. We can talk all night if you want. I'll even help you study for that science test you have to make up."

"Thanks, Kimmy," Corky said with genuine gratitude. She hung up, feeling a little cheered.

"The game's over. You lost," Sean announced as she returned to his room.

"It's okay. I would've lost anyway," she told him, thinking about Kimmy. "Want to play another game till Mom and Dad get home?"

He shook his head. "No, I'm going to play against the machine. It's more fun."

"Oh, thanks a bunch!" Corky cried sarcastically. Then she heard the front door slam downstairs. Her parents were back.

A few minutes later she was in the car, her science text and binder on the seat beside her. She backed the car down the driveway and headed toward Kimmy's house.

It was a cold, clear night. An enormous orange moon hung low in the charcoal sky.

It doesn't look real, Corky thought. *It looks like a moon in a science-fiction movie.* Everything seemed sharper and brighter than it should have been. As she made her way down Fear Street, Corky felt as if she could see every blade of grass, every leaf, in sharper-than-life focus.

She followed the curve of the road, and the Fear Street cemetery came into view on her left. Her headlights swept over it, bringing a row of jagged tombstones into focus.

"Oh!" Corky cried out when she saw someone moving among the graves.

She slowed the car, her eyes on the moving figure. The orange balloon of a moon floated low over the scene. Corky stared hard, startled by the clarity. There were no shadows.

Who is it? she wondered. *Who is there?*

And then she recognized her.

Sarah Beth Plummer.

Without realizing it, Corky had stopped the car in the center of Fear Street. Puzzled, she rolled down her window to see even more clearly.

Sarah Beth was huddled low, moving slowly between the pale gravestones. She was wearing a long black cape that swirled behind her shoulders even though there was no wind.

What is she doing? Corky asked herself. Sarah Beth had told Chip and Corky that she had finished her work in the cemetery.

So why was she there among the old graves tonight?

Her eyes on the dark caped figure, Corky lifted her foot from the brake, and the car began to glide slowly forward. As it moved, Corky realized that Sarah Beth wasn't alone.

Another dark figure stood very close beside her, one hand resting on a tall gravestone.

With a gasp of surprise, Corky stopped the car again. In the bright light from the low-hanging moon, it was easy to recognize the other figure.

Jon Daly.

Jon Daly and Sarah Beth Plummer. Together. In the Fear Street cemetery.

"What's going on here?" Corky asked in a whisper, her eyes locked on the two figures, so sharp and clear despite the darkness of the night.

Sarah Beth gestured with her hands. Jon stood as still as the gravestone he leaned against. Then Sarah Beth pointed to the ground.

What were they saying? What were they doing?

Staring hard, Corky recognized the stone Jon

was leaning against. It was Sarah Fear's grave marker.

As Corky continued to watch, Sarah Beth suddenly pulled off her black cape and draped it over a marble monument. Then she began to twirl, raising her arms above her head, performing a slow, graceful dance.

Sarah Beth danced while Jon still leaned against the gravestone, not speaking, his strange, nearly colorless eyes staring at Sarah Beth.

What is going on? Corky wondered.

With a shudder of fear, she removed her foot from the brake, slammed it down hard on the gas pedal, and roared away.

PART TWO

HERE IS THE EVIL!

12

SURPRISE IN THE SCIENCE LAB

W e'll have to do this on the honor system," Mr.
Adams said, winking at Corky as he handed
her the exam.

Seated on a tall metal stool, Corky leaned forward over the lab table and took the exam from the
teacher. "What do you mean?" she asked, studying
his face.

Mr. Adams was young, in his midtwenties,
but his dark brown hair was already graying at
the sides, and his mustache, which rested over his
top lip like one of the bushy caterpillars they had
studied in biology, was also sprinkled with gray. He
had friendly brown eyes, a nice smile, and usually
dressed in jeans and oversize sweaters. He was a
tough teacher, demanding, but well liked.

"I have to go pick up my car at the service garage," he told her. "I should be back in twenty minutes, half an hour at the most." He lifted his down jacket off a chair.

Corky glanced quickly at the test. Six essay questions. No real surprises. "I'll try not to cheat *too* much while you're gone," she joked.

Mr. Adams chuckled. He pulled the bulky jacket on over his sweater. "Those frogs are noisy, aren't they?" he asked, pointing to the big frog case on the shelf against the wall. Six or eight frogs were croaking throatily. "Whoever told them they could sing?"

"They'll keep me company," Corky replied, watching the creatures hopping around behind the glass. "How long do I have for the exam?"

"It shouldn't take more than an hour," he said. "It's way too easy."

"Yeah, right," she said, laughing.

He gave her a quick wave, pointed to the paper as if to say *Get to work*, and hurried out of the lab.

The room grew silent except for the rhythmic croaking of the frogs. Corky turned her eyes to the windows that ran along the wall to her right. Shards of December sunlight slanted into the room through the venetian blinds, falling onto the large tropical fish tank in the corner. Beside it stood a human skeleton, hunched on its stand, its shoulders slumped forward, its knees bent, as if it were weary.

Shelves beside the skeleton held large specimen jars filled with insects, plant specimens, and all kinds of animal parts. Corky made a disgusted face, remembering the cow eyeball Mr. Adams had shown them earlier that afternoon. It was so enormous, so *blobby*.

She glanced up at the clock. A little past three thirty. Cheerleading practice would be starting in the gym. She tapped her pencil rapidly on the tabletop, thinking about her long conversation with Kimmy the night before.

Then, scolding herself for wasting time, she lowered her eyes to the exam and read the first question. "Good," she said out loud, seeing that it was about osmosis. She had studied osmosis well; she knew everything there was to know about it.

She scooted the stool closer to the counter. Then she wrote the number one at the top of the page.

"Hey!" she cried out, startled, as the door to the room slammed shut.

Had Mr. Adams returned already? She spun around to see.

No one there.

Someone out in the corridor must have closed it.

She glanced up at the clock—it was 3:35.

"I'm wasting time," she said, and began to write.

The singing of the frogs seemed to grow louder. Glancing up with a sigh, Corky saw that the frogs were all hopping around wildly in their glass case, splashing each other, leaping onto one another's backs.

"Thanks for the help, guys," she said dryly, rolling her eyes. "What's your problem, anyway?"

She returned her attention to the test paper.

Then the venetian blinds all slammed shut at once. The clatter made Corky drop her pencil. It fell to the floor and rolled under the table.

"Hey!"

The room was much darker without the sunlight.

Corky slid off the stool and dropped to her knees to retrieve her pencil.

When she stood up, the overhead lights flickered off.

"What?"

Corky blinked. Total darkness now.

The frogs sang louder. Corky covered her ears with her hands.

"What's going on? Is someone here?"

The singing of the frogs was the only reply.

She stood, uncertain, leaning against the tall lab table. Her eyes adjusted slowly to the dim light. "Is there a blackout?" she wondered out loud.

Then she heard an unfamiliar *pop-pop-pop*. It took her a while to realize it was the sound of the glass lids popping off the specimen jars.

She saw the lids fly up to the ceiling, then crash back to the floor, the glass shattering, flying across the floor.

The contents of the jars floated up. Hundreds of dead flies rose up from one jar and darkened the air. Dozens of caterpillars followed them, floating silently in formation like a flock of birds.

The croaking became deafening.

As she stared in disbelief, Corky realized that the frogs were free. Their glass case had also shattered. About two dozen of them were leaping over the countertops, scrabbling toward her.

"Help!" Corky managed to yell.

She gasped as something large and soft plopped onto the counter in front of her, splashed her, spread stickily over her test paper.

The cow eyeball.

It stared up at her as if watching her!

The frogs were on her countertop too, leaping over one another, climbing onto the disgusting eyeball, crying out their excitement.

The venetian blinds began to clatter noisily, open-shut, open-shut, flying out into the room as if blown by the wind even though all the windows were closed. Sunlight flashed on and off, as fast as Corky could blink.

I have to get out of here, she told herself.

She brushed a croaking frog off her shoulder. Another one leaped at her face. The cow eyeball rose up, plopped down again, then rose up as if trying to fly.

With a disgusted cry, Corky ducked as the wet eyeball flew at her face. It floated over her head. She could feel it spray her hair. Then she heard it land with a sickening plop on the floor.

She had started running to the door when something at the front of the room caught her eye. The skeleton. It was no longer hunched over. It was standing straight, straining to free itself from its pedestal.

Corky grabbed the doorknob and pulled. The door wouldn't budge.

"Help!"

She gasped as the room filled with a foul odor that invaded her nostrils, choked her throat. So sour.

As sour as death.

She tried the door again. "Help me! Is anyone out there?"

Silence.

"Please! Help me!"

And then over the clatter of the flying venetian blinds and the mad croaking of the frogs, she heard a disgusting crack. So dry. The sound of cracking bones. And, looking to the front of the room, Corky saw one bony hand break off the skeleton.

She watched, frozen in horror, as the hand, its fingers coiling and uncoiling as if limbering up, floated up over the countertops.

The now handless skeleton continued to strain against its stand, attempting to free itself.

The bony hand flew toward Corky as if shot from a gun.

Corky tried to cry out, tried to duck. But the hand zoomed in on her, flew over the wildly hopping frogs, over the quivering eyeball, through the curtain of dead insects that choked the air.

The hand slammed into her, grabbed her by the throat. The force of the collision sent her sprawling against the door.

"Help me! Somebody!" she shrieked in a voice she no longer recognized.

And then the fingers tightened around her throat. The cold, bony hand squeezed tighter, tighter.

Tighter. Until she could no longer breathe.

13

CUT

Corky noisily tried to suck in a deep breath.

But the bony fingers dug farther into her throat, tightening their already steely grip. The room pulsed with noise. The clanking of the fluttering blinds competed with the frantic croaking of the frogs. The light brightened again, then dimmed.

Then stayed dim as the hand choked off the last of Corky's air.

She whirled around and tried to slam the hand against the wall. Then she reached up with both hands and grabbed the hand at the wrist. It felt so cold. Cold and damp, as if it had just risen from a wet grave.

The room spun. The dark ceiling appeared to lower on her.

Corky grabbed the wrist with both hands and tugged. The bony fingers dug deeper into her throat, squeezing tighter.

She reached for the fingers. Gripped two in each hand.

And pulled with all her might.

The sickening sound of bones cracking gave Corky some hope. Suddenly she could breathe. She noisily sucked in air, exhaled, sucked in more.

The broken fingers grasped frantically for her, but their hold was weak. She grabbed the cold wrist, pulled the broken hand off, and heaved it across the room.

Then, with a cry of horror, of disbelief, of relief all mixed into one, Corky lurched for the doorknob again and frantically turned it. This time the door opened.

She found herself in the dark, silent corridor.

She slammed the lab door hard behind her.

Her heart pounded. The only sound now.

Her eyes were clouded by tears.

She pushed her hair back from her face and started to run.

"Chip," she said out loud. "Chip!"

He had told her he'd be working late in the woodshop. They had made plans to meet there after her exam. "Chip!"

Off-balance, the floor tilting ahead of her, Corky started to run down the long hallway, her footsteps echoing loudly. She was breathing noisily through her open mouth. "Chip!"

She rubbed her throbbing throat as she ran. The bony fingers were gone, but she could still feel them pressing against it, so cold and wet, until she couldn't breathe.

"Chip!"

The shop was downstairs at the back of the building. She stumbled on the first step but thrust out both hands and caught herself on the railing.

Isn't anyone here? she wondered. The vast school building was so silent that she imagined she could hear her thoughts echoing in the hall.

Down the stairs and along a shorter hallway. The double doors to the shop came into view. The silence gave way to a high-pitched roar. A steady whine.

What is *that noise?* Corky wondered.

She pushed her way through the double doors, bumping them open with her body, and lunged into the shop.

"Chip! Where are you?" she cried, her voice revealing her terror. "Chip?"

The steady roar grew louder, closer.

Her eyes darted over the worktables, the pile of

lumber against the side wall, the tall power drills, the safety goggles hanging on their pegs.

"Chip, where *are* you? Are you here?"

She made her way into the center of the big room, her sneakers sliding over the fragrant sawdust on the floor. She came to a halt at a dark puddle.

What is that?

She stared down at it. It took her a long time to realize she was staring at a puddle of blood.

Then she saw two shoes on the floor. Legs. Almost hidden behind a worktable.

Taking a deep breath, she made her way around the dark puddle to get a better view. She cried out when she saw Chip lying facedown in a larger puddle of blood. A lake of dark blood.

"Ohh."

She grabbed the top of the worktable, leaned against it, forced herself not to drop down beside him.

"Chip?"

She could tell that he was dead.

Chip was dead. Sprawled there in his own blood.

She had to look away. She couldn't keep on staring at him.

She glanced up—and saw the power saw. And realized that the steady whirring sound came from the power saw. The blade was spinning loudly.

Louder.

Even louder.

And then Corky's ear-piercing screams drowned out the roar of the whirring saw blade as she caught sight of Chip's severed hand. Chip's hand, cut off at the wrist, rested like a glove beside the blade.

14

WHERE IS THE EVIL SPIRIT?

Corky didn't cry at Chip's funeral.

She was all cried out. She had cried until her eyes burned and her cheeks were red and swollen. And then, suddenly, her tears were gone, as if she'd used up her lifetime's supply. She was hollow now, drained of all emotion.

Except for the sadness.

The sadness remained. And behind it lurked the terror. The frightening memories. The terrifying scenes that she knew would remain forever in her mind.

The thoughts followed her everywhere she went, kept her wide-awake at night. Something was wrong in the world. Something was there. In her life. Something evil, something inhuman. Something out of control.

After the funeral she walked by herself from the small chapel, out into a gray, blustery day. A circle of swirling brown leaves danced over her shoes as she stepped onto the sidewalk.

Dead leaves.

Death. Everywhere.

Corky turned up the collar of her coat, more to hide her face than to protect herself from the gusting winds. She jammed her frozen hands deep into her coat pockets and started to walk.

"Hey, Corky!" Kimmy came jogging up to her, her black crimped hair bobbing, her cheeks bright red, her dark eyes watery and red rimmed. Without saying a word, Kimmy threw her arms around Corky's shoulders and hugged her, pressing her warm cheek against Corky's cold face.

After a few seconds Kimmy stepped back awkwardly, shaking her head. "It's so awful," she whispered. She squeezed the arm of Corky's coat. "And you found him. You were the one who—" Her voice caught in her throat. "I'm so sorry, Corky."

Corky lowered her eyes to the pavement. More brown leaves scrabbled over her shoes, tossed by the wind.

Ronnie and Heather appeared, their faces pale, their expressions grim. Kimmy hugged them both. They offered low-voiced greetings to Corky. Then the three girls headed off toward Kimmy's blue Camry, parked across the street.

"Call me," Kimmy called to Corky. "Okay?" She didn't wait for a reply.

Corky watched them climb into Kimmy's car. She saw all three of them talking at once inside the car. As they talked, they kept stealing glances at Corky.

Corky turned away and started to walk. She had gone several steps before she realized she wasn't alone.

"Hi, Corky," Debra said.

Her cold blue eyes peered out at Corky from under the hood of the black cape she had taken to wearing. Debra had always been pale and fragile, but today she appeared almost ghostlike.

"Come talk to me," she said, her voice barely rising over the rush of the wind.

Corky shook her head. "I really don't feel like talking." She started to walk again.

Debra hurried to keep up with her. The wind blew back her hood, revealing her short blond hair. "We *have* to talk, Corky. We have to," she insisted.

"But, Debra—"

"Over there." Debra grabbed Corky's arm and pointed toward a small diner across the street. "Just for a few minutes. We'll grab a hamburger or something to drink. I'll buy. Okay?"

Debra was pleading so hard that Corky felt she had no choice. "Okay," she said, sighing. "Actually, I haven't eaten today."

A pleased smile crossed Debra's face as she grabbed Corky's arm and pulled her across the street.

A few minutes later they were seated in a tiny booth, their coats folded beside them. Debra was eating a bacon cheeseburger and french fries. Corky, realizing she wasn't as hungry as she thought, took a few spoonfuls from a bowl of vegetable soup.

"People say such dumb things at funerals," Debra said, wiping ketchup off her chin with a napkin. "I heard someone tell Chip's mom that it was a really good funeral." She shook her head. "Now, what's *that* supposed to mean?"

Corky stared down at the soup. "I don't know. I think people feel so uncomfortable at funerals, they don't know what they're saying," she told Debra. "People said some pretty weird things to me at Bobbi's funeral."

Bobbi's funeral.

Chip's funeral.

There had been so many funerals in her life recently.

She forced down a few more spoonfuls of soup. It didn't taste great, but the warm liquid was soothing on her throat.

"We have to talk about the evil spirit," Debra
said suddenly, lowering her voice even though they
were the only customers in the diner.

Corky sighed. "Yeah. I know." She stirred her
soup, but knew she couldn't eat any more.

"You and I both know that the evil spirit killed
Chip," Debra said heatedly. "He didn't accidentally
cut off his hand and stand there bleeding to death
without calling for help or anything."

"The doctors said he probably sawed off his
hand and then went into shock," Corky said.

"Do you believe that?" Debra demanded.

Corky hesitated, then shook her head. "No."

"For one thing, Chip was a careful guy. He
wouldn't stand there and slice off his entire hand."

"I know," Corky said, her voice catching in her
throat.

"Also, do you know how hard it would be to
slice your hand clean off? If you just nicked your
wrist, you'd pull it away immediately. You wouldn't
keep right on sawing!" she exclaimed.

"Debra, please." Corky turned her eyes to the
front of the diner. Through the window she could
see that wet flakes of snow had started to fall.

"The evil is still alive, Corky," Debra continued. "I know it, Kimmy knows it, and you know
it. We can't just ignore it. We can't pretend it isn't

there and hope it'll go away and everything will be nice again."

"I know, I know," Corky wailed. "I know better than anyone else, Debra."

Debra reached across the tabletop and squeezed Corky's hand. "Sorry. I just meant—"

"The evil revealed itself to me," Corky told her. "Just before Chip—just before I found Chip."

Debra lowered her cheeseburger to the plate. She stared at Corky as if trying to read her mind. "What do you mean?"

Corky took a deep breath and told Debra everything that had happened in the science lab, starting with the door slamming shut and the lights going out, ending with her desperate struggle with the skeleton's hand.

Debra listened in silence, resting her chin in her hands. Both girls ignored their food while Corky told her frightening story.

"I don't believe it," Debra said softly. "I don't believe it."

"There's more," Corky said, raising her eyes to the window in front. The snow was turning to a bleak wet drizzle.

"Go on," Debra urged. "Please."

Corky told her about her encounters with Jon Daly and Sarah Beth Plummer. Then she told about driving past the Fear Street cemetery, about seeing Sarah Beth and Jon in the cemetery together.

"What were they doing?" Debra asked, removing her chin from her hands and sitting up straight.

"I don't know," Corky told her. "It was so strange. I saw Sarah Beth perform a dance on Sarah Fear's grave."

"You mean while Jon was watching?" Debra asked.

"Jon leaned on the gravestone and watched," Corky said. "It was so creepy."

"The evil spirit is definitely alive," Debra said in a whisper.

"But where?" Corky asked. "Why didn't it stay down in the grave? Where is it?"

"I think I know how to find it," Debra said mysteriously.

15

RAZZMATAZZ

"We've got razzmatazz!
Pep, punch—and pizzazz!
Hey, you—you've been had.
Shadyside Tigers got razzmatazz!
RAZZMATAZZ!"

As they repeated "razzmatazz," the five cheer-leaders performed flying splits. Then they landed on their feet and, with a whooping cheer, ran to the sideline clapping.

"Wow! That was *awesome*!" Corky cried, push-ing up the sleeves of her Tigers sweatshirt as she moved toward them.

"How about the flying splits?" Kimmy asked, her expression concerned. "High enough? I had the feeling Megan and I were a little late."

"Looked excellent to me," Corky told her, grinning. "Don't be so hard on yourselves."

"Yeah!" Ronnie piped up. "If Corky says it was
awesome, it was awesome!"

Everyone laughed.

Kimmy has really improved, Corky thought
happily. *She's much more graceful. She's even lost
some weight.*

It was nearly four weeks after Chip's funeral,
and Kimmy had persuaded Corky to come to cheerleading practice once again. "We all have to stick
together," Kimmy had urged Corky. "If we're going
to find the evil, if we're going to fight it, we have to
work together. If you're not on the squad, you're not
really with us. You're alone."

Kimmy's words had touched Corky, had con-
vinced her. Now here she was, ready to give it
another try.

The girls, dressed in tights, denim cutoffs, and
oversize T-shirts, seemed relaxed and enthusiastic,
and glad to see Corky again.

"You ready to try the routine now?" Kimmy
asked Corky.

Corky didn't hesitate. "Yeah. I'm ready." This
time she wasn't going to be stopped.

She knew that next Saturday night was one of

the last basketball games of the season. If she was going to get back on the squad, it was now or never.

Corky glanced across the brightly lit gym. Standing against the wall outside her office, Miss Green flashed her a thumbs-up sign.

Corky returned the signal and stepped into line next to Kimmy. "You have to help me with the hand claps," she said. "I think I'm straight on everything else."

"I never get them right either," Kimmy joked, giving Corky an encouraging smile.

Waiting for Kimmy to begin the cheer, Corky felt a moment of panic. The bright gym seemed to fade behind a curtain of white light. Silence seemed to encircle her.

I'm all alone, she thought. *All by myself out here.*

But then the cheer began, the white light dimmed, and the rest of the world returned.

> *"We've got razzmatazz!*
> *Pep, punch—and pizzazz!*
> *Hey, you—you've been had.*
> *Shadyside Tigers got*
> *RAZZMATAZZ!"*

Shouting at the top of her lungs, Corky moved easily through the routine. And when it came to the finale of flying splits, she timed her jump perfectly and leaped higher and more cleanly than any of the other girls.

The routine ended with a whooping cheer, and the girls jogged to the sideline clapping. Corky took a deep breath—and realized she was laughing, laughing from sheer joy, from the happiness of being able to perform an entire routine.

Before she could process what was happening, she was surrounded by the others. They were laughing too, eager to congratulate her, to compliment her on her performance, to welcome her back.

"Now that you're back, we can do the diamond-head pyramid again," Kimmy exclaimed. "You know, the one you and your sister invented."

"Yeah, let's try it," Corky said with enthusiasm.

"Now?" Kimmy asked, expressing her surprise.

"Yeah, right now," Corky insisted, smiling. "If we're going to do the pyramid Saturday night at the game, we'd better start now."

"You'll have to run us through it," Kimmy said uncertainly.

Corky saw Debra and Ronnie whispering intensely near the wall. "No problem," Corky said, signaling everyone to follow her to the center of the floor. "Bobbi and I spent so much time on this routine, I think I could do it in my sleep."

"Who's going to take the top?" Ronnie asked, stretching her legs.

"I will," Corky told her.

She saw the doubt form on Kimmy's face. "Corky," Kimmy whispered confidentially, leaning close, "are you sure? Don't you want to take it easy?"

"No." Corky shook her head emphatically and stepped back from Kimmy. "Either I'm going to be back on the squad just like before, or I'm not," she insisted.

Kimmy quickly relented.

"Maybe we should warm up a bit first," Debra suggested. "You know. Do some roll-ups into partner pyramids before we try the big pyramid?" She cast Corky a pleading look.

"We're already warmed up," Corky replied.

"Corky's right," Kimmy told Debra. "Let's just do it, guys."

Corky outlined the pyramid to them. Three girls—Kimmy, Debra, and Heather—formed the bottom tier. Two girls—Megan and Ronnie—would stand on their shoulders, then move into liberties, each girl raising her outside foot and holding it up as Corky mounted to the top to stand on Megan's and Ronnie's shoulders.

They all worked on shoulder mounts and dismounts for a few minutes; then Corky guided them into position for the pyramid.

I wish Bobbi were here, she found herself thinking. *She was the real expert at getting this going.*

But then she pushed Bobbi from her mind, shaking her head hard as if shaking her thoughts away. "Ready?" she called. "Let's try it now. Take it slowly. Don't worry about the timing."

"Heather, bend your knees," Kimmy instructed as Megan and Ronnie performed their shoulder mounts to form the middle tier.

Then it was Corky's turn to move.

Before she realized it, she was climbing into position. Off the floor. Climbing so high.

And even with all of her concentration, the thoughts came rushing back. The fears. The memories.

The questions.

Will I start to hear the screaming girl again?

Will I freeze up at the top?

Will the room start to spin or go crazy?

Megan and Ronnie each grabbed one of Corky's hands and tugged. Corky stepped off Kimmy's shoulders and climbed.

Higher.

Uh-oh, she thought. *Now is when the trouble comes.*

Uh-oh. Uh-oh. She held her breath. Her temples throbbed.

She could feel the panic well up. Could feel it deaden her legs—could feel the fear rise up from her stomach, tighten her throat. She could feel it pulse at her temples, hear it ring in her ears.

Uh-oh. Now is when the trouble comes. Now. Now. Now.

She stiffened her knees and raised her hands high.

Balance. Balance. She concentrated with all her will.

Uh-oh. Now. Now!

And there she was—on top of the pyramid!

Shaky. But there.

No voices. No spinning walls. No shrieks of terror.

No evil.

"Congratulations!" Corky heard a voice call from the floor. "Excellent!"

She peered down to see Miss Green applauding, a broad smile on her usually dour face. "Now watch the dismount. Take it slow, okay?"

A few seconds later the girls were on the floor, congratulating one another enthusiastically. Even Miss Green joined in the celebration.

"We did it—and no broken bones!" Corky exclaimed.

To Corky's surprise, Kimmy threw her arms

around Corky and smothered her in a warm hug. "I knew you could do it!" Kimmy gushed. And then, in a whisper, she added in her ear, "Maybe the evil has left us—maybe the nightmare is finally over."

"Carry these for me," Debra said, handing the bundle of slender red candles to Kimmy. Debra wrapped her black cloak tighter around her neck.

The full moon rose over the trees. The wind sent dry leaves scampering over the weeds and tall grass. Behind them on the street, a car rolled silently by, only one headlamp lighting its way.

"I can't believe you talked me into this," Kimmy said grumpily. "This is so stupid."

"We'll go back to my house afterward," Corky offered. "We can order pizza."

"Stop complaining. The weather's not so bad," Debra said, leading the way up the hill.

The dead grass clung to their boots. Somewhere in the distance the wind toppled a garbage can. The lid clattered noisily. A cat wailed, sounding human, like a baby.

The three girls stopped at the front walk, the concrete broken and crumbling. They stared up at the ruins of the old mansion.

"Wow," Corky whispered. "I've never been this close."

The stone walls of the mansion were charred black, evidence of the fire that had destroyed it decades before. All the windows had been blown out. Only the front one was boarded up with a large sheet of plywood. The rest were gaping holes, revealing darkness behind the crumbling walls.

"Hey, look!" Kimmy bent down and picked up something from the dead grass beside the broken walk.

Corky shone the flashlight on it. It was a doll, wide-eyed and bald, one arm missing.

"It looks old," Debra said, examining it closely.

Kimmy dropped it to the ground. "What are we doing here?" she repeated. "*Look* at this dump."

"I know what I'm doing," Debra replied mysteriously. She gripped a large black-covered book in her hand, gesturing with it toward the door. "Let's go inside."

"I don't think so," Kimmy said unhappily, her eyes surveying the burned walls.

"Come on," Corky said, tugging at Kimmy's arm. "It's worth a try."

"I know what I'm doing," Debra repeated seriously. "Visiting the Simon Fear mansion makes perfect sense to me."

"None of this makes perfect sense," Kimmy

grumbled, shifting the candles to her other hand. "How can going into this burned-out old wreck on the coldest night of the year make any sense?"

"Do you want to locate the evil spirit or don't you?" Debra snapped, losing her patience for the first time.

"We do," Corky answered quickly.

"What makes you think we're going to find it here?" Kimmy demanded. She kicked the old doll away. It bounced across the walk and lay sprawled facedown in the grass.

"Sarah Fear spent a lot of time in this house," Debra explained. "If the evil spirit is hers, this is the most logical place for it to hang out."

"Logical," Kimmy muttered sarcastically.

"You're being a bad sport," Corky scolded. "This is better than studying for the history exam, isn't it?"

Debra focused on Corky, a hurt expression on her face, which was shrouded in the black hood of her cape. "You don't believe me either? You're not taking this seriously?"

"I take the evil spirit *very* seriously," Corky told her in a low, somber voice. "I want to know where it is. That's why I agreed to come with you."

"I take it seriously too," Kimmy insisted. "But I don't think we're going to get anywhere by poking around and lighting a bunch of candles in this burned-out old mansion."

"Well, we have to do *something*!" Corky cried heatedly. "Maybe Debra's idea *is* dumb—and maybe it *isn't*. Let's face it, Kimmy—we're desperate. We've got to act. We can't just sit around and wait to see which one of us it kills next!"

Corky's speech appeared to affect Kimmy. "You're right," she said softly, and her expression turned thoughtful as she followed the other two toward the house.

"I've been reading a lot," Debra said, making her way through the tall weeds to the front door, holding the book in front of her, pressing it against her chest as if for protection. "This old book tells how to raise a spirit. This house is *the* place to raise Sarah Fear's spirit."

She tugged at the old wooden door, and it suddenly pulled open easily. A damp, sour smell invaded their nostrils.

"I can't go in there. Really," Kimmy said, taking a few steps back, her features twisted in disgust.

"Here, I'll give you the flashlight," Corky offered. "Trade you for the candles."

"Having the flashlight won't help," Kimmy replied, staring into the darkness behind the open front door. "Don't you know the stories about this place? This whole house is evil!"

"The spirits are alive here," Debra said, her eyes glowing in the beam of the flashlight. "I can feel them. I know we're going to succeed."

Corky followed her into the house. Kimmy, her hand on Corky's shoulder, reluctantly entered too. "Yuck! It smells in here," she complained.

"You'll get used to it," Debra said quietly. She led them through the wide entryway that opened into a large sitting room.

Corky shone the flashlight around the room. Wallpaper curled down from the walls, streaked with black. Dark stains covered the ceiling, which bulged and drooped. The floorboards were cracked and broken. "Watch your step," Corky warned. "Look—there are holes in the floor."

The air felt heavy and wet. The smell of mildew and decay surrounded them. The rotting floorboards creaked as the girls made their way to the center of the room.

"This is great!" Debra exclaimed, taking a deep sniff of the sour air, her eyes glowing with excitement. "I can feel the evil spirit. I really can."

"I can *smell* it," Kimmy said sarcastically.

"Hand me the candles," Debra said. She placed the book on the floor and took the candles from Kimmy.

"Shine the light down on the book, okay? I've got to find the right page," Debra instructed as she flipped through the pages.

Corky felt a cold chill run down her back. "It — it just feels so evil in here," she said, surveying the fire-stained walls, the broken floorboards.

"We each take a candle," Debra instructed. She handed Corky and Kimmy each a red one, then lighted all three. "We kneel in the center of the room," she said, lowering her voice to a whisper.

Corky and Kimmy obediently knelt beside Debra.

"Hold the candle in your left hand," Debra instructed. "Then we put our right hands forward and clasp them in the center."

The girls followed these directions.

Suddenly the flames dipped low and nearly went out. Corky gasped and let go of Kimmy's hand.

"You felt it too?" Debra asked, excited. "You felt the spirit?"

"It was just the wind," Kimmy said, rolling her eyes. "Give us a break."

"Try to concentrate, Kimmy," Debra scolded. "We need total concentration. I can locate the spirit here. I know I can. But we have to concentrate."

"I'm concentrating," Kimmy muttered.

They held hands again. The candle flames

dipped once more. This time none of the girls reacted.

"I'm going to chant now," Debra told them. "When I finish the chant, the book says we should know where the evil spirit is."

Corky swallowed hard. The rotting floorboards creaked. The candle flames dipped, then stood tall again.

This is going to work, Corky thought. *The spirit of Sarah Fear* has *to be somewhere in this frightening old place.*

"Give it the old razzmatazz," Kimmy told Debra.

Debra glared at Kimmy. "Shhh." She raised a finger to her lips and held it there. Then, closing her eyes, she wrapped both hands around her candle and began to chant.

The flickering light played over her pale, pretty face under the black hood. She chanted in a language Corky didn't recognize. At first her voice was soft, but it grew louder and stronger as she continued to chant.

Her eyes still closed, Debra began to move the candle in a circle in front of her, still gripping it with both hands. Around and around, slowly, slowly, while chanting louder and louder.

Gripping the candle in her left hand and

Kimmy's hand in her right, Corky stared straight ahead, concentrating on Debra's strange musical words.

After a few minutes, Debra finished her chant. She opened her eyes.

And all three girls cried out as the evil spirit rose from a hole in the rotting floor.

16

HE DISAPPEARED

Corky leaped to her feet, staring straight ahead through the darkness as the creature struggled to rise into the room.

Her mouth open in horror, Kimmy grabbed the flashlight and aimed it at the hole in the floor.

The creature whimpered and scratched at the floorboards.

"It's a dog!" Corky cried.

Debra's face fell.

Corky and Kimmy rushed forward and worked to pull the dog out of the hole in the floor. "You smelly thing," Kimmy said, petting its head and scratching its ears. "How did you get stuck down there?"

The dog, a forlorn-looking mutt with damp

tangles of long brown fur, licked Kimmy's nose appreciatively.

"Don't let him lick you, Kimmy," Corky teased. "You don't know where he's been."

"A dog. I don't believe it," Debra said, sighing.

Wagging its shaggy tail, the dog circled the room excitedly, sniffing furiously along the floor.

"Maybe he *smells* the evil spirit," Kimmy said sarcastically to Debra.

"Not funny," Debra muttered, gathering up the candles. "I really thought we were close to something."

"Me too," Corky said, watching the dog as it loped out of the room. "I was so scared when we heard the thing start to come up from the floorboards."

"Bowwow," Kimmy said dryly, rolling her eyes.

"I'm not giving up," Debra insisted.

"I am," Kimmy said emphatically. "I'm freezing." She handed the flashlight back to Corky and started toward the front door.

"Kimmy, wait," Corky called. "Want to come to my house?"

Kimmy turned back and shook her head. "No, thanks. I'm going home and getting into a hot bath."

"But—"

"Let her go," Debra said glumly.

"See you in school tomorrow," Kimmy called from the front entryway, then disappeared from view.

Corky turned back to Debra, who slammed her book shut and tucked it under her arm. "I was so psyched," she told Corky. "So psyched."

"Me too," Corky said.

"We're the only ones who know the evil spirit is loose," Debra said, heading to the front. "The only ones."

"Yeah, you're right," Corky agreed sadly. "My own parents change the subject every time I try to tell them the truth."

"That's why we have to do something," Debra said.

"I just keep thinking about Sarah Beth Plummer and Jon Daly," Corky said with a shudder. She pulled up the collar of her down coat and buried her face inside it like a turtle as she followed Debra to the door.

They stepped outside, surprised to find it warmer there than in the house.

"Yeah. That sounded like a pretty bizarre scene, the two of them in the cemetery," Debra said thoughtfully. Her expression brightened. "You know what? We should check them out."

"You mean go talk to them?" Corky asked, following her toward the street.

Debra nodded. "Yeah."

"Right now?" Corky asked, glancing at her watch. It was nearly ten.

"Why not?" Debra asked.

"Well . . ." Corky hesitated. That nice hot bath Kimmy had talked about sounded pretty good to her too.

"Come on. We'll take my car," Debra urged, pulling Corky by the arm. "It'll only take a few minutes to drive to Jon Daly's house."

"Yeah, but what do we say when we get there?" Corky asked. "We can't just barge in and say, 'Jon, what were you and Sarah Beth Plummer doing in the cemetery the other night?'"

"Why not?" Debra said. She pulled open the back door to her car and dumped the candles and book onto the seat. "That's exactly what we'll ask." She tossed back her hood and brushed her sleek short hair with one hand. "Come on, Corky. Get in."

Corky hesitated for a long moment, then pulled open the passenger door and climbed in. Debra slid into the driver's seat and rested her hands on top of the steering wheel.

The glow of the streetlight fell over Debra's pale, slender hand.

And Corky thought of Chip.

Of Chip's hand. Lying forlornly beside the power saw.

She saw the hand, severed neatly at the wrist. And then the puddles of dark blood.

And then Chip lying facedown in his own blood.

"Corky, what's the matter?" Debra cried, seeing Corky's horror-filled expression.

Corky shut her eyes tight, erasing the picture. "Let's go see Jon Daly," Corky said, her voice a dry whisper.

The Dalys lived in the wealthy section of Shadyside known as North Hills, a few blocks from the high school. Debra pulled up the driveway to the house, a sprawling redwood ranch-style house behind a neatly trimmed front lawn.

At the end of the drive, the garage door was open. A Volvo station wagon was parked inside. Two bikes hung on the wall. Corky wondered if one of them had belonged to Jennifer.

So much death, she thought, climbing out of the car. *The evil has claimed so many victims.*

Corky and Debra walked side by side up the flagstone walk to the front door. Debra raised her finger to the doorbell, then hesitated.

"Go ahead," Corky urged. "We're here. We might as well talk to Jon."

Debra rang. They heard voices inside the house, then approaching footsteps.

The porch light went on. The front door was pulled open. Mrs. Daly's head appeared in a rectangle of yellow light, her expression quickly turning to surprise. "Why, hello, girls."

Her faded blond hair was wrapped in a red bandanna. Her features seemed to melt together in the harsh light.

"Hi, Mrs. Daly," Corky said, clearing her throat. "Remember me? I'm Bobbi's sister?"

"Of course," Mrs. Daly replied, eyeing Debra.

"We came to see Jon," Corky said.

Mrs. Daly's mouth dropped open.

"Who is it?" Mr. Daly's voice floated out from the living room.

"Do you have news about Jon?" Mrs. Daly asked Corky, ignoring her husband's question.

"Huh?" Corky couldn't hide her confusion. "News?"

"Who is it?" Mr. Daly said again as he appeared behind his wife. He was tall and balding. He had on a Chicago Cubs T-shirt and straight-leg corduroys. His forehead was furrowed.

The house smelled of stale cigarette smoke.

"They have news about Jon," Mrs. Daly told her husband. She gripped his hand.

"No," Corky corrected. "We came to *see* Jon."

"We need to talk to him," Debra added, self-consciously adjusting her cape.

"Oh." Mrs. Daly's face fell. The light faded from her eyes.

"Jon isn't here," Mr. Daly said sternly.

"We're worried sick about him," Mrs. Daly added, gripping her husband's hand. "It's been two days. Two days. We called the police."

"Huh? The police?" Corky glanced at Debra, who looked as startled as Corky felt.

Mr. Daly nodded sadly. "Yes. Jon disappeared two days ago. We don't know *what* happened to him."

17

FEAR

After dinner the next night, Corky waited for Debra at Alma's, the small coffee shop where she and Chip had talked to Sarah Beth Plummer. The restaurant was bustling now, the booths and long counter filled with college students, laughing and talking, their voices competing with the clatter of silverware and china and the saxophones of a salsa band pouring out from the jukebox.

Debra came hurrying in, ten minutes late, her cheeks flushed from the cold. She was wearing several layers of sweaters over blue corduroys. Her eyes swept over the crowded restaurant until she located Corky in the next-to-last booth.

After making her way past a white-uniformed

waitress holding a tray of glasses over her head, Debra slid into the booth across from Corky and sighed. "Sorry I'm late."

"No problem," Corky told her, her hands encircling a white mug of hot chocolate. "Where's Kimmy?"

"She's sick," Debra announced. "Her mom says she has a temperature and everything. That's why she wasn't in school today."

Corky's mouth dropped open in surprise. "Sick? Will she be okay for the game tomorrow night?"

Debra shrugged. "I hope so."

The waitress appeared, pad in hand, and stared down impatiently at Debra. "You need a menu?"

Debra shook her head. "Just a Coke, please."

"Sarah Beth Plummer lives right across the street," Corky said after the waitress left. "She pointed out the house to Chip and me that night— we sat over there." She indicated the rear booth. "And she told us about Sarah Fear."

Debra glanced at the booth Corky had pointed to. It was now occupied by four girls having hamburgers and french fries. "You think this Sarah Beth will be helpful?"

Corky sipped her hot chocolate. She made a face. It tasted powdery. It hadn't been stirred enough. "I just had the feeling that night that Sarah

Beth knew a lot more than she was telling us. There was something suspicious about her, you know. Something *devious*."

Debra's Coke arrived. She picked up the straw and blew the paper covering at Corky. "This Sarah Beth Plummer. Is she old?"

Corky shook her head. She brushed a strand of blond hair from her eyes. "No. She's young—early twenties, I think."

"What makes you think she'll talk to us?" Debra asked.

"I don't know," Corky replied. "But I think we have to try to talk to her. I mean, I saw her dancing over Sarah Fear's grave with Jon Daly. And now Jon has disappeared."

"Do you think Sarah Beth knows where the evil spirit is?" Debra asked, sipping the Coke.

"I intend to ask her," Corky said, and sighed. "This is a crazy conversation, isn't it? If anyone overheard us, they'd think we were *nuts*."

"But we're not nuts," Debra said quickly, gesturing with both hands, accidentally bumping her glass and spilling a small puddle of Coke onto the tabletop. "The evil is real. We know that."

"I know," Corky agreed quietly.

"Let's go see what Sarah Beth Plummer knows," Debra said.

Both girls slid out of the booth and, after paying, hurried out of the restaurant.

There was no name over the doorbell, but Corky remembered the house. It was a narrow two-story semidetached redbrick structure, part of a row of small houses, most of them occupied by students from the nearby community college.

The two girls hesitated on the small concrete front stoop, staring at the curtained window beside the door. Corky raised her finger to the doorbell, then lowered it.

"What's the matter?" Debra asked in a loud whisper.

A car rolled by quickly, its headlights sending a wash of white light over them, fixing them in a bright spot.

"I just keep picturing Sarah Beth dancing in the cemetery," Corky replied. "With Jon leaning over Sarah Fear's grave." She gripped the sleeve of Debra's sweater. "She could be dangerous, Debra. I mean—*she* could be possessed by the evil." Corky shuddered. "We could be walking in to our death."

"We have to find out," Debra said in a tense whisper. "We've got to know the truth." Taking a deep breath, she reached forward, pressed the doorbell, and left her finger on it for a long time.

They could hear the buzzer inside the house. A light went on. They heard soft footsteps; then the door was pulled open.

Sarah Beth Plummer poked her head out. She had a bath towel wrapped around her hair. *She must have just washed it,* Corky realized.

Sarah Beth's eyes fell on Debra first. Then she recognized Corky. "Oh, hi." Her expression was a mixture of surprise and confusion.

"Hi. Remember me?" Corky asked meekly.

"Yes. You're . . . Corky," Sarah Beth said after some hesitation.

"This is my friend Debra Kern," Corky said.

"Come in, come in," Sarah Beth said, shivering. "It's freezing out, and I just washed my hair."

The two girls followed her into a small living room filled with antique furniture. Corky carefully closed the front door behind her. The room was hot and smelled of oranges. Two old oversize armchairs and a large plum-colored couch nearly filled the space. A low coffee table in front of the couch was stacked high with books, papers, and files. The walls were lined with crowded bookshelves that almost reached to the ceiling.

Sarah Beth rewrapped the towel on her head, staring at the two girls. She was wearing a man's white shirt over black leggings and woolly white tube socks.

"Can we talk with you?" Corky asked awkwardly. "I mean, is this a bad time or anything?"

"No. I guess not," Sarah Beth replied, her expression still confused. "I was just making some coffee. Would you care for some?"

"No, thanks," Debra answered quickly.

"Take off your coat," Sarah Beth told Corky. "You can just toss it over there." She pointed to one of the armchairs.

"I thought—well—maybe you could tell us more about Sarah Fear," Corky stammered, obediently tossing her coat onto the back of one of the big chairs.

Sarah Beth's mouth formed an *O* of surprise.

"If it isn't too much trouble," Corky added.

"Sarah Fear?" Sarah Beth said, eyeing both girls thoughtfully. "Well . . ."

"It would really mean a lot to us," Debra said. "Anything you know about her."

"Okay," Sarah Beth reluctantly agreed. "I mean, I don't know that much. But sit down." She gestured to the couch. "I'll just go turn off the stove. Then we can talk. I'll tell you what little I know."

"Thanks a lot," Corky replied gratefully. "I know we're barging in—"

"No problem," Sarah Beth said, waving to them to sit. She rushed to the kitchen.

"She has such an old lady's voice," Debra whispered.

"Yeah. I know," Corky whispered back. "She looked surprised to see us—but not *that* surprised," she added, her eyes on the doorway to the kitchen.

"She didn't even ask us *why* we want to know about Sarah Fear," Debra whispered.

Debra edged past the armchairs and sat down on the edge of couch, sinking into the plush cushion.

Corky tried to make her way to the other side of the couch. But she accidentally bumped the coffee table with her leg, sending a tall stack of files toppling to the carpet.

"Nice move, ace," Debra joked. She tried to get up to help Corky pick up the files, but the low, soft cushion made it difficult for her to stand.

Corky dropped to her knees and began hurriedly to pile the manila files back on the table. A bunch of envelopes fell out of one of the folders.

She scooped them up and started to replace them—and then stopped. Her eyes widened in surprise.

"Debra, look!" she gasped.

"What is it?" Debra asked.

"These envelopes . . . ," Corky said, her voice trembling. "They're all addressed to Sarah *Fear*!"

18

SUNK

Sarah *Fear*?"Debra grabbed an envelope from Corky's hand and pulled it close to study it. "But this letter was postmarked only a few weeks ago!" she exclaimed.

Corky glanced nervously to the doorway. "Do you think Sarah Beth Plummer is really Sarah Fear?" she whispered, frantically stuffing the envelopes back into the folder.

"You mean—is she over a hundred?" Debra asked.

"The furniture is all so old," Corky remarked. "Sarah Fear would feel comfortable in this room."

"I'm back." Sarah Beth reappeared, carrying a cup of steaming coffee. She stopped just past the doorway. "Corky, what are you doing down there?"

"Uh . . . I accidentally knocked some stuff over," Corky confessed, staring hard at Sarah Beth.

"Oh, don't worry about it," Sarah Beth said, moving toward one of the armchairs. "This place is a mess. I'll pick it all up later."

"Uh . . . Sarah Beth?" Corky started. She held up one of the envelopes. "I couldn't help but see. These letters—they're all addressed to Sarah Fear."

Sarah Beth's eyes narrowed for a brief second, but she quickly resumed her friendly expression. "I know," she told Corky.

"But—"

Sarah Beth lowered herself carefully into the big armchair, sinking deep into the cushion, resting the coffee cup on the padded arm. She sighed. "Well, I guess you know my secret. I'm a Fear."

Corky gasped.

Sarah Beth laughed. "It isn't *that* terrible! It doesn't mean I'm some kind of demon, you know!" She seemed to find Corky's reaction very amusing.

Corky climbed to her feet and joined Debra on the couch. "So your real name is Sarah Fear?" she asked, staring into Sarah Beth's eyes as if trying to read her mind.

Sarah Beth nodded. "I don't use it. Most of the time I use my mother's maiden name—Plummer." She took a sip of coffee. "The Fear name is such a curse."

"What do you mean?" Corky asked, clasping her hands tightly in her lap.

"Your reaction said it best," Sarah Beth replied, smiling. "When I said I was a Fear, you practically fainted on the floor!"

All three of them laughed.

"I was just . . . surprised," Corky explained.

"Surprised and horrified," Sarah Beth added. "Everyone in Shadyside knows that the Fear family is filled with weirdos and monsters. The name is a curse." All the amusement drained from her face. She took a long sip of coffee. "A *curse*."

"Are you related to the first Sarah Fear?" Debra asked. "Are you named after her?"

"I'm related to her somehow," Sarah Beth said. "I don't know if my parents named me after her or not—I don't think so." She reached up with her free hand and pulled the towel off her head. Her black hair, still wet, fell down around her face. She tossed the towel over the chair.

"I've spent my whole life trying to get away from that dreadful name," she said with emotion. "Fear." She made a disgusted face. "But it's funny— I find myself drawn to the story of the Fears. I'm fascinated by my ancestors, drawn to them, pulled to them as if by an invisible force."

"When we talked the last time," Corky started,

"across the street, at the restaurant—"

"I didn't tell you everything," Sarah Beth interrupted. "I confess." Her dark eyes burned into Corky's. "I didn't reveal everything I know about Sarah Fear. I just didn't want to." She paused, and then her expression hardened and she added, "I really don't want to now."

Corky recoiled at the young woman's sudden coldness. She glanced at Debra, who was staring intently at Sarah Beth.

"We really need your help," Corky said, her voice cracking with emotion. "My sister and my friends—Bobbi and Chip and Jennifer—they've all lost their lives. And I don't know. Maybe I'm next."

Alarm registered on Sarah Beth's face. She set her cup down on the carpet at her feet.

"Something evil killed Bobbi and Chip," Corky continued. "Something evil from beyond this world. And we think it has something to do with Sarah Fear."

"That's why we have to find out all we can about Sarah Fear," Debra said, shifting her weight on the couch. "We need to know everything you know so that maybe we can stop this evil."

Sarah Beth stared at Debra as if seeing her for the first time. "I don't understand," she said finally.

"I really don't think my dredging up ancient history will do you any good."

"Please!" Corky cried, not intending to sound so shrill, so desperate. "Please, Sarah Beth, please help us. Please tell us what you know."

Sarah Beth raised both hands as if surrendering at gunpoint. "Okay. I'll talk, I'll talk!" she cried. "Don't shoot."

"First tell us what you and Jon Daly were doing in the cemetery the other night," Corky said. The words just burst out of her. She hadn't really intended to ask that question till later.

Sarah Beth acted surprised. "You were there?" she asked Corky. "In the cemetery?"

"No. Just driving by," Corky explained.

Sarah Beth blushed. She took a deep breath. "I didn't think anyone saw us." She stared at Corky.

She's stalling, Corky thought. *She's thinking fast, trying to think of a good lie.* "I saw you dance," Corky said, staring back at Sarah Beth, challenging her with her eyes.

Sarah Beth chuckled and shook her head. "It was all so silly."

"Silly?" Corky asked. She was determined not to let Sarah Beth off the hook.

"I've known Jon for years," Sarah Beth said, her cheeks still pink. "We were in school together.

We even dated for a while, but I lost touch with him. When he called me a few weeks ago, I was really shocked."

"He called you?" Corky asked.

Sarah Beth picked up the coffee cup and took a long sip. "Yeah. Out of the blue. He was really pumped, sounded a little crazy to me. But Jon was never exactly what you'd call calm."

"What did he want?" Debra asked, tucking her legs under her.

"He wanted me to meet him. In the Fear Street cemetery," Sarah Beth replied, reaching up and fluffing her still-damp hair. "Jon knows that I'm a Fear. And he knows about my interest in my ancestors— and my interest in spirits and the occult."

She finished her coffee and set the cup back down on the carpet. "So I met him at the cemetery," she continued. "He was definitely acting weird. I mean, really weird. Even for Jon. As soon as I got there, he started asking me if I knew the truth—the truth about his sister, Jennifer. I really didn't know what he was talking about."

Corky stared intently at Sarah Beth, listening, studying her eyes. *I don't think she's telling us the truth,* Corky thought. *There's something wrong with this story.*

"Then Jon started asking me if I believed in

evil spirits. I told him I believed in all kinds of things—but that didn't seem to satisfy him. He knew I studied the occult and the spirit world. He asked me if I knew how to summon spirits from the grave. At first I just laughed at him. I thought he was kidding me."

She shook her wet hair. "Are you two okay? Do you think it's too warm in here? I could turn down the heat."

"No, we're fine," Debra said quickly. "Please— go on."

"Well, I didn't really want to continue. But Jon was so insistent. He was really out of his head. I told him I'd read about a dance you do on some- one's grave to summon the dead person's spirit. He demanded that I show it to him. I felt ridiculous, but he wouldn't take no for an answer. So I showed him a little bit of the dance. I mean, actually I made up most of it—I don't really know it." She turned to Corky. "I guess that's when you drove by."

But you seemed to be really into *it,* Corky thought skeptically. *You didn't act like it was some kind of goof, Sarah Beth. You looked really serious to me.*

"Then what happened?" Corky asked.

"Nothing," Sarah Beth replied with a shrug. "Nothing happened. No spirit appeared—big surprise, huh? I thought Jon would be disappointed, but he looked very pleased. Really happy, for some reason. Then we said good night and went our separate ways. I haven't seen or heard from him since."

Something's wrong here, Corky thought. *There's something wrong with this story.*

"What a strange guy," Sarah Beth said thoughtfully. "He's scary, I think. Really scary."

The room grew silent. A clock somewhere in the back started to chime. Corky glanced at her watch. Nine o'clock.

"Sure I can't get you some coffee?" Sarah Beth offered. "It's all made."

"No, thanks," the two girls said in unison.

"Then I guess I'll tell you about Sarah Fear," Sarah Beth said, stifling a yawn. "That's why you've come, right?"

"Yes. We really need to know about her," Corky said, studying Sarah Beth's face.

"I'm afraid you'll be disappointed," Sarah Beth told them. "I don't know all that much. Most of it I got from old newspapers and what few family records I could find. One of Sarah's cousins, Ben Fear, kept a journal. That was helpful up to a point. But believe me, there are a lot of gaps in the story. A lot of gaps."

She tucked her legs beneath her in the big

chair, leaned on one of the overstuffed arms, and began to talk, moving her eyes from Corky to Debra, then staring down at the dark carpet as she spoke.

"I guess I'll begin with Sarah's death. Or I should say '*near*-death.' That would be in . . . uh . . . 1899, I guess. Up to that point, I think you could say that Sarah had managed to escape the curse of the Fears. Meaning she had had a fairly happy life.

"In his journal, Ben Fear described her as a lovely flower of a young woman. That's the way Ben wrote. He was pretty flowery himself. But I guess it can be said that Sarah was beautiful in every way. She was a lovely young woman, kind, generous, and loving.

"I'm starting to sound like Ben Fear," Sarah Beth muttered, rolling her eyes. "Oh well, bear with me. According to family records, Sarah was happily married. For a brief time, anyway. She never had any children.

"She and her husband lived close to Simon Fear's mansion. Their house was always filled with people. Cousins, friends, servants. It was quite a life.

"And it didn't change much, even after Sarah's husband died of pneumonia. She mourned him for an entire year. Then she resumed her busy, people-filled life.

"Then in early 1899, the good life abruptly

came to an end. Poor Sarah fell ill—deathly ill. I don't really know what the sickness was. Perhaps no one back then knew either. In his journal, Ben Fear described it as a 'wasting disease.' Old Ben had a way with words, didn't he?

"Well, the doctors gave up on Sarah. She was given up for dead. In fact, a grave was dug in preparation, in the Fear Street cemetery. And a minister was called upon and told to prepare a funeral ceremony.

"But then there was some kind of miracle. To everyone's surprise, Sarah Fear didn't die. In fact, she made a remarkably fast recovery. Her strength seemed to return overnight. And despite the pleas of her family for her to rest and regain her energy, she pulled herself out of bed the very next day and returned to her duties of running the house.

"Here's where the story gets strange. After her illness, Sarah changed. She wasn't the same sweet 'flower' anymore. According to Ben Fear's journal, she became withdrawn, reclusive. She developed a terrible temper and was known to throw tantrums for no apparent reason. She turned away from all her friends.

"The details in the diary become sketchier and sketchier toward the end of her life. My theory is that Ben Fear was no longer invited to Sarah's house, and so he had little firsthand information about her to write in his journal.

"He did tell of rumors that Sarah and a servant had become lovers.

"There were reports of strange gatherings in her house. Late-night meetings. Séances. Wild parties. The police reports are very discreet. Don't forget—Simon Fear was still around, still a powerful figure in the town. Nevertheless, the scandalous stories about Sarah began to spread.

"The newspaper became full of frightening stories about the events that took place at Sarah's house. One spring day a kitchen maid was found murdered in the garden, stabbed through the heart with an enormous pair of hedge shears. A houseguest was also murdered, his leg severed, cleanly cut off his body and found lying beside him on the floor of the stable.

"Sarah Fear was never under suspicion for these murders. And the mysteries were never solved.

"Then came the biggest and most tragic mystery of them all. The pleasure boat trip. Sarah Fear's final trip. It took place on Fear Lake. You know. Tranquil, flat Fear Lake. The tiny, round lake behind the Fear Street Woods.

"There were five people on the boat. Sarah Fear. Three of her relatives. And one servant. According to the newspaper report, it was a beautiful summer day, a perfect day, no clouds, no wind.

"Sarah's large pleasure boat sailed away from the shore. And a few minutes later it happened— from out of nowhere. A mysterious hurricane-force gale. Totally unexpected—on the calmest, most beautiful day of the summer. A wind so powerful that it capsized the large boat. Turned it over in a flash.

"And everyone drowned. Everyone, including Sarah Fear. Within view of shore—only a five- or ten-minute swim at most. And yet all on board Sarah's boat were drowned. There were no survivors.

"Which brings us to the strangest part of all," Sarah Beth said, leaning forward in her big chair, staring at the two girls across from her on the couch, lowering her voice to just above a whisper. "The strangest part of all. When the bodies were pulled ashore, their skin was bright red, blistered, and scalding hot—as if Sarah and her companions had all drowned in *boiling water*!"

19

DID YOU HEAR ABOUT JON?

Drive around," Corky said. "I don't feel like going in just yet."

"Let's park and talk," Debra said. She pulled the car halfway up Corky's driveway and cut the lights and the engine.

Corky turned her eyes to the house. The lamp over the door cast a yellow triangle of light onto the front porch. All the other lights were out. Her parents either were in the back or had gone to bed early.

"Did you get the feeling that Sarah Beth was holding something back?" Debra asked, tapping her gloved hands on the steering wheel.

Corky slid down low in the passenger seat, raising her knees to the dashboard. "Yeah. I think she knows more than she let on," she agreed. "But I don't know what it would be."

"I asked her if she thought Sarah Fear had been possessed by an evil spirit," Debra said. "She just looked at me as if I were from Mars or something."

"She wouldn't answer any of my questions either," Corky complained. "You heard me when I asked what had happened to the servant who was supposed to be her lover. And all she would say was that Sarah Fear's secrets were buried with her."

Debra sighed and rubbed her glove against the side window, which was starting to steam up. "Weird lady," she said quietly.

They had left Sarah Beth's house a little after ten o'clock, their heads spinning with the bizarre details of the story she had related to them.

"I hope I've been helpful," Sarah Beth had said as she'd walked them to the door. "If I come across anything else, I'll get in touch with you."

But Corky and Debra had left with more doubts and suspicions than when they had arrived. They had driven the short distance back to Corky's house in silence, each going over in her mind what she had heard. And now they sat in Corky's driveway, eager to share their thoughts, as the car windows steamed up around them.

"It's just too perfect," Debra said, squeezing the steering wheel with both hands. "She's telling us about Sarah Fear—and *her* name is Sarah Fear. It's too perfect, and too strange."

"They died in scalding hot water," Corky said thoughtfully, closing her eyes. "That's how my sister died. In the shower. In scalding hot water."

"I know," Debra said in a whisper, staring straight ahead.

"And remember the teakettle? That afternoon when I scalded my hand?" Corky cried, her mouth dropping open in horror as the memory flew back to her. "Again—scalding hot water."

"I remember," Debra said, putting a hand on Corky's trembling shoulder. "You're right. Hot water is a clue. It's definitely a clue."

"But a clue to *what*?" Corky asked shrilly, feeling her frustration build. "A clue to *what*?"

"What about those gross murders at Sarah Fear's house?" Debra asked, turning in her seat to face Corky. "The houseguest with his leg cut clean off. Just like Chip. Just like Chip's hand."

Corky swallowed hard. "I—I hadn't thought about that, Deb. But you're right."

The two girls sat silently for a long moment, staring at the steamed-up windshield.

"So what are we proving?" Debra asked finally.

"Well . . ." Corky thought hard. "I guess we're proving that it's the same evil spirit doing the same horrible things—then and now."

"And how does that help us?" Debra demanded, staring intently at Corky.

Corky shrugged. "I don't know." She shook her head unhappily. "I just don't."

"There has to be another clue in the Sarah Fear story," Debra insisted, her features tight with concentration. "There has to be a clue about how to defeat the evil spirit. Somehow the spirit ended up in Sarah Fear's grave; we know that. Somehow it was forced to stay down there for more than a hundred years. But how? How did Sarah Fear defeat it?"

"She didn't," Corky said dryly. "She didn't defeat it. It killed Sarah Fear—remember?"

"Oh yeah," Debra said softly.

They lapsed into silence again.

"Now, more than a hundred years later, more death," Corky said, staring at the clouded windshield. "Jennifer, Bobbi, Chip . . ." A loud sob escaped her throat.

"I wonder who'll be next," Debra muttered, her eyes dark with fear.

Corky's parents were watching TV in the den in back. After pulling off her coat, she went in to say hi to them. They were engrossed in some cop show, and she could see that they didn't want to chat. So Corky said good night and headed up to her room.

She didn't feel like talking to anyone. Her head felt as if it weighed a thousand pounds, weighted down by all she had heard and by her confused thoughts and theories.

If only we could trust Sarah Beth Plummer, she thought, starting to pull off her clothes and get ready for bed. *But I know we can't trust her. For all we know, Sarah Beth herself could be the evil spirit!*

If only we could trust somebody.

She pulled on a long nightshirt and deposited her clothes in a neat pile on the chair across from her bed.

Debra and Kimmy and I—we're all alone, Corky thought. *We're all alone against this ancient evil force. We're the only ones who know about it. The only ones who* believe *in it. And what can the three of us do?* What?

I don't know what *to think,* she told herself, heading to the bathroom across the hall to brush her teeth. *We shouldn't have gone to Sarah Beth's. Now I'm even more confused than before.*

And more frightened.

She had just started to put toothpaste on

the brush when she heard her phone ringing. She dropped the toothbrush into the sink, dashed back into her room, and picked up the receiver. "Hello?"

"Hi, Corky. It's me. Kimmy."

"Kimmy!" Corky cried in surprise. "Hey, how are you feeling?"

"Better, I guess," Kimmy replied uncertainly. "My temperature is down. But I didn't call about that." She sounded breathless, excited.

"What's happening?" Corky said.

"Did you hear about Jon Daly?" Kimmy asked, nearly squeaking the words.

"What about Jon?" Corky demanded. "Did they find him?"

"Yeah, they found him all right," Kimmy said. "They found him in Fear Lake. Drowned."

20

A CHEERLEADER FALLS

How do you feel?" Kimmy asked.

"Kind of fluttery," Corky told her, swallowing hard.

Kimmy took the maroon-and-gray pom-pom from Corky's hand and helped her untangle it. "You'll do fine," she said, flashing Corky an encouraging smile as she handed it back. "Once the game starts, you won't even think about how nervous you are."

I hope she's right, Corky thought, glancing up at the scoreboard, which was being set up for the game. The scoreboard lights were all flashing, and the clock was going haywire, the numbers running backward faster than Corky could read them.

I hope the game goes that quickly, Corky

thought, fiddling with the cuffs of her white sweater. She could feel her heart racing. She took a deep breath and tried to calm herself.

A few early arrivals entered the gym and made their way to the bleachers. Corky watched them, then turned her eyes back to the scoreboard clock. About half an hour until game time.

The cheerleaders spent the next fifteen minutes stretching in silence. Just as Corky was standing up from reaching down to touch her toes, someone grabbed her shoulder. She jumped, startled.

"Sorry," Miss Green said. "I just wondered if you needed a pep talk."

Corky grinned. "Thanks. But I think I'll be okay."

"Nervous?" the advisor asked, studying Corky's face.

Corky nodded. "Yeah. But I can handle it."

"You'll be great," Miss Green said, glancing at the gym door as more people entered. "Practice has been terrific. The new pyramid routine should tear the roof off."

"If I don't fall on my face," Corky joked.

Miss Green chuckled. "You'll get your old confidence back once the game starts. You'll see." She gave Corky a thumbs-up, turned, and jogged back toward Kimmy and the other cheerleaders.

By now the bleachers were nearly half-full. The scoreboard clock showed twelve minutes till game time. The teams were warming up at opposite ends of the floor, shooting running layups; several balls were thundering off the basket and backboard at once.

"Showtime!" Kimmy called, clapping her hands, gathering the cheerleaders together. Corky moved quickly into the circle, wiping her perspiring hands on the sides of her short skirt.

"Energy up!" Kimmy shouted. "Let's get this crowd warmed up. Let's see some *spirit*!"

The girls all cheered. Debra gave Corky an encouraging smile and a slap on the back. Forming a line, they trotted to the bleachers and began their warm-up chant:

"Shadyside High!
Shadyside High!
Can you dig it?
Everybody's here.
So everybody CHEER!"

Then again. Louder. Encouraging the crowd to join in, to clap, to get loud.

And again. And again. Even louder.

And the crowd picked up the chant, picked up

the enthusiasm, stomping and clapping until the nearly filled bleachers bounced and shook.

> "Let's get a little bit rowdy!
> R-O-W-D-Y!"

And again. They repeated this chant until the Shadyside fans were screaming out the word. Then the cheerleaders ended with synchronized back handsprings, all six girls performing backward flips in unison, and landing perfectly before jumping up and starting the chant again.

It's going great, Corky thought with relief as the shouts and cheers echoed off the walls. *I'm doing fine. I'm going to be okay.*

She looked down the line of girls and saw Kimmy grinning back at her. *I'm going to be okay,* Corky thought.

The game started. The gym reverberated with the pounding and squeaking of ten pairs of basketball shoes and the steady thud of the ball against the shiny hardwood floor.

Corky knelt on the sideline with the rest of the squad, watching the game, waiting for a break when the cheerleaders would go into action. She could feel her heart racing, but from excitement rather than nervousness.

The game was going quickly, a close match in which the lead kept changing sides. Corky watched intently and, when it came time to do a cheer, performed with her old enthusiasm and grace.

Standing in front of the cheering fans, the crowd stretching up nearly to the rafters, she felt as if she were shouting away her problems, roaring back at all the terrors that had plagued her.

Just before halftime she turned to see Kimmy behind her. Kimmy leaned down and spoke into Corky's ear, struggling to be heard over the thunderous crowd noise. "About the pyramid," Kimmy shouted.

Corky cupped her ear and smiled up at her.

"At the end, when you're ready to dismount from the top, count to three, okay? So I can be sure I'm in position to catch you."

"Okay, gotcha." Corky nodded. "Have I been coming down too fast?"

"I just want to make sure I'm in position," Kimmy said, putting a hand on her shoulder. "So count to three, and then jump, and I'll be there."

"Thanks," Corky said. And then she added, "I'm really grateful, Kimmy. For everything."

Kimmy didn't hear her. She had moved on to give instructions to Ronnie and Heather.

It was halftime before Corky realized it. The

time *did* seem to be moving as fast as the score-board clock when it was being set before the game.

The visiting cheerleading squad performed first. They had come with a ten-piece band and did a lot of rap cheers and club-type dancing.

"They're good," Corky heard Megan say as they waited on the sideline.

"They're *different*," she heard Heather reply. She didn't mean it as a compliment.

A few minutes later Corky felt her excitement surge as she followed the other girls to the center of the floor to begin their performance.

The opening routines went well. Then Ronnie mistimed a backflip and landed hard. But Debra helped her up quickly, and the routine continued without a pause. There were no other mishaps.

We're doing okay, Corky thought happily. She suddenly wondered if her parents were somewhere up in the bleachers. They had talked about coming to the game and bringing Sean.

I hope you're here, Corky thought. *I hope you're seeing how great everything is going. My big comeback!*

And then it was time for the pyramid, the grand finale.

As the girls began their shoulder mounts, the crowd hushed expectantly.

Corky crossed her fingers for a brief second, took a deep breath, and began her climb.

Up, up.

And she was at the top. And the pyramid was formed.

Perfect.

And the crowd shouted its appreciation.

Corky smiled and thrust out her arms.

And as she focused on the top of the bleachers, the gym began to spin. The entire room began to twirl, like a carnival ride out of control.

She uttered a low cry. She felt her knees start to buckle. "What's happening?"

The walls were whirling. She was inside a spinning cyclone of light and color and noise. "No! Please!"

Struggling to keep her balance, she closed her eyes.

When she opened them, the gym was still whirling.

Faces suddenly came clear as the bleachers spun around in front of her. She saw a red-haired boy with freckles. Saw him so clearly.

The room spun around again. The whirling lights grew brighter, brighter. Swirls of red and yellow and white.

And she saw a man with a red wool scarf tossed

around his neck, sitting close to the floor.

And the gym spun around again.

The shouts and cries seemed to circle her, press in on her, suffocate her as the blindingly bright gym whirled faster and faster.

And then stopped.

And she saw Sarah Beth Plummer standing just inside the double doors.

Sarah Beth Plummer?

What is she *doing here?*

I've got to get down, Corky thought, feeling cold perspiration run down her forehead, feeling her knees tremble. *Got to get down.*

She turned her eyes to the floor, and there was Kimmy. Ready for her. In position already— waiting. Giving her an encouraging nod.

Corky took a deep breath.

Her legs felt rubbery, weak. She leaned forward, raised her knees, tucked her legs.

And leaped.

Kimmy's face twisted into a mask of horror.

She didn't move to catch Corky. Didn't raise her arms.

And Corky hurtled to the floor and hit hard with a sickening *thunk!*

21

NOT OKAY

Corky opened her eyes to silence.

White silence.

The gym had become so quiet.

Faces emerged and came slowly into focus— blurred, distorted, shadowy faces.

"I couldn't move!" she heard a shrill voice crying somewhere above her. "I couldn't move. I couldn't raise my arms!"

It was Kimmy's voice.

The shadowy faces brightened. Corky realized she was lying on her back, staring up at the gym ceiling.

The pain was like a raging river, rolling over her entire body.

Miss Green peered down at her, her features tight with worry.

Other faces stared down.

Ronnie's face was drawn and pale. She had tearstains on her freckled cheeks.

Debra stared down at Corky, her cold blue eyes wide, her lips pursed in fear.

She could hear Kimmy sobbing now, loud sobs.

It was so cold now. So cold and silent. And the pain was everywhere.

"I wanted to catch her," she heard Kimmy tell someone, her voice shrill and trembling. "I *tried* to catch her. But *something held my arms down!*"

That's what Bobbi said, Corky thought.

The faces above her slipped back into darkness.

That's what happened to my sister, she realized.

Something had held Bobbi's arms down. Something had paralyzed Bobbi. Only, no one would believe her.

I believe you, Bobbi. I believe you.

Because I know what was responsible. I know what did it.

It was the spirit.

The evil spirit is here.

It's right here.

But where?

It tried to kill me. It tried.

And then the most horrifying thought: *Maybe it did kill me.*

The faces darkened even more.

She heard Kimmy sobbing.

And then the darkness swallowed her.

When Corky opened her eyes, a different face stared down at her.

"Mom!"

Her voice came out choked and dry.

Mrs. Corcoran, her eyes watery, smiled down at Corky. "You're going to be okay," she said, putting a cool hand on her daughter's forehead.

Corky tried to sit up, but pain forced her back onto the pillow. "Where am I?"

"You're in the hospital," her mother said. Her smile appeared frozen in place—it didn't fade, even when she talked. "The emergency room." She dabbed at the corner of one eye with a wadded-up tissue.

The room came into focus. Actually, Corky saw, it wasn't a room. Just a small rectangular cubicle with gray curtains for walls.

"You're going to be okay," Mrs. Corcoran repeated, still offering Corky that forced smile.

No, I'm not, Corky thought glumly.

"You bruised a rib. And you broke your arm.

That's all," her mother informed her.

So the spirit didn't kill me, Corky thought, turning to stare at the gray curtains. *It didn't kill me. This time.*

But next time . . .

"Your father is filling out some forms," Mrs. Corcoran said. "When he's finished, we can go home. Isn't that great? You're going to be okay."

Corky forced a smile back at her mother. *I'm not going to be okay,* she thought. *I'm never going to be okay.*

The evil spirit killed Bobbi.

And tonight it was in the gym. Tonight it tried to kill me.

I'm not okay. Not okay. Not okay.

A dark-haired young intern in a white coat appeared suddenly above her. "Can you sit up?" he asked, smiling. "I'd like to check the cast one more time."

Holding her by the shoulder, he helped Corky to a sitting position. To her surprise, she saw a large white cast encasing her right arm.

"I wouldn't try to do any backflips for a while," the doctor joked.

"Sean, what are you doing up this late?" Mrs. Corcoran scolded.

Corky's brother, who had greeted them eagerly at the front door in his pajamas, shrugged his slender shoulders.

"He refused to go to bed," explained Mrs. Barnaby, the neighbor who had been babysitting. "He said he had to see his sister's cast."

"Well, back away from the door so your poor sister can get inside," Mr. Corcoran exclaimed.

Sean's eyes grew wide when he saw Corky's cast. "Wow! Can I touch it?"

Corky extended it to him. "Go ahead. If that's a thrill for you."

"No, wait," Sean said excitedly. "I want to sign my name on it. You're supposed to sign casts, right?"

"Not tonight, please!" their mother begged.

"Corky's had a rough night," Mr. Corcoran told Sean. "Give her some space."

"Can I write a message on it?" Sean asked, ignoring his parents as usual. "You know. Something funny."

"Tomorrow," Corky said shakily. "I'm really feeling kind of weird right now."

Sean made his pouty face, but backed off.

"You got two calls," Mrs. Barnaby told Corky, pulling her wool coat over her shoulders, adjusting her scarf. "I wrote them down. One from a Debra;

one from Ronnie someone. I told them you were still at the hospital."

"Thanks," Corky said wearily. "I'll call them tomorrow."

Mrs. Barnaby said good night and headed for home.

Sean argued for a short while. Then he agreed to let Mr. Corcoran tuck him into bed. "Tomorrow I'm going to write something really stupid on your cast," he warned Corky.

"Thanks. Can't wait," his sister replied dryly.

"I'm going to run you a hot bath," Mrs. Corcoran told Corky. "The doctor said it would be good for your sore muscles."

Corky shrugged. "Okay, I guess."

I've been attacked by an ancient evil force, she thought scornfully, *and Mom thinks a bath will help!*

"You just have to be careful not to get the cast wet," her mother warned.

"I'll try," Corky muttered.

She followed her mother up the stairs. After entering her room, she lowered herself carefully into a sitting position on the edge of the bed.

Her ribs ached. Her arm throbbed under the cast.

I can't do anything, she thought, uttering an exasperated cry. *I can't even undress myself.*

She heard the rush of water in the bathtub across the hall. A few seconds later her mother appeared in the doorway, shaking water off her hand. "Let me help you change."

Corky felt embarrassed to be undressed by her mother, but she was too weary to protest. Her mother slipped a cotton robe around Corky, then helped her tie the belt. "This isn't going to be easy," she told her daughter. "But we'll manage."

Corky sighed in response and started toward the bathroom.

"Do you want me to help you get into the tub?" Mrs. Corcoran called after her. "You've got to be very careful."

"No, thanks, I'll manage," Corky said.

She stepped into the bathroom and closed the door behind her. The room was steamy and warm. The steam felt good against her cheeks.

She bent and turned off the water with her left hand.

"Just call me Lefty," she said aloud.

She stared down into the deep aqua tub. The bath looked inviting. Every muscle in her body ached.

This is going to feel good, she thought.

She had started to pull off the robe when she realized that someone was standing behind her. She turned quickly.

First she saw the maroon-and-gray cheerleader outfit.

Then she saw the girl's face.

"Kimmy!" Corky cried in surprise. "What are
you doing here?"

22

CORKY'S BATH

The white steam rose up around Kimmy. Her dark eyes glowed in the misty light.

"I wanted to get rid of you forever," she said coldly, speaking in a low, husky voice.

Corky backed up against the closed bathroom door. "Kimmy—what? What are you saying? You're *frightening* me."

Kimmy's normally pink cheeks flushed scarlet. "I'm not Kimmy," she announced in the strange, husky voice.

"Kimmy, listen—" Corky started. Her ribs ached. Pain throbbed down her arm. "I'm so tired. I—"

"You didn't cooperate," Kimmy said, taking a step toward Corky. "You were supposed to die—like your sister."

"Now *wait!*" Corky cried. "Kimmy—"

"I'm not Kimmy!" she snarled, then let out a roar that blew away all the steam. "I am what you fear most!"

"No!" Corky tried to shriek, raising her good hand to fend off the menacing figure before her.

The puzzle is solved, she realized, feeling paralyzed by dread, unable to move, to call for help, to take her eyes off the advancing girl.

The puzzle is solved.

The evil spirit is revealed.

It's been inside Kimmy.

"Where is Kimmy?" Corky demanded, finding her voice. "What have you done with Kimmy? Did you kill her?"

At first the creature didn't respond. Her dark eyes reddened, then glowed like fire. Her hair—Kimmy's black hair—rose up around her head, flew up like dark flames.

The low, raspy voice declared, "I have been in Kimmy ever since that night. That night in the cemetery. The night *you* thought you sent me back to my grave!"

Corky stared in silent horror into the creature's eyes, glowing like coals in a fire, stared at the dark hair flying wildly around its face.

"You thought you were defeating me," the evil

spirit continued. "You should have known better. Ronnie was there too. And Debra was there. And Kimmy, lucky Kimmy."

"You moved from Jennifer's body to Kimmy's," Corky whispered, slumping weakly back against the door.

Kimmy's eyes grew even brighter, so bright that Corky had to look away.

"Why?" Corky asked. "Why are you doing this? Why did you kill Chip and Jon? Why are you trying to kill me?"

"Kimmy's enemies became *my* enemies," the voice rasped. "I paid Chip back for dumping Kimmy and for liking you. Jon was following me everywhere. He was coming too close to the truth. I knew that when I saw him with Sarah Beth." She paused. Her dark eyes narrowed icily. "He's gone now."

"But why kill *me*?" Corky cried in a shrill, frightened voice she didn't recognize.

"I have to pay you back for that night in the cemetery. You tried to destroy me. Now you must be destroyed."

"No!" Corky cried. She reached for the door-knob.

But the door wouldn't budge.

"Time for your bath," the husky voice said. "So

nice of you to draw a hot, steamy tub. Now, Corky dear, you can die like your sister."

With startling strength, Kimmy grabbed Corky by the hair, jerked her toward the tub, and started to force her head down into the hot water.

23

DOWN THE DRAIN

*O*hh!" Corky tried to pull back as Kimmy pushed her head down toward the steaming tub.

But Kimmy was too powerful.

The steaming water seemed to rise up to meet Corky.

I'm going to drown, she thought.

I'm going to die now.

She closed her eyes as her face met the water.

So hot. So burning hot.

She held her breath. Twisted her body. Tried to force her head up.

Kimmy pushed with inhuman strength.

Deeper. Corky felt the water fill her ears. Rise up over her hair.

I'm drowning now.

I'm dead.

Pictures whirred wildly through her mind. Faces. All her friends. People she didn't recognize.

Her chest ached.

I can't hold my breath much longer. My lungs are going to explode.

More pictures raced through her mind. A jumble of faces. She saw her family. She saw Sean. Sad-faced Sean.

Now he won't get to sign my cast, she thought.

He'll wake up, and I'll be dead.

Dead, dead, dead.

And Sean will be alone.

No! A voice screamed in her head.

No—I can't let this happen! *I can't let the evil win again!*

As her fear turned to anger and her anger flamed to desperate rage, Corky reared up against the powerful force with all her strength—and swung the heavy cast.

"Oh!" Kimmy groaned as the elbow of the cast clubbed the back of her head.

As she was momentarily stunned, her fiery eyes faded to black. She stumbled forward.

And as she stumbled, Corky stood up, water pouring off her head. She grabbed Kimmy's wildly flying black hair with her left hand, jerked the head downward with all her might—and pushed Kimmy's face into the steaming hot water.

Corky turned and, still grasping Kimmy's hair with her good hand, leaned the cast on Kimmy's head. And pushed.

Down. Down.

Kimmy's head was entirely submerged.

She struggled to get up. Her arms flailed frantically. She kicked with her legs. She strained to raise her head.

Her chest heaving, the pain shooting through her body, Corky leaned all of her weight against Kimmy's head, pushing, pushing it down, bearing down with the heavy cast.

Kimmy thrashed and fought.

She pushed up with inhuman strength, pushed up, up, strained against Corky's cast, struggling to remove her head from the water.

"Drown! Drown!" Corky said without even realizing it. "Drown! Drown!"

And then Kimmy's mouth opened wide.

A raging wind poured from her mouth.

Into the water.

A wind so hot, so fierce, the water instantly began to boil and bubble.

And still Corky pressed down. Battling the force, she pushed Kimmy's head back down, submerging it so the raging wind made boiling tidal waves roll across the tub.

The tiny room filled with steam. Thick white clouds of it rose up from the tub, scalding hot. Corky began to choke on it.

I can't see, she realized. *It's thicker than any fog.*

She couldn't see her own arm. Couldn't see the cast. Could no longer see the head she was holding under the water.

The white steam grew even thicker.

Corky blindly choked, gasping for air.

And hung on.

Hung on to the struggling head as the wind raged and the bathwater tossed and churned. Hung on blindly.

I'm suffocating, she thought. *I can't breathe. I'm drowning in a cloud. Drowning in a thick, scalding cloud.*

Suffocating . . . like Bobbi.

But she held on. And pushed. Pushed with her remaining strength, pushed in spite of her pain, pressed the head under the rolling hot water.

The steam cleared. Corky could see again.

Under the water Kimmy uttered a loud groan.

A disgusting green liquid poured from her mouth. The stench of it rose up from the tossing water.

Corky gagged, struggled to hold her breath, trying not to breathe.

The thick green liquid oozed out of Kimmy's mouth. Took shape. Formed a long snakelike figure.

Longer, longer.

It coiled around the bottom of the tub. More. More rolled out of Kimmy's open mouth.

"Drown! Drown! Drown! Please—drown!" Corky screamed.

Leaning on Kimmy's head with the cast, she reached down and pulled open the drain.

She heard a gurgling sound.

And stared in disbelief as the foul-smelling green liquid snake was sucked down the drain.

24

THE END?

As it oozed down the drain, the thick green liquid made a disgusting sucking sound that grew louder and louder, echoing in Corky's head, vibrating, vibrating until the walls appeared to shake.

Still holding Kimmy's head down even though the water had been drained, Corky held her breath, trying to avoid the putrid odor that invaded her nostrils.

The white steam, rising from the tub, rolled over her, wrapped her up like a hot, wet blanket.

The last of the undulating green gunk gurgled into the drain.

Corky shut her eyes. When she opened them, the steam had vanished. The room was clear.

Silence.

She stared down into the tub.

The green ooze was gone.

The water had drained out too.

Kimmy uttered a low cry.

With a sob of relief, Corky loosened her grip on Kimmy's head.

"Hey!" Kimmy cried. In her old voice, not the frightening raspy voice of the evil spirit.

"Hey!" Bent over the empty tub, Kimmy shook her head, beads of water rolling off her black curls.

Reluctantly Corky let go of Kimmy's head and backed away from the tub, her arm throbbing under the heavy cast, her entire body aching.

Kimmy turned around slowly, her dark eyes wide with confusion. She pushed herself up from the tub and stood, breathing hard, her chest heaving. She stared at Corky as if she didn't recognize her.

"Corky?" she cried uncertainly, squinting, her mouth dropping open. Her eyes darted around the small room. "Where am I? What am I doing here?"

Despite her weariness, Corky let out a whoop of joy. "Kimmy, is it *you*?"

The question seemed to confuse Kimmy even more.

Corky offered her a hand. "Kimmy, I don't *believe* it!" She helped pull Kimmy to her feet.

Kimmy gripped the sink to steady herself. "But how . . . ? I mean, I don't understand." She suddenly reached up and grabbed her hair with both hands. "I—I'm wet. I don't—"

"Take it easy," Corky said softly. "Let's get out of here. Let's go downstairs, and—"

"But how did I get here?" Kimmy demanded. "I was in the Fear Street cemetery. You were struggling. Wrestling with Jennifer over that open grave."

"That's the last thing you remember?" Corky exclaimed. "Kimmy, that was months ago!"

"Huh?" Still gripping her hair tightly in both hands, Kimmy gaped at Corky. "Months? What do you *mean*?"

Corky started to reply, but a loud pounding on the bathroom door made her stop.

"Corky, are you okay?" her mother called. "What's going on in there?"

Corky pulled open the door.

"Mom, it's okay."

Mrs. Corcoran gasped in shock. "Kimmy, what are you doing here?"

"I—I don't know," Kimmy told her, still dazed.

"Kimmy's okay," Corky told her mother. "She's okay. Let's get her downstairs."

"But she's all *wet*!" Mrs. Corcoran cried in confusion. "And so are you!"

Corky managed to calm her mother. They helped Kimmy down the stairs and onto the living room couch. Mrs. Corcoran went into the kitchen to call Kimmy's parents to come and get her.

When her mother was out of the room, Corky moved next to Kimmy on the couch and whispered to her. "The evil. It's gone."

Kimmy started to say something, but Corky put a hand on her arm to silence her.

"Just listen to me. The evil is gone. I drowned it. Really, I drowned it. I saw it disappear this time. Maybe now the nightmare is over. Maybe it really is gone for good."

A few hours later Corky lay awake in bed, watching the shadows play across her ceiling. Her ribs ached. Her arm throbbed and itched under the cast. She shifted her weight uncomfortably.

Poor Kimmy, she thought. *She was so dazed, so confused. I don't think she'll ever believe the truth.*

Corky tried to turn onto her side, but a stab of pain shot across her chest. She rolled onto her back again, tugging the covers with her good hand.

Is the evil spirit really gone forever? she wondered, closing her eyes. *Will my life finally return to normal?*

Yes.

She answered her own question. *Yes. Yes. Yes.*

Happily repeating the word over and over, she fell into a fitful sleep.

The next morning she slept late. The clock on her night table said 11:55 when she pulled herself out of bed, yawned, and stretched her one good hand.

She stood up, feeling stronger. A little unsteady. But definitely stronger.

She looked out the window. Bright blue skies.

A sunny day, she thought, smiling.

At last! A sunny day.

The days will all be sunny from now on, she thought cheerfully. She smiled at herself in her dresser mirror.

I'm starving, she realized, pushing her hair back from her face before rubbing the sleep from her eyes.

Still in her long cotton nightshirt, she padded down to the kitchen, humming to herself. "Hey, anybody home?"

No reply.

She started to open the refrigerator, but stopped when she saw the morning mail on the kitchen counter. Shuffling through the stack of bills and mail-order catalogs, she pulled out an envelope addressed to her.

It was hand-printed in light blue ink. There was no return address.

Curious, Corky struggled to tear open the envelope with her good hand. She pulled out a folded sheet of paper. It appeared to be a note.

"Who is it from?" she wondered aloud.

And then she gasped in horror as she unfolded it and read the brief message:

IT CAN'T BE DROWNED.

THE THIRD EVIL

PART ONE
TEAM SPIRIT

1

IN THE SOUP

Miss Green's whistle echoed off the high ceiling of the gym. The cheerleaders stopped in midcheer as their advisor raised both hands to her head and pretended to tear out her frizzy brown hair. Her eyes were wide with exasperation.

Corky Corcoran sighed. *That routine was going really well,* she thought. *Why did Miss Green stop us?*

She cast a glance down the line of cheerleaders to her friend Kimmy Bass. Kimmy mopped her forehead with the sleeve of her T-shirt. She also appeared to be annoyed by the interruption.

It was warm for early April. The air in the gym felt hot and damp. Corky had her blond hair pulled straight back and tied in a high ponytail. She and the five other Shadyside High cheerleaders were dressed in Lycra shorts and loose-fitting T-shirts, which were drenched in perspiration from the after-school practice.

"Hannah, do me a favor," Miss Green said. "Step forward and show my *veteran* cheerleaders the proper way to do a roundoff back tuck."

Hannah Miles bounced forward obediently, a broad smile on her pretty face. "I like to start in this position," she said, not at all embarrassed at being singled out. "You know—with my knees bent a little so I get more spring."

A slender, graceful freshman, Hannah was the only new member of the Shadyside High squad after spring tryouts. She'd replaced Megan Carman, who was graduating in June.

Hannah had long, straight black hair that she wore in a single thick braid to her waist, and dark brown eyes that were constantly flashing with excitement.

She performed her back tuck, flipping high off the floor and landing perfectly on both feet. Then, without a pause, she performed a second back tuck just as stylish as the first.

"How was that?" she asked innocently, straightening her T-shirt.

"She thinks she's really great," Ronnie Mitchell whispered bitterly to Corky.

"She *is* great," Corky whispered back. *Hannah's making us all look like clumsy elephants,* Corky thought. She watched Hannah flash Kimmy a smile as she rejoined the line of girls.

Kimmy and Debra Kern were co-captains of the squad, and Hannah had started playing up to them, asking for advice and fishing for compliments.

We all know Hannah is good. Why does she have to show off all the time? Corky wondered. Then she had to admit to herself: *I guess I'm a little jealous.*

At the beginning of the year Corky and her sister, Bobbi, had been the stars—the flashiest, most enthusiastic, and most talented cheerleaders on the squad. But so much had happened since then.

So much horror . . .

Bobbi was dead. And so was Corky's boyfriend, Chip.

Both of them murdered by an ancient evil spirit. An evil spirit that had inhabited two of the cheerleaders. First Jennifer Daly. Poor Jennifer, also dead. Then Kimmy.

Corky had rescued Kimmy from the evil.

Afterward Corky thought she could push away the terrifying memories by throwing herself into her cheerleading. By making herself go on with her life.

But sometimes it was hard. Hard to forget. Hard to go on. And hard to be just one of the squad members.

I'm not even co-captain, Corky thought, glancing unhappily at Debra.

I'm a better cheerleader than Debra, she thought. *Everyone knows it.*

But before spring tryouts Miss Green had explained her decision to Corky. "Corky, I'm afraid you just don't need the pressure of being co-captain," she had said with genuine concern. "I mean, after . . . all that has happened."

All that has happened.

Corky shook her head, tossing her ponytail, trying to shake away her bitter thoughts.

Debra's my friend, she told herself. *There's no point in being jealous of her.*

"Corky—did you hear one word I said?" Miss Green's husky voice broke into Corky's thoughts.

"Yes. Of course," Corky lied, feeling her cheeks grow hot.

"Then let's try the football chant again," Miss Green said, staring hard at Corky.

Kimmy leaped forward, clapping her hands, and turned to the five other girls. "Okay. Ready? On three."

She counted to three, and they began their

chant, their voices rising with each repetition, stomping and clapping in the rhythm they had practiced:

> *"Tigers, let's score!*
> *Six points and more!"*
> *Stomp, stomp.*
> *"Tigers, let's score!*
> *Six points and more!"*
> *Stomp, stomp.*

"Louder!" Kimmy urged, cupping one ear with her hand. "I can't hear you!"

> *"Tigers, let's score!*
> *Six points and more!"*

"Still can't hear you!" Kimmy shouted.

As they repeated the chant even louder, Corky glanced down the line to Hannah. Shouting enthusiastically, her hands in a high *V*, Hannah ended her chant and then spontaneously leaped into a tuck jump, rising high off the floor and slapping her knees at the peak of the jump.

What a show-off! Corky thought. *Hannah knows we don't do a tuck jump here. Miss Green is going to get on her case now.*

Corky turned her eyes expectantly to Miss Green. But instead of seeing anger on the coach's face, Corky was surprised to see approval—even a smile.

"I like that, Hannah," Miss Green declared. "That's a very clever finish." She turned to Kimmy. "What do you say? Let's try it again, and everybody do a tuck jump at the end."

"I don't believe it," Ronnie muttered to Corky, shaking her head.

"I believe it," Corky replied dryly.

"Hannah the Wonder Cheerleader!" Ronnie said under her breath.

Corky laughed and looked down the row of girls. Heather Diehl was leaning close to Debra, whispering something into her ear. Kimmy flashed Corky a meaningful glance, then stepped forward, changing her expression of disapproval to a smile. She began the chant again.

"Tigers, let's score!
Six points and more!"

The girls repeated the chant, getting louder each time. Then they all ended with tuck jumps.

Corky watched Hannah out of the corner of her eye. Her tuck jump was the highest of all. Her

dark eyes sparkled and her face radiated enthusiasm as she landed gracefully, clapping her hands.

"That was *great*!" she exclaimed. "Can we do
it again?"

"What's her problem anyway?" Kimmy asked, twirling her water glass between her hands.

"Her problem is that she's terrific," Corky
replied, squeezing against the wall as Debra slid
beside her into the red vinyl booth. "And we're
jealous."

"I'm not jealous of her," Ronnie said quickly. A
thoughtful look creased her face. "Well, maybe just
her hair." Ronnie had tight copper-colored curls, a
tiny stub of a nose, and a face full of freckles. She
was in ninth grade but looked about twelve. "Hannah has awesome hair."

"She's stuck-up," Kimmy offered. "She's so
stuck-up, she probably knows we're talking about
her right now."

The four girls laughed. Practice had ended at
four thirty, and they had driven to the Corner, a
new coffee shop a few blocks from school that had
quickly become a hangout for Shadyside students.

"Hannah isn't so bad," Debra remarked, her
eyes lowered to the menu. "She's just enthusiastic."

The other three stared at Debra in surprise.

"Since when are *you* her best friend?" Kimmy asked sarcastically.

Debra raised her icy blue eyes from the menu. "I'm not. I just said she isn't so bad. She isn't mean or anything." Debra had straight blond hair cut very short. She was thin, almost too thin, and seldom smiled, an unlikely combination for a cheerleader.

"So we have one vote for Hannah," Kimmy said, making a one in the air with her index finger. "Anyone else?"

Before Corky or Ronnie could cast a vote, the waitress interrupted to take their orders. Kimmy and Ronnie ordered hamburgers and Cokes. Debra ordered a plate of french fries and a chocolate shake. No matter what she ate, she never put on weight.

When Corky ordered a bowl of split-pea soup, the others erupted in disapproval.

"Yuck!" Ronnie exclaimed, sticking a finger down her throat. "I may *hurl!*"

"I happen to *like* pea soup," Corky insisted.

"You're weird," Kimmy told her. "You're definitely weird."

"Is Hannah going out with anyone?" Corky asked, deliberately changing the subject.

"You ever see the guys hanging around her locker after school every day?" Ronnie asked. "It's disgusting. Their tongues hanging out of their mouths. They practically drool on her!"

"Tsk-tsk." Debra clicked her tongue. "Sounds to me like you're jealous, Ronnie."

Ronnie stuck her tongue out at Debra. "So?"

"I think she's going out with Gary Brandt," Kimmy offered. "At least, I saw them together at the mall Saturday night."

"Gary's kinda cool," Ronnie said, fiddling with her silverware.

"Kinda!" Debra agreed with unusual enthusiasm.

"Hey, can you picture Hannah making out with Gary?" Ronnie asked, grinning. She performed a cheer: "Go, Gary, go! Go, Gary, go! Yaaaay!"

Everyone laughed.

"Know what?" Kimmy added. "Every time he kisses her, she probably does a tuck jump!"

More laughter.

"Hey, are you guys ready for next week?" Corky asked, changing the subject again.

"I'm already packed," Ronnie said. "I can't wait. This'll be the best spring break ever!"

"A whole week away from home," Corky said, sighing. "A whole week away from my pesky little brother."

"Maybe we'll meet some guys," Ronnie said, grinning. "You know, college dudes."

"You guys are in for a shock," Debra said dryly. "There'll be no time to hang out and meet guys. Cheerleader camp is *torture*. You work your buns off exercising in the morning, practicing new cheers all afternoon, going to workshop after workshop. Then at night you kill yourself competing against the other squads."

"Bobbi and I went to a cheerleader camp one summer in Missouri before we moved here," Corky recalled. "We worked hard. But we also did some partying."

"The Madison College campus is supposed to be pretty," Ronnie said. "My cousin told me the dorm we're staying in is brand-new. Maybe we'll all room together! It's going to be awesome!"

Everyone agreed except for Debra. "It's hard work and a lot of pressure," she warned. "You have to be enthusiastic and have a smile plastered on your face all day long."

When Ronnie and Debra got up to go to the restroom, Kimmy slid in beside Corky, a troubled expression on her face. "How are you doing?" she asked quietly.

"Okay, I guess." Corky shrugged.

"No. I mean *really*," Kimmy insisted, her dark eyes staring into Corky's, as if searching for something.

"I'm doing a little better," Corky replied, fiddling with her silverware. "I don't think about things as much. I force myself not to think about Bobbi or Chip or—"

"I *can't* stop thinking about it," Kimmy said emotionally, clasping her hands tightly together on the Formica tabletop. "I keep thinking, what if the evil spirit is still around? What if it's still *inside* me?" Her voice cracked as she said this. She swallowed hard.

"Kimmy—" Corky started, resting a hand on Kimmy's arm. "I saw the evil spirit pour out of you. I saw it go down my bathtub drain. It's gone. You're okay now. You don't have to worry—"

"But how do we know it's gone for good? Corky, you got that note. The one that said it can't be drowned. And, Corky, sometimes—sometimes I feel so strange," Kimmy whispered, her eyes watering. She gripped Corky's arm and held it tightly. "Sometimes I—I just don't feel right."

The door to the coffee shop opened, and some guys from the basketball team walked in. One of them, John Mirren, a lanky boy with short brown hair and a goofy grin, waved to Kimmy before sliding into a booth with his pals.

"Kimmy, we just have to pray that the evil spirit is gone for good," Corky said.

"But what if it isn't?" Kimmy demanded again.

Corky shrugged and felt a sudden chill. "It's *got* to be gone," she said, lowering her voice to a whisper. "I can't take any more death. I can't . . ." Her voice trailed off.

Debra and Ronnie returned, giggling and pushing each other playfully. They stopped when they saw the grim expressions on Corky's and Kimmy's faces.

"Hey—what's wrong?" Debra demanded. "You two still talking about Hannah Miles? Give the poor kid a break." She slid in across from Corky and Kimmy. Ronnie lowered herself into the booth beside Debra.

Corky forced a smile. "No, we weren't talking about Hannah."

"Do you know what other schools are going to be at the cheerleader camp?" Ronnie asked Kimmy.

Kimmy shook her head, tossing her crimped black hair. "I think there's going to be a squad from Waynesbridge. And maybe the cheerleaders from Belvedere."

"The ones that do all that rap stuff?" Ronnie asked.

"Wow, they're excellent!" Corky exclaimed. "Who else?"

"I don't know," Kimmy replied. "About a hundred cheerleaders total, I think."

The waitress appeared, carrying their orders on a metal tray. "Who gets the pea soup?" she asked, staring at each girl.

Making disgusted faces, all three of her companions pointed to Corky.

"Give me a break," Corky muttered. "I had a craving for pea soup. What's the big deal?"

The waitress set the food down and left.

"John Mirren waved at you," Debra said to Kimmy, squeezing the ketchup dispenser over her french fries. "I saw him as I was leaving the ladies' room."

"So?" Kimmy asked defensively.

"So maybe he likes you," Debra said. She put down the ketchup and reached for the salt.

Kimmy shrugged.

"He's a funny guy," Ronnie said around a mouthful of hamburger. "He's a riot in science lab. Were you there last week when he spilled the hydrochloric acid?"

"That sounds hilarious," Debra said sarcastically.

"You had to be there," Ronnie said. The tomato slid out of her hamburger. She struggled to push it back in.

Suddenly Corky uttered a loud gasp.

The others looked up from their food. "Corky—what's wrong?" Kimmy cried.

Corky's eyes were wide with surprise. "Look—" She pointed down at her soup bowl.

The other three turned their eyes to the bowl. The thick green soup appeared to be bubbling.

"Why is it doing that?" Ronnie asked, leaning forward to get a better look. "Oh!" she cried out, and pulled her head back as a gob of soup spurted up from the bowl.

"Hey—!" Corky cried in alarm.

The thick soup was tossing in the bowl, rising up against the edges like green ocean waves, bubbling higher and higher.

"Gross!"

"Yuck! It's alive!"

"What's going on?"

Like a green volcano, the soup rose up and spurted high in a thick, bubbling wave. Hot and steamy, more and more of it made a green tidal wave that began to ooze over the table.

"Hey—!"

"Help!"

"Get up, Kimmy! Let's *go*!"

The four girls scrambled from the booth as the steaming green liquid rose like a fountain, to plop onto the table and then ooze quickly onto the floor.

"What's that?"

"What's happening?"

"Where are they going?"

Voices rang out through the small restaurant. Confused kids gaped as Corky and her friends lurched down the narrow aisle, pushed open the front door, and fled to the sidewalk.

"The evil—" Corky managed to say, breathing hard, her heart thudding in her chest.

It's back, she thought.

The evil spirit is back.

Their anguished faces revealed that all four girls realized it.

The ancient evil spirit was back. It had been right at their table.

Was it inhabiting one of them? Possessing one of them?

Corky stared from face to face.

Which one? she wondered. *Which one?*

2

A CORPSE

*C*orky glanced out at the crooked rows of gray stones in the Fear Street cemetery. "I still miss her," she told Kimmy, her voice breaking with emotion. "I still think about Bobbi all the time."

Kimmy shivered despite the heat of the late afternoon. She shielded her eyes against the lowering sun with one hand, her gaze following Corky's up the sloping hill of the old cemetery.

Debra and Ronnie had driven straight home, eager to get away from the restaurant, eager to get away from the evil that had erupted in front of them.

Kimmy had driven Corky home, to her house on Fear Street, but when they'd gotten there, neither had wanted to be alone. They'd gone out for a walk and ended up just a block beyond the house at the cemetery.

The cemetery where Corky's sister, Bobbi, was buried.

Where Corky's boyfriend, Chip, was buried.

Both victims of the evil. The ancient evil that was still alive and refused to die.

"Come on," Kimmy urged, tugging on the sleeve of Corky's T-shirt.

With a sigh Corky turned away from the cemetery and began walking slowly back along the narrow, cracked sidewalk toward her house. "That was so *disgusting!*" she exclaimed, shaking her head. "All that hot green slime bubbling over everything. I'll *never* eat pea soup again!"

Shadows from the old trees overhead danced on them as they made their way slowly past the graveyard. The air suddenly grew cooler.

"The spirit was warning us," Kimmy said softly, "telling us that it's still here." She stopped beside her car and uttered a loud sob. "Oh, Corky—what if it's still inside *me*?"

Corky turned quickly, her features tight with fear, and hugged her friend. "It can't be," she whispered soothingly. "It can't be. It can't be."

"But how do I *know*?" Kimmy asked, and pulled away from Corky. Her round cheeks were pink and glistening with tears. Her crimped black hair was in disarray. Her dark eyes, locked on Corky, revealed her terror.

"I watched it leave you," Corky said, trying to calm her friend. "I watched it pour out."

"I don't remember any of it," Kimmy admitted. "All of those weeks. That whole part of my life. I don't remember a thing. It's as if I wasn't there."

"But now you're *you* again," Corky insisted. "Now you feel like *you*, right?"

Shadows washed over Kimmy's face. Her expression grew thoughtful. "I—I guess," she replied uncertainly. "Sometimes I don't know. Sometimes I feel crazy. Like I want to scream. Like I want to throw myself onto my bed and just cry."

"But you don't, do you?" Corky demanded.

"No, I don't." She grabbed Corky's arm. Kimmy's hand, Corky felt, was ice-cold. "Corky—what if it wants to kill someone else? What if it wants to kill us all?"

"No!" Corky cried with emotion. "No! We'll find it. We'll stop it. Somehow we'll stop it, Kimmy."

Kimmy nodded but didn't reply.

Corky stared hard at her. She wanted to reassure Kimmy. She wanted to convince Kimmy that the evil spirit no longer possessed her.

As Corky studied her friend's face through the

thickening shadows, doubts began to gnaw at her mind.

Would Kimmy know if the evil spirit was still inside her?

If she did know, would she *admit* it?

As Corky stared at her, Kimmy's face began to glow. Her blue eyes lit up as if from some inner light.

Corky shut her eyes.

When she opened them, her friend appeared to be normal again.

"Call you later," Corky said, and took off at a run up to her house.

"Hi, I'm home!"

Corky closed the front door behind her and stepped into the living room. "Anyone home?"

No reply.

The house smelled good. Corky inhaled deeply. She recognized the aroma of a roasting chicken from the kitchen.

Home, sweet home, she thought, feeling a little cheered.

She turned toward the stairway. A pile of neatly folded clothing lay on the bottom step. Laundry day. Corky stooped to pick up the bundle, then made her way up the stairs to deposit it in her room.

Cradling the freshly laundered clothes in both arms, she stepped into her bedroom. Her eyes went to the windows, where the white curtains were fluttering. Then to the bed.

"No!"

The clothing fell from her arms as she began screaming.

Lying in her bed, tucked under the covers, was the hideous bloated head of a corpse.

3

NIGHT VISITORS

*C*orky stood gaping in horror at the lifeless, distorted face. She didn't see the closet door swing open.

"April fool!" Her little brother Sean leaped out and began laughing uproariously.

"Sean!"

He slapped his knees, then dropped to the floor and began rolling on the carpet, uttering high-pitched, hysterical peals of laughter. "April fool! April fool!"

"Sean—you're *not* funny!" Corky cried angrily. She swung her arm, playfully trying to slug him, but he rolled out of her reach, still laughing.

"Stop it!" Corky snapped. "Really, Sean! You're not funny. You're just *dumb*."

Stepping over the clothing she'd dropped, Corky strode over to the bed.

How could I have fallen for this? she asked herself. *The stupid head doesn't even look real. It's all green and lumpy. And it has only one ear!*

"Gotcha!" Sean taunted, getting the most from his victory.

"I only pretended to be scared," Corky told him, turning away from the bed.

"Yeah. Sure," he exclaimed sarcastically. "I gotcha, Corky!" He climbed to his feet, ran to the bed, and grabbed up the head in two hands. "Think fast!" He heaved it at her.

Corky stumbled backward but caught it.

"Cool, huh?" Sean asked, grinning. "I made it myself. Out of papier-mâché. In art class."

Corky turned it in her hands, examining it, a frown on her face. "What kind of grade did you get for this mess?" she demanded. "An F?"

"We don't get grades in art, stupid!" Sean replied.

"Don't call me names," Corky snapped.

"I didn't. I just said you were stupid."

She tossed the disgusting head back to him. "Watch out. I'm going to pay you back," she warned playfully. "It's my turn next."

"Oooh, I'm scared. I'm soooo scared!" he said sarcastically.

She hurried over to him, and before he could escape, she reached up with both hands and messed up his blond hair. He punched her hard in the shoulder.

Then they went down to dinner.

That night, with a full moon casting a wash of shimmering pale blue light into the room, Bobbi floated through Corky's bedroom window.

Corky watched her sister hover over her bed, her long blond hair glowing in the pale light, floating around and above her in slow motion as if underwater.

I'm dreaming, Corky thought.

But Bobbi seemed so real.

So alive.

Bobbi's eyes opened wide. She stared down at Corky, her arms undulating slowly as if she were treading water.

She wore a long loose-fitting gown, like a nightgown, sheer and shimmering in the pale light filtering through the open window.

"Bobbi—what are you doing here?" Corky asked in the dream.

Bobbi's dark lips moved, but no sound came out.

"Bobbi, why do you look so sad?" Corky asked.

Again Bobbi's dark lips moved, dark blue lips reflecting the cold, cold moonlight. Her hair billowed slowly around her head.

Corky sat straight up and reached out toward her sister. But Bobbi floated just out of reach.

"I—I can't touch you," Corky cried, her voice breaking with emotion. She leaned forward, stretching, reaching as high as she could.

Still Bobbi floated inches away.

The blue light swirled around them now, becoming a whirlwind, silent and cold.

"Bobbi—what do you want?" Corky demanded. "Tell me—*please!*"

Bobbi, her lips moving, locked her cold eyes on Corky. She seemed intent on telling Corky something. But Corky couldn't hear her, couldn't read her lips, couldn't understand.

"Why are you here?" Corky pleaded. "What are you trying to tell me?"

Bobbi floated lower toward her sister. The blue light continued to swirl around them, closing them in, shutting out the rest of the room.

"You look so sad, Bobbi. So sad," Corky said, feeling her breath catch, ready to cry. "Tell me. Please. Tell me why you're here."

Without warning, without displaying any emotion, Bobbi reached up and grabbed her own hair.

She tugged hard. The hair lifted up, removing the top of Bobbi's head with it.

"Oh—*no*—!" Corky shrieked in surprise.

Bobbi remained silent, holding the top of her head by the hair, gesturing with her other hand.

"Bobbi, what are you *doing*?" Corky cried, frozen in place, too horrified to watch, too curious to turn away.

Bobbi bent down and floated even closer.

Closer.

Corky peered up into her sister's open skull.

"What is it, Bobbi? What are you showing me?"

Corky stared inside Bobbi's head. And gasped.

In the darkness the inside of Bobbi's skull appeared to pulsate and throb. But Corky's eyes adjusted quickly to the pale light, and she saw what was moving in there.

Thousands of squirming, crawling cockroaches.

Packed into Bobbi's head like coffee in a can. Their slender legs scrabbled over each other as their bodies bumped and slid in a horrifying silent dance.

"Ohhh."

Corky woke up, choking.

She struggled to catch her breath.

"Bobbi—?"

Her sister had vanished.

The blue light was gone, replaced by ordinary white moonlight.

Her nightshirt, Corky realized, was drenched with sweat. Her whole body trembled, chilled and hot at the same time.

"What's going on?" she wondered aloud, blinking hard, trying to clear her head. "I haven't dreamed about Bobbi in weeks and weeks."

She waited for the trembling to stop. Then, deciding to get a glass of water, she lowered her feet to the floor.

And stepped on something warm. Something crackly. Something moving.

"Oh!"

Corky jumped.

Something crunched under her foot.

Something crawled over her toes.

She stared down.

"No! Oh, no!"

Cockroaches.

Thousands of silent cockroaches, scuttling over the floor, over one another. Climbing over her feet. Starting up her legs.

Their bodies glistened dark blue in the moonlight as they swam silently over the floor. An undulating, bobbing, throbbing carpet of cockroaches.

4

BURNED

"Help me!"

Kicking furiously, trying to force the prickly cockroaches off her feet, Corky stumbled to her door.

"Mom! Dad! *Please!*"

With each step she could feel the cockroaches crackle and squash beneath her bare feet. Nausea swept over her.

"Help me!"

Bending to brush the glistening insects off her legs, she burst out of her room into the dark coolness of the narrow hallway.

"Mom! Dad!"

"Hey—what's going on?" Mr. Corcoran appeared down the hall in his bedroom doorway, wearing only pajama bottoms, rubbing his eyes, looking like a bear coming out of hibernation.

"Dad—!"

"Corky, what's the big idea?" He stepped into the hall, stretching his arms above his head with a loud groan.

"Cockroaches!" Corky managed to blurt out, still feeling sick, still feeling the prickly legs crawling up her legs.

"Huh?"

"Cockroaches!"

"Corky, I hope you didn't wake me up because there's a cockroach in your room," he warned. "This is an old house, and old houses sometimes—"

"What's all the racket?" Mrs. Corcoran interrupted, appearing suddenly behind her husband, brushing her blond hair back off her forehead. "Corky, what on earth—?" She ran to Corky and threw her arms around her. "You're shaking all over. What *is* it, dear?"

Corky tried to answer, but her voice caught in her throat.

She pulled away from her mother and grabbed her hand. Then she tugged her toward her bedroom.

"Cockroaches, Mom," she finally managed to say.

Her father followed, shaking his head. "That's all she keeps saying. 'Cockroaches.'"

They followed Corky to her room. "Look," Corky said. She stepped into the doorway and clicked on the ceiling light. She took a deep breath, trying to hold down the waves of nausea, and pointed to the floor. "Just look."

All three of them peered down at the wine-colored bedroom carpet.

"I don't see anything," Mr. Corcoran said quietly.

Mrs. Corcoran stared hard at Corky, concern troubling her face.

The cockroaches were gone.

"Hey, you guys woke me up!" Sean's angry voice echoed in the hallway.

They turned to see his blond head poke into Corky's room.

"Sean—did you play some kind of practical joke on your sister?" Mr. Corcoran demanded sternly.

Sean's face filled with genuine innocence. "Who—me?"

"Wow! We're here!" Corky exclaimed, staring out the bus window as it bumped through the small campus of Madison College, where the cheerleader camp was being held. The ride from Shadyside had been nearly an hour, and the girls had laughed and joked and sung the whole way.

"It's perfect!" Hannah declared excitedly. "All the brick buildings covered with ivy. Like a movie set!"

"But where *is* everyone?" Debra asked, leaning over Corky to see out the window.

"Spring break," Kimmy told her from the front seat.

"You mean—*no guys!*" Ronnie cried.

She looked so devastated, everyone laughed.

Simmons, the young blond bus driver, showed them the large domed gymnasium, then drove to a tall brick dormitory about a block from it. As the bus pulled to a stop, a young woman, a cheerleader camp employee, hurried out to greet the girls and give them their room numbers.

A few minutes later Corky, Kimmy, and Debra found themselves in their assigned room.

A large picture window overlooked the campus. The walls were lime green, the low ceiling bright yellow. Two small desks were pushed back-to-back in the middle of the room. A third desk stood against one wall between two low dressers. Over one of the dressers, someone had tacked up a poster of Harry Styles.

"I claim this bed," Debra declared, tossing her backpack onto the narrow bed in front of the window. "I have to have a window."

Corky spotted the bunk bed on the opposite

wall. "Do you want the top or bottom?" she asked Kimmy.

Kimmy shrugged. "Top, I guess."

"The campus is so much bigger than I thought," Debra said, staring out the window at the green quadrangle, a grassy square surrounded by brick classroom buildings and other dorms. "What a shame there's no one here."

"Just cheerleaders," Kimmy said. "Dozens and dozens of cheerleaders." She opened her suitcase and began to unpack, unfolding tops and sweat suits and balled-up socks, and jamming them into the top drawer of the low maple dresser beside the bunk bed.

Corky laughed and pointed. "You sure you brought enough socks?"

Kimmy's cheeks turned pink. She brushed a strand of hair off her forehead. "My feet sweat a lot." She glanced up at Corky. "Some of us don't like to wear the same socks for a month!" she teased. She pulled a worn brown teddy bear from the suitcase and tossed it up onto the top bunk.

"Oh wow," Debra exclaimed from across the room. "Kimmy, don't tell me you still sleep with your teddy bear!"

"Even my little brother gave up his teddy bear," Corky teased. "But your bear is really cute!"

Kimmy's cheeks burned even redder. "I don't need it to sleep with. I just . . . take it places. It's sort of a good-luck thing."

"I guess we can use some good luck," Debra said wistfully.

Her comment brought a chill to the room.

Everyone became silent. Debra, her arms crossed over her chest, continued to stare out the window, her suitcase still unopened.

Corky knew they were all thinking about the evil spirit. Had it followed them to camp? Was it in the room with them now, hiding inside one of them?

Without realizing it, Corky stared hard at Kimmy. Kimmy seemed so nervous. She'd been so tense on the bus that had brought them from Shadyside that she hadn't joined in on the songs or any of the kidding around.

Sitting next to Debra at the back of the small bus, Corky had confided her dream. She'd told Debra about Bobbi pulling off the top of her head, about the cockroaches inside and the cockroaches she thought she'd seen on her bedroom floor.

She knew that Debra wouldn't laugh at her. Ever since the evil spirit had been revealed the previous fall, Debra had become obsessed with the occult, with ancient superstitions and spirits.

She had begun wearing a crystal on a pendant around her neck, a crystal that she believed had special powers. And she read book after book on spiritualism, the occult, and the dark arts.

"I've been studying dreams," Debra had replied seriously, her icy blue eyes staring into Corky's.

"What could that awful dream mean?" Corky demanded. "I mean, it was just so *gross*."

"Bobbi was trying to tell you something," Debra replied in a low voice. "She was trying to show you something."

"Show me what? Cockroaches?" Corky asked. "Why would she want to show me cockroaches?"

Debra chewed thoughtfully on her lower lip. She shook her head. "I don't know, Corky. I don't get it."

Corky wanted to forget the dream and enjoy the cheerleading camp. But the dream was hard to shake. It had followed her to the campus.

Had the evil spirit followed her too?

All three girls were shaken from their somber thoughts by a loud knock on their door.

Debra reached the door first and pulled it open. "Hannah! Hi!" she exclaimed.

Wearing a green T-shirt over black leggings, Hannah marched past Debra into the center of the room. She was lugging two large leather suitcases, one in each hand. She plopped them down and sighed. "Ugh."

"What's going on?" Debra demanded, closing the door and following Hannah back to the center of the room. Kimmy and Corky both stared at Hannah curiously.

"Can I room with you guys?" Hannah asked, reaching back to adjust her long braid behind her shoulders.

"Huh?" Corky cried in surprise.

"There's no room for me with Ronnie and Heather," Hannah declared. "They both filled up the dressers before I could start to unpack. And look at all the stuff I brought." She gestured to the two bulging suitcases.

"Your room is bigger," Hannah continued, gazing around. "There's nowhere for me to put my stuff in the other room."

"But, Hannah—" Kimmy started to object.

"And get this," Hannah said, ignoring Kimmy. "Ronnie took the top bunk even though I told her I can't sleep on the bottom. I mean, it just creeps me out to have someone sleeping above me. You know? But she was so stubborn—she refused to move down."

"What about the other bed?" Kimmy suggested. "There's a third bed, right?"

"Yeah. Sure," Hannah replied heatedly. "But Heather claimed it. She says she has to be by the window or else she can't breathe."

"I can understand that," Debra said, glancing at the bed she had staked out by the window.

"So can I room with you guys?" Hannah asked.

"But there are only three beds," Corky protested.

"Yeah. These rooms are designed for three," Kimmy added, gesturing around. "Three desks, three dressers, three beds."

Hannah sighed again and rolled her eyes unhappily, her face drooping into a pout. "Well, would one of you trade with me?" she asked reluctantly.

"I'm all unpacked," Kimmy protested. She clicked her empty suitcase shut.

"Come on," Hannah urged in a tiny voice. "Somebody trade places with me. You've *got* to. I'm just too claustrophobic in the other room. I'll freak. I'll totally freak. Really."

She glanced from Debra to Corky, then back to Debra.

"Well . . . okay," Debra finally relented. "If it means that much to you, Hannah—"

"Yes, it does! Thanks, Debra!" Hannah cried. And to Debra's surprise, Hannah rushed over, threw her arms around Debra, and hugged her. "You're a real pal!" she squealed.

"No big deal," Debra said, casting an uncomfortable glance at Corky. She started to collect her things.

Hannah dragged her suitcases over to Debra's bed by the window.

"Hey, we're going to be late," Kimmy cried, glancing at her watch. "We're supposed to be in the gym at two o'clock."

"See you down there," Debra called. The door slammed behind her.

"Where's the gym?" Hannah asked, opening one of her suitcases and starting to unpack.

"It's that big gray building with the dome. Remember? We passed it on our way here," Corky told her.

"I'll never get unpacked in time," Hannah said. She turned to Kimmy. "Which dresser is mine?"

Kimmy pointed. "You've got to hurry. We get points taken off for being late."

"Even for practice? That isn't fair," Hannah protested. "Do we have to be in our uniforms?"

"Not for practice," Kimmy said. "Only at night for the competitions."

"We're going to win every night!" Hannah declared. "I just know it."

"That's the spirit," Corky said dryly.

"Corky, would you do me a big favor?" Hannah asked, unfolding a pair of jeans from the suitcase, the third pair she'd pulled out.

Why did she bring so many jeans? Corky wondered. *Why did she bring two suitcases for a one-week stay?*

"Sure. What?" she asked Hannah.

"Would you run me a hot bath?"

The request caught Corky by surprise. "What did you say?"

"Would you run a tub for me? I feel so grimy after that long bus ride. But I've got to get this stuff unpacked. And I don't want to be late. Please?"

Corky glanced at Kimmy. Kimmy made a funny face, crossing her eyes.

"Yeah, sure," Corky told Hannah. She started toward the bathroom in the corner.

"You're a pal," Hannah said, pulling two pairs of denim cutoffs from her suitcase.

I don't believe her nerve, Corky thought angrily. *She really thinks she's a princess or something.*

Corky pushed back the white plastic shower curtain, then bent down to turn on the water.

First Hannah complains that the other room is too small for her, Corky thought, getting even more annoyed. *Then she orders me around like I'm a servant. It's really* unbelievable!

She put her hand under the faucet to gauge the water temperature, then turned the knob to make it a little warmer.

"Okay, it's going," she told Hannah, returning to the main room.

"Thanks," Hannah muttered distractedly. She was arranging her makeup and other cosmetics on a dresser top.

"We'd better hurry," Corky said to Kimmy. She walked to the mirror and pulled a hairbrush back through her straight blond hair. "You ready?"

"In a sec," Kimmy replied. She disappeared into the bathroom, closing the door behind her.

"I guess we'll meet you in the gym," Corky told Hannah.

"Yeah, fine," Hannah said, starting to unpack her second suitcase.

Kimmy emerged from the bathroom. "Don't take too long," she warned Hannah.

Corky followed Kimmy out to the hallway. She closed the door behind her. She heard the latch click as Hannah locked the door from the inside. "Do you *believe* Hannah?" Corky asked as they started to walk toward the elevator.

Kimmy stopped short. "Oh no! I forgot the

pom-poms. Miss Green said she was counting on me to remember them."

They both turned and made their way back to the room. "That was a close call," Kimmy said.

Kimmy reached for the doorknob.

But her hand stopped in midair as a scream rang out.

Both girls froze.

Another high-pitched shriek.

It was Hannah, Corky realized at once.

Hannah inside the room. Screaming in horror.

5

"I COULD JUST MURDER HER"

Corky fumbled in her bag for the room key. Kimmy pounded furiously on the door. "Hannah—what's wrong? Hannah!"

Her hand trembling, Corky finally jammed the key into the lock and pushed the door open.

As she and Kimmy hurtled into the room, Hannah came running out of the bathroom, a large maroon bath towel wrapped around her. Dripping water, she pointed an accusing finger at Corky, her eyes wide with anger.

"How *could* you?" she shrieked in a shrill, high-pitched voice. "How *could* you?"

"Hannah—what happened?" Corky demanded, gaping at her, bewildered.

"What happened?" Kimmy repeated right behind Corky.

"How *could* you? How *could* you?" Hannah said frantically. "You tried to *scald* me!"

"Huh?" Both Corky and Kimmy cried in unison.

"The water. It was so hot! I didn't know. I stepped right in. I trusted you."

"But, Hannah—" Corky started.

"Look at my legs!" Hannah screamed. "Look!" She lifted the towel to give the other two girls a better view. "You tried to *scald* me!" she repeated.

Corky lowered her eyes to Hannah's legs. Still dripping wet, both legs were bright red from the feet nearly up to the knees.

"But that's impossible. I *tested* the water," Corky protested.

Hannah glared furiously at Corky. "That's just so *mean*! I—I—I don't—" she sputtered.

"The water probably started coming in hotter after Corky left," Kimmy said, coming to Corky's defense.

"Really. I tested it. I did," Corky insisted, staring at the scarlet flesh of Hannah's legs.

Hannah pulled the towel around herself more tightly. She didn't reply.

"I wouldn't deliberately hurt you," Corky muttered.

"Should we get you to a nurse or something?" Kimmy asked.

Hannah shook her head. "They're starting to feel better. I was just shocked, that's all."

"I'm really sorry," Corky said, "but I know the water was okay when I left it."

Hannah shrugged. "Okay. Guess I overreacted."

"You sure you're okay?" Kimmy asked.

"Yeah. Fine," Hannah replied. She took a few steps into the center of the room. "I guess I'm okay. Sorry I freaked like that." She turned and disappeared back into the bathroom.

"See you at the gym!" Kimmy called. "We'll explain to Miss Green why you're late."

Corky's mouth dropped open in a silent gasp as her sister suddenly flashed into her mind. Bobbi had died because of scalding-hot shower water, Corky remembered.

"I really did test the water," Corky said, more to herself than to Kimmy.

Kimmy picked up the carton of pom-poms. Then they headed out the door.

"Weird," Kimmy muttered, shaking her head as they walked quickly down the long corridor to the elevators. "Weird."

It sure is, Corky thought.

And then she remembered that Kimmy had gone into the bathroom while the water was still running.

That's right, Corky told herself. *Just before we*

left the room, Kimmy went into the bathroom.

She glanced at Kimmy as the elevators came into view. Kimmy stared straight ahead, her face expressionless, revealing no emotion.

Did Kimmy go into the bathroom and turn the hot water up? Corky wondered.

Did Kimmy try to scald Hannah?

> *"Hey, America—the time is here!*
> *Shadyside, stand up and cheer!*
> *Here we come. We want the world*
>   *to know*
> *Shadyside is the HIT OF THE*
>   *SHOW!"*

Cheering loudly, the six Shadyside cheerleaders ended the routine with synchronized back handsprings.

"Ow!" Ronnie cried out, losing her balance and landing hard on her arm.

Miss Green blew her whistle as the other squad members clustered around Ronnie. Kimmy and Debra helped her to her feet.

"I'm okay," Ronnie insisted. "Really. I'm all right." She tested her shoulder, rotating her arm like an airplane propeller. "It feels okay."

"Then let's try the routine again," Miss Green

said brusquely. She glanced at the sideline, where one of the camp officials was scribbling notes rapidly on her clipboard.

Miss Green blew her whistle again.

Whistles were blowing all over the enormous gym. Cheerleading squads from fifteen different schools were shouting, dancing, leaping. Sneakers squeaked and thudded on the polished floor. Chants echoed off the tile walls.

What an amazing sound, Corky thought. *I'll bet it doesn't sound like this anywhere else in the world!*

A few feet away the cheerleaders of the Redwood Bulldogs were practicing roll-ups into partner pyramids. Their blue-and-gold uniforms, which they wore even though uniforms weren't required, looked fresh and new.

"Look at that girl. Their captain," Corky said to Kimmy, practically having to shout into Kimmy's ear to be heard. She pointed to a cheerleader with beautiful long red hair. "She's really *awesome*!"

"I *know* her!" Kimmy exclaimed. "She used to go to my Sunday school. Her name is Blair O'Connell. She *is* awesome—and she knows it!"

They watched Blair perform an astounding cartwheel, then flip herself effortlessly up onto her partner's shoulders, her red hair flying like a victory pennant.

"Wow," Corky said, shaking her head in admiration. "She is really outstanding!"

"We can beat her!" Hannah cried, suddenly appearing behind Corky and Kimmy. "We'll just have to work harder, that's all! Come on, everybody!" she shouted, clapping her hands. "Let's show the Bulldogs they're not so hot!"

Hannah acts as if she's *the captain,* Corky thought scornfully. But Corky found herself caught up in Hannah's enthusiasm anyway. Clearing her mind of all unpleasant thoughts, Corky threw herself wholeheartedly into the routine.

"Hey, America — the time is here!
Shadyside, stand up and cheer!"

As the Shadyside squad practiced its cheer, Corky saw Blair O'Connell watching, her arms crossed over her chest, a sour look on her face. As the routine ended and Ronnie again mistimed her backflip and fell, Corky saw Blair laugh gleefully as she pointed Ronnie out to one of the other Bulldog cheerleaders.

Kimmy stepped up beside Corky. She had obviously been watching Blair too. "I never liked her," she said in Corky's ear. "She's so stuck-up, she's disgusting."

"But what a figure!" Corky exclaimed. "She's so tall and—and—look at that tiny waist and—"

Miss Green's angry voice interrupted their conversation. "We're not here as spectators," she scolded. "Let's start again. Ronnie, are you going to land on your feet or your butt this time?"

Ronnie blushed. Her upper lip glistened with perspiration. She tugged at her curly copper-colored hair and uttered a cry of exasperation. "I'll get it this time," she promised.

"Let's go! Let's go! Let's go!" Hannah cried, jumping up and down and clapping.

She's the cheerleader's cheerleader, Corky thought sarcastically. Her eyes went from Hannah to Blair. *Two of a kind,* Corky thought bitterly. *Except that Blair is more talented.*

Corky lined up with the others to begin the routine again. The gym grew hotter, the air thick and damp. The shouting voices, the cheers, the singing and clapping—it was all starting to make Corky's head spin. She closed her eyes for a brief moment, but the bright lights didn't fade. The echoing sounds only grew louder. She reopened her eyes and began the routine.

It went better. At least, Ronnie didn't fall.

Again Corky watched Blair O'Connell in her sleek blue-and-gold uniform, an expression of superior amusement on her beautiful face.

They did the routine one more time. Then Miss Green suggested they work on handsprings.

As they practiced, camp officials circulated and studied each team carefully, jotting down notes, having brief conversations with coaches and advisors.

Corky performed a handspring, then moved into a spread-eagle jump.

Pretty good, she thought, breathing hard. *This is quite a workout, but I'm really getting into it.*

She wiped the perspiration off her forehead with the back of her hand.

"Corky, can I give you a little advice?" Hannah said loudly, stepping up in front of her. It wasn't a question, Corky realized immediately. "You need to get more lift on your spread-eagle jump," Hannah instructed. "You're still a little too low."

"Huh?" Corky wasn't sure she was hearing correctly. Was Hannah, a freshman, really giving her advice in front of the entire squad?

"If you bring your feet in closer together, you can control your jump better," Hannah continued. "Watch. I'll show you."

She proceeded to perform a spread eagle, jumping high off the floor, her eyes on Corky the

whole time, her long braid flying. She landed gracefully, a pleased smile on her face. "See?"

"Thanks, Hannah," Corky said without enthusiasm. "I'll try it." She turned quickly and walked
over to Debra and Heather.

What unbelievable nerve, Corky thought
angrily.

*I don't mind taking advice from the other girls.
But Hannah really thinks she's queen of the world!*

*She's only a freshman, after all. Bobbi and I
were all-state in Missouri. I think I can get along
without advice from Hannah.*

"Hey—lighten up!" Debra called, seeing
Corky's angry, tight-lipped expression. "People
are watching," she teased. "Ten points off if you
lose your smile for a second."

Corky plastered a big, phony smile onto her
face for Debra's benefit.

"That's better," Debra said, laughing. She was
fingering the crystal she always wore around her
neck. She flashed Corky a thumbs-up sign, then
returned to working on partner pyramids with
Heather.

Corky hadn't noticed that Kimmy had come
up behind her. She jumped, startled, when Kimmy
started to talk. "Someone has to take Hannah down
a peg or two," Kimmy said with surprising bitterness.

"Huh?" Corky hadn't realized that Kimmy had observed her jumping lesson from Hannah.

"She's the pits," Kimmy said through gritted teeth. "Sometimes I could just murder her—couldn't you?"

The way Kimmy said those words gave Corky a cold chill.

Sometimes I could just murder her.

Corky shrugged. "Hannah is Hannah, I guess."

Kimmy stared at her with no expression.

Whistles blew. The cheerleaders were being called to a meeting to hear about the evening competition. There would be minor competitions each evening. On the fifth and final night a major competition would be held. Each squad would perform its most complicated routine, and awards would be presented to the winners.

After the meeting Corky walked alone back across the quadrangle to the dorm. Her legs ached. She was hot and sweaty. *What a workout!* she thought.

Well, Debra had warned her that cheerleader camp was mostly hard work.

A cool late-afternoon breeze did refresh her as she made her way across the nearly deserted campus. A few college students circled the quadrangle on bikes.

She pulled open the glass doors to the dorm and stepped inside. Her sneakers squeaked on the marble floor as she crossed to the elevators. The lobby was deserted and quiet, but somewhere far down the hall, country music was playing.

Thinking about taking a long, cool shower, Corky stepped onto the elevator and rode up to the sixth floor. She stepped out and began walking along the dark carpet to her room.

To her surprise, her sneakers stuck to the carpet.

"What's happening?" she cried out loud, looking down.

The carpet appeared to be moving, undulating like waves.

"Hey!" Corky shouted.

She blinked. Once. Twice. Waited for her eyes to adjust to the dark hallway, to stop playing tricks on her.

She tried to walk, but the floor was sticky and wet. The carpet still moved in waves, thick and black, rolling over her sneakers.

"No!" Corky screamed. *Can anyone hear me?* she thought. *Is anyone up here?*

The entire carpet had become a dark, thick sea, rolling and tossing, swaying back and forth.

"I can't walk!" Corky screamed. "Is anyone here? Can anyone help me?"

Like bubbling tar, the thick liquid rose up and over her sneakers, over her ankles.

It's pulling me down, Corky realized.

I can't move.

It's so sticky.

It's pulling me down.

"Help!"

6

FIRST CHEERS, THEN SCREAMS

It's so sticky!" Corky cried again. "I—I can't move!"

She looked up to see Debra staring down at her, her normally calm features twisted in alarm.

"Corky—what *is* it? What are you *doing* down there?" Debra dropped to the floor and wrapped an arm around Corky's trembling shoulders.

"It's so sticky," Corky repeated, still dazed.

"Huh? What's sticky? What's happening?" Debra demanded frantically.

Corky realized she was on her knees. On the dark carpet.

The still carpet.

It was no longer rolling and tossing.

Confused, she rubbed the dry carpet with her palms. "Debra?"

Debra's eyes were locked on Corky. She kept her arm protectively around Corky's shoulders. "Why are you down here, Corky? Did you fall?"

Corky raised herself back up onto her knees. She shook her head. "No. I didn't fall. It pulled me down."

Debra's mouth dropped open. "Huh?"

"The carpet. It started to roll back and forth; then it turned into a sticky liquid. And tried to pull me down." Corky stared intently at Debra, trying to read Debra's expression, trying to see if Debra believed her.

Debra shut her eyes. "The evil spirit," she said, lowering her voice.

"Yes," Corky quickly agreed.

"It's here," Debra whispered. "I can feel it." Letting go of Corky, she moved her hand to the crystal that hung around her neck. With her eyes still closed, she twirled the crystal rapidly in one hand, then squeezed it tightly.

She opened her eyes and climbed to her feet, reaching down with both hands to Corky. "Here. Let me help you up," she said softly. "Let's get you back to your room."

"Who's doing this to me?" Corky asked,

unsteadily resting one hand against the wall. "Who is *torturing* me?"

Debra shook her head, her expression tight-lipped and thoughtful. "I don't know, Corky," she replied, guiding Corky to her room. "I really don't know."

The Bulldogs won the evening competition easily. They performed an endless rap routine that wowed the judges. Blair O'Connell, with her beautiful red hair floating behind her, appeared to defy the laws of gravity with her jumps and flips.

The other cheerleaders, dozens of them, huddled with their squads, waiting to compete and gaping in obvious admiration as Blair confidently performed her flashy solo part of the routine.

"What a show-off," Kimmy whispered to Corky as Blair and the Bulldogs ended their rap routine with a series of synchronized flips. "Blair's not really graceful. She's just an acrobat."

Corky laughed. "The judges look impressed. Maybe they *like* acrobats."

Kimmy scowled and walked away.

"We can beat them! We're the best!" Hannah was shouting, clapping excitedly. "Tigers rule!" she cried.

The other girls picked up the rhythm, clapping with Hannah. "Tigers rule! Tigers rule!"

But when it came time for the Shadyside squad to perform, everyone was just a bit off. When both Ronnie and Heather mistimed their final tuck jumps, Corky realized that it wasn't their night. The Tiger cheerleaders trotted off clapping, to join the audience to watch the next squad perform.

"We'll get 'em tomorrow night!" Hannah shouted enthusiastically. "We're psyched now! We're *psyched*!"

"Yeah! We'll get 'em!" Kimmy echoed, but she couldn't muster up the same enthusiasm as Hannah.

After Blair and the Bulldog squad received their first-place award, the red-and-white-jacketed judge raised her hand for quiet. The roar of excited voices in the enormous gym became a hushed rumble.

"On the final night we will award a spirit stick to each member of the winning squad. The sticks will be painted with your school colors, and can be used to help inspire spirit at pep rallies," she announced, straining to be heard. "But on every other night we'll award a red spirit ribbon to the most spirited cheerleader on each squad. There's so much spirit in this gym tonight, it's *unbelievable*!" she cried, holding up the red ribbons in both hands.

"I want you all to give yourselves a cheer and a round of applause!"

The gym practically shook from the exploding voices, stomping feet, and clapping hands.

When the cheering stopped, the judge called out the name of the red-ribbon winner on each squad. Blair O'Connell accepted hers casually with a broad smile and wave at her cheering teammates.

The winner on the Tigers was Hannah. She squealed with delight when her name was called, and drew a cry of surprise as she performed a cartwheel on her way to collect her prize.

Corky glanced at Kimmy, who rolled her eyes to the ceiling. Then Corky noticed that Debra was smiling broadly and clapping heartily for Hannah.

When Hannah came bounding back, holding the ribbon triumphantly over her head, Debra rushed forward and gave her a hug. The two girls walked off together, heading toward the exit.

Wow, Corky thought, following them with her eyes as everyone began filing out noisily. *Since when is Debra such pals with Hannah?*

Corky realized she was feeling a little jealous. Debra was *her* friend, after all.

"Corky—catch you later!" Corky looked up to see Kimmy calling to her, shouting over the excited voices of the crowd. Kimmy said something else, but the words were completely drowned out.

Corky slowly made her way through the crowd. As she passed Blair O'Connell, she overheard Blair boasting to another Bulldog cheerleader, a tall, pretty girl with a dramatically short hairdo. "Not much competition this year," Blair said snootily.

"It was better last year," her companion replied.

"Everyone's just so tacky," Blair complained.

She's deliberately talking loudly so people will overhear her, Corky realized, frowning.

"Did you *believe* that nursery-rhyme routine?" Blair exclaimed, hooting and shaking her head. "What *is* this? Kindergarten or something?"

"There aren't even any cool guys around," the other cheerleader complained.

They drifted out of Corky's hearing.

They really are snobs, Corky thought. *Especially Blair. She's good, but I've never seen anyone so stuck-up.*

I'd like to beat them one night, Corky told herself, feeling her anger rise. *Just once. I'd like to show Blair O'Connell what real cheerleading is like.*

Just once. I'd like to wipe that snobby, superior smirk off her perfectly perfect face.

Maybe tomorrow . . .

Later that night, tossing in her unfamiliar

dorm bed, Corky again dreamed about Bobbi.

Bobbi floated in through the window, her long, nearly transparent nightgown fluttering around her, her blond hair flying out around her face, circling her head in light.

"Bobbi!" Corky exclaimed in the dream.

As before, she reached out to her sister with both hands. And again felt the frustration, the heart-breaking frustration, of not being able to touch her.

"Bobbi, why are you here?"

Her dead sister hovered above Corky's bed, gazing down at her mournfully.

"Please, Bobbi—can't you tell me? Can't you tell me why you're here?"

Again Bobbi spoke, and again no sound came out of her mouth.

"Bobbi, you look so sad, so troubled. Tell me what's bringing you here," Corky pleaded.

Bobbi descended until she was just inches above the bed, staring down at Corky with mournful eyes.

And then, as in the previous dream, she grabbed her hair with both hands and tugged hard.

Her scalp pulled off, taking with it the top of her skull. Holding her scalp to one side, she leaned down so that Corky could see inside her head.

"No!" Corky didn't want to look. "Bobbi, please—don't make me—!"

She shut her eyes tightly, but couldn't keep them shut.

Corky couldn't help herself. She had to see what was inside.

Peering into Bobbi's open skull, she saw snakes, brown snakes, slithering over one another, hissing and rattling, snapping their venomous jaws.

Snakes rose up, lifting their slender triangular heads out over Bobbi's skull. Snakes poured down past Bobbi's ears, slid down the back of her neck.

Hissing louder and louder, the snakes stared down menacingly at Corky with their flat black eyes.

Corky snapped awake in the heavy gray light of morning.

She bolted upright in bed, her heart pounding like a drum.

She heard hideous screams.

It's me. I'm screaming. Because of my dream, she thought.

I'm screaming and I can't stop.

Blinking hard to gaze through the dim light at the unfamiliar room, it took Corky several seconds to realize that she *wasn't* the one screaming.

The horrifying cries were coming from Hannah.

7

A BAD CUT

Hannah—what *is* it?"

Hannah's high-pitched shrieks continued.

Kimmy slid down from her top bunk just before Corky leaped out of her bunk. In the pale morning light washing in around the curtains, Corky could see Hannah sitting on her bed, her head bent forward.

As Corky moved closer, still half in her dream about Bobbi, almost expecting the floor to writhe with snakes, she saw that Hannah had both hands at the nape of her neck.

"Hannah! What's *wrong*?"

Hannah screamed again, staring at something on her lap.

"Are you dreaming?" Kimmy demanded.

"My hair!" Hannah screamed.

"Huh?"

"My hair! My hair! My hair!"

Corky reached up and turned on a bedside lamp.

She and Kimmy both cried out when they saw what was in Hannah's lap.

It was her braid.

"My hair! My hair! My hair!" Hannah shrieked, covering her face with her hands.

"But how—?" Corky started.

Kimmy stared down at the braid in open-mouthed horror. "It—it was cut!" she stammered.

Hannah sobbed loudly into her hands.

"But who *did* it?" Corky cried, staring at Kimmy. "You and I are the only ones who . . ." Her voice trailed off. She couldn't finish her sentence.

Suddenly Hannah grabbed the braid in one hand and thrust it up accusingly at Corky and Kimmy. "One of you did this to me," the girl said in a low, trembly voice. Tears ran down her cheeks as her entire body convulsed in an angry tremor.

She recovered quickly and jumped to her feet, holding the braid high, forcing Corky and Kimmy to step back. "Who?" she demanded, her horror giving way to fury. "Who? Who? Who?" she repeated, pushing the braid first in Corky's face, then in Kimmy's.

"No!" Corky cried. "I didn't. I *wouldn't!*"

"I didn't!" Kimmy also protested, glancing at Corky.

"Who?" Hannah repeated, sobbing. "Who? Who? It was one of you. It *had* to be. First the scalding bath. Now *this!*"

"We didn't do it," Corky exclaimed. "You've got to believe us, Hannah." She reached for Hannah's shoulders, intending to comfort her. But Hannah recoiled violently, her face twisted in anger.

"Why would we do such a horrible thing?" Kimmy asked. "Why?"

"Because you're jealous of me," Hannah snapped back. She held up the black braid. It looked like a small dead animal in her hand.

"Hannah—"

"You're both jealous of me," Hannah said, lowering her voice. She wiped the tears from her cheeks with her free hand. "You know I'm the best cheerleader at Shadyside. You know you can't compare."

"Hey, that's not fair!" Kimmy snapped. "We're all good."

Corky could see Kimmy's anger building, her muscles tightening, her hands balling into fists at her sides.

"You're new on the squad, Hannah," Kimmy said heatedly. Her cheeks were bright red, even in the morning light. Her chest heaved and she was breathing hard. "You don't know us very well. And I'm sorry to say it, because I know you're really upset, but you don't know as much as you think you do."

Hannah's eyes flared. "I know *one* thing for sure," she said through gritted teeth, lowering her voice. "I know one thing. You want me out—you want me off the squad. So you think you can scare me—"

"That's not true!" Corky insisted shrilly.

"Well, I'm not quitting," Hannah declared, ignoring Kimmy and Corky. "No way. No way you're frightening *me* off the squad."

She stormed to the dresser and deposited the dark braid carefully on the dresser top. "I'm staying on the squad even if I have to cheer bald!" Furiously she pulled out the top drawer and began rummaging in it.

"Hannah—wait," Kimmy pleaded. "I didn't mean to lose my temper. What are you going to do?"

Hannah tossed a pair of denim cutoffs onto the bed and continued rummaging. "I'm going to get dressed," she answered, her voice tight. She glanced at her wristwatch, which lay beside the sad-looking braid on the dresser top. "It's almost breakfast time. I'm going to get dressed. Then I'm going to show Miss Green what you did to me."

"But, Hannah—" Corky started.

"Shut up!" Hannah screamed. "Both of you—just *shut up!*" She uttered another loud sob and pulled off the oversize T-shirt she'd been sleeping in.

Corky started to say something, but a sharp glance from Kimmy made her stop. Slowly Corky retreated to her bed and lay down on top of the tangled covers, with a loud sigh.

Her eyes followed Kimmy as she made her way across the room to the window and drew the curtain open. Her cheeks on fire, Kimmy pressed her face against the morning-cool glass and shut her eyes.

Corky shivered. She pulled the thin wool blanket up over her legs. She continued to stare at Kimmy, her mind spinning with unpleasant thoughts. Frightening thoughts.

It was obvious to Corky that Kimmy was the culprit.

Kimmy *had* to have been the one to cut off Hannah's braid while she slept. No one else had been in the room.

That meant that Kimmy was also guilty of changing the bathwater, turning up the hot water so that Hannah would scald herself.

Kimmy had confided to Corky that she'd like to murder Hannah. And here she was, torturing Hannah.

The evil is here, Corky thought miserably.

The evil is in this room. Still inside Kimmy. Poor Kimmy—she doesn't know.

It was all too horrifying, too horrifying to put into words. But words popped into Corky's mind:

Kimmy is not in control of her body. The ancient, evil force controls her now.

The door slammed shut then, jarring Corky from her thoughts. It was Hannah leaving the room.

Corky's eyes went to the dresser top. Hannah had taken the braid with her.

Kimmy turned away from the window, looking drained, lifeless. "Guess I'll get dressed too," she muttered.

"Kimmy—what are we going to do?" Corky demanded.

Kimmy shrugged and shook her head sadly. "Hey, Corky?" Her voice caught in her throat. She stared intently into Corky's eyes. "I'd remember if I cut off Hannah's braid, wouldn't I?"

It wasn't just a question. The words were too heavy with fear for it to be just a question.

She wanted Corky to reassure her, to tell her she was okay, she was normal. But Corky couldn't bring herself to lie to her distressed friend.

"I'd remember something like that, wouldn't I?" Kimmy repeated, sounding even more pitiful, more desperate.

"I don't know," Corky said softly, lowering her glance to the floor.

A short while later Kimmy, dressed for the morning exercise workout in Lycra shorts and a red tank top, headed out of the room. She stopped at the door and turned back to Corky. "You coming down to breakfast soon?"

"Be right there," Corky replied.

After Kimmy left, Corky stood up and stretched. Then she walked to her dresser, her mind spinning. She pictured Miss Green listening to Hannah's story. She imagined the shocked expression on the advisor's face.

Then what?

Will Kimmy and I be kicked off the squad?

Frowning, Corky pulled open her dresser drawer, started to reach for a clean T-shirt, and stopped, her hand poised in midair.

She stared open-mouthed at the pair of scissors on top of her clothing.

Scissors?

She picked them up with a trembling hand.

She brought them close to her face to examine them.

There were strands of straight black hair caught on the blades.

Hannah's straight black hair.

8

A CONFESSION

*C*orky sat by herself at the far end of the table, staring down at her bowl as the cornflakes turned to mush. The brightly lit dining hall echoed with excited voices and laughter, but she didn't hear them.

At the other end of the table Kimmy, Debra, Ronnie, and Heather ate quickly, downing stacks of pancakes and French toast, spooning up bowls of cereal as they talked enthusiastically. They all kept glancing down the table at Corky, but she lowered her eyes, avoiding their curious stares.

Turning her eyes to the food line, Corky saw Hannah approach Miss Green, who had just entered and was standing near the back wall. Miss Green, her arms crossed over the chest of her gray sweatshirt, had a grim expression on her face and kept shaking her head. Hannah was talking rapidly, her face flushed, gesturing wildly with the sad black braid in her hand.

Corky realized that Miss Green was staring at her, her face drawn into a tight frown.

What's going to happen now? Corky wondered, a heavy feeling of dread in the pit of her stomach. *What is Miss Green going to do to Kimmy and me?*

What should I do? Corky asked herself. *Should I tell her that Kimmy cut off the braid? Should I tell her that Kimmy put the scissors in my dresser drawer to make it look as if I had done it? Should I tell her that Kimmy is inhabited by the evil spirit?*

I have to tell someone, Corky thought glumly, hearing a burst of loud laughter from the girls at the next table. *I can't let Kimmy go any further.*

Hannah was still talking furiously, waving the braid in the air, pacing back and forth in front of Miss Green as she talked.

Just then the Bulldog cheerleaders erupted in a long cheer. Corky turned her eyes to their table to see Blair O'Connell, a peppy smile on her face, energetically leading the chant.

Doesn't she ever *quit?* Corky thought bitterly.

The cheerleaders were supposed to show pep

and spirit every moment of the day, from the time they woke up in the morning. *But give me a* break! Corky thought, shaking her head. She dropped her spoon into the soggy cereal with a *plop.*

The cheer ended at the Bulldogs' table, and another cheer, even louder, erupted at the next table. Corky noticed that Hannah had returned to the Shadyside table, taking her place beside Debra. She was red-faced and looked as if she'd been crying. She and Debra were whispering together.

Kimmy was at the head of the table, chewing on a slice of buttered toast, her expression troubled. Heather leaned forward then to ask Kimmy a question, but Kimmy didn't seem to hear her.

The evil is here at this table, Corky thought, staring hard at Kimmy. Corky shuddered. Two other cheers started up just then at two different tables. The shouting voices echoed off the yellow tile walls and high ceilings.

Corky suddenly felt terribly frightened. And terribly alone.

Who can I talk to? she asked herself. *Who can I confide in?* Debra would understand, she realized. Debra knew all about the evil spirit. Debra had been changed by it too.

Corky pushed her chair back and climbed to her feet. Ignoring the happy cheers at the other tables, she edged her way down the aisle and stopped behind Debra.

"Debra—can I talk to you?" she asked, bending down so that Debra could hear her over the shouting voices.

Debra turned around slowly. "Hi, Corky. Can it wait?" Debra asked, shouting over the noise. "I'm talking to Hannah right now."

Stung by Debra's words, Corky stepped back.

Ignoring Corky, Debra leaned close to Hannah as the two of them continued to whisper together.

Surely Debra can see that I'm upset, that I've been sitting off by myself, Corky thought angrily. *What kind of friend is she?*

And since when is Hannah so important to Debra that Debra can't interrupt her conversation to talk to me when I really need her?

On the verge of tears, Corky started toward the dining hall door. *I can't deal with this,* she thought. *I've got to get out of here!*

She was halfway to the door when she heard Miss Green calling to her.

Corky stopped but didn't turn around. *I can't face this,* she thought. *This is going to be horrible.*

She took a deep breath and held it. Letting it out slowly, to calm herself, she turned. Kimmy had climbed to her feet and was starting away from the table. Miss Green had called her too.

A stern expression on her face, Miss Green motioned for the girls to join her against the far wall. Corky walked slowly, her mind racing. *What am I going to say? How am I going to explain?*

Glancing back to the table, Corky saw that the other four Tiger cheerleaders were staring at Kimmy and her, not talking now, just watching intently to see what would happen.

The cheers seemed to fade into the distance as Corky approached Miss Green, walking slowly, her heart thudding in her chest. She glanced at Kimmy, who was staring straight ahead, lost in her own thoughts.

"Hannah has brought a serious complaint against you two," Miss Green said without any other greeting. She stared first at Corky, then at Kimmy, her dark eyes searching for some kind of answer. "I—I really can't believe this happened. I mean, what Hannah told me. It's just so—cruel. So incredibly vicious."

Neither Corky nor Kimmy said anything. Corky could feel her chin quivering. She tried to stop it but couldn't.

"I know both of you girls," Miss Green continued finally. "I like you both. And I—I'm just flabbergasted. That's the only word I can think of. I can't believe that either of you . . ." Her voice trailed off.

Time seemed to stand still. Corky couldn't breathe. It was as if her lungs were ready to explode.

"Cutting off someone's hair can be described only as an attack," Miss Green said sternly, narrowing her eyes at the two girls. "A truly vicious attack."

Corky lowered her eyes to her hands, which were ice-cold, she realized. She had balled them into such tight fists that her fingernails were cutting into her palms.

"I have to know," Miss Green said. "I have no choice. I have to find out which of you did this terrible thing to Hannah."

She turned her hard gaze on Kimmy. "Kimmy — was it you who cut off Hannah's braid?"

Kimmy cleared her throat. "Yes," she said.

9

THE BLOOD FLOWS

Miss Green's mouth dropped open in shock.

She wasn't expecting Kimmy to confess, Corky thought. *At least, not that fast.*

Corky turned her eyes to Kimmy, who gave her a meaningful glance. Kimmy was telling her: *Go along with this. Don't contradict me—I'm covering for you.*

Kimmy thinks she's protecting me! Corky realized. *No. No way. I can't let her do this.*

Kimmy is the guilty one, Corky knew. *But it isn't Kimmy's fault; she isn't in control of her own body. I can't let Kimmy take the blame for this alone.*

"No, Miss Green," Corky said. "I did it. I was the one."

Miss Green's face turned hard and cold. "Follow me," she said, motioning for both of them to go with her.

She led them through the double doors into the hallway. It was quiet out there, and cooler.

Miss Green stopped abruptly and spun around, anger on her face. "I want the truth," she snapped. "I don't want you covering for each other. I want to know the truth. Who's responsible?"

"I did it," Kimmy said in a low voice, darting a quick glance at Corky to tell her to keep quiet.

"No," Corky said, ignoring her friend. "It's not true."

"Then, *you* did it?" Miss Green demanded, stepping up close to Corky, so close that Corky could smell the coffee on her breath.

"No." Corky shook her head and took a deep breath. She had to tell Miss Green about the evil spirit, she decided. She really had no choice. "The truth is—"

"Yes, what *is* the truth?" Miss Green urged impatiently.

"The truth is that neither of us did it," Corky blurted out. "You see—"

"Stop!" Miss Green interrupted, holding up both hands. She sighed—a long, exasperated sigh. "I'm going to deal with both of you when we get back to Shadyside."

"Miss Green—" Corky started. But the advisor raised her hands again to cut Corky off.

"We'll do a complete investigation when we get back," Miss Green said, lowering her voice to a whisper as two of the judges walked by. "When we get back to Shadyside, both of you will be disciplined. Disciplined strongly." She slowly shook her head.

"Miss Green, we're really sorry," Kimmy said softly.

"No apologies," the advisor said sharply. "Let's just try to finish the week, okay? With no further incidents? I-I'm just flabbergasted. I can't imagine what could have gotten into your heads!"

I can, Corky thought glumly.

She and Kimmy watched as Miss Green, taking a few long, angry strides, hurried back into the dining hall. Then Corky turned to Kimmy, her chin quivering again. "I . . . uh . . ." She couldn't think of what to say.

"This really makes me feel like going out and giving it my all," Kimmy muttered sarcastically.

"Yeah, I know," Corky agreed.

"I mean, what's the point?" Kimmy cried, throwing up her hands. "Why should we work on routines and go ahead with all this? We're both going to be thrown off the squad when we get back to school."

Corky started to agree, but her voice caught in her throat.

"I was so psyched for this camp," Kimmy said sadly, pushing back her dark hair. "But now . . ." Her voice trailed off.

The hallway suddenly exploded with loud voices, calls, and laughter. Breakfast had ended, and everyone was heading to the gym for the morning workout.

Walking together in silence, Corky and Kimmy followed the others out onto the quadrangle. It was a bright, clear day, the sun already high in a cloudless sky.

A Frisbee sailed past Corky's head. A cheerleader in a gold uniform, gleaming in the sunlight, leaped to catch it. Then the girl spun around and flung it back in an easy motion.

The beautiful day didn't help cheer Corky. She knew it would take more than sunlight to make her problems go away.

She and Kimmy both saw Blair O'Connell at the same time, and both stopped on the path to stare at her.

Blair was performing a set of perfect cartwheels on the grass, rolling joyfully just for the fun of it.

"She really makes me sick," Kimmy declared,

leaning close so that only Corky could hear. Corky found herself startled by the angry heat of Kimmy's words.

"I mean, she *really* makes me sick," Kimmy repeated, making a disgusted face as she watched Blair's exuberant performance. "Someone should do something about her."

"We can't let the other girls down," Corky told Kimmy, pulling at the bottom of her cheerleader sweater and brushing a piece of lint off the big maroon *S* on the front. "We've got to give it our best."

"I guess you're right," Kimmy agreed half-heartedly.

They had practiced all afternoon, working to get a complicated new rap routine to come together. But neither of them had practiced with her usual enthusiasm and spirit.

Now it was seven thirty, time for the evening competition. The enormous gym rang out with excited voices. Corky could *feel* the tension, could feel everyone anticipating performing in front of the judges.

Hannah and Debra were clapping and stamping their feet in rhythm, practicing. Hannah had hurried into town and returned with a new, short hairstyle—she seemed as pert as ever. Ronnie was kneeling on the floor, frantically trying to repair a broken sneaker lace. Heather was several feet away, doing leg stretches.

"The show must go on," Corky said, forcing a smile.

"Why?" Kimmy asked.

Corky shrugged. "Beats me."

They both laughed. Their first laugh of the day.

Whistles blew. The gym slowly became quiet. A judge, a young woman with striking blond hair, called the captains to the center of the floor. The captains drew straws to determine the order of the competition.

"Yaaaay, Bulldogs!" Blair O'Connell, holding a red straw, screamed.

"Guess who's going first?" Kimmy whispered sarcastically to Corky.

Corky rolled her eyes. "Blair is unreal!" she muttered.

Secretly she admitted to herself that she was more than a little jealous of Blair. Blair was happy. . . . She was having a great time. . . . She was really into the competition. Blair was at her best . . . and she knew it.

That's the way I used to feel, Corky thought. *That's the way Bobbi and I always felt when we were cheering. We always felt so confident, so ter-*

rific, *so on top of everything whenever we put on our uniforms.*

But now . . .

Now she could only watch Blair and the other happy, enthusiastic cheerleaders and envy them.

"Clear the floor!" a voice cried over the loudspeaker. The cheerleaders scrambled up into the bleachers, sneakers thudding and squeaking. The eight Bulldog cheerleaders remained on the floor, huddling beside the bleachers.

Corky found a seat on the very end of a bench, about eight rows up from the floor. Debra sat beside her, nodded to her, smiling, but didn't say anything.

Corky turned away from Debra, still feeling hurt and angry by Debra's behavior toward her that morning. She looked down from her vantage point and watched Blair O'Connell encourage her squad. Blair went from girl to girl, saying something to each one.

A spotlight came on high in the ceiling rafters, throwing a white circle of light onto the gleaming polished floor. The bleachers grew quiet.

"The Redwood Bulldogs will go first tonight," announced the voice on the loudspeaker. "Whenever you are ready . . ."

The judges raised their clipboards as if at attention.

After a long pause the Bulldogs came running out, clapping, from beside the bleachers. They entered in a single line, Blair O'Connell in the lead.

As Blair ran into the spotlight, she performed a handspring. She dove forward onto her hands, flipped her body over, and landed effortlessly on both feet. Still on the run, she started into a second handspring.

But as she leaped this time, she appeared to trip over something.

Startled, her eyes grew wide. Her arms flew up.

She plunged forward, falling.

Her arms flailed in the air helplessly as she landed — on her face.

Corky heard the sickening *crack* as her face hit the hardwood floor.

Her arms continued to thrash about wildly, but Blair made no attempt to get up.

The silence in the gym hung heavily. The spotlight flooded her still form with glaring white light.

When Blair finally raised herself up, her eyes wild with confusion and fright, bright scarlet blood was gushing from her mouth like spurting water from a fountain.

Even from where she was sitting, Corky could see the cut in Blair's lip. And she could see that Blair's two front teeth had been broken in half.

Blair's head rolled about as blood continued to flow from her mouth, down the front of her uniform.

Her teammates ran over to huddle around her. Two girls put their arms around her waist.

Horrified shrill voices rang out. "Where's the doctor?"

"Somebody help her!"

"Her teeth! Her teeth are broken!"

"Stop the bleeding!"

"Her lip . . . it's cut wide open!"

And then Blair's anguished cry rose up over the other frantic voices. "Somebody tripped me!"

At first Corky assumed she hadn't heard correctly.

But Blair repeated her accusation. "Somebody tripped me!"

The cheerleaders in the bleachers had all jumped to their feet. The rumble of distressed voices rose to a roar.

Leaving a smeared trail of blood on the floor, Blair was half carried and half walked out of the gym. The judges and Blair's teammates moved her quickly toward the medical office down the hall.

As they passed beside her, Corky heard Blair repeat her accusation, the words burbling out like the blood from her mouth. "Somebody tripped me! Somebody tripped me!"

Repeated over and over like some kind of tragic cheer.

And then Blair was gone. Only the smeared trail of blood remained under the hot white glare of the spotlight.

Corky stared at the floor until it became a white blur. Then she forced herself to lift her eyes and focus down the row on Kimmy.

To her surprise, Kimmy was staring back at her, the strangest look on her face.

10

THE SCISSORS AGAIN

Let's do the diamond-head pyramid," Kimmy
suggested. "That's always a winner."

Corky stared at Kimmy in surprise. The
other girls cheered enthusiastically.

It was the next afternoon, a gray, overcast day
of low-hovering clouds. But inside the gym, spirits were as bright as ever. The afternoon practice
was underway—cheerleaders in shorts and T-shirts
were beginning to work on routines for the evening
competition.

"Kimmy, are you sure—?" Corky started, but
her words were drowned out by loud chants from
the squad a few feet away.

Suddenly gripped with fear, Corky remembered the last time they had performed the

diamond-head pyramid. She and Bobbi had taught the squad how to do it. It was complicated and dangerous, with three girls standing on the bottom, two girls standing on their shoulders, and one girl on top of them.

When they were in position, the girls all performed liberties, posing with one foot raised to their heads. Then the top girl did a tuck jump into the arms of the girl on the right end.

We haven't done the pyramid since that night, Corky thought with a shudder. *The night I was on top. When I made my jump, Kimmy deliberately let me fall.*

She wanted to kill me.

She was inhabited by the evil spirit, and she wanted to kill me.

Why is she suggesting we do the pyramid again tonight?

"Kimmy—do you really think it's a good idea?" Corky asked, staring hard at her friend.

"Yes!"

"Let's do it!"

"Let's try!"

The others all voiced their enthusiasm.

"Let me be on top!" Hannah shouted eagerly, her pleas directed at Kimmy. "Please!"

"Okay. You're on top," Kimmy answered quickly.

Too quickly, Corky thought.

Is Kimmy planning on letting Hannah fall? Is that her plan? She's already tortured *Hannah. Is she intending to* kill *her too?*

Corky decided she had to act. She pushed her way past Ronnie, who was struggling with a shoelace, and walked up to confront Kimmy.

"What's going on?" Corky demanded. "I've always been on top in the pyramid."

"Let's give Hannah a chance," Kimmy replied softly, almost innocently.

"Yeah—come on, Corky, give Hannah a chance," Debra interrupted.

Wow, thought Corky, *Debra has certainly become Hannah's pal in a hurry.* She turned her gaze on Debra. Fingering the crystal she always wore around her neck, Debra stared at Corky as if challenging her.

"I really think I should be on top," Corky insisted, turning back to argue with Kimmy. "I mean, we only have this afternoon to practice. There really isn't time to break in someone new."

But Kimmy insisted: "Let's give Hannah a chance." And the other girls quickly agreed.

Corky backed off as Hannah flashed her a triumphant smile.

The smile cut Corky like a knife. It was a cold

smile, a cruel smile. It said: *I'm the star now. . . .*
I'm the favorite now—and you're nothing. No one
wants to hear your *opinion.*

Dread swept over Corky. Staring at Hannah,
she had a heavy feeling in her stomach. She realized her hands had suddenly become ice-cold.

Hannah is doomed. The words flashed through
Corky's mind. *Kimmy cannot be stopped. Hannah
is doomed.*

"Didn't you hear me?" Kimmy's shout interrupted Corky's frightening thoughts.

"S-sorry," Corky stammered. "I was just
thinking . . ."

"Let's try the pyramid," Kimmy said. "We'll
practice the shoulder stand—in case anyone forgot."
She turned to Hannah. "Watch carefully. Corky and
Debra will be in the middle. We'll help you make
your climb."

"This is so exciting!" Hannah squealed.

"More exciting than you think," Corky muttered under her breath.

"Corky—did you say something?" Kimmy
asked, a challenge in her voice.

Corky shook her head and stepped forward to
demonstrate the shoulder stand.

A few minutes later five girls were in position
and Hannah began to make her way to the top.

Balancing on Ronnie's and Heather's shoulders, Corky felt a chill run down her back. She forced away a shiver of dizziness.

Was Kimmy planning to drop Hannah now? In practice?

Or was she going to wait until the evening competition?

Corky wanted to warn Hannah, to tell her the truth, to tell her about Kimmy. But what was the point? She knew that Hannah would never believe her.

Hannah reached up with her hands. Corky grabbed them and tugged. Hannah's hands were hot and wet. She was breathing noisily as she hoisted herself up and moved into position to the top of the pyramid.

"Excellent!" Miss Green called, jogging across the gym. She had arrived late but didn't seem at all surprised to see the girls practicing the pyramid. "Hold it. Don't move!" she shouted up to them, smiling. "Hannah, don't move. Just get a feel for it—get a feel for your balance."

"I'm fine!" Hannah declared. "This is easy! Really!"

"Okay. Liberties!" Kimmy instructed.

"Slow. Take it slow. Hold your balance," Miss Green called.

Corky, Debra, Ronnie, Heather, and Kimmy slowly raised one leg each.

"Steady, Ronnie," Miss Green urged. "Keep your other knee locked. All right, legs down."

Corky could feel Hannah sway unsteadily above her.

She realized she was holding her breath. *Is Kimmy going to drop Hannah? Is she?*

Time seemed to slow, then freeze.

Corky finally exhaled, took another deep breath, and held it.

"Lean forward just before you begin your tuck jump," Miss Green was telling Hannah.

"No problem," Hannah declared.

"Debra will have to shift her weight and balance on one leg," Miss Green instructed. "Then Kimmy will step out from under her and forward to catch you."

"I get it," Hannah called out. "I'm ready."

"On three," Miss Green said, her expression set, her eyes narrowed as she stared up at Hannah. "One . . . two . . ."

Kimmy stepped forward to catch Hannah.

Corky closed her eyes.

"Three."

Corky felt the pressure on her shoulder as Hannah pushed off for her jump.

Corky opened her eyes in time to see Kimmy catch Hannah easily.

Smiling happily, Hannah bounced to the floor, clapping.

The pyramid collapsed. Corky jumped down, feeling another shiver of dizziness.

Everyone was cheering and congratulating Hannah.

Miss Green, usually somber-faced, was smiling too. "Take a five-minute break!" she called.

Corky began to make her way to the water fountain in the hall.

"Are you okay?"

She looked up to see Kimmy staring at her, concerned.

"Are you okay?" Kimmy repeated.

"Yeah, I guess," Corky replied unsteadily. *I don't want a confrontation now,* she thought. *I can't handle a confrontation with Kimmy now.* "I'm okay."

Kimmy stared at her coldly, her eyes glowing. "Good," she said. "I'm glad. I think some people are in for a surprise tonight—don't you?"

"This skirt is so wrinkled," Kimmy said, holding the maroon-and-gray cheerleader skirt up in front of her. "Think anyone brought an iron?"

Corky, brushing her hair in front of her dresser mirror, raised her eyes to examine Kimmy in the mirror. "It doesn't look so bad."

Hannah was in the shower. Corky could hear her humming to herself over the steady rush of water.

Shaking her head, Kimmy pulled the skirt on. "We're late," she said, adjusting the bottom of her sweater over the skirt. "We're all late."

"I'm almost ready," Corky replied, setting down the hairbrush.

"What do you think is for dinner?" Kimmy asked, fluffing her black hair with both hands. "Hope it isn't chili. After dinner last night I felt like I weighed a thousand pounds—I could barely get off the floor."

"Yeah, I know," Corky said, reaching for her lip gloss.

"I'm going down," Kimmy said, taking one last look at herself in the mirror, adjusting her skirt. "Meet you in the dining hall, okay?"

"Okay," Corky told her. "I'll only be a minute."

Kimmy hurried out. As the door slammed behind her, the bathroom door opened, and Hannah stepped out, surrounded by warm steam, wrapped in a large maroon bath towel, her newly short black hair wet and dripping.

"We're going to win tonight," she said enthusi-astically. "I just know it. With Blair gone, the Bull-dogs are out of it." She sat down on the bed and began rubbing her hair with the towel.

"Blair won't be cheering tonight?" Corky asked, having trouble clasping her watch onto her wrist.

"No. Didn't you hear?" Hannah replied from under the bath towel. "She went home. She had ten stitches on her lip, and she's got to have dental surgery."

"Too bad," Corky said softly. She stood up and stretched.

Hannah dropped the towel, pulled on her underwear, and then sat back down on the bed to put on her maroon uniform socks. Her back was to Corky.

"With Blair out of the way, we *have* to win!" Hannah declared.

Corky quickly pulled open her top drawer. Her hand fumbled through the T-shirts inside until it found the scissors.

Wrapping her hand around the handle, she lifted the scissors from the drawer.

Hannah was still talking excitedly about the competition, her back to Corky.

Raising the scissors like a knife, Corky took a step toward Hannah.

This is my chance to finish what I started,
Corky thought.

Silently she made her way across the floor and
stopped behind her unsuspecting roommate.

No more teasing, Corky thought. *No more fool-*
ing around. This is it.

Goodbye, Hannah.

I can't say it's been a pleasure knowing you.

As Hannah leaned forward on the edge of the
bed to pick her other sock up from the floor, Corky
brought the scissor blade down quickly, aiming for
the tender spot between Hannah's shoulder blades.

11

CORKY'S SURPRISING DISCOVERY

You're dead, Hannah. You're dead!

The door swung open.

"Would you believe I forgot the pom-poms again?" Kimmy said, hurrying in breathlessly.

Corky let the scissors drop to the carpet and quickly kicked them under Hannah's bed.

Hannah spun around, surprised to find Corky so close behind her.

Feeling her face grow hot, Corky stepped back to her bed. A strong wave of nausea rose from the pit of her stomach. She held her breath, forcing it down.

Her head spun. She saw brilliant red lights. The entire room flashed, red then black, red then black.

Still struggling to fight down her nausea, she turned to Kimmy, who was searching the front closet. "I think you shoved the box over here, by our bed," Corky said, pointing.

"Thanks." Kimmy hurried over and picked up the carton. "Hey—aren't you two ready yet? What's taking so long?"

"I'll be ready in two seconds," Hannah said, pulling on her skirt.

"I . . . I don't feel so hot," Corky said weakly.

"Huh?" Kimmy's mouth dropped open in surprise.

"Really," Corky insisted. "My stomach. I don't feel right." She dropped down onto the edge of her bed.

The room flashed red then black, red then black.

She had a roaring in her ears, like a rushing waterfall. The back of her neck felt prickly and hot.

"You're not coming to dinner?" Kimmy asked shrilly.

"I'll be down as soon as I feel better," Corky told her. "Tell Miss Green, okay?"

Another wave of nausea sent her running to the bathroom. She slammed the door behind her and gripped the sink with both hands. The porcelain felt cool under her hot, wet hands.

Her entire body convulsed in a powerful tremor.

Red then black. Red then black.

She shut her eyes, but the flashing colors continued on her eyelids.

The roar in her ears grew louder.

She thought she heard laughter, evil laughter, somewhere far away.

Suddenly the sink became scalding hot, and with a cry more of shock than pain, she jerked her hands away.

Steam rose from the empty sink, putrid and thick, smelling of mold and decay. The porcelain shimmered and melted from the heat as she gaped in disbelief at it.

A hideous, low gurgling sound rose from the drain, growing louder and louder until it became a moan.

Corky turned and ran. She burst out of the bathroom and threw herself down onto Hannah's bed.

The room was empty. Hannah and Kimmy were gone.

I nearly killed Hannah, Corky realized. *I nearly murdered her.*

And then the horrifying words pushed their way into her consciousness:

I am the evil one now.

PART TWO
COLD FEAR

12

USING HER POWERS

Back in Shadyside, Corky could barely remember the last days of camp. Everything was a blur since she had discovered the awful truth. This Saturday afternoon found Corky in her room.

"Corky, what are you doing?" her mother's concerned voice called through the closed door.

"Just resting," Corky called back, raising her head from the pillow. Dressed in faded jeans and a sleeveless yellow T-shirt, she had thrown herself onto her bed after lunch. Thoughts washed about in her head like unruly ocean waves—strange thoughts, thoughts that weren't entirely her own.

"Are you sick?" her mother called in. "It's not like you to rest on a Saturday afternoon."

"I'm just tired," Corky replied impatiently. "You know . . . from cheerleader camp."

She listened to her mother pad down the stairs. Then she buried her head deep in the pillow, trying to drown out the roaring in her ears.

Cheerleader camp. What a dreadful week.

She'd stayed in her dorm room after she had made her horrifying discovery. She'd told everyone she was sick.

What choice did she have?

She couldn't go to any of the workshops or practices; she couldn't perform in the evening competitions. She was too afraid she might hurt someone.

Or worse.

She stayed in bed when Kimmy or Hannah was in the room. She tried to talk to them as little as possible.

Miss Green got a doctor to come examine Corky. But, of course, he found nothing wrong.

Nothing wrong. *What a laugh,* she thought bitterly.

Sometimes the evil force faded a little. Sometimes it let her think clearly. Sometimes it gave her just enough time to herself to become afraid, truly afraid.

And then the roar, the endless roar, would

return, and her memories would leave her. And she would move in a world of deep red and darker black, and not remember.

Not remember anything at all.

Except the fear.

Lying on top of her bedcovers, tossing uncomfortably, feeling the weight of the ancient evil, she remembered everything now.

So clearly. Too clearly.

She remembered sitting in the coffee shop with the other girls, making the pea soup spurt up over the table.

Why? Because they had teased her. And just because she *could*.

She remembered reaching out across the gym, reaching, reaching to trip Blair O'Connell. What a pleasing sight that was. And what a pleasing sound. That *crack*. That *crunch*. The sound of her face hitting the floor, her teeth breaking.

How satisfying, the shimmering red blood that flowed from her wounded mouth.

And there was more. More!

She remembered getting up in the early hours of morning, the sky still heavy with night. She remembered creeping to the desk drawer and silently removing her scissors. She remembered working carefully to cut off Hannah's disgusting black braid. She remembered the soft, nearly silent *snip, snip* as she moved the blades through the thick hair. And she remembered placing the severed braid neatly on top of Hannah's covers so she would see it the moment she woke up.

That was fun.

But later her fun was interrupted.

Kimmy burst in to spoil her fun, spoil her chance to murder Hannah.

That made Corky so angry that the roar drowned out all her thoughts. She disappeared inside herself, somewhere far away.

And now . . . now . . .

Corky sat up, uttering a low cry.

She suddenly understood the dreams, the dreams about Bobbi.

She understood what Bobbi had been trying to tell her in those sickening, awful dreams.

When Bobbi had opened her skull and pointed to the horrors inside, Bobbi had been telling Corky: *Look inside your own head. Look inside yourself. The horror is inside YOU!*

"Now I understand, Bobbi," Corky said out loud.

And as she said this, her bed rose. She grabbed the covers as the bed began to writhe and toss like a bus on a bumpy road.

No. Oh no. Please—nooooo.

The foot of the bed bucked as if trying to throw her off. Then the covers began to roll over her, the bed trembling and shaking.

No. Oh, please. Stop!

She clung to the bedspread, tightening her grip, holding on for dear life. The headboard slapped loudly against the wall. The covers flapped as if being blown by a hurricane wind. The mattress buckled and bumped.

Help me! Please—stop it! STOP it!

Terrified, she rolled off the bed and toppled onto the floor.

As she hit the floor, landing on her elbows and knees, the carpet began to undulate in waves, rising and then buckling back down, flapping noisily.

The curtains beside her windows flew straight out as if reaching for her. The windows rose, then slammed down.

Please—stop! STOP!

Her perfume bottles and cosmetics flew up from her dresser top and hovered near the ceiling.

The windows opened and shut more rapidly as the curtains continued to flap wildly. Struggling to her feet, Corky was tossed helplessly about by the rocking, undulating carpet.

She reached up toward her dresser, but the

moving carpet pulled her back. The mirror above the dresser burst into flames, then appeared to melt. She gaped in open-mouthed horror as the silvery lava poured down over the front of the dresser onto the throbbing, bucking floor.

And then she saw the puddle of dark blood on the carpet just in front of her.

"Please—SOMEBODY! Please, stop!"

As she stared down at it, struggling to focus her eyes, the puddle began to bubble and then expand. The dark wetness crept wider until it was underneath her, until it spread over the throbbing carpet, until she was *swimming* in it.

Drowning in it. Drowning in the thick dark blood . . . thrashing her arms and legs . . . kicking frantically . . . trying to swim . . . but feeling herself pulled down, sucked down into the bubbling, dark ooze.

"Noooooooooooo!"

Thrashing wildly, Corky struggled to keep her head up as the blood bubbled, red waves rocking and crashing over her, sweeping her away, pulling her down.

"Why are you doing this to me? Why are you torturing me? Leave me ALONE!"

Was she screaming the words? Or only thinking them?

The bedroom door opened.

Someone stood over her.

Panting loudly, she raised her eyes.

"Sean!"

Her little brother stared at her, hands in his jeans pockets, his blue eyes wide with surprise. "What's going on? What are you doing down there?"

Gripping the carpet tightly between her fingers, crouched on all fours, Corky stared up at him.

"Man, you're messed up!" he exclaimed, laughing.

"I . . . uh . . . I guess I had a bad dream," Corky explained weakly. She pulled herself up to her knees.

Red then black. Red then black.

The roar in her ears was a steady rush in the background.

She let her eyes dart around the room.

Normal. Everything was back to normal.

Of course.

"Come to my room," Sean demanded, grabbing her hand and tugging it.

"Why?" she asked. The roar grew louder. Closer.

"I want to show you something." He tugged harder. "Something I did on the computer."

She tried to stand up, but the dizziness pushed her down.

Her head weighed a thousand pounds. The roar drowned out her thoughts.

Red then black. Then red again.

The world was only two colors.

"Come *on*!" Sean cried impatiently.

And suddenly, without realizing it, she was hugging him, holding on to him, pulling him close. Closer. Holding on to him because he was real. Because he was good. So good.

"Hey—what's the big idea?" he cried, trying to squirm out of her grasp.

The roar made everything vibrate, every breath echo loudly in her mind.

Red then black. Then red. Then black.

Holding on to Sean, she wrestled him playfully to the carpet.

He laughed and squirmed. He reached up and put a headlock on her with his bony arms.

Sean liked to wrestle.

She ducked out of his hold and grabbed a slender arm. *I can break his arm,* Corky thought. *Yes. I can break both his arms.*

It would be so easy. So easy to just snap them in two.

YESSSSSSS, said the roar, the insistent roar in her head.

It would be so easy.

Crack, crack.

YESSSSSSSS.

Feeling the strength, the awesome strength of her powers, Corky grabbed Sean's arm and started to bend it back.

13

"WE HAVE TO KILL THE OTHERS"

Corky bent Sean's slender arm behind his back. "Ow!" he protested, struggling to free himself. "You're *hurting* me!"

He wasn't strong enough to loosen her grip. She pulled the arm up, listening for the shoulder to crack.

"*Ow!* Stop!" Sean screamed.

She bent the arm up even more. Then, suddenly, she let go, and Sean burst free.

"Get out!" Corky screamed to her startled brother. "Get out! Get out *now!*"

He ran to the door, his blue eyes wide, his expression bewildered. Turning, he glared back at her. "What's your problem, jerk?"

"Get out, Sean! Get *out!*"

He tossed his blond hair back angrily. "First you want to wrestle. Then you kick me out. You're a jerk!"

"Just get out," she moaned, feeling her entire body start to tremble.

He was already out the door and heading down the stairs.

I almost hurt him, Corky thought, terrified. *I almost broke his arm.*

Somehow the evil backed off just before . . . before . . .

She heard laughter, cold and dry. Almost a cough.

Corky glanced around the room. But she knew immediately that the laughter was inside her head.

It grew louder. Cruel laughter, taunting her. She covered her ears with her hands. Pressing hard, she tried to shut the evil sound out. But it grew louder still.

"Leave me alone! Leave me alone!" she screamed, not recognizing her own voice.

She fell onto her bed and pulled the pillow down over her head.

But the cold, dark laughter inside her mind grew louder and louder.

Corky dreamed that she was on a boat. She could feel the gentle swaying, the rise and fall of the wooden deck beneath her feet.

It was a bright day, sunny and warm. The cloudless sky was a vivid blue. The sun, reflected in the water, sent trickles of gold leaping around the white boat.

Corky could see herself standing on the swaying deck, leaning gently against the polished rail. She was dressed all in white. Her dress, floor-length and old-fashioned, had long sleeves with lacy cuffs. The skirt billowed in the soft wind. The frilly top had a high-necked lacy collar. On her head she wore a wide-brimmed straw hat, with a red ribbon around the crown tied in a bow to hang down her back.

How strange, Corky thought, *to be in the dream and be able to watch the dream at the same time.*

The colors were all so lovely. The sparkling gold-blue water, the white pleasure boat, the pale sky, her shimmering dress.

There were two children with her, slender and blond, also dressed in white Victorian clothes. *Very dressy,* Corky thought. *Not for sailing.*

The boat slid gently through the shimmering calm waters.

The children called her Sarah.

The sun felt warm on her face.

I'm not me, Corky thought. *I'm someone called Sarah.*

"Sarah, watch me," the little boy said. He hoisted himself onto the deck rail and struck a brave pose.

"Get down from there," Sarah scolded gently, laughing despite herself. "Get down at once."

The boy obediently hopped down.

Corky watched him chase the little girl along the bright deck.

Sarah lifted her face to the sun.

Suddenly the boat heeled hard to the right. Sarah grabbed the deck rail to steady herself, to stop herself from toppling over.

What's happening? Corky wondered, feeling Sarah's alarm.

Why is the boat tilting?

The boat lurched, then heeled up in the other direction. Sarah clung tightly to the rail.

She could feel the fear creep up her back.

The boat began to spin rapidly as if caught in some kind of whirlpool.

What's happening? Where is the sun? Why are we spinning like this?

The sky was suddenly black, as black as the swirling, frothing waters that lapped up noisily against the twirling boat.

Corky felt Sarah's fear. It washed over her, weighing her down, freezing her in place.

"Sarah! Sarah!" the children's voices, tiny and frightened, called to her.

She grabbed the deck rail with both hands now.

But the rail was no longer a rail. It had transformed itself into a thick white snake.

The snake raised its head, opened its venomous jaws, and started to hiss at Sarah. . . .

Then Corky woke up.

Drenched in cold perspiration, she sat up straight, gasping for air. She blinked and rubbed her eyes, rubbing away the vision of the hideous hissing snake.

I'm back, she thought. *Back in my room.*

The dream had been so real. It hadn't felt like a dream. More like a memory. A powerful memory.

She looked over at her bedside clock. Seven thirty. Outside her windows, the sky was the color of charcoal.

I've slept right through dinner, Corky realized.

What a frightening dream.

But why did it seem so familiar, almost as if she had lived it before?

And why had the children called her Sarah?

Still feeling shaky, still feeling the frightening pull of the boat as it spun, Corky lowered her feet to the floor.

She opened her mouth in a wide yawn.

And as she yawned, she heard a hissing sound—the hissing of the snake?—like a strong, unending wind escaping from deep within her.

She tried to close her mouth, but it wouldn't close.

The hissing grew louder, and Corky could feel something pour from her mouth.

A disgusting, putrid odor invaded her nose as green gas spewed from her open mouth.

From inside me! she thought in horror. *And I can't stop it.*

She sat helplessly as the green gas poured out of her mouth, filling the room with its powerful stench.

Help me. Oh, help me!

I can't stop it. I can't close my mouth.

It smells so bad!

The green gas roared out of her mouth. More. And more.

I'm going to vomit forever. Forever! Corky thought, her entire body trembling as the green gas spewed out.

When it was finally out, the hissing stopped. Weak, Corky fell back against her headboard, dizzy and drained.

The room was filled with the putrid mist. It

hovered, hot and wet, like a heavy fog.

"Don't sit back. We have work to do," said a voice that crackled like wind through dry leaves.

"Huh? Work? What w-work?" Corky managed to stammer breathlessly, pressed up against her headboard, trembling violently, unable to stop her body from shuddering.

"We have to kill the others, the ones who betrayed you," whispered the voice in the disgusting green fog. "Let's start with Debra."

14

KILLING DEBRA

N o!" Corky screamed in a high-pitched voice she'd never heard before.

She pressed her back against the headboard, trying to escape the foul odor, the smoky green shadow that hovered over the room. Shaking all over, chills rolling down her back, she realized that her room had become icy cold.

"I won't kill Debra," Corky insisted, crossing her arms protectively over the front of her T-shirt. She stared hard at the shadow as it billowed silently in front of her.

"But Debra turned against you. She chose Hannah over you," came the dry whisper. "Now Debra must pay."

"No! I won't let you!" Corky screamed shrilly.

The evil voice laughed, dry laughter like breaking twigs. "You won't let me?" The heavy mist rose up toward the ceiling. "But you *are* me!"

"No!" Corky protested.

"You are me—and I am you!"

"No! Please!"

The voice laughed again. The green fog folded in on itself, billowing and bending in the dark, cold room.

And then it floated rapidly up to the ceiling.

Corky's entire body shuddered violently, gripped in panic. Her breath caught in her throat. She stared in horror as the green gas spread over the ceiling, blanketing the light fixture to darken the room.

Corky grabbed her bedspread and pulled it up to her chin.

She thought of burrowing beneath it—but she knew that it wouldn't hide her from this powerful evil.

Above her the gas bubbled and billowed. Then, suddenly, it began to rain down on Corky, a heavy green dew, foul-smelling and damp.

Corky closed her eyes and covered her face with both hands.

The heavy dew descended over her, smothered her with its odor. Heavier. Heavier. Weighing her down as if it were a heavy old quilt.

I can't breathe, she thought. *It's* suffocating *me.*

Heavier. Heavier.

She felt so sleepy. So far away. The room seemed to fade into the distance. *She* seemed to fade with it.

As the sickening green liquid fell on her, Corky was floating away from herself.

Floating, floating into grayness.

Floating far away as the green gas filled her up, filled her mind, took over her body.

In a short while Corky was gone.

The evil force was completely in control.

She stood up, straightened her T-shirt, and walked over to her phone, taking long, steady strides.

Picking up the receiver, she punched in Debra's number. A few seconds later Debra was on the other end.

"Can you meet me?" Corky asked calmly. "I have something important to tell you."

Debra agreed.

Corky pulled a brush through her hair, then hurried downstairs. She grabbed up the car keys and called to her parents that she'd be back in a few hours.

Then she headed out to kill Debra.

15

SO EASY TO KILL

Gripping the steering wheel tightly in both hands, Corky leaned forward against the shoulder belt and headed the blue Accord along Old Mill Road in the direction of the Shadyside Mall.

I'm coming, Debra, she thought.

I'm coming to get you.

A smile passed across her face as she blinked her eyes in the white glare of oncoming headlights.

Debra and Hannah. They were quite a team at camp. Just about inseparable.

Well, I think I can separate you now, Corky thought darkly. *I think the grave will separate you from your pal Hannah!*

The thought pleased Corky greatly as she remembered how Debra had refused to interrupt her conversation with Hannah to come talk with her. How Debra went everywhere with Hannah, forgetting entirely about Corky. How Debra defended Hannah. How Debra voted that Hannah should have the top spot on the pyramid.

Debra, Debra, Debra. What a bad choice you made, Corky thought.

She sped up to pass a slow-moving station wagon filled with kids. Shadows rolled across her smiling face as the tall streetlamps whirred past.

After waiting at the stoplight, she made a left onto Division Street, unexpectedly crowded with cars inching along.

Debra had explained over the phone that she had to pick up some things for her mother at the mall. "Mom had kids just so she'd have slaves," Debra had complained. "That's all she does ever since I got my driver's license — sends me off to the mall to buy stuff for her."

Corky had tsk-tsked sympathetically, thinking all the while about how much she was going to enjoy seeing the end of Debra. Debra and her cold blue eyes. Debra and that chic short haircut. Debra and that goofy crystal she was always fingering as if it had some strange power.

Power? What a laugh. *I'll show her power,* Corky thought gleefully.

She had arranged to meet Debra in the far corner of the parking lot in back of the big Dalby's department store. No one parked back there, Corky knew, unless the rest of the lot was filled. It would most likely be deserted this time of night.

Corky turned the Accord into the mall and headed for the back. She saw two boys from school standing at the ticket window to the sixplex movie theater.

She stopped to let a woman pushing a filled shopping cart pass, then continued behind the department store.

This vast lot was nearly deserted, dotted only with cars that probably belonged to store workers.

Corky's eyes eagerly roamed the dimly lit lot.

Yes. There was Debra. Standing in a puddle of gray light, all alone at the back of the lot, her hands stuffed into her jeans pockets.

This is so easy, Corky thought. *So totally* easy!

Aiming the car at Debra, she pushed her foot down hard on the gas pedal. All the way down!

The car lurched forward with a roar.

Debra, staring at the other end of the lot, didn't notice Corky at first.

Then her mouth dropped open in a silent scream and her eyes bulged with fright as she realized the blue Accord was roaring at her.

So easy, Corky thought gleefully. *This is* so easy!

16

TRY, TRY AGAIN

As the car roared toward its target, Corky leaned forward against the shoulder belt, her eyes glowing with anticipation, her lips twisted in a triumphant grin.

Captured in the twin white headlights, Debra's face was a perfect portrait of horror.

She knows she's dead, Corky thought gleefully. *She can already feel it. She can already feel the car as it crushes her, the pain coursing through her body, the gasping for breath that won't come.*

Die, Debra! Die!

As the car roared toward collision, Debra leaped away. Out of the light. Onto a low concrete divider.

Corky's car slammed into the divider with a

deafening *crunch*. Then it bounced off and lurched into a lamppost.

"Ooof!"

Corky was jolted hard: forward so that the steering wheel shot into her chest; then she was jolted back, her head slamming against the head-rest with jarring force.

She stared straight ahead into the darkness, waiting for the pain to stop shooting through her body.

Silence.

The engine must have cut off.

Where's Debra? Corky wondered, unfastening the seat belt.

Did she get away?

The pain melted quickly. The ancient powers pushed the pain away.

Maybe Debra is under the car, Corky thought hopefully.

Loud, insistent tapping on the window beside her head startled her. She turned to see Debra, alive and healthy, tapping with one hand, a wor-ried look on her face. "Corky—are you okay? Are you hurt?"

Sighing in disappointment, Corky pushed open the car door. "I'm okay." She climbed out into the sultry night air.

TRUE EVIL   519

"What *happened*?" Debra demanded. "I—I was so scared. I thought you were going to mow me down!"

"The accelerator stuck," Corky told her. "I couldn't get the car to slow down. I—I completely lost control."

"How awful!" Debra exclaimed. Impulsively she hugged Corky. "You're really okay? You hit that post pretty hard!"

Corky took a step back and examined the car. The left side of the bumper had been crushed in. "Dad'll have a cow!" she said, shaking her head.

"But you're okay? Your head? Your neck?" Debra's face revealed her concern.

"I'm fine. Really," Corky replied impatiently. "How about you?"

"My heart is still racing, but I'm fine," Debra told her.

"Get in," Corky said, motioning toward the passenger door. "I've got to talk to you. It's pretty important."

"Maybe we should call a tow truck or your dad or something," Debra suggested.

"No. The car will probably still drive," Corky said, lowering her eyes to the damaged bumper. "I'll test it. Come on, get in. This is important."

"Why don't we take my car?" Debra insisted,

pointing to her red Subaru on the other side of the divider.

"I want to try *my* car," Corky snapped angrily. "I'll drop you off at your car when we're finished— okay?"

Debra stared at her intently. "Wow, Corky— I've never seen you like this."

"Well, I'm very worried about Kimmy, and I need to talk to you," Corky said. She lowered herself back into the driver's seat and slammed the door shut. Drumming her fingers on the steering wheel, she waited while Debra made her way around the car and climbed into the passenger seat, a thoughtful expression on her pretty face.

"Kimmy? What about Kimmy?" Debra asked. "I talked to her this afternoon. She seemed fine."

Corky didn't reply. She turned the key, and the engine started right up. Turning her head to the back window, she eased the car away from the divider.

"The car's okay now?" Debra asked. "The gas pedal—it's—"

"It's fine," Corky told her, shifting into drive and heading toward the mall exit. "Isn't that strange?"

"Yeah," Debra agreed, studying Corky. "I'm glad. That was a close one." A nervous giggle escaped her throat.

"I was so scared," Corky said, heading the car back in the direction she had come.

"Where are we going?" Debra asked, turning to face the front, pulling on her seat belt.

"Let's go to the old mill," Corky suggested. "It's so quiet there. A good place to talk."

Debra seemed reluctant. "That broken-down old mill? It's completely falling apart."

"It's quiet," Corky repeated.

A good place to kill you, Debra.

"Are you feeling better?" Debra asked, her eyes on the shadowy trees rolling past in the darkness. "I mean, since cheerleader camp. We were all so worried about you."

"That was weird, wasn't it?" Corky said. "It must have been a virus or something. Some kind of bug."

"But you're okay now?"

Corky shrugged. "I guess. I still feel a little knocked out. I completely vegged out this afternoon . . . took a long nap. Like a two-year-old. Would you believe it?"

Debra tsk-tsked. They drove in silence for a few moments. "When you were sick at camp, Hannah did such a good job of taking up the slack," Debra gushed. "I wish you could have seen her. She was awesome."

Corky nodded but didn't reply.

"What about Kimmy?" Debra demanded a short while later, turning in her seat to stare at Corky.

"We have to do something," Corky said, lowering her voice. "I'm just so scared."

She turned off Old Mill Road onto the gravel path that led through the trees to the deserted mill.

"You mean—?" Debra started, her lips forming an *O* of surprise.

"You still have all those books on the occult?" Corky asked.

The deserted mill, a two-story wooden structure with a tall wheel at one side, rose up in the headlights. Corky cut the engine and the lights and pushed open her car door.

"Yeah, I still have them." Debra reached reflexively for the crystal she wore on a chain around her neck. "I'm still really interested in all that stuff. But—"

Corky's sneakers crunched over the gravel as she led the way to the mill and the almost dry stream beside it. She was pleased to see there were no other cars there—Shadyside students often used the mill as a place to make out.

The fresh spring leaves rustled in the trees behind them. The air was fragrant and soft. The old mill loomed in front of them, black against a dark purple sky. The pale moon was cut in half by a wisp of black cloud.

"Do you think—I mean, do you think the evil spirit is in Kimmy again?" Debra asked reluctantly, hurrying to catch up to Corky.

"I think so," Corky replied somberly. Taking longer strides, she made her way past a broken gate, stepping over the fallen door, and walked into the old mill yard.

"That's *horrible!*" Debra exclaimed breathlessly. "Hey, Corky—wait up!"

Ignoring Debra's plea, Corky picked up her pace. Stepping over loose boards and other debris, she carefully crossed the yard to the towering mill wheel. It stood like a black Ferris wheel against the purple sky.

"Corky—where are you going?" Debra demanded. She had to jog to catch up. "I thought you wanted to talk."

"It's all so scary," Corky said, gazing up to the top of the rigid old wooden wheel. She raised her hands and gripped a wooden slat just above her head. "It feels good to use up some energy . . . nervous energy. You know."

"Hey, Corky, stop," Debra said, breathing hard. "I don't feel like climbing tonight."

Corky had already hoisted herself onto the wheel and was pulling herself up slat by slat to the top. The owners had locked the wheel so that it no longer moved.

Climbing the wheel was a popular sport among Shadyside teenagers. Sometimes they had races to see who could get up to the top first. Sometimes kids did a high-wire act, walking along the top of the wheel with their arms straight out, balancing precariously as they moved. Sometimes they had competitions to see how many people they could squeeze onto the top.

"Hey, Corky—this is dangerous," Debra protested.

Corky, halfway up the wheel, was pleased to see that her companion was following. She began to climb even more quickly.

"Corky—stop! It's slippery on this thing . . . from the rain yesterday. Corky! Why do we have to climb up here?" Debra cried.

Corky pulled herself up to the top of the wheel and stood up. Stretching, she glanced around. *Great view,* she thought. She could see the dried-up stream and entire mill yard, cluttered with trash and broken boards. Beyond the high fence, her car parked at the end of the gravel path. Beyond that, dark trees.

Darkness. Darkness stretching forever.

She reached down and helped Debra climb onto the top. Debra rested her knees on the damp wood, then reluctantly got to her feet. "This is dumb," she said, catching her breath.

"Great view," Corky replied softly, staring out at the trees.

"You said you wanted to talk," Debra complained, shaking her head. "We could talk on the ground too, you know?"

"You afraid of heights?" Corky asked, turning her eyes on Debra.

"No. Not really."

You should *be,* Corky thought, studying her friend. *You* should *be very afraid of heights, Debra.*

"Why are we up here?" Debra asked, leaning forward, bending her knees and resting her hands on her thighs.

"To get a different perspective," Corky said seriously.

"Huh?"

"I don't know." Corky shrugged, smiling. "I feel *safer* up here. Weird, huh?"

"Safer? You mean from Kimmy?" Debra asked, wrinkling her forehead.

"Yeah, from Kimmy. From everything," Corky told her.

A gust of warm air fluttered through Corky's hair. She edged closer to Debra, balancing carefully.

"Well, I don't know what to say about Kimmy," Debra said, still hunched forward. "It's all so frightening."

That's okay, thought Corky. *You won't have to be frightened anymore.*

Bye, Debra. It's been nice knowing you. Have a nice flight. And happy landings.

She reached out both hands and grabbed Debra's shoulders to push her over the side.

17

SOMETHING TO LOOK FORWARD TO

As Corky put her hands on Debra's shoulders, Debra smiled up at her, unaware of her intentions. "I'm okay," she said.

No, you're not, thought Corky. *You're not okay. You're dead.* She tensed her arm muscles and started to push.

"Hey, you girls—get down from there!"

The man's voice startled Corky back.

"Oh!" she cried out, and nearly toppled off the wheel.

"Get down!" the man shouted angrily. A bright light from a flashlight shone onto Corky's face, then darted over to Debra. "Don't you know it's dangerous?"

Corky squinted down to see a man in a

sweatshirt and denim overalls, staring up at them, moving his flashlight from one to the other.

"We're not doing anything!" Debra called down.

"You're trespassing," the man yelled up. "Now get down before I call the police."

"Okay, okay. We're coming," Debra said. She lowered herself to a sitting position. Then, flipping over onto her stomach, she carefully climbed down the side.

Corky remained standing at the top, her anger surging, the ancient evil rising up until her entire body felt as if it were on fire.

I'm going to explode! she thought. *Then I'm going to twist that guy's head around until I hear his neck crack. Then I'll rip his head off and pull the brains out through the neck.*

The angry thoughts crackled like electricity in her mind.

But as Corky stared down at Debra making her way slowly to the ground, Corky's fury cooled. *Why waste my time on that idiot?* she thought.

Debra's my real target. Debra is the one who must die.

Corky lowered herself quickly down the side of the old mill wheel. Stepping onto the soft ground, she glowered at the man with the flashlight.

"I know you young people think you'll live forever," he said, keeping the light on her face, "but you really shouldn't test your luck up there."

I will *live forever!* Corky thought, feeling her anger begin to seethe again. But she kept herself under control. "You can skip the lecture," she said dryly, then hurried to catch up with Debra, who was already crunching over the gravel to the car.

A short while later Corky dropped Debra off at her car in the deserted parking lot behind the mall.

"We didn't really get to talk," Debra said quietly, pushing open the car door.

"I'll kill you tomorrow," Corky told her.

Debra's eyes opened wide. "Huh? What did you say?"

"I said 'I'll call you tomorrow,'" Corky replied, realizing her slip.

"Oh." Debra's eyes narrowed again. She giggled nervously. "I guess I didn't hear you right." She gave Corky a wave and slammed the door behind her.

You heard right. I'll kill you tomorrow, Corky thought. *Something to look forward to. I'll kill you tomorrow, Debra,* she thought, turning and heading the car toward the exit.

Then Kimmy will have to die.

Kimmy knows too much. Way too much.

And all that knowledge is a dangerous *thing.*

So, goodbye, Debra. And goodbye, Kimmy. Goodbye, cheerleaders. I'm afraid that from now on, I'll be the only one with something to cheer about.

Corky chuckled to herself, pleased with her amusing thoughts.

So much to look forward to, she told herself, turning onto Fear Street, heading for home.

Hannah's smiling face flashed into her mind.

"Don't worry, Hannah," Corky said aloud. "I haven't forgotten you. I'll be looking in on you real soon . . . to finish what I started."

18

SINKING DEEP

*C*orky awoke. Wide-awake. Alert. She saw the brass light fixture with its white globe above her head. The curtains, hanging straight and still in front of the dark windows. The hairbrush resting on the edge of the dresser top.

Everything was so clear. In such sharp focus. As if all that had come before had been a blur, a dream.

She sat straight up and gazed at her bedside clock. It was 3:07. The middle of the night.

What had awakened her? And why did she feel so . . . light?

Something is different, Corky realized. *Something has changed.*

Pale shadows flitted over the ceiling. They were so clear, so amazingly clear.

And then Corky realized.

The evil spirit was gone.

She was herself again. Seeing things for herself. Thinking her own thoughts.

I'm me! she thought.

It's gone! It's really gone!

Excitedly she pushed down the covers and started to jump up.

But a heavy feeling held her back. A feeling she couldn't locate. A presence. Somewhere . . . somewhere inside her.

She sank back onto the bed.

It's still there, she knew. *Is it sleeping?*

Did the ancient evil have to sleep too?

How long do I have? she wondered sadly. *How long do I have before it awakens and takes over again? And I am back to being a prisoner, an unwilling prisoner inside my own body?*

Thoughts raced through her mind. Desperate, frightened thoughts. Corky closed her eyes and took a deep breath.

How can I get rid of it? she asked herself. *How can I get my body back again . . . before I kill my friends?*

The evil stirred within her. Stirred but didn't waken.

When it's awake, it's like I'm dreaming, Corky

thought. *I'm asleep somewhere, somewhere in my own body. Dreaming everything that's really happening.*

She thought suddenly of her dream. She was on the pretty sailboat, in the long white dress. Sailing on the sparkling gold water.

And the children called her Sarah.

Sarah . . . Sarah *Fear?*

Corky struggled to remember the story of Sarah Fear.

Months before, a strange young woman named Sarah Beth Plummer, a descendant of Sarah Fear, had told Corky the story. Or part of it, before the young woman had left town.

Sarah Fear, Corky remembered, was a young woman who'd lived in the late 1800s. She, too, had been inhabited by the evil spirit. In the summer of 1899 she had gone sailing on Fear Lake. A beautiful, calm day. But her pleasure boat had capsized, and all aboard—including Sarah—had drowned.

Yes. Corky knew this story. This story had formed her dream.

Only, it wasn't really a dream. It was a small chunk of memory. A small chunk of Sarah Fear's memory.

Is that crazy? Corky asked herself. *Is it possible that Sarah Fear's memory was revealed to me while I slept?*

It *had* to be a memory, she decided. It was too clear, too *real* to be a dream.

Excited by these thoughts, Corky climbed out of bed and started to pace back and forth over her bedroom carpet.

What does the dream mean? Why did I dream it? How did I get inside Sarah Fear's life?

Again she could feel the sleeping evil stir.

She stopped pacing. Waited. Not breathing.

It continued to sleep.

Breathless with anticipation, she sat down gently on the edge of the bed. She pictured Sarah Fear in her wide-brimmed straw hat and her long white dress, leaning on the rail of the gently bobbing sailboat.

How did I see all that? Corky wondered, closing her eyes and trying to see it all again. *How did I see it so clearly?*

Poor Sarah Fear. She had been inhabited by the evil spirit until she died.

Corky opened her eyes, excited by a new thought.

The spirit inhabited her—and it kept her memory.

The evil force must have Sarah Fear's memories inside it, Corky realized. *It must have all the memories of all the people it inhabited over the years.*

It took over their minds. It *possessed* their minds. And that meant that it also possessed their *memories*.

So somewhere deep within the mind of the ancient evil spirit, somewhere deep inside that sleeping evil, Sarah Fear's memory remained.

And a little bit of it had escaped, had come to Corky while she slept.

How can I get to the rest of it? Corky asked herself. *How can I get back into Sarah Fear's mind?*

She stopped, suddenly chilled.

Why do I want to get into poor Sarah Fear's memories? What would be the point? Sarah Fear died more than a hundred years ago.

As quickly as she asked herself the questions, Corky knew the answers.

Sarah Fear had been the only one to *defeat* the evil spirit.

When Sarah Fear had died, the evil spirit had gone to the grave with her. And the evil had remained inside her grave for more than a hundred years.

I want to send the evil force to its grave, Corky thought, breathing hard, her mind spinning with ideas.

I want to send the evil away just as you did, Sarah. But how? How did you do it?

Sarah Fear had died with that secret. But,

Corky knew, the secret must live on in Sarah Fear's memory.

And Sarah Fear's memory was somewhere inside Corky's mind.

I just have to find it, Corky thought. *I have to search until I find Sarah Fear's memory.*

I have to let myself sink down, down, down into Sarah Fear's memory. And then maybe I can learn from Sarah Fear how to defeat this evil.

Corky suddenly realized that her entire body was trembling. Her hands and feet were ice-cold. Her heart was thudding loudly in her chest.

As these wild ideas continued to whir through her mind, she returned to bed, lowered herself between the cool sheets, and pulled the covers up over her chin.

She closed her eyes and waited for her body to stop trembling, for the chills to stop, for her breathing to slow.

Then, with her eyes still closed, she tried to concentrate.

She pictured Sarah Fear. The swaying sailboat. The shimmering blue-gold water of the lake.

Forcing herself to breathe slowly, slowly . . . she sank into the evil spirit's memory.

Slipping into shadows darker than any she had ever experienced, she sank. Darker—and even darker.

Such darkness, such depths inside her own mind.

Deeper. Until she heard low moans and soft whimpers. Cries of despair. And still deeper, into the ancient memory, into the memory of evil. The cries became howls. Anguished yelps of pain and suffering.

The darkness grew heavy and cold. Ghostly wisps of gray mist slithered like wounded animals in front of her. The howls of pain encircled her, pulled her down, down. . . .

As the anguished cries grew louder and the darkness became a living thing, a monstrous presence, a hungry, groping shadow that threatened to swallow her whole, Corky felt overwhelming fear.

As if all the fear from all the people inhabited by the evil spirit had poured into her.

Endless fear. Endless pain. All inside her own mind.

Crying out to her. Reaching for her. Trying to grab her and pull her down into untold horrors from centuries past.

No, I want to get out, Corky thought, struggling against the darkness, against the agony inside her. *I don't want to be here. I don't want to hear this, to see this.*

But she had no choice now. Now it was too late.

She was slipping back in time, deep into the memory of the foul thing inside her. . . .

19

SARAH FEAR'S SECRET

Standing at the rail, the sails rippling pleasantly beside her, Sarah Fear stared into the sparkling waters of Fear Lake.

The boat created gentle blue-green waves as it cut through the water. Sarah stared down at the water, sprinkled with the gold of reflected sunlight.

Such a calm day, she thought. *So little wind. It will take forever to cross the lake.*

That was okay with Sarah. She was in no hurry.

Sighing, she raised her pale face to the sun, closing her eyes. She stood still for a long time, letting the warmth settle over her.

"Aunt Sarah?" A young boy's voice interrupted her peace. "Come sit with Margaret and me."

Sarah opened her eyes and smiled down at

Michael, her young nephew. Bathed in yellow sunlight, he seemed to sparkle and shimmer like the water. His starched white sailor shirt and blond curls glowed in the bright light as if on fire. "Come sit with us."

"In a while," Sarah replied, placing a hand on his curls gently, reluctantly, as if they truly might be as hot as fire. "I'm enjoying the light breeze here. I feel like standing for a while."

"Where is Father?" Michael asked, searching the deck.

"He went below," Sarah said, pointing to the stairs leading to the lower cabin. "He has a dreadful headache, poor man."

"We are moving too slowly," Michael complained.

"Yes—we want to go fast," his sister Margaret called from her seat across the wide deck.

Sarah laughed. "We can't go fast if there isn't any wind," she told them.

"Michael—would you like to take the wheel?" Jason Hardy called from behind them. Sarah turned, startled by his voice. She had almost forgotten he was on the boat.

Jason Hardy, Sarah's personal servant, was a tall, stern-faced man. His black mustache, waxed stiff, stuck out like bird wings on either side of his face. Dressed in a blue admiral's cap, matching blue blazer, and white sailor pants, he stood behind the wheel, motioning for Michael to join him.

"Me too!" cried Margaret, jumping up from her seat and starting toward the wheel.

"No, Margaret," Sarah scolded, laughing. "Piloting a sailboat is a man's job. That wouldn't be ladylike, would it?"

"I don't care." Margaret pouted, hands on her waist. But she stopped obediently halfway across the deck.

Michael, beaming excitedly, grabbed the big wheel with both hands as Hardy instructed him on how to steer.

Sarah turned back to the rail, taking a deep breath. In the near distance she could see the green pines of Fear Island, the small round island in the center of the lake.

The children look so good, so healthy, she thought wistfully. *It's the happiest I've seen them since their mother died.*

Something fluttered near Sarah's face. Startled, she took a step back. It was a butterfly. Black and orange—a monarch butterfly.

You're a long way from shore, Sarah thought, admiring it as it hovered just over the rail. *Did you follow us onto the sailboat this afternoon?*

The butterfly fluttered silently just in front of her, hovering in place.

Such delicate beauty, Sarah thought. She reached out, wrapped her fingers around it, and crushed it.

A voice inside her head laughed. Cruelly.

It was a laugh Sarah had heard many times before.

"Aunt Sarah!" Margaret's surprised cry drowned out the sound. "What did you do to that butterfly?"

"Butterfly?" Sarah turned to face the little girl, a look of innocence on her face. "What butterfly, Margaret? I didn't see it."

She opened her palm and let the crushed remnants of the insect drop into the water. She wiped her hand on the rail.

One more murder, Sarah thought bitterly. *One more . . .*

A small cloud drifted across the sun. The rolling waters darkened around the boat.

How many more murders? Sarah wondered silently, squeezing the rail with both hands.

"Many more," came the reply. "As many as we desire," the familiar voice told her.

Sarah shuddered. "I want you gone," she said aloud into the wind.

Laughter. "I will never leave you," said the voice, the voice of the evil that shared her body.

"I want you gone."

"I am part of you," the evil force declared.

"No!" Sarah protested.

"Aunt Sarah?" A hand tugged at her long skirt. "Aunt Sarah? Are you okay?"

"Yes . . . fine," Sarah answered quickly, turning to Margaret, who was staring up at her, concern on her pretty, pale face. "I'm fine, Margaret."

Sarah turned to Jason Hardy. "Give Margaret a turn at the wheel. We won't tell anyone."

Margaret gave a squeal of joy and hurried to join her brother, her heavy black shoes loud on the wooden deck.

Sarah's hands wrapped tighter around the rail, and she leaned forward until she could feel cold spray on her face. So refreshing, so . . . clean.

She closed her eyes and remained still, her face catching the drops of spray. She loosened her grip on the rail and pressed hard against it with her corseted waist.

I know how to kill you, she thought. *I know how to get rid of you. I know how to free myself of your evil.*

She waited for the voice inside her head to reply. She didn't have to wait long.

"You cannot kill me, Sarah."

A bitter smile formed on her pale lips. *I know how.*

And then a cold shudder of doubt made her grip the rail again.

I know how. I just don't know if I can bring myself to do it.

The evil laughter echoed once more in her mind. "I will move to the children," the evil spirit said. The cruelest threat of all.

"No!" Sarah screamed.

"Yes. I will live inside the children. First one, then the other. My evil shall live on, Sarah."

"No!"

She looked down at the mirrorlike surface. So clear, so pure.

And as she stared, visions of the deeds she had been forced to do seemed to float up to the surface. They were shadowy at first and murky, but as they floated nearer to the top, the pictures became bright and clear.

Sarah found herself facing her own evil.

She saw herself murdering the man at the mill, the man who had caused her husband's accident. She saw the expression of utter disbelief on the man's face as she grabbed him and shoved him from behind. And she heard the *crack* and *splat* as she pushed his head under the mill wheel. And his head was ground up as fine as the corn.

The woman who lived in the big house on the hill was even easier to murder. And what pleasure Sarah had taken in the crime. What delight. After all, the woman had insulted the Fears, insulted Simon Fear, insulted Sarah's dead husband, insulted the entire family.

The woman couldn't utter any insults with that length of clothesline wrapped around her neck. Sarah had pulled the clothesline tighter and tighter, until the woman's face was bright purple, as purple as the violets in her garden. So tight that the rope actually disappeared under the woman's skin. And the blood had flowed out in a perfect ring.

The tiny town of Shadyside was in an uproar now. Who could be doing these ghastly murders?

They were all frightened of the Fear family. But they'd sent the young police constable anyway. He was so young and handsome, Sarah thought. And he asked so many questions.

Too many questions.

How lucky that Sarah was boiling an enormous pot of potatoes when the young police officer arrived. She had only to shove his head deep into the boiling water, and wait.

What a struggle he'd put up. Thrashing his arms.

But Sarah had held his head under until the thrashing had stopped. Until his breathing had stopped, until he was dead, and he slumped, lifeless, over the black cast-iron stove.

All of his hair had floated off, floated to the top of the pot. And when she finally pulled him up, his head was as white as a boiled potato and nearly as soft.

So much for the police investigation.

The residents of the town grew quiet and fearful. Neighbor avoided neighbor. Rumors were whispered, but few words of accusation were murmured aloud.

These pictures surfaced in the mirrorlike lake water as Sarah leaned over the rail and stared down.

"No more," she whispered aloud.

"There will be more," the evil spirit inside her promised. "There will be many more."

"No more," Sarah repeated, shaking her head.

I know how to kill you, she thought, taking a deep breath.

I know how to get rid of you.

"I will move to the children," came the ugly threat once again. "I will live inside Michael. I will live inside Margaret."

No, you won't, Sarah argued.

No. You will die, evil spirit.

I know how to drown you.

The cruel laughter rang in her head. "Fool. I cannot be drowned."

Yes, you can, Sarah told it, a twisted smile spreading on her pretty face. *Yes, you can. You can drown. You can.*

"I cannot be drowned."

You can be drowned, Sarah told it silently, *if* I *drown first.*

"No," the voice inside her quickly replied, but doubt and surprise colored the single word for the first time.

If I kill myself with you inside, Sarah told it, *then you will die with me.*

Sarah turned back to the children. Jason Hardy stood between them as they enthusiastically guided the wheel together.

So innocent, she thought.

They don't know anything at all about their evil aunt Sarah. And I hope they never will.

Sarah had known for a long time how to rid herself, how to rid the world, of the ancient evil force. She had known that she had to die in order for it to be killed.

But ending her own life had been too frightening to think about. Too frightening to imagine — until the evil spirit had mentioned the children.

I have to save them, Sarah thought. *I have to save them* now.

Her throat constricted as she stared down into the water. She uttered a low cry and leaned forward a little farther.

And as she leaned, the boat tilted in the opposite direction, reared up as if facing a strong wind.

Sarah was tossed back. She landed sharply against the mast and toppled to the deck in a sitting position. She struggled to get back up as the craft began to twirl.

"What's happening?" She heard Margaret's frightened voice behind her. "Why are we spinning?"

"It isn't windy!"

"What's wrong with the boat?"

Sarah knew what was wrong with the boat. The evil spirit was working hard to keep her from throwing herself over the rail into the water.

Around and around, like a carousel, the boat spun. Picking up speed, it sent up a high wall of water around it.

Dizzy and terrified, her heart thudding, Sarah reached for the mast. She grabbed it to pull herself up.

The boat reared up violently then, and dipped low into the tossing water. Sarah's hand slipped off the mast, and she fell hard to the deck once again.

The sky was black now, as black as night.

The ring of water tossed up by the spinning boat encircled the boat and threatened to roll over it.

"You cannot drown me!"the evil voice screamed inside Sarah's head. "My evil lives forever!"

As the boat spun faster and faster, Sarah heard the terrified cries of her little niece and nephew.

"You will not get to them," she said out loud through gritted teeth. This time she pulled herself to her feet.

Water crashed down heavily and washed over the deck like a tidal wave. The boat heaved as it twirled, and the waters tossed up high, frothing eerily in a circle around it.

"You will not get the children!" Sarah Fear declared, shouting at the evil inside her.

She shut her eyes tightly and lunged blindly to the rail.

"Aunt Sarah!" She heard the children's shrill voices, distant now, as if miles away. "Aunt Sarah! Come back!"

"You cannot drown me!"

But I must!

"You haven't the courage to drown yourself!"

Was the ancient evil right?

Did she have the courage?

Could she sacrifice her life, her young life, for Michael and Margaret?

"There will be more evil to come, Sarah. There will be much more evil."

"Noooooooo!"

And Sarah Fear dove under the rail. Into the dark, tossing waters under the black sky.

Down into the cold water. Churning and bubbling.

Down she plunged, gulping in water.

Inhaling the heavy water.

Taking in mouthfuls as she descended, her hair loose and floating gracefully above her head like a kind of sea creature, her arms pulling her deeper into the darkness.

Her lungs filling with the heavy water.

Choking. Sputtering.

No longer breathing.

No longer seeing.

I'm drowning, she thought. *I'm not breathing now. Soon I will be gone. Soon, I hope.*

And as Sarah drowned, the evil thrashed inside her, fighting desperately. As the water invaded her lungs, the spirit struggled to free itself.

She felt it try to thrust itself out from her throat. The water bubbled as a stream of green gas erupted from her mouth.

The eruption was so powerful that it forced Sarah to the surface. She saw the sailboat over-turned, upside down.

The children, she thought.

And then she was underwater again.

The water was hot. Boiling. Scalding hot.

Burning her skin. So unbearably hot.

And the green gas poured into the tossing, boiling water.

"Up. Rise up," the voice told her. *"Rise up and save us both!"*

But Sarah plunged lower, forcing herself down.

Now she could feel two fears at once. Her own and that of the ancient spirit.

Both frightened now. Both about to die.

Both dying.

Both.

The boiling, bubbling water churned around her. The flowing green gas encircled her, shutting out all light. The spirit was trapped in Sarah's drowning body.

The evil voice cried out. "NOOOOOOOOOOO!"

A wail of rage, of disbelief.

The cry was strong at first. Then weak. Then a whimper of faint protest. The green gas bubbled away.

Sarah Fear's eyes were bulging wide. But she saw nothing now.

Not even the still, still blackness.

For she — and the evil — were dead.

· · ·

Then—more darkness. Rapidly swirling darkness. Black moving against black.

Corky slept without moving, as if in a coma, her breathing slow and silent.

Deeper, she sank. Deeper into old memories.

Shadows formed, twisting and bending in the darkness.

Deeper.

Deeper.

No longer in Sarah Fear's memory.

Sinking deeper inside the mind of the ancient evil.

Deeper.

Until she entered the memory of the evil spirit itself.

Now Corky looked out through the evil spirit's eyes.

And stared in bitter horror at the velvet-lined walls of a coffin.

She was inside the coffin. Six feet under the ground. Trapped inside. Hunkered low against the closed lid.

Inside the rotting corpse of Sarah Fear.

Yes. Sarah Fear was dead. Drowned in Fear Lake. And up above, poking up through the loamy cemetery ground, stood Sarah's gravestone.

Surrounded by four other stones. Stones for Michael, for Margaret, for their father, and for Jason

Hardy. All dead. All drowned in the boiling waters of the lake.

And now the evil spirit shared Sarah's grave. Imprisoned beside the foul, decaying body it had once possessed.

Defeated by Sarah's courage. Trapped by Sarah's final sacrifice.

It waited.

Waited eagerly for a live body to come along and free it.

Waited. Waited.

Staring at the worms that invaded Sarah's grinning skull.

Corky woke.

She sat up, alert, wide-awake. Trembling. Her sheets were tangled, hot, and damp from perspiration.

She could still see Sarah Fear's corpse, the decaying walls of the small coffin. She could still hear the roar of the churning lake in her mind, still hear the hiss of the escaping green gas, still hear the hideous howl of the evil spirit dying.

Corky swallowed hard. She realized she was crying. Hot tears rolled down her even hotter cheeks. *Sarah Fear has told me all I need to know,* she thought, letting the tears fall.

To kill the evil, I have to kill . . . myself.

PART THREE
HOT WATER

20

KIMMY MUST DIE

*C*orky drifted back into a troubled sleep. When she awoke again, sunlight was streaming in through her bedroom windows, the curtains fluttering in a soft breeze.

She sat up, stretching, and stared down at the foot of her bed into the bulging eyes of a hideous orange-fleshed face covered with stitched-up scars.

Corky opened her mouth to scream. But then recognized the intruder as Sean's rubber mask from Halloween.

Sean must have placed it on the bedpost while she slept.

"Way to go, Sean," she said out loud, shaking her head. She reached over, pulled the disgusting mask off its perch, and tossed it into the corner.

My little brother is a real monster, she thought.

As she lowered her feet to the floor and stretched again, the images of her dream, the images from Sarah Fear's memory, came back, forced themselves vividly into her mind, as vividly as if she had lived them herself.

But how can I kill myself? she asked herself, staring at the rubber mask she had tossed to the floor.

Never see Sean again? Never see my parents again? Never go out? Never fall in love? Never get married? Have a family? Have a life?

I'm only sixteen, Corky thought miserably. Sixteen. Too young to die.

"No!" she declared aloud. "No way!"

She thought of Bobbi. Poor Bobbi—she didn't live long enough to . . . to *do anything!*

I owe it to Bobbi, Corky thought, standing up unsteadily, her mind racing. *I owe it to my poor dead sister to go on living. To have a full life—a full, happy life.*

But how?

She could sense the evil stirring inside her. Waking, it started to dull her thoughts, and she began to fade into the background.

She began to drift away—inside her own body.

I'm going to ignore it, Corky decided.

That's how I'll deal with it. I'll ignore it, and it'll go away.

If it tries to do something terrible, I can deal with it. I know I can. I just won't cooperate.

If I ignore it. Or if I fight it. I mean, I'll ignore it. And then . . .

She knew she wasn't thinking clearly. But how could she? Her room was so far away . . . the windows so tiny and distant . . . the light so dim.

"No!" she cried, struggling to resist the force taking over her mind. "No! I'm ignoring you!"

She heard cruel laughter. Then her bedroom walls began to quake.

"No!"

The flowers—the red carnations, the blue gardenias—all the flowers on the wallpaper started to spin.

"No!"

The flowers spun wildly, then flew off the wallpaper, spinning up to the ceiling.

"No! Please—no!"

Corky heard the laughter again, loud laughter inside her head as the red and blue flowers rained down on her. Another peal of cruel laughter.

Turning away from the wall, Corky quickly pulled on a pair of gray sweatpants and a wrinkled blue T-shirt. Then she ran out onto the landing and started down the stairs. But as she stepped onto the first one, a row of razor blades popped up from the carpet.

"Ow!" She cried out as her bare foot just missed getting sliced.

Leaning on the banister, she stared as razor blades popped up with a loud snap on each step.

She flung herself onto the banister and slid down on her stomach. The banister was burning hot by the time she leaped off at the bottom.

"Corky—what on earth?" her mother exclaimed. She was standing in the hallway, a bundle of dirty clothes in her arms.

"Oh. Sorry, Mom," Corky said, swallowing hard. She looked up at the stairs. The razor blades were gone.

"You slept so late," Mrs. Corcoran said, dropping the clothing by the basement steps. "It's almost noon."

Corky opened her mouth to speak. But what could she say? No words came out. She followed her mother into the kitchen.

"I'm going to fry up a couple of eggs for you," Corky's mom said, gazing fretfully at her daughter. "You look hungry."

"Yes," Corky said weakly. She hoped her mother didn't see how hard she was breathing, how her entire body was trembling. Trying to steady herself, to appear calm, Corky climbed onto a stool at the kitchen counter and watched as Mrs. Corcoran made two eggs.

"Toast? Juice?" her mother asked.

"I guess," Corky replied, struggling to keep her voice low and steady, struggling against the wild swirling thoughts in her head.

Her mother stared at her, as if examining her. "You feeling okay, Corky?"

"No, Mom. I'm inhabited by an evil spirit. It's inside me, controlling me, and I can't do anything about it."

"Very funny," Mrs. Corcoran said sarcastically, rolling her eyes. She tapped her metal spatula beside the frying pan. "Do all teenagers develop such gross senses of humor, or is it just a specialty of yours?"

I'm telling the truth, Mom! But you don't want to hear it, do you? You don't want to believe it.

"Where is Sean?" Corky asked. The words weren't hers. The evil spirit was forcing her to change the subject.

"He and your dad are at his baseball game," Mrs. Corcoran said. She scraped the eggs from the pan. "You haven't spent much time with your brother lately."

"He left me a little reminder of himself this morning," Corky said, picturing the gruesome rubber mask.

Her mother deposited the two fried eggs onto a plate and set it down in front of Corky. "Get your toast when it's ready," she said, and disappeared to deal with the laundry.

Corky stared down at the eggs, then reluctantly picked up her fork.

As she gazed at the plate, the eggs shimmered, then transformed themselves. Corky's mouth dropped open as she now stared at two enormous wet eyeballs.

"No!"

The eyeballs stared back at her. Their color darkened to gray. Then the gray became a sickening green, the green of decay, and a foul odor rose up from the plate. As the putrid aroma filled the air and the eyeballs shriveled and wrinkled, Corky gagged and leaped off the stool.

The laughter, the cruel, cold laughter, followed her as she ran blindly back up to her room.

I give up, she thought, flinging herself facedown onto her bed. She started to sob, but her breath caught in her throat. A wave of nausea swept over her as she felt the evil force move within her.

The phone rang. It took her a while to recognize the sound. It rang again. Again.

"Hello?"

"Hello, Corky? It's me." Kimmy.

"Hi, Kimmy. How's it going?" She tried to sound casual, but her voice broke.

"Okay. I was just worried about you," Kimmy replied. "I haven't seen you since—since camp. And you were so sick and everything. I mean, it was just such a *disaster*. Are you better? I mean, are you okay?"

Why is Kimmy calling? Corky asked herself bitterly. *She isn't my friend,* she thought, her features tightening in an unpleasant expression of hatred. *Kimmy has never been my friend. She tried to kill me once. Tried to drown me.*

"I saw Hannah yesterday, and she said she hadn't seen you either," Kimmy continued brightly. "So Hannah and I were just wondering—"

Don't worry, Corky thought coldly. *I'll be seeing Hannah soon. Very soon. And when I see her, Hannah won't be happy to see* me.

"I'm feeling better," Corky told Kimmy.

"Oh good!" Kimmy exclaimed. "I really was worried about you. I mean, after all that went down. You know."

Yes, I do know, Corky thought angrily. *I do know what you're talking about, Kimmy.*

And I do know that you know too much.

You have to die, Corky decided. *You have to die now, Kimmy.*

"Hey, Kimmy, are you doing anything this afternoon?" Corky asked, winding the phone cord around her wrist.

"No, not really," Kimmy replied. "Why? You want to hang out or something?"

"Yeah," Corky answered quickly. "I really want to talk to you."

"Great!" Kimmy said. "I want to talk to you too."

"Can you meet me up on River Ridge in about half an hour?" Corky asked. River Ridge was a high cliff overlooking the Conononka River.

"River Ridge?" Kimmy sounded surprised. "Sure, I guess. See you in half an hour."

Corky untwisted the cord from her arm and replaced the receiver.

Kimmy must die in water, she decided, picturing the high cliff and the river flowing beneath it.

Kimmy must die the way Sarah Fear died.

The way my sister, Bobbi, died.

Now.

21

KIMMY DIES

*P*ark storm clouds filtered out the sun, casting a wash of eerie yellow over the afternoon sky. The air was heavy and wet . . . and very still. There was no wind.

Corky left her car at the end of the road and walked across the hard ground to the cliff's edge. Behind her, the silent woods darkened as the black clouds hovered lower.

There was no one else around.

Standing on the rocky ledge that jutted out over the steep drop, Corky stared down at the wide brown river below. The Conononka, she saw, was high on its banks, flowing rapidly, a steady rush of sound rising up the cliff.

Ever since moving to Shadyside, Corky had

enjoyed coming up to River Ridge. It was the highest spot around. Beyond the river she could see the town stretched out like some kind of model or miniature. To the north, the woods formed a winding dark ribbon on the horizon.

It's so peaceful up here, Corky thought. Even though she could still see Shadyside, she felt far away from it. As if she were floating over the town in a tranquil world of her own.

Corky took a step back and glanced at her watch. Where was Kimmy?

Let's get this show on the road, she thought impatiently. She gazed up at the darkening sky, the black clouds so low now over her head. *It's so humid,* she thought. *The air is so still and sticky.*

She realized she was perspiring, her T-shirt clinging to her back. The back of her neck started to itch.

Come on, Kimmy. Don't you want to see the surprise I have for you?

I'm going to give Kimmy a flying lesson, she thought, her lips forming a cruel smile.

A flying lesson. And then a *drowning* lesson.

Hearing a car door slam behind her, Corky turned. Kimmy, dressed in a cropped red shirt over blue Lycra bike shorts, walked quickly toward her. Kimmy's car was parked next to hers at the end of the road.

"Think it's okay to park here?" Kimmy called.

"Sure," Corky answered. "There's no one else around." *And you won't need it to leave,* Corky added to herself.

Kimmy's round cheeks were bright pink; her crimped black hair was damp and disheveled. "I thought it would be cooler up here," she complained, brushing a strand of hair from over her eyes.

You'll be cooler in a moment, Corky thought. "There's no wind at all today," Corky said. "Look at the trees."

They both turned to gaze back at the woods. "Not a leaf moving," Kimmy said, and focused on Corky, a questioning expression on her face. "What are we *doing* up here?"

Corky chuckled. "I don't know. I thought it'd be a nice place to talk. You know."

Kimmy glanced up at the rain-heavy clouds. "We're going to get drenched."

"That would feel good," Corky said, and took a step toward the cliff's edge. Kimmy followed her.

"You're feeling better?" Kimmy asked with genuine concern.

Corky nodded. "Yeah. A lot." *And I'm going to feel even better in a few seconds,* Corky thought.

"That was so terrible at camp," Kimmy said. "I mean, you getting sick like that. What a disaster."

"Yeah . . . what a disaster," Corky repeated with a grim smile.

"And all that stupid stuff with Hannah," Kimmy added, avoiding Corky's eyes. "You know I didn't do any of that stuff to her. You believe me, don't you?"

"Yes, of course," Corky replied. "I didn't do it either."

"So . . . what do you think?" Kimmy asked, turning to face Corky, searching her face. "I mean, what do you think happened?"

"I think Hannah did those things to herself," Corky told her, forcing herself to keep a straight face.

"The scalding bath? The braid?"

"I think she faked the scalding bath," Corky said in a low voice. "I think she just screamed and carried on. I don't think she was really burned—just a little red."

"And you think she cut her own hair?" Kimmy asked.

Corky nodded solemnly.

"But *why*?" Kimmy asked shrilly.

"To get both of us in trouble," Corky said. "To make us look bad. To get us kicked off the squad so she could be the star."

"Wow!" Kimmy's mouth dropped open in dismay. "I never thought of that. Never. It never occurred to me that Hannah . . ." Her voice trailed off as she thought about it.

"Well, what *did* you think?" Corky asked sharply.

"That I did it? Did you suspect me, Kimmy?"

"No!" Kimmy protested, her cheeks reddening. "No, I didn't, Corky. I—I didn't know *what* to think. I knew the evil spirit had to be around. I knew the evil had to be responsible. But I didn't know where. I mean, I didn't know *who*. I just . . ."

Corky felt a drop of rain on her forehead. *Enough stalling,* she thought. *I'd better get this over with.*

"The evil is around," Corky said, lowering her voice to a whisper. She felt another large raindrop, this time on top of her head. Then one on her shoulder.

"Huh?" Again Kimmy's mouth dropped open in surprise. "You mean—Hannah? Do you think it's inside Hannah?"

"Maybe," Corky said mysteriously.

"It's starting to rain," Kimmy said, holding out her palms. "Maybe we should go back to your car and talk."

"Okay," Corky replied. "But first look down there." She pointed straight down over the cliff's edge. "I've been trying to figure out what that is, but I can't."

"What?" Kimmy leaned over and peered down at the rushing river.

Corky reached out and shoved Kimmy. Hard.

Kimmy uttered a loud shriek as she went over the side. Her arms thrashed wildly as she dropped headfirst.

A grin spread over Corky's face as she stood, hands on hips, and watched Kimmy plunge to her death.

22

TRIUMPH OF EVIL

Kimmy is dead."

Corky said the words out loud, a triumphant smile spreading across her face.

Raindrops fell gently, a few at a time. Standing on the cliff's edge, Corky peered down at the brown flowing river water.

"Kimmy is dead."

Still smiling, Corky started to leave. But from somewhere deep inside her a muffled voice shouted: "No!"

She hesitated.

I have to leave now. Kimmy is dead. Now I have to take care of Debra.

And again the distant, muffled voice cried out: "No!"

The smile faded on Corky's face, and her eyes narrowed unpleasantly.

"No!"

The rain fell harder. The gentle *ping* on the ground became a steady drumroll. *I have to finish Debra now.*

"No!"

The protesting voice was Corky's. The real Corky trying to make herself heard, struggling to regain control.

"No! I can't let this happen!" The real Corky's voice grew stronger.

"*I am in control now!*" the evil force cried out. "*Stay back! I'm warning you!*"

"No!" Corky called out with renewed strength.

"No!" From somewhere deep in her own mind Corky lashed out, pushed her way forward, pressed against the heavy evil.

The horror of Kimmy's death—the horror of what Corky had just done—had reached through the evil, had brought Corky to life. She knew she had no choice. She had to fight it. Now.

"*Stay back!*" the ancient evil warned. "*Stay back where you belong!*"

"No!" Corky fought back, struggling within herself, struggling blindly as the ground disappeared, along with the sky, the trees, everything.

She was nowhere. In a gray limbo. Fighting a foe she couldn't see . . . fighting herself.

"I have to die!" she told herself. "I have to die now!"

And another part of her said, "No. I cannot die! I am too young. I want to *live!*"

"Die—and force this evil to die with you!"

"No—I can't die! I'm too afraid! I want to live!"

"You cannot live with this ghastly thing inside you! You must die to save your friends, your family!"

"*Get back!*" growled the evil inside her head. "*Get back now!*"

"No!" Corky cried. "Kimmy!" she screamed. "Kimmy—I'm so sorry!"

I am evil, Corky told herself. *I am evil, and I must die!*

"*I must live!*" the evil force declared. "*Get back or suffer a thousand deaths inside your own body!*"

"Nooooo!"

With a final scream Corky spun around—and stepped to the cliff's edge.

She stopped to peer down, her chest heaving, her blood pulsing against her temples.

No! I can't do it!

"I can't!" she screamed. "I'm too young! I can't!"

She felt the evil stir, rising up heavily, triumphantly, inside her.

"I can't! I can't!"

She took a step back.

Defeated.

"I can't die! I won't die!"

"Others will die," the evil spirit said inside her. *"We will live forever!"*

23

INTO THE WATER

Let us go," the evil said. "We have work to do."

Corky obediently took another step back.

Then suddenly, impulsively, courageously, she stopped. Raising both fists to the dark sky, she shut her eyes and uttered a howl of anguish.

And plunged off the cliff.

The fall was like a dream.

Was that *her* screaming all the way down?

She hit the water hard and instantly sank into the murky brown depths.

"*I must live!*" the evil protested.

But Corky dove toward the river bottom. The strong current swept her along. Down, down, down.

She started to choke. The thick muddy water

poured into her open mouth. She tasted the grit, the sourness of it.

I'm choking. I'm going to die.

But I don't want to die.

I want to live!

I can't drown. I can't die!

I have to live! I have to!

But I can't. I have no choice.

I have made my choice.

To die!

She gasped in another mouthful of the thick disgusting water.

And choked violently as she thrashed help-lessly in the dark waters.

As she choked, the evil began to erupt from her mouth.

She thrashed blindly as the force flowed out of her, blasting the water, churning it, heating it with its evil.

Hotter.

The water grew hotter as Corky thrashed and choked.

Hotter.

Until the river boiled.

And still the evil poured out.

The evil flowed into the thrashing brown waters, protesting its fate, a howl of fury rising in

Corky's ears, raging through the tossing waters.

Hotter.

The brown water bubbled and boiled up. Tall geysers erupted toward the black sky. Even hotter.

Corky writhed in pain as the water scalded her struggling body.

I'm dying — dying. . . .

She felt suddenly light. The evil had departed.

And then heavier again. Heavy with the thick water that choked her, filling her lungs.

"I'm drowning!"

She heard the evil spirit's startled cry.

"I'm drowning!"

And then Corky drowned. She felt as if she were shrinking.

Shrinking until she was nothing but a tiny acorn floating in the water. Then a dot. A lifeless dot. She knew the evil spirit had shrunk too.

And knowing this, she died.

24

ANOTHER DEATH

Raindrops pelted the tumultuous tossing waters. Steam rose up from the boiling surface, forming an eerie white ceiling of fog over the river.

Corky's body floated to the top and bobbed like a small rubber raft.

Watching from the depths, the evil spirit uttered its own death cry, an unending wail of despair.

Its power boiled the water, pushed the river over its banks, sent high waves crashing against the cliff beside it.

The thunder of the crashing waves drowned out the thunder in the sky. The anguished howl of the ancient evil weakened and began to fade. The waters still bubbled and steamed.

"*You can't die!*" the spirit wailed, tossing Corky's body on the surface.

"You cannot die. You cannot betray me! I am you, and you are me! You cannot die!"

Weaker.

The waters began to cool. The eerie white steam drifted apart in the heavy rain.

Weaker.

"*I won't let you die!*" the ancient force declared. Gathering its strength, it pushed the waters beneath Corky, pushed her up, up—until she rose above the water, suspended in the white mist.

"I won't let you die! You are free now! You are out of the water! You are free!"

Hovering over the water like a sagging helium balloon, Corky's body slumped lifelessly, her head back, her eyes staring blindly up at the storm clouds.

"*NOOOOOOOOOOOOOOOOOOO!*" The evil spirit's wail of defeat rose like a siren, then faded to silence.

Corky's body dropped back into the water without making a splash.

"You are dead," the spirit admitted. "And in dying, you have killed me."

Now the thunder in the sky roared louder than the crash of the ebbing waves. In that crash, the spirit was thrown from her body.

The river flowed quietly again.

The water quickly cooled.

The evil faded, then disappeared. Washed away forever in the rain-stirred brown river current.

25

A SMILE

Kimmy had hit the water hard, on her stomach, and then plunged to the bottom. Paralyzed from shock, she could do nothing but let the current move her.

But the cold water quickly revived her. Raising both arms and kicking off from the soft river floor, she forced her way to the surface—in time to see Corky's dive.

Sheets of rain blinded Kimmy as she struggled against the current to get to her friend.

The tossing waves pushed her back.

The water heated up, boiled, and swirled.

What's going on? Kimmy wondered, ducking under the waves, stroking desperately, her feet kicking the hot, frothy water.

What is happening?

I can't get to you, Corky.

I can't get there.

Please be okay. Please. Please. Please.

Please.

The word became an endless chant in her mind. The sky darkened as the torrents of rain pelted down. Kimmy searched in vain for Corky.

And then—to her amazement, to her horror— she thought she saw Corky rise up from the water.

Squinting through the rain, pulling against the current, Kimmy stared at the figure hovering in the white mist, floating over the surface of the water, suspended in the air.

"Corky!"

Kimmy swallowed a mouthful of the hot brown water.

Choking and sputtering, she struggled to breathe.

When she looked back up, Corky was gone. Had she slipped back into the water?

Or had she been some kind of mirage, merely Kimmy's imagination? "Corky! I can't get to you! Where are you? Where are you?"

Be okay. Please. Please. Please. Please.

An object floated on the surface, bobbing on the waves, carried by the strong current.

Kimmy shrieked as she recognized Corky's lifeless form.

Gasping for each breath, her arms aching, her chest about to explode, Kimmy swam frantically toward Corky's body. Remembering her lifesaving course, Kimmy grabbed Corky in a cross-chest carry and paddled desperately against the current.

Dead. Dead. Corky is dead.

Kimmy pulled Corky onto the grassy shore, then stood up unsteadily. Her legs trembled as she gasped, sucking in air, not noticing the cold rain beating down on her.

When she knew her heart wasn't going to explode, Kimmy dropped to her knees, rolled Corky onto her stomach, leaned over her lifeless body, crying, sobbing, trembling.

She pushed down with all her weight on Corky's back. Then released.

Then pushed again, sobbing as she worked.

Pushed and released.

Nothing. No sign of life.

Pushed and released.

Pushed and released.

Until a convulsion of brown water spewed from Corky's lifeless mouth.

Pushed and released.

Kimmy sobbed as she worked, salty tears mixing with cool raindrops on her feverish cheeks.

Pushed and released.

Corky's body rose with another convulsion. Another thick gob of river water rushed out of her mouth. *She's dead,* Kimmy knew. *Corky's dead.*

But she pushed anyway, leaning forward, shivering from the cold, from the wet as she worked, sobbing.

Corky's dead.

I'm not doing any good. I have to stop.

I have to stop. I have to get home. I have to tell someone.

Pushed and released. Pushed and released. Even though it was too late.

Corky groaned as the murky water poured out of her mouth.

She stirred. Coughed. Opened her eyes.

And saw only dirt. Tall grass. Her face was down in the dirt, her eyes covered with a film of water.

She blinked. Choked. Putrid brown water spilled over her chin.

"Corky! Corky!"

Where was the voice coming from?

Corky raised her head. She turned to see a girl on her knees beside her.

"Kimmy!"

Kimmy smiled down at her. "You're alive!"

"Kimmy—you're okay!"

Kimmy tried to reply, but tears choked her words.

Corky coughed. Her mouth tasted sour. She reached up to brush the matted hair off her forehead. The rain pounded down around them, over them. Neither girl seemed to notice.

"I'm so cold," Corky finally said, shuddering.

Kimmy helped her to sit up. "I thought you were dead," Kimmy said, shivering too.

Corky didn't seem to hear her. She sat up and gazed, wide-eyed, around her, ignoring the rain. After a long while she climbed unsteadily to her feet. "Let's go."

"I'll help you." Kimmy wrapped an arm around Corky's trembling shoulders.

"I'm alive," Corky said, still dazed. "I'm alive and you're alive."

"Yes," Kimmy said, and smiled. Slowly she started to lead Corky up the trail to the top of the cliff.

"Oh!" Corky uttered a frightened cry and pointed back at the water. "Look."

Corky turned from her friend, back to the dark waters. Something stirred near the shore. She took a reluctant step closer, squinting against the rain.

A light spot in the water. A circle of light.

And inside it, a reflection.

A face.

Corky stared hard, trembling, breathing hard.

It's Bobbi's face, she realized.

It's Bobbi's face in the water.

It's Bobbi.

And she's smiling.

Corky stared, smiling back, until the reflection broke into tiny pinpoints of light. Bobbi's smiling face dimmed and then shimmered away.

Feeling peaceful, Corky turned back to Kimmy. "Let's go home."

Arm in arm they began to make their way up the cliff through the cool cleansing rain.

EPILOGUE

"Tigers, let's score!
Six points and more!
Tigers, let's score!
Six points and more!"

The cheers rang out through the gym. Corky had done this chant a million times. But now it seemed fresh and new.

"That sounds great!" Miss Green exclaimed from the sideline.

Even she *notices the difference,* Corky thought.

She flashed Kimmy a smile as the girls got into position for the pyramid. "Don't drop me," Corky teased.

"Who—me?" Kimmy replied with exaggerated innocence.

Corky made her way to the top.

"Liberties! In rhythm!" Miss Green called, gripping the whistle around her neck.

The six cheerleaders obediently struck the well-practiced pose.

"Excellent!" Miss Green said. "Straighten your back, Ronnie."

Time for my jump, thought Corky. She glanced down at Kimmy.

Her throat tightened. A moment of panic.

Then she stepped off.

Kimmy caught her easily.

"Perfect!" Miss Green declared.

The girls all cheered.

"Way to go!" Hannah slapped Corky on the back.

"Are you putting on weight?" Kimmy teased.

After practice Corky, Kimmy, Ronnie, and Debra squeezed into a booth at the Corner, all four of them talking at once. One of the basketball players had told Ronnie a dirty joke that she couldn't wait to share. Corky laughed hard at Ronnie's joke even though she'd heard it before. Debra had news about Gary Brandt's new girlfriend. Kimmy wanted to discuss how she should have her hair cut on Saturday.

The waitress stood impatiently, tapping her pencil against her pad, waiting for the four friends to stop talking so she could take their order.

"I'll just have a Coke," Debra said finally.

"Me too," Kimmy said. "A Coke and an order of fries."

The waitress turned her attention to Corky.

"Know what I have a craving for?" Corky asked Kimmy, peering at her over the top of the menu.

Kimmy shrugged. "No. What?"

"Pea soup," Corky said softly.

"No way!" her three companions shouted in unison.

"I'll have a burger and fries," Corky told the waitress.

All four girls collapsed in riotous laughter.

The waitress headed back to the kitchen, shaking her head, wondering what on earth could be funny about pea soup. . . .